Aggrieved, Dillon kicked his townhouse's front door closed and scooped up the calico kitten making a beeline for the exit. "No, you don't," he warned it, before slinging it over his shoulder and heading into the kitchen for a cold beer. "I'm having more than enough trouble with females today; I don't need you adding to the mix." Setting Maisy down on the sofa and taking a long pull, he finally sighed. "Okay, okay, so it's not your fault. And I can hardly blame Anica, she's right about the tear sheets." Maisy reached a paw up to bat at his fingers, unfazed by his suddenly morose tone. "But what the hell is going on with Serena?"

It just didn't make sense. Serena was one of the most straightforward people he knew. Even before he'd started at Lanigan, she'd shown herself to be honest about everything — from work issues to the interpersonal. But lately he couldn't get a read on her at all. She was her usual vibrant self half the time, backing away from him the other half. It just didn't add up.

"Is it me?" he asked the kitten, who blinked and looked away. "I just … I kinda thought things were …." He took another pull on the beer, then had to laugh. He couldn't even articulate his feelings to his sister's cat. No wonder Serena was acting strangely. He was probably feeding her all kinds of assbackwards signals himself, and she didn't know how to react.

How did he feel, though? He shed his jacket, which Maisy promptly started kneading and purring upon, and headed back to the kitchen to throw together some sort of dinner. "Pasta night," he called to the kitten, which ignored him. "Did I talk to myself before you showed up?" he asked it. "I can't seem to keep my mouth shut at home anymore. But as long as you're listening, check it out, 'kay? Here I've known Serena for weeks. And don't get me wrong, I noticed her right off, you know? Second I walked into the interview, as a matter of fact. But I always thought you've got to keep that stuff out of the office." He bit into a carrot and glanced back at Maisy, who was now asleep. "Fine. Ignore me."

He had kept it out of the office, and over time had stopped — okay, practically stopped — looking for Serena as soon as he got to work. Stopped cataloguing the many enticing ways she wore her hair, stopped half-memorizing her schedule, stopped asking her out. Almost stopped, anyway. And they worked closely together; he couldn't go more than a few hours without having to at least shoot an email to Serena, if not engage in some more substantial contact.

Substantial contact. Face it, that was what he wanted.

Also by Melanie Greene

READY TO ROLL

ROCKET MAN

Roll of the Dice Book 1

MELANIE GREENE

GreeneLeaves
Houston, TX

Always, to Robert.
And because I promised her the first, also to Gladys.

ACKNOWLEDGMENTS

It's been an amazing journey getting *Rocket Man* to publication, and would have been one with lower lows and fewer highs if I'd been without a slew of friends and compatriots. Thanks to my WnW cult for years upon years of supportive listening, my CPs for drafts upon drafts of incisive comments, and my local gals for toast upon toast of good cheer. I'm grateful to the invaluable networks of my RWA chapters—West Houston and Contemporary Romance. Most importantly, thanks to my family for their tolerance and support, and maintaining their good opinions of me. (Probably they should stop reading after chapter 5.)

CHAPTER ONE

It was 8:12 on a weekday morning, which meant that Serena Colby was negotiating with the finicky lock to her scummy-butt apartment's front door.

It also meant that she jumped a little at the unwelcome sound of Joey coming up behind her. And jumping a little meant Serena risked dropping either her keys or her mug of steaming Earl Grey. Drop the keys, and the drawing case dragging down her shoulder would follow, and she'd just finished the Mooney account mock-ups. Drop the mug, and she'd be reminded that no matter how much she loved its paprika-and-nutmeg swirl of color, that particular to-go cup had a loose lid, and Serena was wearing sandals.

She dropped the keys, trusting her case's integrity more than her mug's. Catching the strap before her work hit the floor, Serena turned, tight-lipped, to face Joey.

Other ex-boyfriends would have been polite enough to pick up her keys. Of course, other ex-boyfriends would also have been polite enough to remember that Serena left her apartment at 8:12 every morning, and would avoid their common hallway for the three minutes it took for her to get out to her car. Or at the very least, other ex-boyfriends would have been polite enough to wait until she was done locking her apartment door before approaching.

One thing that was sure about Joey: he wasn't like Serena's other ex-boyfriends. Not that she'd been stuck living two doors down from other ex-boyfriends before, so maybe she was giving the others too much credit. She counted to six before speaking, since that was the number of weeks she had left before her lease was up. When she'd regained some patience, she greeted him. "Joey."

He was barefoot. Khakis and his work polo, but barefoot on the sticky hallway linoleum, just in case Serena thought it was coincidence that he was leaving for his store at the same time that Serena was headed out to Lanigan Printing and Advertising.

"Hey, I was wondering if I could borrow some coffee."

"I don't drink coffee." Which should have been apparent after eight and a half months of dating.

"But you have that instant stuff in your freezer."

"I threw that out." On the first morning of January, actually, cursing herself for keeping it throughout December, just in case he came knocking. A long, fun, revelatory New Year's Eve with her former college housemates had been the push she'd needed to get up the next morning and throw out Joey's coffee, Joey's toothbrush, and Joey's Christmas present (she'd bought it the week before he broke up with her, which she did confess to the gals; she hadn't admitted to wrapping it, prettily, post-breakup). In the weeks since, Serena's early rising and Joey's later working hours had kept the hallway encounters to a minimum. But every time they did meet, Serena ended up with a longer list of prohibitions about the next guy. Not younger than her. Not a coffee addict. Not afraid of cockroaches. Not laid back about being on time. Not a food mooch. Not obsessed with his stupid gaming. Not living in a scummy-butt apartment within steps of her own scummy-butt apartment.

"Why'd you do that?"

"Throw it out? Because I don't drink coffee."

"You could have given it to me. The Brackenbridge kids were having some sort of tennis match all morning."

"It was a sword fight." The Brackenbridge family lived in the apartment between theirs. The walls were thin. Cammie Brackenbridge had pointed out, early in Joey and Serena's relationship, that the boys and Joey shared a bedroom wall. Serena had averted her eyes around the kids for a good long while. On the up side, Serena was petty and the boys hated waking up at seven for school. Each whining protest about missing shoes and bad-mood-induced loud game that floated on the air waves while she got ready for work delighted her, knowing that Joey was piling pillows on his head and grumbling into his mattress about it.

"It was loud. And I ran out of coffee last week."

"Well, you're up now. You should have time to go buy some before work." Serena retrieved her keys and finessed the lock before shouldering her drawing case again. "Gotta go."

"Where'd you get it, though?" Joey was walking alongside her.

"Get what?" She knew. But she liked irritating him. More proof of her pettiness.

"The coffee."

"I threw it out."

"I mean where'd you get it to start with?"

She'd told him, at least twice. Probably more. It was bad enough that she'd once spent a couple of hours online researching instant coffee brands, searching for something flavorful, fair trade, organic, and also available from a locally owned store somewhere in Houston. Never mind that it was at the same place where she got her olive oil and shampoo, and she might have just grabbed the coffee off their shelves without the research time. But she'd told him the whole story when he'd complimented the flavor. Joey had even gone to the co-op with her, back when they sometimes ran errands together.

"Oh, just the grocery store. I think it was HEB." The chain carried organic coffee; it wasn't impossible that Joey would find the same stuff there.

"Okay. Fine. I guess I have to go shopping."

"Bye, Joe." He hated being called Joe. Serena took the stairs instead of waiting for the elevator. Sure, her case banged repeatedly against her thigh and a few drops of tea spilled out onto her hand, but the thud of the fire door slamming shut between her and her ex-boyfriend was more than worth it.

Despite the Joey delay, Serena was at work early enough to grab a minute to herself. She spent it rearranging her poster frames. The first thing she'd done when she was hired by Lanigan was to install two rows of a deep crown molding along a couple of her office walls, which she used in place of an easel to display client mockups, past campaigns, and some of her own personal, more artistic work.

Right at nine, Serena's friend Janice came in and caught her repositioning the Mooney account frames.

"You know, Toots, I'll have those Mangoes and Moonshine posters for you tomorrow at two. You're just going to want to move everything around again." Janice was Lanigan's Operations Manager. She knew the schedules for a million things at once, and how to deal when any of those million processes threatened her deadlines. If Janice promised a poster at two, Serena would have a poster at two.

Serena laughed. "Yeah, I know. But Anica took my HouGreen mockups to give to Mr. Kenzi, and I can't leave these poor walls with a big gaping hole showing, can I?"

"Your walls aren't sentient, Toots."

"Shh! They'll hear you."

"They don't really have ears, you know. I'm beginning to think you're clinically disordered here. Or maybe it's clinically ordered? Ducks don't come in rows that straight. Some people let paper stack up in their in-boxes, or keep the 'to be filed' pile hidden behind the door." Janice made a show of looking, but of course only found a white board outlining the quarter's work flow. "Seriously. I dare you to just leave your walls the way they are until Monday."

As if she'd leave them a mess for four days. Janice was toying with her, but Serena could play right back. She knew Janice's obsessions as well as Janice knew hers. "I dare you to only go to the gym once this weekend."

Janice cocked her head, considering. "Does Friday count?"

"If it's after five, it counts."

"No deal. I'd miss my kickboxing class."

"You have a sickness."

"Which I think was my point to you." Janice sighed. "We need boyfriends."

"Speak for yourself," Serena said, and turned to nudge one of her collages to the left an inch. "You're addicted to exercise endorphins, so a nice physical outlet is just the ticket for you. As for me, there's nothing wrong with making my environment nice. And besides, even if I could find anyone worth dating, I'd still keep my filing done."

Janice snorted. "I want to know which one of your thirteen evil stepparents beat you black, blue, and purple unless you folded your laundry on time. You have a deeply scarred psyche, my friend."

"There were only seven stepparents, and I never even lived with Number Seven. I mean, Zane. I promised Mom I'd stop calling him Number Seven. What's your point?"

"Want to go for Cuban food and talk about it?"

"Is that a subtle way of making me go out dancing with you tonight?"

"Maybe."

"Will you glare at me for the poor dietary choices I will definitely make?"

"Not if you promise to shake your hips afterwards."

Serena grinned and tapped the last frame a tiny bit to fix the spacing. "You're on."

Before Janice had even cleared the room, Anica called Serena in for an unexpected meeting, and told her to bring everything she was working on. Not always a good thing, being summoned by the boss, but Serena's conscious was clear. And as it turned out, Anica had only slightly nerve-wracking news.

"I need you to sit in on these interviews today for Margaret's replacement."

Serena blinked. Margaret, one of the copy writers, was moving to Alabama rather suddenly, but Anica had always done the hiring on her own. "You want my help?"

Anica stopped flipping through the paperwork Serena had handed over and glanced up. "It looks like these spots can go to Eddie as-is, and I'll have Philip and Johnnie do some initial mock-ups of the gala brochure based on your notes. That should give you a few hours free to talk with the copy writers."

"Right," Serena tried not to sound as nonplussed as she felt. It didn't seem bad, exactly, but it was unexpected, and Anica was many things, but few of them were spontaneous.

Anica smiled at her. "Relax. I've decided to groom you for more responsibility, and I thought you'd benefit by sitting in. It's hardly a death sentence. Besides, you worked most closely with Margaret, so you'll know the essentials we're looking for in a replacement."

Well, then. Serena smiled back, hoping she looked at ease. She'd been eyeing the management tier; after almost four years at Lanigan she was eager to do more than strictly graphic design, but hadn't yet formulated her plan for approaching Anica about it. Seems that first step had been taken without her realizing it. Trying to expel her nervous energy, Serena picked up the applicant's folders. "Okay, then, thanks. Just these three? Can't HR rustle up anyone else?"

"Oh, Emily had several applicants. Of the ones she put through to me, these are my top choices. If this process goes well, next time we have to hire I'll show you how I go through the applicants to decide who to talk to. Listen," Anica took off her glasses and tossed them to the side, "I know everyone is used to

Margaret, and the way she works, and maybe your team will resent the new guy a little...."

"Or gal," Serena added, reading the applicant names. "But if I'm one of the interviewers, I'll stand up for him or her and smooth things over, yes, I get that. It's not subtle."

"I never said it was."

Serena tried to get ahold of her mouth before it shot her in the foot. "No, no, of course not. It's a solid plan. I'll do what I can, but there is going to be some fallout. I'm not the only one who's going to miss Margaret, or her efficiency. For the group's sake, I can't be seen as rising up solely on the back of her departure. So, how else will you be giving me more oversight?"

Anica swept her hair back from her forehead and put her glasses back on. "You're not so subtle yourself, Serena. But this isn't a fast track, so don't get too rebellious on me. For now, you will sit in on sales meetings between Eddie and me, and take over some of the direct communication with clients. Select clients. Lanigan wants to build a stronger base in the hospitality industry, and we think you can help with that. For now, these interviews. The first one's in about thirty minutes—have a seat over there and look over the resumes and portfolios."

Moving to the small conference table Anica had indicated, Serena checked the time on her cell phone. There were two interviews before lunch. And while their talk with the first applicant took most of the hour between ten and eleven, the next guy was so monosyllabic and almost hostile that Serena and Anica both were happy to shut the door behind him a half-hour after he first walked in.

"What was that? Misogyny?"

Anica shook her head. "I do not know. What year is it again? Do they still make blatant chauvinists in this millennium? Let's hope that Dillon has a little easier time with the idea of female bosses."

"Cheri was fine with us, at least."

"My only question with her is her experience. She has talent, but her resume just isn't very deep."

"Okay. Dillon at one?"

Anica nodded. "See you then."

1:10 rolled around; Dillon Hamilton was late.

Anica shot Serena a wry look and made noises about the file of other applicants, but before they could open it, Hamilton was announced. He propelled himself into the office, jacket flying behind him, and seemed anchored to the earth only via the messenger bag he wore over one shoulder. He was all apologies, kinetic charm and a tumble of dark hair.

"What a disaster, I'm so sorry. Do you still have time for me? All my fault, inexcusable. But not typical." He turned to Serena. "Sorry, I didn't know I'd meet you, too, just Ms. Sands. Dillon Hamilton, hi."

"Serena Colby." They shook, his long fingers wrapping around the back of her hand, enveloping it. His height when they were right up close was a little overwhelming, but he was lanky, only his broad shoulders filling up his otherwise flapping blazer. At her name, he grinned one of those lights-up-the-face grins. Charm. The guy had dangerous levels of charm.

"Right, hi, Serena, nice. I saw your picture on the Lanigan site. You did their new logo, right?"

Serena confirmed she had, and Dillon complimented her before turning his eyes (Serena hadn't decided if they were cobalt or Egyptian blue) and his attention back to Anica. "I feel bad I kept you waiting. My references will tell you, I'm really prompt. Oh, you have my samples there, good. Let me show you a couple of other things. This is recent, similar to what Lanigan did for McMahan Foods, I think. Similar tone. I've just done some food writing, and I'm not sure my application materials show you enough of that."

They discussed his work, Lanigan's history, Houston, and the industry.

"Why are you looking to move from freelance to a permanent position?" Serena asked. Over the course of the day she'd gotten more comfortable with questioning the applicants, but something was tying her tongue a little with this one. She didn't want to think that it was the fact that he was gorgeous, so she refused to think about it and kept her eyes on his resume and on Anica.

"It's what I always wanted. I moved to Houston to be near my sister, she's having a baby soon, and they're my only family. Anyway, I came here because she's here, and I'm staying because she's here. And I like it. I'm a huge Rockets fan. I've been searching for a permanent position since I got here, looking at different companies, and Lanigan is just perfect for me. The size and the team and the work you've all done. The location. It's exactly what I hoped for."

His enthusiasm was sweet. And she'd never fault a fan of her hometown basketball team, since she was rather rabid about them herself. Serena remembered her own interview at Lanigan; she'd probably been about Dillon's age, and was just as eager to be hired on. But she didn't think she'd come across as open about it. Not that it was a bad thing. He was just so...so there. So tall and happy and that dark hair and those cobalt eyes and Serena was not inclined to gladness that she was so aware of his thereness. But he interviewed well, and they'd liked his work best of the three candidates. As Dillon packed up, Serena and Anica shared a relieved smile behind his back.

"We should be making a decision in the next couple of days," Anica said, returning to her desk. "Serena will show you out. Nice to meet you, Dillon."

"And you. I'll look for your call."

They strolled to the lobby, chatting. Lanigan's halls were lined with completed campaigns—not updated as frequently as Serena's office walls, but still a strong recommendation for the work they did there. And it gave her a secret little smile that several of the pieces Dillon commented on had her graphics. At the front desk, he turned fully towards her. "Thanks, Serena. I can call you Serena? I know I said it, but I can start right away."

"That's great." Despite being fairly sure Dillon would be their hire, Serena didn't want to give anything away. Plus she'd caught sight of Philip, their other writer, headed into Margaret's office with a grim look on his face. Clearly the word of Margaret's potential replacements and, with it, Serena's semi-promotion, was spreading through the building. She was mentally running damage control, but Dillon still stood facing her, blue eyes unwavering.

"I can ask you a question?"

Serena nodded.

"I don't want to come on too hard. And I know it's maybe stupid of me to mention this. But," he ducked his head some, rubbing the back of his neck. "Can I call you?"

"Well, sure. Like Anica said, we're going to contact all the candidates by early next week, but if you want to just check in, that's fine."

"No. I appreciate that, but...I mean, you, specifically. No matter what happens with the job decision, can I call you? For coffee or something?"

"I don't drink coffee." What a stupid response. Serena sent a mental slap to her forehead, but this adorable puppy of a man was asking a maybe future boss on a date? What if Anica had been the one to walk him out, would he have asked her instead? Was this strategy, or just strange? And why did the idea of his offering Anica a coffee set Serena's mind at disgruntled alert? "I like tea."

"Well, for tea then."

"Sorry. I mean, sorry, it's not the coffee. I appreciate it, Dillon, but I don't...it's not...."

"You're with someone?" He shook his head. "Never mind. You said 'no' and I'll let it go. I just didn't want to wait until I started working with you and have to wonder how to fit my asking you out in with the job stuff. Or if I don't get it, for you to think I'm trying to get a second chance. I mean, when I say it like that, it's obvious the right answer is to not ask you out at all. Which is what you're trying to say. I was right to start with and it was stupid to ask. Forget it all, please. What an impression I make. Show up late and won't go away and incapable of biting back my words when I should."

"No. It's fine. Nice of you to ask." Unsettling, but nice. Serena was not looking to date. The post-Joey list of things to avoid was too long, and she had a promotion to chase, and Dillon was too young and too handsome and too likely to be her subordinate and too much a whirlwind and anyway, Serena was not looking.

He took her hand in hers, squeezed. Serena resisted pulling away from the warmth of it. "I'll leave now. Thanks for your time today. And when you choose someone else for this job, I'd still like to hear from you. If you want. I won't pester you. Thanks, Serena. You're really nice. And pretty. But mainly nice. I'm going, I promise. Bye."

And like that, he slung his messenger bag around his neck and strode away, shoulders set, not looking back.

CHAPTER TWO

FRIDAY'S HAPPY HOUR AT FRIJOLES, where the Lanigan crew usually went, doubled as Margaret's farewell party. They took over a couple of tables, and it didn't escape Serena's notice that Philip maneuvered so that they were sitting together. She prepared to be grilled. It was her own fault for avoiding Philip all day, even after Dillon had accepted Anica's job offer.

But Philip bored Serena half to death. He was a fine, even a clever writer, but dull. Same turkey club and bag of chips every day. Annually updated studio portraits of his family. Made a fuss if he ran out of medium point blue ballpoints. Serena never understood why someone so entrenched in his routines even wanted a creative job, but apparently, at some point, Philip had made that decision. And upon deciding something, Philip stuck with it, and was willing to expound on why. So she'd put off the obligatory gossip as long as she could, and as a result she was stuck in a corner with only a frozen margarita to hide behind while Philip tried to persuade her to recreate every line of Dillon's resume.

"Toots, leave her alone," Janice interjected, finally. Janice called everyone but the company's owner 'Toots.' "The poor woman's given you all the details she can. Unless you want her to draw a picture of him, but you'll meet him for yourself on Monday."

Serena stopped herself from saying that the set of markers she carried in her bag didn't include the right shade of blue for Dillon's eyes. And then she got distracted thinking about doing a pencil sketch, with a heavy line, and the only color the pop of his eyes. Purely as a creative exercise, not because she remembered how the blue glinted when he asked her out.

Philip was not leaving her alone. "I only wanted to know if he's worked on any annual reports before? It's just that my team has been given more of them than yours, and Anica said she was going to redistribute them. But then Margaret's husband was transferred and now I don't know if Anica will stick to that."

"You're really going to have to bring that up with her," Serena said, shooting Janice yet another exasperated look. She should have just taken Dillon's portfolio and dropped it on Philip's desk.

"A toast to Margaret!" Eddie burst in before Philip could think of any more questions. Not that Eddie was trying to spare Serena; he was just grandstanding as usual. Fantastic head of sales, Eddie was, but overwhelming in social groups. "Drink up, Margaret, this is the last good margarita you're ever getting. Do they even have tequila in Birmingham?"

"I'm pretty sure they do," Margaret replied placidly, but she was smiling.

"Well, just in case, let me buy another round."

"None for me, thanks," Serena said, sliding back her chair. "I'm meeting my realtor first thing in the morning."

She gave Margaret a final hug, and avoiding Philip's eye, Serena escaped.

Dillon showed up uninvited at his sister's house Friday evening. It was typical of him, but also typical of Shannon and Justin to include him in whatever they had going on. This time, it was nursery arranging. Shannon and Justin's long-anticipated first baby was due in mere weeks, and Shannon was finally feeling confident enough to set up his room.

"Why is it so yellow? You know he's a boy, you could do blue walls."

"Because I like yellow," Shannon said, tossing a stuffed rabbit at him. "Put that on the shelf next to the changing table."

Nursery arranging took the form of Justin—and now Dillon— wandering around the room as directed, while Shannon sat in the rocking chair taking things out of the succession of storage bins the guys placed on the table beside her.

"But I got him that spaceship mobile, and the glow-in-the-dark stars. Yellow walls don't look like outer space."

"Wait, are you saying that if the baby was a girl you wouldn't have given her space toys?"

"No. Have daughters. I'll give them cool sci-fi stuff, too. Paint all the kid rooms blue, is what I'm saying."

"Maybe my kids won't be a sci-fi geeks, Uncle Dillon."

"Maybe your kids won't be cool, you mean? Why don't you want your kids to be cool?"

"Justin, explain to my brother that his version of cool is skewed."

"Justin, explain to your wife that everyone knows that space is the final frontier of coolness."

"Justin, explain to my brother that even the sci-fi geeks no longer think *Star Trek* is cool."

Justin was about to break in, but Dillon had already upended a bin full of onesies and tiny socks over Shannon's head, so he wisely took his usual course when the siblings started bickering, and retreated. Shannon was pelting Dillon with the rolled up socks, laughing, and Dillon was dodging them as well as he could, but also scooping them up and shooting them into the open dresser drawer.

"You are such an idiot."

"You're an idiot."

"I'm nine months pregnant. You can't insult me or I'll burst into tears."

"And what are you going to hide behind when my nephew shows up?"

"Postpartum hormones."

"Come on, Shan, eventually that's not going to work. You may as well let me insult you now. It makes me happy, and you know there's nothing in the world you like more than making me happy."

"Idiot," she replied, but didn't deny it.

Not that she could. They'd been through a hell of a lot, he and Shannon, since the night a decade before when a drunk driver ran their parents off the road. He'd been sixteen, Shannon twenty-one, in her third year of college, but fortunately for Dillon, still in LA. She'd rearranged her whole life so she could move back home with him, whereupon she made Dillon's emotional equilibrium her life's mission. Her very new boyfriend Justin had ended up at the house, too, as often as not, exhibiting his uncanny ability to solve every practical problem in their lives.

Shannon had fallen in love with Justin for—well, for whatever reasons women fall for smart, decent, intuitive guys—but Dillon loved him because he'd kept the house from being silent, and kept their meddling Uncle Bob supplied with information without making Dillon talk. Plus he got Shannon stop asking Dillon how he was doing seven or ten times a day.

"Dinner in fifteen minutes," Justin said, stopping short in the nursery doorway to watch his very pregnant wife attempt to stack tiny refolded outfits on the shelf of her belly.

"That gives you two just enough time to finish emptying those boxes," Shannon said, beginning to rock forward in the chair.

"Where are you going? Why do we have to keep working when you're leaving?" Dillon asked, but he'd already taken the clothes from her and was helping Justin lift her.

"I have a baby on my bladder and you don't, that's why. Don't forget to put the empty boxes in the hall closet."

"We're not idiots," Dillon said, but Shannon only snorted as she slow-walked away.

Once they'd served themselves lasagna and shooed the kitten out of the dining room, Justin turned his 'I know you've got something on your mind' look on Dillon. "Go on. What's up?"

"I've got news."

"You got the job," Justin said, nodding.

"You got it! Dillon, that's super!"

"Thank you, sis. That's the kind of excitement I was looking for." Dillon side-eyed his brother-in-law.

"It's not like we didn't expect this."

"And what if I'd lost it, what then? Wouldn't you feel bad for me?"

"Nope. If you didn't get it, it'd just because you fucked up the interview."

"Justin. Language," Shannon said, rubbing her baby bump.

"He can't understand."

"He can hear your voice and your inflections," she said.

"Wait. Hold up. Are you seriously going to stop cursing when he isn't even here yet?" Dillon asked his sister. "No fucking way I'm stopping cursing, you know that, right?"

Justin said, "You want to be near my baby, you stop cursing."

"You just now said I fucked up the interview!"

"So you did fuck up the interview. Thought so."

"I did not fuck it up."

"Stop saying 'fuck,'" Shannon said.

"Now the baby heard his mommy say fuck," laughed Dillon, glad that Shannon was across the table, and therefore out of hitting range. He'd forgotten to fold his legs out of her way, though. "Ouch!"

"Serves you right for making me say bad words. How exactly did you mess up your interview, anyway?"

"I did not mess up my interview. I got the job, didn't I?"

"But?" asked Justin, who was way too perceptive.

Dillon shoved more lasagna in his mouth, but then his plate was clean and Justin pushed the casserole out of his way so he couldn't have seconds.

"Aw, Dill, it's okay. What happened? Are you okay?"

She had to have done it deliberately. Shannon knew how much he hated when she asked him that. Dillon closed his eyes a second, sighing, but when he opened them, Shannon was just watching him. They had the same blue eyes—their father's—and the same square jaw—their mother's—and he could read her concerned love as well as if she'd shared every thought in her head.

"Aw, Shan. It is okay," he echoed back at her, lightening his tone. "I was ten minutes late, but they were cool about it. Anica and Serena, those are the ones who interviewed me. Anica's my boss now. Well, starting on Monday."

"Ten minutes?" Justin was a banker, and had a knack for turning into a serious professional the second the suit jacket went on. Normally he didn't burden Dillon with fatherly-seeming advice, but when it came to work, he had his standards, and readily passed them along.

"It wasn't my fault."

"Did you at least call to let them know?"

"It was just a freight train. I didn't think it would stop traffic that long."

"So you didn't call?"

Dillon reached for the lasagna. "I said I was sorry when I got there. Anica said it was fine. Serena, too, she walked me out and was really nice."

Justin shook his head, still clearly flabbergasted that Dillon would allow himself to be late to an interview. And sure, Dillon had felt like an idiot about it. More than an idiot. He'd covered okay, mostly. He'd gotten the job. Nothing else really mattered. Certainly not impulsively asking out the cute interviewer like some sort of impulse-asking idiot.

"Who's Serena, then?" Justin, naturally, picked up on everything. "If Anica's the boss?"

"She's so cute."

"Dillon!" Shannon kicked him again.

"Stop that."

"It's only fair. The baby keeps kicking me."

"That doesn't make it fair. Your feet are a lot bigger."

"Plus she's wearing shoes," Justin added.

"Hey, whose side are you on?"

"Yours, always." Justin refilled Shannon's water glass. "But I want to know about the cute girl."

"She's not—she's just someone at work. I mean, she's a graphic designer, so I'll be working with her, but not like she's my boss. Anica's my boss. I double-checked, after."

"After?"

He stabbed a forkful of food. "After I asked her out." And then he shoved the pasta in his mouth, so he couldn't answer any of Shannon's questions.

Justin knew how to wait, though. He stretched across to the sideboard to snag the container of baklava Dillon had brought over, and he didn't even look up until Shannon had stopped her barrage of words and Dillon had drained his beer.

"You didn't bring any chocolate ones?"

Dillon shrugged. "They were out."

"Your sister's going to have a baby. You bring her chocolate, idiot."

"Yeah. Idiot."

"They were out."

"And speaking of out. Why did you ask Serena out? Are you an idiot? Why did they even give you the job? Did she say yes?"

Damn Justin and his calm and reasonable act. It's not like his questions were any different from Shannon's. It's not like they were any different from the ones he'd been asking himself for the previous twenty-nine hours. But Justin had some sort of mojo that made it impossible for Dillon to be evasive.

"Look, it's no big deal. It just happened, okay? The interview was over, and she was walking me out, and I felt like I'd screwed up too much by being late—yeah, and not calling—so I figured

I'd never get the job. And she's really pretty. And I like her designs, I mean, the ones I've seen, and her hair smells nice and she was wearing this orange shirt. Remember how Mom always wore orange? I just liked it. And then, I don't know, I just asked her out for coffee."

What he wouldn't give for another beer, but he was driving back, and anyway, like cursing, drinking was something Shannon made them all cut back on because of the baby. As if his unborn nephew would care that Dillon had a second beer.

"What'd she say?" Justin was nonchalant again.

"She doesn't drink coffee." Dillon was scraping the label off his longneck, so he didn't have to catch the knowing glances his family was undoubtedly sharing.

"What are you going to do when you see her on Monday?"

He shrugged. "Apologize? Pretend it never happened? I don't know. Come on, stop hogging the pistachio ones."

"Should have brought me some chocolate ones then," Shannon said, not releasing the baklava. "Idiot."

The problem with house hunting was Natalie, Serena's realtor. Actually, the problem was Becky, Serena's mom. Or to be most precise, it was her mom's attitude about her realtor.

Natalie was one of Serena's best friends; they'd lived together in college and been close ever since. She had also, for almost a year when they were twelve, been Serena's stepsister. It was five years after her parents had divorced; her dad's third marriage, and third stepchild.

By then, Becky Lofthouse-Colby was on her own second marriage, and might have given Serena's new stepsister a little slack. Alas, no. Rides from Dad and Elaine's house to Mom and Erik's house were a finely balanced trek on a ledge with 'don't admit to any fun or comfort' on one side and 'don't give her reason to rant about Dad's failures' on the other, and the surest way to cross safely involved bitching about Natalie.

Honestly, Serena wasn't sure that Natalie ever did a thing wrong, back when they were stepsisters. She was a little clingy at times with Serena's dad, but Serena was well over being Daddy's Little Girl, so it didn't bother her like it had when he'd let Alice's demon spawn twins curl up on either side of him for story time, leaving her to stand behind him if she wanted to see the pictures.

All that was over half Serena's lifetime ago, but Becky was still snippy about Natalie. She'd been snippy when Serena and Natalie had reconnected in college, and remained snippy throughout the decade of their adult friendship. Serena's impulse had been to keep Becky far away from her house hunting, but she'd gone and recommended Natalie to one of Becky's current stepkids, and it had gotten back to Becky. So now, unless she could be very clever about the timing, Becky Lofthouse-Colby-Russo accompanied Serena whenever she and Natalie looked for Serena's ideal home.

"I don't understand why you won't even look outside the Loop," Becky said, far from the first time. The Loop was a freeway that circled Houston's downtown. Being outside it meant a more suburban and a more traffic-intensive lifestyle that made Serena shudder to imagine it.

"You do, too. You just don't believe I know what I want."

"We never lived inside the Loop."

"I did, with Dad and Tennessee."

"Tennessee," her mom snorted. It hadn't been a stretch at all for Serena to bitch about Tennessee.

"And him and Fran, for that matter; before Fran had Jonas, he still lived in West U." Between them over the years since their divorce, Serena's parents had introduced her to seven stepparents, but Jonas was her only half-sibling, so Fran was the only stepparent she actively kept in touch with.

"That wasn't a house, it was a hovel."

"It was just small."

"Too small for kids."

"Too small for a baby, that's why they moved. But it was fine for me. I liked it."

"Well, I didn't. Every time I picked you up it took forty-five minutes just to get back on the freeway."

Serena laughed. "Well, your bad luck that as soon as I learned to drive, they moved. Let it go, Mom. I want to live in Montrose, and I'm going to live in Montrose, and Natalie said today's houses are maybe perfect."

"Well, if you're trusting to her judgment. She just wants her commission."

There was only so much laughing at her mom's attitude Serena could handle, and it wasn't good to hit the limit before they'd even set foot in a property.

Serena liked the first place, even though Becky said its energies were blocked by the front door to driveway configuration. She didn't quite like it enough to sign up for a lifetime of her mom's mentioning the front door/driveway thing, but it appealed. The second place had residents who refused to let them in because they didn't think their landlord gave them enough notice of the showing (only fourteen instead of their requested twenty-four hours).

"Anyway, it looked like the whole place is carpeted. That's terrible for your allergies, Serena. Imagine if they have cats, all those years of dander trapped in the fibers. You'd be sick every day."

"I could replace the carpets."

"And you want to start by incurring those kinds of expenses? You know, Ridley and Neera are making a point of looking for newer construction. There are so many pitfalls about older houses."

Ridley was Becky's oldest stepkid. Serena didn't really know any of the Three Rs (she'd been in college when Becky married Ridley, Regina, and Rufus Russo's dad Zane), but she'd observed them growing up, going to college, and getting married via her mom's Facebook feed. So many pictures of the happy family, Becky right in the middle of them all. Sometimes Zane even called Serena's mom 'Rebecca' so he could include her in his list of 'Beloved Rs.' Zane liked to post status updates along the 'one of the Beloved Rs baked my favorite muffins for breakfast! I am blessed!' lines.

Still, it might have been excessively petty of Serena to skip Ridley and Neera's wedding reception. It was three days after the Joey break-up and she'd exaggerated a work crisis to get away. Allowing Becky to stickle-burr herself to house hunting was penance she had to pay, but Serena regretted making Natalie pay alongside her.

Natalie kept on her calm collected professional face. "I'm so glad that Neera and Ridley are finding some good options. I think we're really closing in on the perfect location for them. Good schools, too."

Becky was flustered. "Schools?"

"I hope I didn't let a cat out of the bag! Neera mentioned it was important to them, but that's all I know. Probably she's just looking to the future," Natalie said, even offering a reassuring pat to Becky's arm.

Great. Just what Serena needed after all the 'proud mama of the groom!' photos: Ridley to have a kid who would decide forevermore what Becky's grandmother name would be. They'd probably settle on 'Beloved Granny R' or something, and when Serena had children they'd be stuck with the same name.

Two houses later (former duplex badly remodeled to single-family; roof with missing tiles and water-stained ceilings), Becky had to leave to meet Zane for their couples meditation class.

"I'll email you some of the places that were too small for Ridley; they might be just the ticket for you. It would be so nice if you moved out closer to them so we could all visit more easily."

"Bye, Mom." Sometimes Serena was really really excellent at restraint.

"Natalie," Becky said, offering the briefest of handshakes.

"Lovely to see you again, Becky."

Serena waited until Becky's car was around the corner before giving in to the growl that had been building for hours.

Nat was shaking her head. "I shouldn't laugh. It's terrible of me to laugh."

"Better to laugh than scream. My throat hurts now."

"Come on, she's been worse."

"That's no consolation."

"Remember when she first saw our apartment senior year?"

"I've blocked that out."

"She tried to give you Regina's old princess bed."

"Regina was fifteen! Why was there still a princess bed in their attic even?"

"I know. Craigslist that shit already, right?"

"Don't give it to your twenty-one year old daughter, anyway."

"'We're making room for some of my stuff in Zane's house,'" Natalie mimicked.

"Like you didn't snag the triple-mirror vanity table for yourself."

"I felt like the fanciest girl in all the land every time I sat there." Natalie laughed, nudging Serena. "You were so jealous but you wouldn't say anything in case it meant you appreciated Regina's castoffs."

"Was not."

"Was too."

"Was not, shut up." But Serena was grinning again, and finally leaned back against Natalie's car with a sigh. "Okay, so do you have more for today, or are we done?"

"Sorry, I've got another appointment, but I'll send you some listings to look at tonight."

"No rush. Mom's readily available for the next four days, so I may not look again until Thursday."

Natalie put on her mock-scolding voice. "Cynic. You'll change your mind when you get home and Joey is haunting the hallway."

"Ha! I'll have to text Cammie to send the boys out for an epic jousting match, that'll scare him."

"Thank goodness they haven't grown out of their knights and squires phase."

"I'm grateful every day." And petty. Every day, petty. Serena really needed to rein that in. Sometime. Soon.

CHAPTER THREE

OVER THE REST OF THE WEEKEND, Serena was twice forced into evasive maneuvers to keep from having to talk to Joey; it annoyed her even though one retreat had led her to a thrift shop where she'd found a box of nearly perfect tangerine Fiesta-ware serving pieces. They'd go perfectly with the spice-hued dishes she'd been collecting for years.

And on Monday morning her landlady denied Serena's proposed three-month extension of her lease.

"You'd think she'd take any excuse to keep ignoring the broken bathroom door," complained Serena. She'd run into Janice in the Lanigan parking lot, and was feeling free to vent expansively as they headed inside.

"Did she explain why?"

"Supposedly scummy-butt apartments are so desirable she's turning people away. But she said I could renew for the full year with only a seven percent rent increase."

"Did you tell her to stick her seven percent where the sun don't shine?"

"No, I ignored her."

"Toots."

Her gut reaction had been a flat refusal, but she was scared to close that door. "Well, what if I can't find a place to buy? It's not that I don't need out of that apartment. But I don't want to rent anywhere at all. I've been saving and saving for so long and I swore to myself I'd own my own house when I was thirty."

"You've only been thirty for like a week, Toots."

"And if I sign a year lease, I'll be thirty-one before I'm out of it." The very thought of it was enough to curdle everything in her stomach. She couldn't fail to get her house. She just couldn't. "Nope. My only options are to buy something now, or hope she'll change her mind. I could put up with Joey and the bugs and the door and all, if she'd give me a few more months to buy something."

Janice shook her head. "Or slacken up on the reins a little and admit there's no law you have to buy now, and find someplace decent to rent for another year."

Janice was right. Serena knew she was right. But admitting it was such a reversal of all the plans she'd made. Practically her whole life, the roofs over Serena's head had felt temporary. No matter if her dad moved her familiar old iron bed from house to house, no matter if her mom let her chose the paint color for every new bedroom, Serena knew that sooner or later, she'd be sleeping elsewhere. If not for custody reasons, then because one of her parents was divorcing or remarrying. Every new or newly-dead relationship meant someone was about to move, and that someone was usually Serena.

So all through her twenties she'd put up with weirdo roommates and her landlady's reluctance to schedule repairs and Joey down the hall and any number of inconveniences and indignities, with one goal and one goal only in mind: saving for that down payment. Serena wanted her own house. Her very own, all hers, no sharing, no negotiating, no noisy neighbors or desperately in love or desperately unhappy parents, none of that. And her twenties were over, so it was time. Serena was going to buy a house. Hell and high water could try in vain to stop her.

"Hey, Serena, hold up," Dillon said behind her. Serena actually bit her tongue when she realized she'd recognized the warm tenor voice before seeing who'd greeted her. The pain was meant as a sharp reprimand to her libido, but it just made her more aware of her skittery nerve endings.

"Oh! Hey. Good morning. Ready to start?" He was wearing the same slate blue jacket and carrying a different messenger bag. The fast once-over he gave her had Serena happy she'd worn her favorite kicky orange patterned skirt with sleek black top and tights. Not for him. Just because it made her feel strong and vibrant and competent. If the new guy liked it, that was no skin off her nose.

"Ready as I'll ever be." He hitched up his shoulder strap and turned to Janice. "Dillon Hamilton."

"Our new copy guy," Serena added. "Janice is the operations guru. She knows everything."

"Including where to bury the bodies," Janice agreed.

"Got it. First rule of the new job: don't make Janice mad."

"Oh, I like him. Good call," Janice told Serena.

They all moved into the waiting elevator, Dillon hanging a half step back until Janice and Serena preceded him. Serena absolutely did not sway her hips as she stepped forward. Not much, anyway.

"You live far from here?" Janice asked.

"Me?"

"Yes, Toots, you. I know where Serena lives."

"Right. Sure. In the Heights. I bought my sister's townhouse when they moved to the suburbs."

"Near Serena and Joey then."

"Joey?"

"I don't live with Joey," Serena said, not that she ought to be clarifying. And not that Janice should be telling this guy she'd barely met where Serena lived.

"Joey works here, too?" Dillon's eyes weren't quite as blue in the elevator's dismal lighting, but that also could have been because of the satin chrome walls. Serena knew her own reflection in their surface was often duller than expected. Probably her skirt read almost as sienna, to Dillon. Not that it mattered.

"No, we just live in the same building. But not for long."

"She's looking for a house," Janice said.

"And since we're sharing, Janice lives on the far side of downtown, and my dad is in Baytown and Miguel is in Garden Oaks and Emily from HR is probably way out in a suburb somewhere, but I'm not sure where," Serena said, shooting Janice a look that even in the dim elevator light ought to be clear enough.

"Miguel doesn't live in Garden Oaks," Janice told her, stepping into the well-lit reception area as if she'd never seen a chiding look in her life.

"He doesn't? Oh, Miguel's the production manager, I'm sure you'll meet him soon," Serena explained to Dillon.

"Nope. He was just staying there when his mom got sick. She's better now so he's back in Sixth Ward at his place."

"Aw. That's sweet."

Janice rolled her eyes. "I'll do you a favor, Toots, and never tell him you said that. Noon?"

"Noon," Serena confirmed as Janice took off towards her office. She turned to Dillon. "Do you know where Emily from HR's office is?"

"The suburbs?"

She laughed. "Not quite. Come on, I'll give you the grand tour on the way."

"Show me everything."

Had that been suggestive? Serena couldn't decide. Possibly Dillon was a bit nervous, between his faux-pas after the interview and first day jitters. She decided to ignore it, instead detailing the members of her team and Philip's as well. Anica usually separated them into two distinct groups, but they crossed over depending on what jobs were to hand.

They moved down the main corridor, Serena pointing out various offices and keeping to herself any wayward thoughts. Like whether Dillon had been flirty with Janice, or if he just projected an extroverted kind of easy charm. She stopped at the lunchroom.

"Did you bring anything to eat?"

"A sandwich," Dillon said, patting his messenger bag.

"Well, there are plenty of places to grab something nearby, if you want. And a roach coach shows up outside the main dock at nine forty-five each morning, so you can always grab something from there."

"Does it have anything edible?"

She shrugged. "It's not terrible. Chips and candy bars and drinks, plus some heated things. Tacos, fries, burgers."

"Decent burgers?"

"Nothing I would touch with a ten-foot anti-salmonella pole, but you're welcome to try for yourself."

Leaning against the counter, Dillon nodded at the coffee pot. "I'll be cautious. Is there a coffee fund or anything?"

She showed him the cabinet of sugars and stir sticks. "All courtesy of Lanigan Printing and Advertising. I'm told it's good enough—well, unless you're very picky—and all you have to provide is your own mug. I have a couple here if you want to borrow for now."

"Thanks. You're making this place more and more appealing by the moment."

"I live to serve. Lanigan, that is." Serena was going to have to bite her tongue again. And Dillon really needed to stop with the blue-eyed smile. She tapped the chart taped inside the cabinet door. "If you're going to drink the coffee, you have to go on the coffee list. They rotate weeks to keep the coffee maker clean and the pot full. If you screw up you have to do two weeks in a row. Do you want to just put your name in place of Margaret's?"

He shrugged. "May as well. Got a pen?" She handed him one and Dillon leaned over her to make the change. He smelled like coffee, and something fruit-based, too, maybe a citrus scent.

"And while you're taking over Margaret's desk and coffee job, you may as well take over her fridge shelf, too," Serena said, giving herself a little more personal space by moving to open the refrigerator door. "The stuff in here isn't communal—nothing else is, really, other than coffee. Not to say you can't borrow some of my milk until you bring in some of your own. Assuming you can handle my fat-free soy, that is. Some guys balk."

"I'm not just any guy."

Oh, dear. The charm again. She'd turned down his coffee date, so this had to be just harmless. But it would be fine with Serena if Dillon stopped flirting. Not that he wasn't cute as all get out, but it wasn't what she was looking for. Too young, too tall and charming, too much in her daily orbit. She'd fallen for all of that with Joey, and then when it had fallen apart she'd been stuck limping along in the relationship while they figured out how to end it and still deal with living two doors apart.

She put on her professional, neutral smile. "So that's the lunchroom. Any questions?"

"These places nearby?"

"I think Jay at the front desk keeps the take-out binder up to date, and he has a whole alert system set up for the fancy food trucks in the area."

"For all my gourmet roach coach needs."

"Some of them are pretty great, actually."

"Yeah?" He had eye-crinkles.

"Yep. There's a fusion burrito one that is freakishly tasty."

"Freakishly tasty. I don't think anyone's ever given me that recommendation before. Can I persuade you to let me take you there, if Jay can track it down?"

Serena smoothed down her skirt. "Look, Dillon...It's not that I don't appreciate it."

"To celebrate my first day and all? You don't want me to sit all alone with my dry old sandwich, do you?"

"No, I know. I mean, I'm sure some of the others will be around."

"But not you?"

"Janice and I always go for smoothies on Mondays." It was true, too. Mostly.

"Tomorrow then?"

"Tuesday lunch basketball game down next to the dock."

"You play?"

"As if." Serena was barely five three. Janice was even shorter. "But we watch."

"Maybe I'll join in. I was a decent power forward in my day." A lot of his height was in his legs, Serena realized, and those broad shoulders would be an asset on defense.

"In your day? You're not exactly over the hill."

He shrugged and handed back the pen. "I had an, um, setback after my sophomore year in high school. I kinda quit the team after that. But I still love the game."

Serena stuffed the pen back in her bag. "Thanks. Well, I'm sure the guys would love to have you join them. You should ask Miguel about it, or Eddie."

"But not you, and no lunch with you, is what you're saying?"

He was blunt and persistent and it was possible he had dimples lurking, and Serena just really wanted the resolve to not be charmed.

"Thanks but no, no lunch. I've got to get to work; is there anything else I can show you? Oh, first aid is over there, beside the door. And the microwave overcooks everything, be careful. But if you get burned, there's aloe cream in there. Come on, I'll show you the stairs down to the warehouse on the way to HR."

Once she'd deposited Dillon for safety training, Serena retreated to the ordered calm of her office, picking up the morning's proof sheets with a distinctly relieved sigh.

Tuesday, right as Janice stopped by Serena's office to walk with her down to the basketball game, Serena's cell rang. "Hang on."

"Only because it's still cold out," Janice said. Once it warmed up some, several of the guys would play shirtless.

"Are you sitting down?" Natalie asked over the phone.

"Um, sure."

"Seriously, Serena sit down. No, never mind. Don't sit. Get out the door. I'm texting you the address."

"What address?" She shrugged at Janice, mouthed Natalie's name.

"They barely even posted this house, and Carter's the one who got the listing, so you know how much I love you that I'm even telling you about it, but get your ass over here now. Can you?"

"Now?"

"Now, yes, now. Cancel whatever boring meeting you have and get over here. I'll meet you in ten minutes."

"Nat, you haven't even sent me the listing."

"Doesn't matter. I know you. Get over here."

"Yeah, yeah. I'm missing the basketball game for this, you know." Raising her eyebrows, Serena pointed at the phone, then reached for her bag. Janice waved and headed off.

"It's a two bedroom bungalow built in the forties and renovated six years ago. Move your damn ass."

"Just listed?" Now Serena's heart was pounding in time to the excitement in Natalie's voice.

"Twenty minutes ago, twenty-one now, and Carter is emailing everyone in the universe about it."

"I'm in the car."

"Liar."

"I'm in the stairwell, it's the same thing. The forties?"

"1944. All of the electrical is updated."

"Windows?"

"I don't know, I'll be there in five minutes, but it's got a trellis over the carport, covered with trumpet vine."

"Shit!" Serena would have skidded down three stairs if she hadn't grabbed the rail. She had no time for a sprained ankle; Natalie was telling her about the furnace and insulation and there was a back patio. A patio!

"Oh, hell, Serena. Hell and triple damn."

She stopped dead in front of her car. "What?"

Natalie was grim. "Just hurry. Carter's here already. Bastard. He's walking some smiling young couple out, and the windows. Oh, Serena, hurry. It has a stained glass dormer window."

CHAPTER FOUR

"JORGE, OLD MAN, YOU'RE OUT. Dillon's my guy now," Eddie said, slinging his sweaty arm up around Dillon's sweaty shoulders.

Eddie was the head of sales. Jorge was a photographer. Johnnie was the other graphic designer. Ida was from accounting. The last player from the office lunchtime basketball team was Philip, another writer. Philip had been benched to make room for Dillon, who was busy figuring everyone out, befriending his coworkers. There'd always been something about the literal teamwork of hoops that made it easier for Dillon to find his place in a crowd.

It wasn't a full game, given that they all had just an hour to change, play, clean up, eat, and get back to work, but two fifteen-minute halves were enough to get his blood pumping and to get Eddie into quite the lather. Not that Eddie hadn't been hustling. They'd all been hustling, trying to keep up with their opponents on the makeshift loading dock court.

Apparently Dillon had helped them not be trounced as badly as normal by Miguel's warehouse team, and it earned him a gold star in office politics. Even Philip claimed to be glad to have Dillon there, since Philip's knees gave him some sort of problems that

Dillon only half-noted as Philip explicated them. Philip had cornered him a few times already, and it wasn't all that charitable of Dillon, but he was looking to form bonds that he'd honestly enjoy, in this new job, in this relatively new town. And Philip was wearying, with his long stories and longer complaints.

Dillon reached over to shake Jorge's hand. The man was a quiet, but efficient, shooting guard, and it was obvious that he and Ida were practically telepathic as they dealt with the backcourt. "Did Ricky—that was Ricky, right?—did he trip you up too bad?"

"Nah," Jorge said, though he did reflexively rub his shin. "And Ricky'll get his own back next week."

Dillon nodded. The office team retreated to a small clump of trees next to the dock while the warehouse team claimed winner's rights to first use of the washroom. The day was January-cool, but Dillon was glad to sit in the shade and let his heart rate return to normal. This Tuesday game was an unexpected bonus of Lanigan; it had been a good while since he'd played with any regularity, but there were years when Dillon had spent more time on a court than anywhere else.

Back then he'd been able to get through a half-hour of play without being quite so winded, but he'd get back in shape. Eddie, the sort-of captain, had welcomed Dillon with open (albeit sweaty) arms; Dillon would do what it took to keep up that goodwill and camaraderie.

The game gave him a clearer in with his coworkers than the whirlwind of introductions over his first day and a half at Lanigan. Other than cursory hellos to several people, he'd pretty much been stuck at his desk, deciphering the somewhat-clear piles left by the outgoing Margaret. He'd communicated regularly with Anica, but only run into Serena in passing a couple of times. She hadn't, despite her earlier claims, shown up to watch the basketball game. Her friend Janice was there, perched in the open back of a delivery truck angled so as to give her and other non-players sun-warmed court-side seats.

He didn't ask about Serena; he'd already been shot down for coffee and for lunch, and he wasn't the idiot his sister and brother-in-law liked to suggest.

But that didn't mean he'd failed to note how her denim skirt had hugged her ass that morning. Her wardrobe, in the few days he'd known her, was barely on the office-casual side of hippie attire, which suited her colorful nature and flowing light brown hair.

"Seriously, Jorge, why're you moving like molasses when I need you to cut out Polk for me?" Eddie asked. One quick fact Dillon had picked up on about Eddie was that a lot of things were about Eddie. He could be funny, though.

Jorge just shrugged and knocked back the last of his water. He'd ignored or downplayed every one of Eddie's jibes without once defending himself. Now he stood and, patting Dillon once on the shoulder, headed to the showers. Slowly, almost pointedly slowly.

Dillon snorted softly, but Johnnie was guffawing, which seemed to be good enough for Eddie.

Dillon caught up to Jorge. After changing, they make their way back to the third floor offices together, discussing a new project. It wasn't until he was on his way out for the day that Dillon saw Serena again.

She stood at the top of the warehouse stairs, clutching Janice's arm and speaking rapidly. Grinning. Serena was grinning. Her face in profile and her mouth wide and her cheeks glowing and since her hair was pulled back into a loose braid; Dillon noticed for the first time that she had a freckle on the base of her right ear. It was a shade darker than the brown of her hair, and maybe it was technically called a mole or a beauty spot or something, but to Dillon it looked like a freckle.

It looked like a great place to place his lips.

Cautioning himself to go past without making a hat trick of three rejections on three consecutive workdays, Dillon strode toward the pair. "Bye, Janice, Serena."

"See ya, Toots."

And then Serena turned the full force of that grin on him. She'd been biting her full lower lip, listening to Janice's reply to whatever had her bouncing off the beige office walls, and it gave her just a bit of an impish air. Like a fun kind of faerie creature; like Arwen that one time in *Lord of the Rings* she smiled instead of being so focused and intense all the time.

"Hey, Dillon. You're off?"

And he stopped walking. Like an idiot. "Yep. Five o'clock and all."

"It's five, that's fantastic. You'll come have a beer—a sparkling water, whatever—with me while I wait, right?" Serena was asking Janice, not him, and Dillon knew that, yet he was somehow standing there. And so maybe it was just because he was in the way, but maybe she meant it when Serena turned to him and added, "We're going to Frijoles, do you know it? It's just down Washington. I've got an hour before the other buyers were told to put their bid in so they could compare. Am I talking nonsense? Sorry, I'm all over the place. It's the house, I saw my house today, and I put in an offer, but Carter's couple was putting in an offer, too, and the seller is Carter's client, so he's advised—advised, strong-armed, I'm sure, Natalie said it wasn't totally ethical to hold up their response to my offer until they got the other one, even though they have days to respond so I guess it's fine?—anyway, he told them to wait for his couple's six PM offer so they could see which is better."

"Toots."

Serena glanced between them, at Dillon's raised brow and Janice's rolling eyes, and took a breath. "I'm a nervous wreck. Sorry. I'll calm down, but you have to keep me company while I wait to hear if the other couple is going to make an offer, okay? Will you?"

Janice agreed, and the three of them started towards the elevator.

"Shit, I forgot my stuff!" Serena whirled around and headed towards her office, but turned back and rushed more words in their direction. "Dillon, Janice can tell you where Frijoles is. If you want to come along, that is. Maybe you've got other plans, I don't think I even gave you a chance to say, but if you want to come along they've got a good happy hour and that way someone will split nachos with me, since Janice won't eat them."

"Maybe Dillon doesn't eat nachos either, Toots!" Janice called at Serena's retreating form, but she'd already rounded the corner, and Dillon was left holding the elevator door open just for Janice.

Frijoles was bustling. Their two-dollar beers and half-off margaritas had plenty to do with the happy hour crowds, but so did their ambience. Serena was full of giddy nerves, and the modern pop soundtrack, heavily adorned walls, and classic mission-style stained glass windows settled her into an upbeat groove as she worked her way to the booth where Jorge had joined Janice and, yes, Dillon.

He'd shown up, then. Good. That was good.

Because of the nachos. And because everyone at Lanigan should know about Frijoles; it had the best nachos of the several Tex-Mex spots within a mile or two of the office. It was just friendly, inviting him along, and she was too busy worrying about the offer on the house to worry about if Dillon thought her inviting him along was some sort of apology for not getting lunch or coffee—tea—with him the times he'd asked her. It wasn't. She was just friendly.

Serena worked to put everything back in their necessary boxes. Dillon was her coworker, and she had to stay professional. She needed that promotion, and the raise that came with it; in the few hours since she'd seen the house, she'd brimmed over with ideas for paint and furnishings and other delightful but not-exactly-free ways to decorate the rooms. She paused to snap a photo of the multi-hued cane rush stools in the bar area, making a mental note to ask Frijoles' manager if he knew where she could buy some; they would be perfect up against the island in her new house.

If she got her new house.

Natalie had carefully eyeballed her rival realtor as he left, and predicted that the couple he'd shown it to were interested, but not ready to commit. Serena had been ready. The house was just about everything she'd had on her dream list, except a magnolia tree and a second bathroom, but she could plant the tree—and since she was going to live blessedly alone, she really only needed one bathroom. Sure, sometimes her half-brother might spend the night, but they'd shared a bathroom when he was a toddler, which had to be worse than occasionally letting him use hers now that he was a teenager.

Janice scooted over so Serena could slide in next to her, across from Dillon and the nachos between them.

"Got a mix of chicken and fajita, since I didn't know which you liked." Dillon handed her a side plate so she could load it with chips and guac. He was wearing that same dark blue blazer again, the one he always seemed to wear, like somehow he knew it enhanced the hues of both his deep blue eyes and his near-black hair.

"Combo is great, thanks," she told him. "Fajita, usually, but I'm not picky."

Janice snorted, earning herself an arch look, but the waiter showed up with beer and distracted Serena from her mock-outrage.

"Here's to your house," Dillon said, lifting his Corona to clink against hers. "Janice told us all about it."

"Well, I made a valiant attempt, anyway. You were going on like your words got caught up in the rapids and washed ashore in a different order."

"Ha ha ha. You're hilarious."

"Call em like I see em, Toots."

Serena's laugh was genuine then. Dillon's warm smile flustered her a bit, and she took a moment to check her phone was on, ready to vibrate the moment Natalie called, and for what felt like the first time all day, let out a deep breath. "Okay, fair enough. I'm just nervous."

"Like a cat on a porch full of rocking chairs," Janice agreed.

"But, I mean, I've been looking and looking and I haven't seen anything this close to perfect. And I can afford it, just, and the location is nice and did I tell you there's granite counters in the kitchen?"

"You maybe mentioned it."

"And my mom didn't even have bad things to say. Well, not many. I should have called her to meet me there so she could have, whatever, judged the psychic vibes and checked for residual spirits or something, but I didn't so she only saw the pictures so I thought she'd be harsher. But she only said it would need a fountain or a bird bath to balance out the front yard, which you know is practically a ringing endorsement from her."

"What'll you do if you don't get it?" Jorge asked. He was practical to the point of pessimism, though his overwhelming sweetness usually made it tolerable.

"Aw, Toots, she's antsy enough."

"It'll work out," Dillon said. Based on what evidence, Serena couldn't imagine, but it was nice of him to attempt to be reassuring. She smiled at him and scooped some more nachos onto her plate.

They were all deep into debate about whether Mr. Lanigan had started coloring his hair when Serena's phone rang. It was still a quarter to six, and her gut clenched. It couldn't be good for Natalie to be calling early. It could only mean that the other buyers had already put in a competing bid.

The table quieted while Serena answered. "Nat?"

"Okay, listen. It's all right."

"All right like my offer was accepted, or all right like you're trying to get me not to hyperventilate before you tell me the bad news?"

"Neither. Well, not really."

"Nat." She reached out and took Janice's proffered hand.

Natalie sighed. "I don't know yet what the sellers will do."

"But?" She gripped Janice's hand tighter, ignoring her inarticulate protest.

"Carter's couple did make an offer, and from the sounds of it, it was full price, but they had contingencies."

Serena gnawed at her now-raw lip. "I didn't have contingencies. I'm pre-approved. You put that on the paper, right?"

Nat's laugh was hardly reassuring. "All the stories I've told you over the years about freaked out buyers, and you're turning into every one of them. You saw the offer; you know everything was ship-shape. So here's what's happening, okay? The owners have two offers to look at. Carter's helping them go over them, but yours is in their best interest. They're motivated and you're pre-approved. We'll know more in a few days—maybe even sooner—and Carter promised to tell me if any other offers come in."

"Other offers?"

"Well, they're hardly going to stop showing it just because they've had some activity already."

"What if someone offers them above full price?" Serena squeezed Janice's hand too hard, and Janice pulled away, and then punched her lightly in the bicep. "Ow."

"Ow?" Nat asked.

"Never mind. Hang on." Serena tucked the phone against her chest and dug in her bag for some cash. "I'm going to take off. Thanks for hanging with me, y'all, you're the best."

Jorge and Dillon and Janice lifted their hands in farewell as Serena stood and put the phone back to her ear. "I'm on my way to my car," she told Natalie.

"Oh, goodie." Natalie used her own Bluetooth constantly, but complained whenever Serena did.

"It's too loud inside, just deal with it. Now tell me again about why the owners are so eager to sell? Will it really matter to them if I can close fast? What contingencies did the other offer have?"

It took Natalie all of Serena's drive home plus another fifteen minutes of pacing in her scummy-butt apartment to calm all of Serena's nerves and answer all of her questions. Finally reassured, Serena thanked her effusively and disconnected. Time to make some noise. She dialed up a kickass dance party playlist, blasting it as she shimmied around the apartment, sneering at the dingy off-white walls that would soon, ideally, hold her no more.

CHAPTER FIVE

SERENA'S HAIR WAS BOUND UP IN A BRAID that wrapped over her skull in some kind of mystical feminine way and she wore another flowy top that reminded him of Elven folk. Normally, Dillon preferred sci-fi, but wasn't averse to crossing the sci-fi/fantasy divide, such as it was, and every day Serena was just a little more of a fantasy kind of woman.

He stood in her office doorway for just one second, watching her. Not so long that anyone in the hall would think he was a moron. Maybe two seconds, but then he reached up to rap on her door frame with his knuckles.

"Dillon, hey." She smiled as she looked around at him.

"You wanted to see me before the meeting?" There was a regular Thursday morning meeting with Anica and the creatives on his team; Margaret's binder of past schedules had been a fount of information on how things worked at Lanigan. Some people's deadlines jumped around from week to week, but Janice's guiding hand reached in so that, in the end, the jobs were on schedule.

"Yeah, thanks. It's about Mooney. I want the 'success stories' page to be more vibrant, and I came up with this deal here," she turned a notebook towards him, "so you have a pull quote and they each expand into a box with the whole story. But it means I need thirty or forty words to pull from each, and maybe they should be no more than three hundred words overall, so the boxes don't overwhelm the rest of the page. Can you do it?"

He was already mentally reviewing that section of the site, and the files bequeathed to him by Margaret. He'd seen something, back when he was first getting into the Mooney work—it was the biggest account he'd been thrown into mid-project—about success stories and the page layout.

"Didn't Eddie say they wanted mostly smiling faces and not so much language on that page?"

"But they're wrong. My way works better and Edgar Mooney will agree as soon as he sees it."

Her brash confidence was infectious. His lips quirked. "So I'm not just doing this for your ego and it'll get shot down?"

"My ego doesn't need Mooney to help it thrive, and thanks for the negativity." But she smiled back at him, and Dillon took one second, again, as if seconds were just laying around to be wasted, to absorb the curve of her gloss-shimmered lip.

He grinned and tapped her sketched plan. "I don't mean it. This is good, it'll look great. When do you want the copy?"

"Tomorrow morning's fine." Serena stood and grabbed a few files. "Ready to encounter your first production meeting?"

"You make it sound terrifying." He stood back to let her lead the way out of her office.

"Sure. So far you've only seen the nice side of Janice. Wait'll Eddie lets her know that Houston Green wants to move their roll-out to tie in to rodeo season."

"Isn't that next month?" The Houston Livestock Show and Rodeo, as Dillon understood it, took place at the end of February and into March. Shannon and Justin had attended every year since they moved to Houston, though their newborn would presumably keep them home this season.

"Yep. You see the problem then."

"Okay, now I'm scared." Dillon glanced down at Serena. He was tall enough to see the whorls of her hair as they were drawn into the braid on the crown of her head, and he wondered if she'd styled it on her own. And if not, who did it for her.

"It's okay, you're a newbie. You'll probably miss all the crossfire."

"'Probably.' Such a reassuring word."

Entering Conference Room B, she winked at him before crossing to one of the table's long sides. "You come sit by me, newbie. I'll protect you."

"Or use me as a shield?"

"No promises."

"I'm so relieved," Dillon said, and snagged the chair next to hers before anyone else could.

He was a lefty. Serena's elbow kept bumping Dillon's as they took notes next to each other. She'd shifted her chair a little to the side, but there was a table leg there, and the bumps kept happening, which probably would have sent tingles up her arm no matter who it was bumping her funny bone.

She focused on mapping out a cleaner version of the new page for Mooney's site, and every time she moved her arm it brushed the sleeve of that one blazer of his. Not that Houston—or Los Angeles, for that matter—was cool enough to merit a large jacket wardrobe. She just was observant, was all. For instance, she kept an eye on him, and was pretty darn sure that he was deliberately reaching for his pencil every time she grabbed a pen.

Ever-so-subtly, he reached over and slid her sketch so it was in front of him, and started to fill in her pull-quote boxes. She tried to read over his obstructing left arm—lefties sure did hold their pencils so that no one could copy from them—but had to wait until he slid the page back over. Then she had to press her lips together to stop from laughing, shooting a glance at Anica to make sure they weren't about to be called out like obstreperous third-graders.

A minute later she'd slid the paper back at him. Next to his quote, "Man in the Mooney Investments says, 'Cattle futures are high!'" she'd drawn a cow jumping over a moon whose visage was remarkably similar to Edgar Mooney's face. She was about to take it back to add a long-nosed coyote next to, "Mooney Investments makes me howl with joy!" and an astronaut giving a thumbs-up next to, "One small step for Mooney Investments; one giant leap for my portfolio!" when Anica said her name.

Serena wasn't positive, because how would she know if his chuckle was low and a little growly, but she thought Dillon used the noise she made gathering herself together to laugh at her. Just see if she ever volunteered to keep him out of the crossfire again.

Right as the meeting was wrapping up, Serena's phone buzzed. It was Natalie; Serena had her hold on while she vamoosed to the quiet of her office. "Yeah? What is it? Did they reject it? Why? Hang on, let me shut my door."

She caught a glimpse of Dillon looking in at her as she swung it shut, a slight furrow between his cobalt eyes, but all she could do was widen her eyes at him and barricade herself in privacy to find out what was happening with her offer on the house. He'd been a respite, during the meeting, from her obsessive worry about what Natalie would have to say, but if she was lucky—or maybe really unlucky—Serena was about to get answers.

"You sitting down?"

"Why do I have to sit down?"

"You don't. I'm just curious."

"No, for the love of Pete, I'm not sitting down, I'm like a caged wildebeest. Can you just tell me why you called? If you called just to say hello, I will kill you. Really violently, too. There'll be gore."

"I'm not calling just to say hello," Natalie said, and she sounded as calm as deserted stretch of beach.

"You're infuriating, you know that? Just tell me, will you?"

Natalie interrupted. "You got it."

Serena gulped. She'd been mid-rant and Natalie had spoken so quietly, like no big deal, how's the weather, I got a new outfit ain't that cool, blah blah blah. But that was just like her.

"I got it?"

"You got it."

"I got it?"

"Yes, yes, you got it!" Natalie laughed.

"You're sure?"

"Serena. Do you need to take six calming breaths and call me back later?"

"No way. Not a chance. You'll just refuse to pick up and then I'll never get the details and I'll never believe you. Tell me everything."

"After you promised me a bloody death?"

"You tell me right now, Natalie Renee East, or so help me, I will never speak to you again." But Serena was smiling so hard her cheeks hurt, and she couldn't sit fully down in her desk chair before she had to get up and pace the confines of her office again. She sure as heck couldn't take notes on whatever Nat told her.

Natalie knew her well enough, though, to promise a follow-up email with everything in writing. And Serena grasped the basics: they'd accepted her offer, they wanted to close at the end of February, Natalie had an inspector she trusted all set up to go through the house on Saturday morning, and Carter hadn't even been too surly when he'd given Natalie all the news.

"I'm going to paint the kitchen kind of a sage green, I think. Or butter gold? What do you think?"

"I think you have a lot of paperwork to deal with before you pick out paint colors."

"But which do you think will go better with those countertops?"

"As if you'd really give anyone else the choice on your wall color."

"Hey."

"Hey, nothing. You didn't even let me pick the paint for my own house; why would you let anyone tell you what to do for yours?"

Serena sat back, finally, blowing out a long breath. "My house."

"Your house."

"Mine."

"All yours."

She could feel just how wobbly her grin was. "Mine, all mine."

Well, that was odd. Dillon thought they were doing something fun there, at the meeting. Kind of goofy, sure, but fun. They'd been joking around in the hall, and then it continued during, and he'd kind of figured it would continue on the way back to their offices, too. But she'd run off, just about shut the door in his face, and not emerged for hours. Or not that he'd seen, anyway.

Not that he was particularly looking. But he'd been moving around Lanigan for various reasons, and each time he happened past, her office door remained closed.

He and Jorge were going over how much white space he needed on some HouGreen web ads when she finally walked by, and since it was pretty much the end of the day, Dillon wrapped up with the photographer and headed after her.

"Hey."

"Oh, hey, Dillon."

"I'm still standing, even with all the bullet holes."

Serena stopped and quirked an eyebrow at him. "Bullet holes?"

"Because you left the meeting so fast and I got caught in the crossfire." She didn't look like that cleared things up any, so obviously he was a moron and their banter hadn't meant anything to her.

"Oh, right. Crossfire."

He was going to let it go, but then she smiled a big happy smile at him, and next thing he knew, Dillon was asking if she was headed to Frijoles for happy hour.

"I wish. I was so distracted last time that I barely even tasted the beer. I think those nachos were totally wasted on me."

"So come make up for that now."

"No can do. I can only go once a week."

"Or what, the happy hour police will arrest you?"

"Ha ha. No, it's my budget. Been saving for years for my down payment and then—oh, this is my news, it's the best thing! I got my house! I get to finally move. Finally! What was I saying?" She caught her lower lip between her teeth and slowed down. "Budget. Right. So I have a system. One happy hour, one lunch, and one other social thing per week. That gives me enough going out time so I don't feel deprived, but stops me from spending all my house money on ephemeral things."

He wasn't sure he'd call developing friendships over drinks ephemeral, but okay. She had a goal, that made sense. Even if it didn't quite align with his goal, which, when he thought about it, probably needed to change. He kept asking to get closer to her, and she kept turning him down with a smile.

It was the smiles that kept him on the hook, though. They were great, Serena's smiles. They made him feel welcomed into her world, and something deeper, as well. Something kind of primal. He wasn't used to it, to the way it kept hitting him over and over and over again. Or to the way it took away the filter of common sense, which he knew—when he wasn't standing next to her—informed him that he'd made his attraction to her obvious enough that he should settle back and let her make the next move.

But then they had a few moments alone in the lobby and he saw sparks in her eyes when she smiled at him and he was searching for an excuse to spend more time with her, no matter what his common sense might advise upon reflection.

"That's great about the house, congratulations. Now you have to come to happy hour, and let me buy you a celebratory beer. It's my treat, so your budget won't even notice."

She laughed and damn if she didn't reach up and squeeze his bicep. He felt the warm pressure through his shirt and jacket both. "You are the sweetest guy, Dillon. Thanks so much. But I've got a million things to organize now, to get ready for this. Maybe a million and a half. I don't know. I've been itching to go home and start making lists."

Sweet. Great. "You can't make lists at Frijoles?"

"Don't tempt me."

As if he would obey that directive.

But Dillon's filter finally kicked in enough to shut him up, so he just walked Serena to her car, listening to her ramble on about her lists and boxes and the room idea binders she'd been compiling for years while she saved up for her down payment. When she'd hopped into her little hybrid and left the Lanigan parking lot, he didn't even stand there staring after her like a moron. Not for more than a minute, anyway, before taking himself home. But then home was boring, and Shannon and Justin were at a childbirth class, so he took himself to a superhero movie.

At least there, in the dark with nachos and a soda and explosions and baddies and powers, he was surrounded by a crowd of people on his same wavelength. Sure, not all of them would trudge home alone afterwards, but that wasn't something he had to think about for the entire two hour and thirty-two minutes.

CHAPTER SIX

SERENA WOKE WITH A HAND ON HER BREAST and a stimulating heaviness between her legs. She stretched and indulged in a waking continuation of the dream: Dillon moving over her lazily stretching form, a little stubble scraping her sensitive skin and her hands buried in dark hair she imagined to be thick and soft and warm.

She hummed throughout her shower. No matter that he was tall like Joey and young like Joey and in inescapable proximity like Joey; Dillon was happier dream fodder than Joey had ever been.

Sadly, that didn't change the reality of their relationship. Friday had ended with Anica escorting Serena to Ms. Lanigan's office for a meeting about her future with the company. With no notice, leaving her mentally scrambling together all the scraps of proof that she deserved a promotion, had earned it with her talent and leadership. And it didn't help that tall, gorgeous, young Dillon hadn't given her all of the pull quotes for the Mooney redesign she'd asked for. So much for feeling like she had any semblance of authority over the team. She was left to nod like an automaton throughout the meeting, barely a thing to contribute, and unsure if she was imagining a slightly disappointed look in Ms. Lanigan's eyes.

It was the weekend, though, and time to put her work issues away. Well, except for the occasional fantasy, but that wasn't really work. Serena loaded two more boxes up with books and the art supplies she was least likely to crave over the month before moving. She'd given herself a strict schedule of one box per work day and ten boxes per weekend, and even though she'd already cheated and counted cleaning out a neglected dresser drawer full of winter clothes as packing, she felt okay about it all. Her scummy-butt apartment wasn't nearly large enough to make packing to finally move out of it an overwhelming chore. She did have a whole lot of art supplies, though.

She got so caught up sketching ideas to turn her new second bedroom into a studio with enough space left over for a futon for her half-brother's visits that she had to dash over to the house to meet Natalie and the inspector.

It was an overcast day, but the rain held off long enough for the guy to check the roof and the attics and the crawl space under the house. The floors were, predictably enough, not level, but that and the degraded insulation were easy fixes. More problematic were the critters under the house, the rotten boards all along the north wall, and the wiring that was only updated in the remodeled kitchen and living areas.

"They have to get it up to code, right?" Serena asked Natalie once Carter and the inspector had left.

"Well, they don't have to. But the report will go with the house now, so even if they try to back out of it with you, any other buyer would see that and not offer as much as you did."

Serena put a hand to her racing heart. "Don't talk about other buyers, you're freaking me out."

"Well, sweetie, I'm just telling you the truth." Natalie's pretty green eyes were laughing at her, Serena was sure of it. "Don't go into a frenzy. We discussed this. This is the next stage. Let's figure out how much you want to ask them to do, how much you're willing to let them do or if you want to get bids and ask for the money to do it yourself, all of that. Come on, I'll buy you a sandwich and you can take a deep breath and we'll make lists. I know how you like your lists."

Blowing out a growl of a breath, Serena nodded. "Okay, fine. You're the expert. But I want soup. It's about to rain and my house has a raccoon family under it, so I want soup."

Dillon's whole weekend had been shot to hell. He'd been close to scoring Rockets tickets online, but the guy never called him back after they'd gone back and forth a few times. Then his cable was out so he didn't get to watch the game from the comfort of the deep sofa in his townhouse. And the rain screwed with his plan to surprise Shannon by planting some spring flowers at her house. She wasn't exactly up for a lot of bending and shoveling, and Justin, for all his fine qualities, sucked at gardening. Not that Dillon was a complete natural, but he'd spent more weekends than he'd liked helping his mom with her over-abundant flowerbeds, and had picked up a basic skill set. Plus, getting in spring annuals was the kind of thing his mom would have done during Shannon's last trimester, if his mom were around.

It was weird, sometimes, trying to imagine what his parents would have been like as empty nesters. When Shannon had gone to UCLA, she'd lived on campus, so of course the house was quieter with just the three of them there. None of Shan's girlfriends stopping by, or boyfriends for that matter, and a dramatic decrease in the number of stupid shows on TV. But Dillon's sister had still come home every couple of weeks to do laundry, and was apt to swing by to pick up random items or grab a meal when the dining hall options got boring.

But Dillon was only sixteen when they died, so even though his parents hadn't really been tied to child care or driving him everywhere or any of that, they never made the leap to being on their own. They'd talked about it sometimes, but it was mostly joking stuff, like that if Dillon left town for college, they'd quit their jobs and move to wherever he was, or that they were going to remodel the house like a giant play-land so the grandkids would always want to be with them.

He figured if he and Shannon had ended up both in Houston like this—if he'd moved to Texas on his own accord and not just because she was the only family he had left in the world until he made a family of his own—his parents probably would have sold the house in LA. Especially with the baby on the way. Dillon had been old enough to have known them as adults who were not just parents. Dad's eye-rolling acceptance of Mom's beloved Broadway shows; the fact that they went out for Indian food practically every time they had a meal without their kids; their mutual dislike of organized group travel—all of it sketched in the shape of their older age together. But they'd also clearly imagined being close to their kids when Dillon and Shannon were adults making their own ways in the world.

None of that was possible anymore. So Shannon gave Dillon a good deal on her old townhouse and always made room at the table when he dropped in, and Dillon planted flowers in her front garden. Shannon hadn't ever explicitly said it, but Dillon knew, because for him it was the same: he nurtured Shannon out of genuine brotherly love, but, also, because Mom and Dad didn't have the option to do it themselves.

He hiked his jacket up to mostly cover his neck and the back of his head, and jogged through the Lanigan parking lot, arriving in the lobby dripping only slightly. The forecast called for fairly steady rain over the next few days, which presumably meant no lunchtime bball, no gardening, no going for runs.

Good thing his cable was working again.

"Why so glum, Toots?"

Janice stopped on the landing on her way downstairs, looking not in the least bummed out by the weather or life in general.

"You know of any good gyms around here?"

"Do I know of any good gyms? Toots. I know the best, the worst, everything in between. What are you looking for? Lifting? Training? Circuit?"

He shook his head. "I just want to be able to run when it's raining, and maybe some weights. I guess I could just get a treadmill."

She tapped his arm with her trusty clipboard. "Bite your tongue, Toots. You're not getting any younger, you know, and running doesn't build strength."

"That's what the hoops are for."

"Did you forget the part where you were about to drop after half an hour last week?"

"You sound like Coach Fairbairn."

"Well, Coach Fairbairn was a wise man. I'll hook you up with a pass to my place, then when you want to work with a trainer I can make sure you're with the best."

Dillon sighed. "I should have just Googled it."

"Too late now, Toots. Come downstairs with me, and you can take the stairs two at a time—three at a time, your legs are long— on your way up."

"You're not going to just let me pass, are you?"

"Not a chance."

Dillon grumbled, but only so he didn't have to admit to Janice that it felt good to let her harass him a bit about working out. Dropping basketball after his parents died had been, his counselor and Coach Fairbairn and half the team had told him, a dumbass move. Even Justin, who he hardly knew at the time, pointed out the advantages of the workouts and the time with guys who knew him well enough to not treat him like Sad Orphan Boy.

Now that he was smarter than the average teenager, he wasn't going to walk away from friendships, exercise, or anything else that made him feel good.

A long week divided between new work responsibilities and stolen time preparing for her move meant Serena was more than ready for Friday's happy hour.

"Toots!" Janice popped up and gave Serena a hug, then nudged her into the booth next to Dillon. He gave her his appraising half-smile. She returned the look, a little surprised to note that he'd for once thrown off his blazer and rolled up his shirtsleeves, baring long lean forearms. Great. As if the eyes and the cheekbones weren't enough for her to notice, now she had a detailed visual on his forearms. Reminding herself that Dillon checked practically every box on the 'Joey taught me never to do this again' checklist didn't mean Serena was indifferent to the occasional male charm. And more than occasionally, Dillon was charming.

Janice had pulled up a chair to the end of the booth, and over the rim of her mug was scrutinizing Serena. "Toots, you look like last week's chili reheated and then gone cold." With a nod at their other coworkers, she said, "Someone get this one a drink."

Jorge already had the pitcher of margaritas in hand, but at Janice's words he'd stopped pouring and examined her. Serena ran her hands through her hair and shook it out behind her, rolled her shoulders, and smiled at him.

"Are you sick? Is that why you were out this afternoon?" Jorge asked, still not handing over her margarita. He seemed to be holding his breath waiting for her answer.

"No, Jorge, didn't you read my email? I took off so I meet an electrician at my new house?" Serena's tired smile turned into a suppressed grin as she reassured the hypochondriac photographer. "No germs, I swear it. I even went home afterwards for a shower since that attic is far from dust-free."

"Give her alcohol, that'll kill anything in her system," Eddie said, taking the margarita from Jorge and handing it across. "Did my guy Dan work out for you? I grant you that gold front tooth and the constant pit stains don't always inspire confidence, but he's smart about wires and all that shit."

"Yeah, he was great. Thanks—well, thank Magnolia, since I know you never talked to a subcontractor in your life."

Eddie laughed. The only time Eddie laughed at his own expense was when the joke pointed out good things about his wife. It was one of the reasons Serena tolerated his jackal personality so affably. Also because Magnolia really was excellent, and if she loved Eddie—and to all appearances she really did—he was worth tolerating.

Especially when he was handing over a much-needed margarita. And nachos. She grabbed one of the bright side plates and scooped a few chips onto it, topping them with more than her fair share of the guacamole. Before she could dig in, Eddie asked what she was doing about the additional problems the foundation contractor had found, and Serena heaved a deep breath. "You guys, enough with the inquisition. I can't think for one more second about problems with the house, it's stressing me out. Now, can I please chug this margarita and find out if Mooney threw any last-minute curve balls?"

"Poor Toots. Getting a little grumpy, are we?" Janice asked, ruffling her still-damp hair. Laughing, Serena leant to the side to evade her, almost landing against Dillon, and noticing for the first time that he'd removed not only his omnipresent blue blazer, but also his tie. So informal! Dillon was almost always in jacket and tie, which secretly amused Serena, since the rest of them on the creative side tended to go as casual as they could get away with. Dillon had to be one of the only men at Lanigan to even own more than two ties. He might dress down as he got more comfortable with the job, but until then she was keeping an unofficial tally. She was up to eight ties, but always just the one jacket.

"No one expects the Spanish Inquisition," he said.

"Huh?"

"The Spanish Inquisition? You know, from—oh, never mind." He glanced at Jorge, who smiled in apparent appreciation but didn't speak. Dillon turned back to Serena. "Mooney went great. And more importantly, we're done with it."

"Cheers to that," Eddie said, and they all lifted their mugs for a toast.

"Cheers, y'all," Dillon semi-drawled, which just about made Serena choke on her tortilla chip.

"What on earth was that?" she asked, after a quick clink of her margarita against Janice's. "I don't know how long you've lived in Houston now, but it's not long enough for you to get away with that accent."

He grinned. "Come on. It wasn't so bad."

"Janice? You're our resident country gal, what's your vote?" Janice had grown up in an East Texas town, that was, as she liked to say, too small even for a stoplight.

"Dude, hang ten, like, the voice is totally tubular. Like, you know?" Janice said. Or tried to. She was snorting by the end of her recitation, but so were the rest of them.

Serena, Janice, and Jorge were Texans from childhood, and Eddie had moved to Houston for college and never left. But while Dillon's love for Tex-Mex was all it really took to fit in with his coworkers, it didn't stop Serena from saying, "My point is made. I know all the unfortunate souls not native to this fine state just want to fit in, but butchering our favorite word won't get y'all anywhere with us." Serena, of course, said 'y'all' properly.

"Fine, no accent," Dillon said. "As long as Janice lays off whatever hybrid surfer-valley nonsense that was." He split the last of the margarita pitcher between Serena and Janice, which earned him smiles from both.

Not two minutes after the waiter delivered their second pitcher Miguel showed up, necessitating a badly choreographed shuffling of appetizers and drinks. Janice shoved into the booth next to Serena and suddenly Serena was shoved up next to Dillon. They somehow ended up thigh to thigh more often than not. He reached over her to get to the salsa verde, and she pressed into him while grabbing the salt for her chips. Maybe Serena was off-kilter from all the mental exertion of late, but she found herself rather intently focused on the space between her body and Dillon's. It was...humming. A bit electric. And very nice.

She self-consciously smoothed down her hair, wishing she'd put it up or taken the time to dry it before joining the gang. Not that it made a difference. They'd seen her frazzled and put-together and everything in between, and it was stupid misplaced vanity for her to worry about it now.

Like the most useless mantra ever, Serena reminded herself she didn't even believe in workplace flirtation. It could totally undermine her whole management campaign, making her look unprofessional and maybe like she wouldn't be able to effectively lead a team with Dillon on it. She'd already had to turn into an enforcer for Mooney, not that he hadn't come through, but it was the principle of the thing. Besides, she had enough to occupy her time, what with the house and everything.

Still. As Janice held court with one of her crazy-lady-next-door stories, prompting more of Eddie's hyena laughter that set them all off more often than not, Dillon tilted his mouth close to her ear to ask what she'd heard about an injury to the Rockets' star forward. And oh, he did smell good, and his breath warmed her cheek.

"Nah, it's just rumors," Serena replied, telling her body to stop with the shivers of awareness. "You know everyone's all 'the sky is falling' the second he stops to retie his shoes. Hey, how did you become such a Rockets fan, anyway? I always figured you for a Lakers guy."

"Oh, in my misguided youth, sure. But I was always more of a Bruins guy than a Lakers guy. And my sister moved to Houston when I was in college, so I visited a lot."

"After playoffs, though."

"After playoffs," he agreed. Reaching for another chip, which entailed leaning across her airspace, Dillon threw a smile Jorge's way then refocused on Serena. "Shannon—that's my sister—her company contracts some work for the Rockets, so she is a little up close sometimes. One Christmas I drove here for the break and since I had my car, she hired me as messenger boy for a couple of weeks. I guess you could say I was star struck by Charles Barkley."

She couldn't help it. She sniggered.

"No, listen, he was really nice to me. I mean, the one time I met him."

"Sir Charles?"

"The very one. Come on, tell me you wouldn't be taking his side against Shaq and the Lakers if he'd told you that determination was the key to success."

She laughed outright then. "Was he reading you his fortune cookie?"

Of course Eddie had stuck his nose in then, unable to abide a joke he hadn't instigated. Serena didn't get Dillon alone again (or as alone as a plate of nachos shared by six at a table for four allowed), but there were some serious vibes thrown her way during a story involving Dillon, his high school teammates, two bicycles and a starlit night.

If Serena spent the weekend remembering those vibes, it didn't matter. If the Brackenbridge kids' sleepover meant Serena woke every ten minutes to juvenile wrestling next door, it didn't matter. If Serena's dad's birthday card arrived a month late, it didn't matter.

The odd flash of Dillon's laughter floating through her head was just a distraction. On Saturday he'd emailed the group: "Sis had the baby! He's a giant and all are well and happy"—and her reply, despite how many times she'd re-drafted it, had still been over-effusive. No power on earth could get her to admit how often she'd checked her in-box since then for a reply from him. At thirty, she was for sure too grown up for that kind of foolishness. Plus she didn't need it.

She'd saved for her house for years—certainly she didn't get any help from either of her parents, though she did get a big laugh out of the mortgage people posing the question—and Serena was determined to focus only on getting her promotion, getting out of the scummy-butt apartment, and living the long-desired life of solitude where everything was just the way she wanted it.

Her colors on the walls, her furniture where it suited her, her music playing at whatever volume pleased only her. No parent or stepparent or landlady making her move the moment she got used to the night noises of a place.

Exactly how she wanted it.

CHAPTER SEVEN

MONDAY MORNING, JUST AS THE ELEVATOR prepared to lift her up to the Lanigan offices, Serena heard Dillon's "hold up," and before his blazered arm snaked through the closing doors she was fighting back an instinctive grin. She had yet to figure out how a guy who consistently wore the same jacket and sedate rotation of button-downs could manage to look refreshingly cute each morning.

She found herself edging aside just a little as Dillon squeezed up against her, his arm rubbing, then settling against, her shoulder. Serena reminded herself that she was too busy for a man in her life, and also that she should stop smiling before her face froze that way. She caught a flash of movement in the elevator's reflective walls, only then catching up to the fact that she'd begun flapping her shirt to create a breeze over her blazing chest. Her body, clearly prodding her into backing off from the handsome man beside her, was breaking out in honest-to-goodness hives. As soon as the elevator doors opened, Serena had to fairly sprint down the hall to cool down in front of the open break room fridge.

Jorge gave her the oddest look while moving her aside to put his week's worth of neatly stacked and labeled lunch containers on the half of the shelf he claimed. (Jorge, bless his heart, was morphing from fresh-faced twenty-something into a crotchety old man before their eyes. They all did their best to counteract it, except for Eddie, who preferred to stash prune juice and canisters of Metamucil with bright labels reading "Jorge, Sr." on Jorge's fridge shelf.)

"Morning, Jorge," Serena said, blushing a bit. "What's on the agenda today?"

He handed her the jug of iced tea she indicated before going into detail about the Houston Green account and the relative carbon-neutrality of the shoots they had planned. Fortunately, Serena's hives had settled down by the time they left the break room, but she hadn't breathed easy for long.

For the rest of the week she wasn't able to get near Dillon without the tightness in her throat, the flush across her face and chest, and, once, another full blown case of the hives. It was mortifying, and it was making work both difficult and irritating. She was on the verge of admitting to herself that she was slightly addicted to her interactions with Dillon. Every time she had to back away because being near him triggered a physical reaction, she resented her body for betraying her by noticing him so very much.

Exasperated, she began deliberately testing herself. First, some straight forward, friendly but professional email. That was fine, no big deal, same as her communication with Eddie or Anica or anyone. Then some more personal messages from her office to his—the new nephew was an easy mark for her experiments, bless his little ten-pound, two-ounce soul. And okay, she had to admit that his reply made her smile a little more goofily than she might have at an affectionate joke from, say, Jorge. But it didn't put her anywhere near the vicinity of hives.

Her next test—she wasn't quite ready for it but he took it out of her hands—was when he buzzed her desk to finalize his script for the MediCost spot. So she set her mind to business, and gauged her reactions to his warm voice, to the smile in his tone, to the laugh she deliberately provoked in him. And sure, her stomach fluttered a bit at that point. She was being purely scientific here, and there was no denying it. But she whipped out her compact mirror as soon as they'd hung up, and her complexion was just fine. If she noticed, while examining her chest for hives, that her nipples were a little peaked with anticipation, Serena determinedly ignored it. After all, that was a fairly normal reaction to an attractive man's husky, intimate chuckle in her ear, not these damned abnormal hives.

The fact that she and Dillon had known each other, had even laughed together, for weeks now without her noticing her clearly wanton and wayward nipples' involvement was neither here nor there.

Now Anica had called much of the team, including Serena and Dillon, into Conference Room B for a status report on Houston Green. Just to be safe, instead of sitting next to him as usual, she'd grabbed an empty chair between Anica and Janice. After they'd wrapped up, as people were mingling, Serena caught herself contemplating Dillon.

She pictured herself approaching him, gazing up into his cobalt eyes, running her hands under that omnipresent blazer of his, trailing her fingertips up past his narrow waist to his broad back. Imagined that his long hands cupped her face, pulling her in for a deep, slow kiss before brushing back her auburn hair to kiss her neck, her throat, her collarbone. His tongue gently flicking at her flesh as he nuzzled lower. Her arms pulling his taut body closer, hip to thigh, pelvis seeking pelvis. His chest, pressing against her eager nipples while her abdomen met the answering pulse of his erection....

He caught her looking, held her gaze, quirked an eyebrow from across the conference room.

Serena felt the blush swarming her face, her pounding heart, her breath caught shallow in her chest, but, no, thank goodness, she was okay. She checked her hands—pale as usual, unswollen—then surreptitiously felt her throat. Cool and smooth. She was light-headed, sure, but able to take a steadying breath, to turn away from him and slow her pulse.

"Mental note," Serena thought, "no matter what the libido seems to want, the mind and the body are in total agreement about this not dating thing." She swiped up the rest of her pens and determined to relegate Dillon firmly back into the "work pal only" zone. If that. Hives, honestly!

Dillon raised an eyebrow at Serena. She'd been giving him some funny signals since the previous week at Frijoles. He'd kind of given her a couple of signals then himself, if he was honest about it, but, well, margaritas and work success and proximity to her gently sweet scent. And of course the fact that she was so damned sexy—a fact he usually tried to forget, in the not pissing upriver of your own camp sort of vein. Maybe that was why she seemed to be bouncing between flirt and friend with him now. He supposed he couldn't fault her for it, but damned if he hadn't gotten good and confused in the meantime.

Anica interrupted his reverie with a pointed look. Damn. He recognized that look. It was the "stick around after they're gone so I can tear you down in private" look, and it was not his favorite look to be getting from his boss. He much preferred the "public high-five for solid excellence" look he'd gotten not infrequently in his earliest days at Lanigan. It seemed his learning curve was at an end. And yes, he knew the Houston Green copy wasn't (yet) up to snuff, but it didn't make him any more eager to face the music.

Dillon allowed himself a covert glance at Serena's excellently rounded backside as she and the others cleared out, loosened his suddenly-tight tie, and turned to Anica, glad the day was, at least, nearly over.

Serena dealt with having vivid sex fantasies at work the way she dealt with other importunate distractions: via virtual house-hunting. Sure, she had her precious bungalow almost completely and perfectly planned out on paper. And on her computer. And on lists on her phone. If only the bid from the seller's exterminator wasn't taking so long to come in so they could get back to negotiation on the inspection items.

But working on her lists, while excellent at dealing with low-level jitters, couldn't take her to the full-on peaceful high she required after picturing Dillon nude and spread-eagled over the table in Conference Room B. To calm that particular flush, Serena went straight to the really good stuff: scrolling through the newest real estate listings. And none of the empty lots or new construction, either. She needed wood frames, and converted attics, and ideally, screened-in sleeping balconies.

Natalie had sent out her weekly newsletter that afternoon, so she could be a good friend and generate some click-through traffic while she drooled over hipped rooflines and renovated kitchens that still honored the feel of the original construction. Nat's featured buy was a fairly generic townhouse, one of a line with identical plantation shutters and porches barely deep enough to hold a rocking chair. But below that was another, kind of amazing house. Its porch was authentically deep, and it featured a bow window in the dining room and a claw-foot tub in the master bath. A master bath! Because somewhere along the line—probably the update prior to the most kitchen renovation, if Serena's eye for detail didn't fail her, and it rarely did—someone had converted the smaller bedroom's closet into a tiny but adequate second bathroom, meaning doors could be rearranged to give the original small bathroom room to expand into a proper master bath.

She read the flyer through a couple of times, and clicked through the photos one by one before letting them shrink back into a grid on her screen.

It was too expensive, for one thing. Out of her range, at least at her current salary and keeping her savings and retirement plans intact.

Also she already had a dream house. One without an established magnolia tree blooming profusely in the front yard, like this new place did, but hers already. Almost totally and completely hers. And her house was almost totally and completely good enough.

She just had to get rid of the raccoons and plant a magnolia and, oh yeah, actually close on the mortgage first, and then, for all intents and purposes, it would be perfect.

Sure was nice to let the slideshow of the Magic Bungalow of Perfection scroll past her eyes and help bring her to calm stillness, though.

Aggrieved, Dillon kicked his townhouse's front door closed and scooped up the calico kitten making a beeline for the exit. "No, you don't," he warned it, before slinging it over his shoulder and heading into the kitchen for a cold beer. "I'm having more than enough trouble with females today; I don't need you adding to the mix." Setting Maisy down on the sofa and taking a long pull, he finally sighed. "Okay, okay, so it's not your fault. And I can hardly blame Anica, she's right about the tear sheets." Maisy reached a paw up to bat at his fingers, unfazed by his suddenly morose tone. "But what the hell is going on with Serena?"

It just didn't make sense. Serena was one of the most straightforward people he knew. Even before he'd started at Lanigan, she'd shown herself to be honest about everything— from work issues to the interpersonal. But lately he couldn't get a read on her at all. She was her usual vibrant self half the time, backing away from him the other half. It just didn't add up.

"Is it me?" he asked the kitten, who blinked and looked away. "I just...I kinda thought things were...." He took another pull on the beer, then had to laugh. He couldn't even articulate his feelings to his sister's cat. No wonder Serena was acting strangely. He was probably feeding her all kinds of assbackwards signals himself, and she didn't know how to react.

How did he feel, though? He shed his jacket, which Maisy promptly started kneading and purring upon, and headed back to the kitchen to throw together some sort of dinner. "Pasta night," he called to the kitten, which ignored him. "Did I talk to myself before you showed up?" he asked it. "I can't seem to keep my mouth shut at home anymore. But as long as you're listening, check it out, 'kay? Here I've known Serena for weeks. And don't get me wrong, I noticed her right off, you know? Second I walked into the interview, as a matter of fact. But I always thought you've got to keep that stuff out of the office." He bit into a carrot and glanced back at Maisy, who was now asleep. "Fine. Ignore me."

He had kept it out of the office, and over time had stopped— okay, practically stopped—looking for Serena as soon as he got to work. Stopped cataloguing the many enticing ways she wore her hair, stopped half-memorizing her schedule, stopped asking her out. Almost stopped, anyway. And they worked closely together; he couldn't go more than a few hours without having to at least shoot an email to Serena, if not engage in some more substantial contact.

Substantial contact. Face it, that was what he wanted.

He liked working with Serena, and valued their friendship, but he just wasn't satisfied with it. He wanted to be able to touch her. He needed to be able to touch her. To draw his fingers through the length of her hair then trail them down the slope of her breasts. To smooth his palm down her spine then spread it over her ass. To draw her body close to his as he tasted the creamy skin of her throat. To press his thigh between her yielding legs. His cock. To have her touch his throbbing cock. To have her grasp the base of his cock while his mouth closed over the tight peak of her nipple. To....

"Ow, fuck!" he cried as the fucking pasta boiled over. Maisy jumped up onto the table and mewled at him. "Not funny, cat. Just. Not. Funny." Trying to adjust himself back into some sort of composure, he drained the penne, stirred in a Bolognese he'd nuked, and scooped some into Maisy's bowl before throwing himself against the back of the sofa. Cuing up an old-school *Star Trek* episode off his DVR, he deliberately banished every thought of Serena, and her breasts, from his mind.

CHAPTER EIGHT

THIS TIME WHEN NATALIE ASKED if she was sitting down, Serena sat. There was something about her friend's voice that varied dramatically from the suppressed excitement of the call that said she'd gotten the house.

"What? What's wrong? Are the gals okay? Chris?" Chris, a pilot with one of the smaller airlines, was Natalie's boyfriend. It wasn't the most dangerous profession out there, but things happened, and Natalie didn't always know where he was from one day to the next.

"No, he's fine. Everyone's fine, Rachel and the baby are fine."

"Okay. Good. Good. So…I'm sitting, then." Serena straightened her spine, then reached out to rearrange the folders stacked on her desk, thickest files on the bottom and spread into a fan that allowed her to read the job names printed in the center of each tab.

"Well, I just got off the phone with Carter." The way Natalie spat out the name of her biggest professional rival did not bode well for Serena.

"Oh no." Her mind raced, considering then rejecting the potential problems. The sellers had agreed to the extermination. The bid to level the foundation was low enough that she could swing it, if she had to, though she'd asked them to cover that, too. And all she needed for the electrical was for them to bring it up to code, which they had to do regardless.

"They're not selling."

"They're...what?"

"Not selling, hon. I'm so sorry. It's to do with her job, the owner's. She was offered a good promotion to stay with her company, so now she's not transferring to the East Coast, so now they're not selling."

Serena let her head sink onto the forearm she'd braced on the desk, trying to focus on the sharp edge of the folders poking at her elbow. Anything was better than absorbing this news.

"Not selling?" Dimly aware she was parroting Natalie, Serena cleared her throat and tried again. "But they signed the contract, right?"

"They did, yes. And they'll have to give you back your earnest money, of course, but we can't force them to sell. We can't evict them. And Carter was—well, he was smug, the unrepentant bastard—but he wasn't giving me any reason to think this wasn't a hundred percent. The deal is off. The house—the house isn't yours, Serena. I'm really sorry."

The house wasn't hers. "You're not making this up because it's Friday the Thirteenth?"

"I don't think that's how Friday the Thirteenth works. And it's not April Fool's Day, either."

The house wasn't hers. "Maybe I could talk to her? Get them to, I don't know, use her promotion to buy a bigger house somewhere?"

Natalie sighed. "Sorry, hon, no. I asked Carter if they were considering that, and he was firm. They love the house, they love it more since fixing it up to sell, and they're not moving."

The house was not hers. Serena closed her eyes. Her grip on her phone slackened as she let out a warm gust of air.

"I wish it wasn't happening. I'm sorry."

Not hers. Since she was eight, when Mom had to sell the house once Dad moved out to live with Alice and her demon spawn five-year-old twins, Serena had been dreaming of owning her own home. A dozen different addresses since then, maybe more; a dozen periods of packing up the too-familiar boxes labeled "Serena's bedroom" and learning where the light switches were for late-night trips to the bathroom. Each time she lined her book collection neatly along the back of her dresser and piled her sketchbooks back in her desk drawer, she dreamed of the day when no one would make her pack—or unpack—again. Of not storing a stack of flattened boxes under her bed. Of owning fragile items that would just break in a move. Of navigating dark rooms because she knew them so well she didn't have to turn on the lights.

And she'd worked for her dream. She hadn't just let it be an idle fantasy. She'd made a plan, with a timeline and stages and lists. How much she needed to save, what kinds of places she could afford depending on her income, how to keep her credit score high and her financial life mortgage-friendly. She'd turned her passion for illustration and design into a job with earning potential, and taught herself to pay attention to management and corporate structures in order to maximize that potential. And she'd given herself a deadline: she'd promised herself—sworn to herself as she turned down nights out with friends, the chance for a more dynamic but less secure job, vacations away from the cruelest of Houston's summer heat—that she would own her house at thirty.

And here she was: thirty. And the house wasn't hers.

"Serena?" Natalie was softer now, all sympathy after the sucker-punch. "We can go look this afternoon, if you want. Or tomorrow, I'll rearrange some stuff."

"I thought you and Chris had plans." Valentine's Day plans, plans Serena knew that Natalie was hoping included a proposal.

"That's later, and anyway, I get the feeling I'm going to be grumpy after the date's over. He's not exactly full of secretive smiles or whatever. Besides, girl power, right? I'm not going to abandon a friend in need in favor of some guy."

That got a laugh out of Serena, at least. "Well, if you can, I'd love to look at houses tomorrow. Just let me know what time. Thanks."

Before she could get too much more maudlin about her house—her ex-house—Serena hung up and turned her attention to an absorbing bitch of a layout problem with HouGreen. What the point was, when it was apparently nothing but, well, work, Serena didn't know. She only knew how to work in pursuit of her plans, and with them falling apart, what did it matter that her folders weren't tidy? Why should she be the one who had to gripe at Dillon because he'd ignored her word limit and made it impossible fit his copy into the space she'd designed for it?

Sighing, she hit the button to call his office.

"Hey, Serena, what's up?"

Damn her nipples to hell and back, and damn Dillon's husky voice and damn every thought she'd ever had about making her life the life she wanted. "I told you no more than three hundred words for page two, weren't you paying attention?"

"Wasn't I—hang on, you mean for HouGreen?"

"Of course I mean for HouGreen, what else have I told you three hundred words about?"

"Okay, sure. Nothing else, if you put it like that. So you don't like the copy?"

Even when he was playing at being confused his voice was sexy, so Serena added that to the damn unfair column of life. "I didn't read the copy, because the copy is supposed to be under three hundred words, and it's not. I don't care if it's good, Dillon, that's not the point. I mean, it has to be good, of course it has to be good, but it also has to be three hundred words. Until it is, it's useless, no matter how good it may or may not be."

"So you didn't read it?"

"It's too long. I don't need to read it if it's too long, I need you to make it the right length."

"How long is it, Serena?" Dillon had the nerve to sound amused, and her body had the nerve to heat up when he said her name.

And all this talk of length wasn't in the least amusing. She looked back at the file he'd sent her. "Six hundred and ninety-two words."

"About ninety-two of those words are about half-way through, and they're to explain that I'd written two versions, and asking your opinion about which—of the two, three hundred word versions—you prefer."

Serena sighed. Loudly.

"Sorry, Serena," Dillon said. Not very contritely. "I probably should have asked the question in the email and sent them in two files instead of one. I'll make it clear next time."

"That would be best."

"Do you want me to resend it as two now?" And the damn man felt the need to smile while he asked, Serena could just tell. She straightened the files on her desk again, refusing to give him the satisfaction of admitting he might not have screwed up. Teach him to tease her nipples with his suppressed laughter.

She sighed more gently, and said, "No, just pay attention to my needs next time."

And then she hung up and refused to imagine his interpreting that in anything other than work-related ways.

"Happy Valentine's Day," Dillon said, leaning in to give Shannon a big hug.

"That's pathetic," Justin called from his seat in the living room, where he was cradling baby Toby. Both were in their pajamas. Or, Justin was for sure. It was a little hard to tell with the baby.

"You're pathetic."

"Hey, until two minutes ago I was curled up on the couch with my sexy wife and beautiful son, and no one was being a pain in my ass." Justin handed over the baby, though, in exchange for the white deli bag Dillon was holding.

"I brought you strawberry milkshakes and Cuban sandwiches," Dillon explained, even though Justin had already ripped open the bag.

"Fine, I apologize for saying it's pathetic that you're spending Valentine's Day with your big sister."

"Oh, I'm not here for her. I came by to see my guy Toby here." And what a guy. Dillon buried his nose in Toby's sweet blond curls. He thought the baby would be too young for so much hair, but apparently not. "Do you two want to go out or anything? I can stay with him a while."

Shannon groaned. Glancing up, Dillon saw her staring fixedly at the fries Justin had dumped onto a napkin on the coffee table. "Dig in, it's all for you."

"I can't. I can't even have the sandwich. He doesn't like it when I have fried food." Shannon's voice was full of regret. Presumably not about having the baby, who was a miracle after the miscarriages they'd gone through earlier in their marriage.

"Aw, I'm sorry. I didn't think."

"No, it's okay. I can have the milkshake. And since it's Valentine's Day, I'll even let Justin eat all the rest of it in front of me."

"You're my angel," Justin said, wrapping his arm around Shannon.

"Damn straight," she nodded. "Oops."

Justin laughed, which startled the baby some. Dillon bounced him back into sleep while Justin held Shannon back from standing. "It's Valentine's Day, you get a free pass on the swear jar."

"You have a swear jar?"

"Well," Justin said, "we weren't having much luck stopping with just will power. Turns out you can't have both will power and a newborn at the same time."

Shannon nodded. And nodded, dropping her head against Justin's shoulder. The hand holding her milkshake went slack, but Justin grabbed the drink before it spilled, handing it off to Dillon before cradling the now-snoozing Shannon more deeply into his hold.

Dillon's brother-in-law grinned ruefully. "Maybe not so much on the going out, but thanks for the offer."

"You tired, too?"

Justin snorted.

"Okay, okay, dumb question. Listen, Tobias and I will go hang out in his room a while. You guys chill. For the next two hours, you can stare at the TV and eat fries and nap and not worry about the baby." Dillon handed over the remote so Justin wouldn't have to move. "Want your phone or anything?"

"Nah. Hand me that blanket, though."

Toby kindly stayed asleep long enough to let Dillon get the new parents settled into their stupor before carting the baby off to the nursery.

And then he had two hours alone with his thoughts, only sometimes broken by the fun of figuring out how to change diapers and attempting to get the baby to focus on his funny faces. It wasn't exactly the distraction he'd been hoping for when he'd decided to drop by Shannon's house. It gave him way too many opportunities to replay Serena's inviting him to pay attention to her needs.

If she'd just stop running away every time he got near her, he would be more than happy to oblige.

"Well?" Serena asked Natalie, who'd rearranged her Sunday clients to show Serena houses in the afternoon. Not that she really needed to ask. If there'd been a ring on Nat's finger, Serena would have seen it.

Her friend shrugged. "He gave me a dozen thornless red roses."

"Ick."

"I know. At least there was no teddy bear holding them."

"How about 'I love you' balloons?"

"Not a one."

Serena grinned. "Maybe he's a keeper after all."

"Well," Natalie shrugged. "I love him anyway. Even if he didn't propose. How was your Valentine's Day?"

"Ha. Very funny. The highlight might have been when I ran into Joey on my way back from the market, and he was all kinds of snarky about my roach baits."

"Roach baits make Joey snarky?"

Serena rolled her eyes. "Not the baits themselves. Just the fact that I use them, because he likes to make fun of me using organic cleaners otherwise. He wouldn't kill the bugs for me when he had the chance, either. And somehow the pest control people have never managed to show up, even though it's in our rental agreement that they'll treat the building a couple of times a year."

"One more reason to get you out of there. You ready to house-hunt?"

"So ready."

"Where's you mom?"

Stifling a groan, Serena checked her phone for messages. "She's running late. I'll text her where we are in a half-hour."

"Right, then," Nat said, clapping her hands together and putting on her Efficient Realtor face. "Let's get some house viewings under our belts before then."

But when the half-hour was up, they were still at the first place. The one from Natalie's email. The one with the claw-foot tub, and the magnolia, and the out-of-her-range price tag. Nat was trying to persuade her to offer on it anyway. Or maybe Serena was letting Nat try to convince her. It was Serena, after all, who'd asked to see this place, and to see it first of all. And it was Serena who'd gone from yelling pointlessly at Dillon, after the disappointment of losing her Ex-House, to staring at the listing for this one.

She knew it was too much. Knew it. Although, all it would need was some cosmetic stuff to be perfect. The owners even had the inspection report from when they'd bought it two years prior, with the receipts on the items they'd fixed, so Serena could be confident that the electrical and foundation would be in good shape. But it was twenty percent over her budget.

"What does it hurt to put in a lowball offer?" Natalie asked. "You never know what they'll take."

"And Zane and I will be happy to loan you a few thousand to help with the down payment," Becky added. She'd been talking about the bungalow's happy energy and positive flow since walking in a couple of minutes before. Not that Serena was disputing it; just walking through the rooms felt settled and uplifting.

"No, Mom, but thanks." A loan from her current stepfather— because that's what it would be, Becky not actually having money of her own—would maybe be an easy out for Serena, but it didn't at all fit into her plans. She refused to get a place she couldn't afford on her own; it was contrary to everything she'd been working towards all her adult life. And no matter that Mom and Zane had been married nine years. It could end any day, and Serena would be pressured to repay the loan early. Not worth it, even for the pressed tin ceiling and the subway tile in the second bath.

But, oh, she did love the pressed tin ceiling. And the sconces on the front porch, and the bay window in the dining room, and the red brick fireplace.

They did leave, finally, and looked for the rest of the afternoon (another bad duplex, a house on a terrible street with broken streetlights and sagging fences, a 'sold for lot value' whose pictures had been misleadingly full of potential, and not one but two remodeled bungalows that might actually work, if Serena could just get the Dream House out of her head). Becky rejected them all, except for the lot value home, and Serena was inclined to agree. But Natalie talked her into offering for the Dream House, and also making a low offer on one of the other remodels.

Becky took off after handing over a jar of bee pollen ("So good for your allergies! Just put a spoonful in your morning smoothie.") Natalie watched her go, then talked Serena into meeting the gals for dinner at Rachel's place. Rachel was single parenting her one-year-old, so her house was the default meeting place for the four college friends, and take-out from the Dutch restaurant at the end of Rachel's block was their default meal.

It was all very comfortable, and comforting in its routine, with Natalie's bossy advice and Gillian's snide jokes and snatching baby Hannah up at every opportunity and Rachel griping about her ex but with a lot less vehemence than in the days when Hannah was an infant and the divorce was new.

In the middle of it all, Serena caught herself imagining having them over to her house. Putting some toys for Hannah out on the patio while the friends sat around an outdoor table, drinking iced tea flavored with the herbs from her garden. The Dream House had an entire raised bed along the back fence that had been colonized by peppermint plants. She could put rosemary and thyme pots on the porch, and use the other raised bed for beans and tomatoes and other veggies.

"You're daydreaming again," Gillian pointed out, after kicking at the sole of Serena's shoe to get her attention.

"About lettuces."

"Wow. Fancy fantasy."

"Also about carrots," Serena said.

"Somebody stop her before she taunts us with her visions of cucumbers."

"Mmm, cucumbers! I could definitely grow some of those. Nice and hefty and firm. So juicy when you bite into them."

"You two are depraved," Rachel said, after glancing over to check that Hannah wasn't paying attention.

"What?" Serena said, pretending innocence. "I'm planning my spring garden."

"Planning some kind of spring action, anyway," Gill muttered.

"Woah, springs? I don't know what you're into, Gill, but keep it out of my garden."

"As if you've never had a little fun in the sun."

"That's it, you two are cut off," Rachel declared, taking the empty bottle of wine to the kitchen and returning with the water pitcher.

But it was too late. Already Serena had gone from fantasizing about heirloom tomato seedlings to imagining lounging on the grass in the fenced-in back garden of the Dream House, the sun beating down on her bared skin. And as if by magic, there beside her in her dreamy nudity appeared none other than the delicious Dillon Hamilton. Who was, if her imagination was at all correct, even more delicious when naked.

CHAPTER NINE

IT WASN'T THE BEST DAY, Serena thought as she headed off to the morning meeting. But it wasn't so terribly bad, either.

Natalie had called before she'd finished her morning rituals in her scummy-butt apartment—wiping down bathroom mirror, making the bed, straightening the throw rug in the entry that always liked to drift off-square when she wasn't looking. She'd talked to Natalie the evening before, responding to the counteroffer on the nice but not perfect house. The owners had countered at full price, but agreed to a quick closing. It could be worse, but it wasn't exactly good.

"Hon, far be it from me to jeopardize my commission," Natalie said, "but remember this: you'll be living in this house for years. Decades, maybe. Make sure you're happy, and not just rushing into it to get away from your lease. I'll find you a short-term rental, if it comes to that."

"And then I have to move again?"

"Serena."

"I know, I know. But have I mentioned that I never want to move again, after this next time?"

"Maybe just the once."

"Funny. Okay, I'll think about it. Let me know when you hear about the other."

And then, between pouring her to-go cup of tea and straightening the entry rug, Natalie had called again. She'd heard from the agent about the Dream House—Serena was calling it 'Hakeem' for short, after Hakeem 'The Dream' Olajuwon, former star player for the Houston Rockets and top of Serena's 'if you could have dinner with anyone, living or dead, who would it be?' list.

Hakeem's owners hadn't taken her offer. But they'd countered. They needed a quick sale, and liked that Serena was pre-approved and willing to move fast. But they also wanted closer to asking price, and had come up with a compromise offer. Serena could lease-to-own, her rent going towards her down payment, and if—when—she could afford the negotiated price she would get the house for keeps.

It wasn't the best.

But all things considered, she'd take it.

When he stepped into Conference B that morning, Dillon sucked in his breath a little. Serena was wearing that sleeveless shiny orange shirt and her hair was swept back then fell loose down the curve of her neck. He hardly knew which part of her to avoid staring at first. Was she trying to kill him? Or at least his concentration? But then she flashed him the old 'hey buddy, what's up?' smile that just said friends. But did her eyes linger on him some? They did! They lingered! So, yes, damnit, she was trying to kill him, and just when—after a morning chat with Maisy he'd deny to his grave—he'd given in to his impulse to say the hell with it and go for something a little more with her, coworker or not. They were both fully mature adults. Her thirtieth birthday had been recent enough that Eddie was still wisecracking about her age. Dillon would be twenty-seven in a few weeks, and was already wondering if he could keep his birthday quiet and bypass whatever Eddie would think hilarious to mark the occasion.

It was amazing he didn't make an ass of himself during the meeting. He had to get out of there and regroup, figure out a strategy to get through the day. Maybe on Friday at Eddie's barbecue—Eddie and his wife hosted a monthly barbecue for coworkers—he could get her alone.

But now Anica was holding Serena back, and beckoning him over.

"Hey, tonight I need you two...."

"Can't," Serena said as the same time as Dillon.

Anica shook her head. "Such devoted employees, how did I get lucky enough to have you two on my team?"

Dillon grinned. "Sorry, An. It's just tonight...."

"Detroit game." Serena finished for him. Their eyes met, the glint in hers merry, conspiratorial. Dillon's answering smile faded as what had to be a stupidly inappropriate lustful look crossed his face. Not in front of the boss, dumbass! Or at all, really. He tore his eyes away, back to Anica.

"As I was saying," she continued, "Edgar Mooney sent over two tickets to the Rockets game for tonight, and I need you two to be discreet about the fact that I'm giving them to you. Thank Edgar, of course, but try not to let Eddie hear about it. He can be so grasping about this stuff."

Dillon met Serena's eyes again, sure she was fighting a twin grin to the one he couldn't really suppress. They were third place in the Western Conference and consistently winning at home. He'd been eagerly anticipating the game. He let out the smile, satisfied. Maybe he didn't have to wait until the end of the week to sound out Serena after all.

"Which one of these things is your place?" Serena asked Dillon as she circled another row of semi-identical townhouses, trying to read the dimly lit numbers.

"Twenty-six. Look, I'll flash my porch light," he said into his cell.

"Got it. You ready?"

"Be outside in two seconds." He disconnected, checked he had the tickets, double-checked Maisy had food, and headed down to Serena's car. "Thanks for picking me up."

She shrugged. "No problem. You're on the way. How long have you lived here?"

"About a year. It was my sister's place, but they moved out of the Heights when they were going to start a family and wanted more room." Near downtown, the Heights was a popular neighborhood of Victorian-era homes, neo-Victorian townhouses, independent retailers, and enough run-down residences and shady characters to bring the market values down a little.

"I love the Saturday market over by Onion Creek," she said. "I know it's on the small side, but there are a couple of farmers there who always have brilliant greens."

"Never been."

"It's, like, half a mile from here!"

"Okay. Granted. If it makes you feel better, I've never been to a farmers market anywhere else."

She laughed. He felt it down deep. "I grow what I can at home, but veggies don't do that well indoors. I'm dying to get into my house and figure out what I can grow in the beds, besides carrots. I used to have a real orange thumb with carrots."

Dillon may have zoned out a little when she started talking about beds—he wasn't an idiot, he knew she meant planting beds—but he recognized an opportunity when he saw one. "You should come by on Saturday and drag me to meet these farmer friends of yours. Maybe I'll surprise you and go all organic all of the sudden."

She grinned at him as she pulled into the arena's parking garage. "Stick with me, babe, and I'll have you all organic in no time." It wasn't the words themselves that had him just about ready to convert to vegetarianism if she asked, but the combination of her tone and the sparkle in her eyes. Dillon was beginning to think this was all going to work out very, very well for him indeed. And then they parked and got out of the car and he finally got a good look at Serena's outfit, and his mouth went dry.

Serena kept flea-jumping between edginess and relaxation. It was refreshing to get almost entirely away from work with Dillon, and she was pleased that being with him after-hours without the gang was as easy as when they were buffered by Jorge and Janice and everyone. Friendly. But there was a vibe there—or was she inventing the vibe? Or was her recalcitrant libido just inventing a one-sided vibe? After twenty minutes in the car together she was still breathing just about normally, with no signs of splotchy red patches anywhere, so on the up side, yay, she didn't look like a troll. And Dillon was maybe probably being a little flirty with her, right? And the farmers market on Saturday, that was—well, it wasn't a date, but it was an assignation. And one he instigated. Going to this game was great, but it was Anica who'd set it up. Saturday was the first time they'd ever discussed doing something, just the two of them, outside of work. So until she knew differently, it was going to be an assignation, and she was going to look forward to it.

Unless he meant it completely as a date? When she wasn't looking for dating, she didn't want to date. So why did it deflate her that maybe Dillon didn't mean it as a date?

Disgusted with her inner ramblings, she yanked up the parking brake and checked the garage pass was hanging on her rearview before hopping out of the car and shaking out her jersey. She looked up to find Dillon just a step from her, and the lights in the garage weren't the brightest, but it seemed to Serena that he was definitely on the staring side of the expressions spectrum. So... that was interesting. Watching him, she slowly reached up to pull her hair into a ponytail and twist the band from her wrist around it, and, yeah. He noticed. And despite the way he forced his eyes up to meet hers and grin as he said, "Old school. I like it," she knew he was appreciating the red baby-doll tee and low-rise jeans under her Olajuwon #34 jersey as much as the homage to the Rockets' former star center.

She grinned back. "He's The Dream, you can't top the best."

"Did you live in Houston back then?"

"Sure, yeah, most of my life," she said, and chatted about the good old days of back-to-back NBA Championships when she was a kid as they made their way into the arena.

The game was a nail-biter, but Dillon kept track of his own stats—nine high-fives with Serena, sixteen knees or shoulders brushing against each other, and once when she clutched his arm as a three-pointer rimmed out of the basket just before the buzzer sounded, sending them into overtime—as avidly as he usually tracked the rebound percentage. Sometimes when she jumped up with a yell he could see the curve of her breast moving through the large armholes of the jersey. When she sat forward to follow a play he could steal up-close and very appreciative glances at her jeans-clad rear end. He warned himself to stop staring, repeatedly, and the game was a brilliant distraction. But when the hell had he gotten to the point in his life that the NBA was a distraction from a woman? Damn. And when he saw her again—not work seeing, but social seeing—what was supposed to act as a barrier between his increasingly desperate need to touch Serena every damn where and his last shreds of self-restraint? Eddie's burgers? Organic produce, for fuck's sake? If he could happily envision grabbing Serena and pulling her onto his lap in the fourth quarter when they were down by four points, just to feel her hip and ass pressed up against his cock, to see if he could make her nipples so tight that he could see them, feel them through the layers that separated them from his searching thumbs, to taste her—to finally, finally taste her—then, yeah, the damn farmers were going to have to redefine 'all-natural' once he and Serena got there.

Her gasp startled him back to the game. They'd missed a jumper, they were headed into a second overtime, and Dillon had been too glazed over to catch it. She gave him a questioning look during the break, and he came up with a comment about the forward getting aggressive to prove he was still focused on the Rockets. He just about had his head together by the time the Pistons were defeated and the happy crowd surged to its feet to cheer and then swarm out to contribute to the gridlock getting home.

But it wasn't images from the play on the court that filled his head that night while he tried, frustrated, to fall asleep.

CHAPTER TEN

For the next couple of days of only cursory contact with Dillon, Serena pondered. Okay, maybe obsessed was the more apt word. He'd half-leaned in to her when she pulled up at his door after the game, but stopped short of anything more than a "best thanks from a client ever, right?" grin and shoulder-bump before getting out. It wasn't like she'd expected to be invited in. Or to get a kiss. Or to get naked and show up to work in the morning in her Rockets jersey.

And then their schedules turned into 'ships passing in the night' territory, as sometimes happened—when she was in, he was off-site, and when he was back, she was in a client meeting or at the inspection for the new house. Not that it mattered, since they were just pals. He might have asked her out a couple of times when he'd been new to Lanigan, but probably that was just because he was getting to know people. Almost a month later and Serena was full of inappropriate thoughts she just wasn't sure were reciprocated, since he hasn't asked her out again. He did email her a blurb from his neighborhood e-newsletter about the Saturday market's increasing popularity, with the subject line "High time I followed the trend, right?" So she supposed that was still on.

And no one at work needed to know what was going on.

Or not going on.

Or going on, in explicit, excruciating detail. But only in her fantasies.

That Friday was the third of the month, which meant grilling burgers at Eddie's for whoever could show up. Serena wasn't kidding herself. She didn't know what exactly she wanted to happen—especially with a potential audience—but she wasn't playing it safe and staying away. She'd overheard Dillon offering to bring a six-pack and a couple of bags of chips, and she'd confirmed on her break that the longnecks were cooling on his shelf in the fridge.

"Hey, Toots, what's wrong?" Janice asked, coming to an abrupt halt at Serena's door. "You look like the fates of nations rest on your shoulders."

She wriggled the shoulders in question to loosen them up and grinned up at Janice. "Nothing. It's all good. Just Friday-itis, I suppose." Serena glanced—again—at the clock on her screen. "And it's not even lunch."

"You wanna throw on your cross trainers and take a walk with me at noon?" Janice was always finding ways to fit fitness into her day. The day the smoothie shop opened six-tenths of a mile from the office was one of her best ever—several times a week now she would walk there and place her order, then take off for a two-mile jog to the bayou and back, picking up her smoothie to enjoy on her cool-down walk back to the office.

"You're a maniac. It's getting hot out there. What are you going to do when it hits the nineties next month?"

"Duh, I'll run in the morning and do weights in my office at lunch."

"The Smoothie Shack will go out of business."

"I've warned them. Liza's considering opening a franchise at the end of my block at home."

Serena laughed, and gave in. "Fine, fine, I'll go with you, but I'm not running in this skirt. You'll have to do that part without me. I'll sit in the Shack's a/c and read the free papers until you get back."

"Deal," Janice said, straightening away from the doorframe. "See you in a couple of hours, then, Toots."

Refocused, Serena set aside questions of what to do—if anything—about Dillon that evening and turned to her light table. Get the Atkinson proposal done before lunch, stretch her legs with Janice, then head out for a site survey on the creative for Houston Green at two. The day would end before she knew it, and Eddie had promised to make beer can chicken that night as well as the burgers, so it had to end well for that reason if no other.

Or so she hoped.

Janice amazed Serena—and Liza, the smoothie proprietor—by pulling up a stool to Serena's table instead of hitting the road after they ordered.

"So."

"Soooooo?" Serena echoed.

Janice fiddled with a straw. "I was up early, so I've already run a few miles today."

"Fair enough." As if Janice ever needed to justify opting out of physical activity. Her metabolism ran on high-octane or something—she was never still. Serena tried to run with her at lunch semi-regularly, and dragged herself to a yoga class at the gym on a basic schedule, but Janice put every fitness buff to shame. Serena had been about to launch into rhapsodic rambling about the lack of raccoon infestations at Hakeem the Dream House, but her friend's unusual body language put everything else on the back burner of her mind.

"Maybe I'll just go half the distance," Janice blurted, half-standing.

"Sit your toned butt down, missy, and tell me what on earth's gotten into you," Serena laughed, grabbing at her wrist. "I've got the feeling that your jitters aren't the kind that can be run off as easily as they can be talked out. You were fine this morning, right? What happened?"   Janice slumped—she slumped!—at the table and groaned. "It's stupid."

"Yeah, so?"

"You're going to think I'm dumber than three fence posts."

"Again: so?"

Janice laughed, at least. Liza waved them over for their drinks, and pacing just those few feet seemed to settle her down a little, because she finally gave up a little info. "Okay, you know our forklift guy, Ricky?"

Janice's job kept her hopping between the warehouse, the creative offices, and the print shop, usually in the middle of one call or making notes about another call looming on her horizon. The job would eat alive someone without her boundless energy, at least the way she did it. And the way she did it was kick-ass. Anica had tried to move Janice to an off-site position once, and everyone in Serena's office had threatened revolt.

"Ricky's the one with the faux-hawk who's always losing packing slips, right?"

"Yeah. Or running over them then giving them to me with giant tire treads over the signatures, whichever."

"Okay, then, sure, I know Ricky." Serena stirred her smoothie, trying to work out what had shaken Janice up so much. Her eyes widened, "Oh, he didn't make a pass at you, did he? Or... did you want him to, and he didn't?"

Janice gagged. "Serena. Toots. Faux-hawk, remember?"

"Good. I mean, if you wanted... I won't judge."

"Yeah, well, I will. That dog won't hunt. I'm still waiting for Prince Charming, and I guarantee that Prince Charming's never stolen a hairstyle from anyone on Big Brother."

Serena laughed. She was relieved that Janice was back to joking around, but something had clearly upset her friend, and she wanted to know what it was. After Janice paced a little more while pretending to need napkins from the dispenser at the other end of the tiny Smoothie Shack, Serena pulled her back down onto her stool. "Okay, what did Ricky the unfortunately coiffed tow motor driver do?"

Janice hunched her shoulders up and glared out the window. "He said I was a dyke." Taking in Serena's stunned face, she continued. "He said that only a dyke would work in the warehouse—which, way to get my job right, Ricky—and that if I needed a real man to show me what was what, he was sure he could find me some volunteers on the back dock."

"Oh. My. God."

"I know. I know. I'm furious. Furious, Serena. I've never—I just can't believe...."

Serena was stunned. "So what did Anica say?"

"Why would I tell Anica?"

"Well, then, whoever. Miguel or, I don't know, that HR woman who is always handing out her cards."

"Emily."

"Yeah, Emily."

Janice sighed. "Emily would just make me file an incident report and then stick me and Ricky and Miguel and I don't know who-all in a room for interviews."

"Which, and I know you know this, is the right thing to do in cases of workplace harassment."

"Okay, sure, and I need that kind of paperwork on file? Troublemaker Janice, can't hack it in the good old boy's world of the warehouse?"

"Miguel doesn't run it like that."

"No. But only because he's too macho to let a girl threaten his sense of his own superiority."

"Then isn't he macho enough to put a stop to this crap happening in his warehouse?"

Janice slumped again. "I don't know."

"You should tell him," Serena urged. She didn't know the warehouse manager super well, but she'd always thought he was an upstanding guy, and Janice had never said anything against him, no matter what kinds of problems or hold-ups from that quarter were threatening her sanity at any given time. "Do you think he wouldn't believe you?"

Janice snorted. "It's not like he's never met Ricky before."

"Okay, then?"

"I should be able to handle this kind of crap by myself," Janice grumbled.

Serena smiled. "You're wishing you'd pulled out the roundhouse punch on Ricky, huh?"

"At least. In kickboxing class last week we learned this excellent punch-jab combo."

"And I'm sure it's very effective," Serena said, slurping her smoothie, "but not very appropriate to the workplace."

Janice rolled her eyes. "You're no fun at all sometimes, Toots."

"Granted. But you'll go talk to Miguel?"

Janice nodded briefly before slumping against the table again.

Serena shot a reassuring smile towards Liza, who was watching Janice's extremely uncharacteristic body language with wide eyes, then glanced at her watch and clapped her hands together. "Great! Let's walk a half-mile before heading back. I want to feel guilt-free about whatever I eat at Eddie's tonight."

"He's making beer can chicken," Janice sing-songed, finally smiling as she rose.

"I know. He has to. I told him we'd boycott for the next three months if he didn't stop promising and never delivering. He thought it was funny. Funny! To dangle the specter of beer can chicken in front of me and then withhold." They waved to Liza on the way out the door. "What's funny about that?"

CHAPTER ELEVEN

EDDIE'S WIFE, MAGNOLIA, opened the door then immediately reached up to give Dillon a smack on the cheek. "Baby doll! Good to see you. You have more pics of the little one?"

"Hey, Mags," he returned with a kiss of his own. He'd met Magnolia a couple of times when she'd stopped by the office or happy hour to see Eddie, and they'd bonded quickly over the adorable nature of his new nephew. Dillon handed the beers and chips to Eddie before pulling out his cell. "Let me show you. Here's Toby having his sponge bath—look at his nose!"

Magnolia took the handset and scrolled through the latest uploads from Shannon, cooing.

"Oh, lordy, you've done it now," complained Eddie, sighing dramatically. "Now she's going to jump me tonight for sure."

"Pobrecito," muttered Jorge, who crowded in the door behind Dillon.

"I know, right? Just write it in your calendars for ten months from now, 'Eddie Jr.'s Christening and BBQ.'"

"You're grilling at our baby's baptism?"

"Mags, my love, I'm grilling while you're in labor."

"Best to start rethinking that whole 'Eddie, Jr.' thing then, dear one. Dillon, you're a fine looking young man, and clearly fond of the little ones. Would you care to procreate with me?"

Dillon awkwardly but gamely danced Magnolia into his arms in time to the country music blasting from the next room. He stumbled just a tad when he spun them to see Serena in the doorway, looking quickly up from the level where his butt had been pre-spin, but Magnolia didn't seem to notice, laughing as Eddie pulled her away from him.

"Get your own woman, Dillon-tante, this one's all mine."

"Dillon-tante?" Dillon snorted. "Seriously? That's bad even for you. Hey, Serena, let me help you with that." He reached for the salad bowl. "Grow these tomatoes yourself, did you?"

Serena "mm-hmm"ed at him as she twirled Magnolia away from Eddie to say hello. The two of them linked arms and headed out back. Janice had seen them coming and pulled a couple of beers from the cooler, leaving the men to sort the appetizers and side dishes into some sort of accessible order before the burgers needed tending.

"Well, that's gratitude for you," Dillon grumbled. "I was going to give your wife a baby, and instead I got left holding the salad."

Eddie slapped him on the back. Eddie, it must be said, did more than his fair share of back-slapping on a routine basis. "I've been left holding worse than that whenever I've tried it, my friend. Be grateful."

"I don't think he's that good looking," Jorge put in.

"Eh?"

"Dillon. Mags said he was good looking. I was standing right beside him, but she didn't even look at me. Does she got something against a biracial kid? No Mexican in her precious bloodlines?"

"Her kid with me would be biracial, too," Dillon pointed out. "Our baby will get nothing but pasty Irish white from me."

"First of all, Mags is half Hispanic already, her daddy's from Guadalajara. Second of all, neither of you dumbasses is getting my wife pregnant, so, maybe you could stop talking about it and open the damn salsa, okay?"

Dillon grinned. Like all jokers, there was nothing Eddie hated more than being the butt of a jest. Still, he made damn good burgers, in appreciation of which fact Dillon stopped ribbing him, and opened the damn salsa.

"Anyone for another beer?" Serena asked the group around the fire pit, standing. Not that she'd paced it so she and Dillon finished their longnecks at about the same time or anything. What was she, fifteen?

"Beer me," Eddie said, channeling who knew what juvenile comic actor. She was just as happy to let most of his impersonations go right over her head.

"Dude. Nice try, but, no," Dillon told him, and stood, too. "I think we need to grab some from inside. I'll help you restock the cooler."

She hid the involuntary grin by reaching for Janice's empties. "Thanks, Toots," Janice said, giving her arm a little squeeze. Serena needed to corner her to ask about the Ricky/warehouse situation, but had, at the moment, a more selfish agenda. So far she and Dillon had talked face-to-face, had brushed briefly against each other while loading up their plates, had made, well, more than the completely necessary amount of eye contact while everyone sat around talking. And not even a hint of shortened breath, much less giant red patches burning on her cheeks. Maybe it was just talking to him at work that freaked out her subconscious. Her libido and her dream-brain were getting more and more obsessive about Dillon, no matter what her mind and work-body were saying. So after some thought—okay, a hell of a lot of thought—Serena had decided to let her libido talk her mind into some kind of mature casual sex-and-dating thing. That way she wouldn't have all the "find a husband" pressure or whatever it was that brought on the hives when she contemplated Dillon's body, and also, she presumed, she would get to have orgasms with someone else again.

In the kitchen, alone enough by virtue of the fact that the window looked over the side yard rather than the back, she stood irresolute for just a moment, then moved closer to him.

"Dillon?"

He finished dropping the bottles in the recycling and turned, starting back just a tiny bit to find her so close. But then he wiped his hands down his jeans and leaned in. "Serena?"

Blue smoke eyes, dilated in the low light and maybe, just some, for her, too? Black hair angled over cheekbones so pure and sharp they made her ache to smooth them under her palm. A gentle fresh scent cutting through the lingering hickory smoke on his shirt. Serena drew in a long, careful breath, trying to ground herself. It pretty much failed, though, when Dillon's eyes dropped from her mouth to her swelling chest then shot back up to her eyes. Damn.

"Just...um. Just wondering if you were still up for going to the market tomorrow?"

He just kept looking into her. Just looking, then with a quick glance to the door, he made the half-turn necessary to bring himself in contact with her, and all hopes Serena might once have had of breathing properly disappeared forever.

Finally—finally!—Dillon's internal monologue said 'screw it!' and turned away in exasperation, leaving the rest of him rejoicing as he gave up on holding back, gave up on pros vs. cons, gave up on anything and everything that had stopped him, in the past month, from putting his hands on Serena's body. He touched her lightly, just his fingertips across her lips, her cheek, her hair. Her hair! So smooth, so alive as he wove his hand through it, palming the base of her skull as he lowered his head towards hers. Their eyes met, danced around, met again. Her lips had parted. She wasn't pushing him away, at any rate. Not pushing, no—her hand had gone around his arm, an electric buzz through his shirtsleeve.

Dillon's storm-blue eyes had a wide black rim, Serena noted somewhere in the sidelines of her brain, while most of her was focused on the message in those eyes. He was going to kiss her. Hell, she was going to kiss him! Why wait? Hadn't it been long enough? A day, a week, all the weeks since they'd met—it was beginning to feel as if each of those moments had been wasted, but no more. She slid her palm up to outline his amazing cheekbones, and leaned in, expectant, ready. Time almost stood still, now was forever, they were always in the middle of Eddie's gingham kitchen, Jorge calling in the background.

Damnit.

No, damnit, no, don't want to listen, don't want to return. No!

But it must have penetrated Dillon's haze, too—he did have a haze, didn't he? Serena blinked and tried to focus on the black of his blue eyes. Dillon closed them, though, and drew deeply for air.

"Dillon, are you locked in the john? Get out here!"

Well, trust Eddie to get them to move.

Dillon kept one hand on her shoulder, stroking it slowly. He blinked again then turned towards the kitchen door. "Yeah, coming!" he called back, then looked at her. A quick, sweet smile. "Serena."

"Mmm?"

"Yes, I am up for the farmers market tomorrow."

Despite their longish absence, Janice hadn't moved over to the seat beside Jorge, so they once again sat with her between them. So much for bumping legs together on the sly, Dillon thought, handing Eddie the cold beer. Maybe he and Serena could just head out quickly. His townhouse wasn't more than ten minutes from Eddie's house; he could bear to wait ten minutes to get her in his arms. Maybe. He might fucking well explode on the spot, actually, but he thought he could manage ten minutes.

"I've got some stuff in the morning, so," he began, but Jorge reached out a hand to his chair.

"Hang out another minute, okay? I need to tell you all some news."

"Aw, come on, Jorge, you've got to have at least another year before retirement! You haven't even joined AARP yet," Eddie smirked. Not for the first time, Dillon wondered why Jorge—who was actually younger than he was, so Eddie could practically be his very young uncle or something—put up with Eddie's BS. They were both great guys, and Dillon had very few friends in Houston outside of work, so he was glad they got along decently. But Eddie's 'humor' always found a target in Jorge, and Jorge, instead of fighting back or keeping away, just put up with it. Classic bullying. Dillon tried to stay out of the middle, but he'd once or twice told Eddie to back off, and Jorge to step up. As far as he could tell, it didn't make a difference, but at least he tried.

"Hush, Eddie Senior, and let the man tell us. Good news, I hope, Jorge, hon? Are you going to make someone's baby, because I wasn't scorning you earlier," Mags said. "I'd be honored to grow your fruit in my womb."

Janice practically did a spit-take, which, if nothing else, broke the tension between Dillon's friends. "'Scuse me?"

Dillon leaned over to her and stage-whispered. "Eddie apparently can't father children. Very hush-hush. Magnolia is going to draw straws to see if Jorge or I will do it instead."

"Har har har." Eddie, not happy at the bottom of the joke again.

"Thanks, Magnolia, I am honored. We'll return to that in private, yes?" Jorge smiled, that rare event; even Dillon appreciated it as benevolence upon them all. "Not quite that news, no. But I am engaged."

"Toots!" Janice was the first voice of surprise and delight, but the rest followed.

"I didn't even know you were with someone," Serena added to the general chorus.

Jorge was rubbing the back of his neck, blushing a little. "We weren't going to get engaged until it was legal here, but Bubba says if the mayor can run off to California to get hitched, so can we."

"Bubba? His name's Bubba?" Eddie was clearly about to start riffing, but Magnolia pulled him back.

"Jorge, honey, we're so happy for you," Mags said, shooting Eddie one of those marital looks that clearly said, 'Get with the program, buddy.'

"Congratulations, man," Dillon said, standing to shake Jorge's hand.

"Oh, Jorge," Serena said, elbowing Dillon aside to give his friend a hug. Dillon reacted viscerally, surprising himself with the 'get your hands off my woman' thud of his heart, even in the midst of this happy news. When Janice and Magnolia joined the hug he didn't even blink, other than noting that they pushed Serena closer to Jorge in the group. He sighed.

Okay, okay, the correct friends thing to do was take Jorge out to celebrate—one-on-one, because he'd early on figured out that Jorge's normally quiet reserve shed like snakeskin once he was out of a group situation. A true photographer at heart, Jorge sat back and observed rather than participated, given the option. But here Jorge had hardly ever mentioned Bubba, and they were engaged, and that meant it was time to remove Jorge from the group around Eddie's fire pit and give him a chance to talk it out to his heart's content.

Dillon shot Serena a wryly apologetic look he hoped sharp-eyed Janice couldn't interpret, and extracted Jorge from the press of women. The best he could manage was a longish squeeze of Serena's warm hand as they said their goodbyes, and he and Jorge headed to the nearest of several nearby Starbucks.

CHAPTER TWELVE

SERENA PULLED HER LITTLE CAR into a street space a block or two from Dillon's townhouse and texted him her location before she got out and checked her appearance. She was not—not—going to keep breaking into infantile grins once he met up with her. Not. She took some deep centering breaths and willed the feeling of last night's near-kiss from her mind. Totally not thinking about it. Not remembering the fine-grit sandpaper of his jaw. Not conjuring up his scent. Not feeling a significant anticipatory pull in the general vicinity of her thighs. Nope. Deep, calm breaths, an appreciation of the warm, sunny day, nary a lustful thought in her head.

It worked so well that when she spotted him walking towards her, Serena didn't even plaster herself to him, much less send her tongue spelunking down his throat. She was absolutely in control.

Even if his answering grin did mean that she'd failed on the infantile thing.

Dillon stopped a few inches shyer of her than she'd expected, which pulled Serena up a little short herself. He seemed to notice and make a leap to recover, gesturing to the main street with one arm while reaching for her with the other, which only made her feel like they were about to waltz or something. Considering his adorably lead-footed performance in Magnolia's foyer the night before, Serena figured that dancing wasn't his aim, but something of the momentum was, nevertheless, lost.

"Morning," she chirped (chirped? oh but she was losing all semblance of herself today; was this all a terrible idea?).

"Hey, you made it."

"I did."

"It's good to see you," he added, then gave his head a half-shake and turned to face her full-on. "I'm sorry. I'm being awkward. Let me start again."

Serena laughed. "You can't go back, but you can always go forward." She suited action to words, stepping the inches necessary to give him a brief hug. "Hi."

"Is that some sort of ancient wisdom?"

"What? The go forward thing?"

"Yeah."

She scoffed as he took her arm and they set off towards the market. "Not exactly. I think I read it on the tag of a tea bag, but I'm pretty sure it wasn't handed down from the prophets or anything."

"My illusions are shattered."

"I'm so sure."

"Hey, you think you know a woman. She shops at farmers markets, eats organic, does yoga, right?" Serena nodded. "So, she does yoga, grows tomatoes; I have to figure there's an ancient wisdom component in there just waiting to show itself."

"I grow herbs, too."

"Just what I'm saying. Drinks tea, grows tea, packages tea in bags with fortunes hanging off the end of them. The dots connect themselves."

"You, sir, are a laugh riot."

He pulled her closer, and not only, she hoped, because of the passing pedestrians. "Anything I can do to put a smile on your face."

And then they were stopped, facing each other. Serena glanced away, caught a reflection of the two of them in a shop window. As tall as he was, he didn't tower over her so much as draw her up to him. It was more unbearable to watch the image of the two of them together than to look directly at him, so Serena turned back. She wasn't exactly afraid. It wasn't that. But she felt poised on a precipice.

Here, on this sun-and-people-filled street, she and Dillon were deciding on a direction forward. His looking at her like that meant there was a direction, there would be movement, the night before hadn't just been an interlude between burgers and dessert.

So not 'afraid'—but 'nervous' would work. Yep. Definitely nervous. She faced him, chin up, eyes wide. She licked her lip. "Hi."

"Hi," he answered, and pulled her in for a proper hug.

He would have breathed a sigh of relief, if he wasn't trying to avoid further embarrassment. God, that had been excruciating. Unaccountable. Why hadn't he hugged her as soon as he'd seen her? What the hell had he been doing with his arms? Spent half the night flashing to memories of touching Serena in Eddie's kitchen, then acted like a fucking preadolescent when he saw her on the street, glowing brighter than the day should have allowed. But now. Now his wayward arms were around Serena, and felt right. It shook him a bit, if the truth were told, the rightness he felt. What minuscule parts of his brain that were functioning beyond the rightness were pushing back at him. Nagging at him: isn't it too much? Doesn't this feel too good? Shouldn't he back off some?

And also, they were in the middle of the street. So he held her to him a moment longer before letting go. She moved back enough to look into his eyes, and he didn't censor himself by looking away too soon, by hiding too much. At least, he thought not. Her eyes—almost silver in this daylight!—were a shade wary, but warm. Bright and warm and clear on him. Well, that was Serena down to the ground, no games.

He smiled, reassured. The nagging was just an immature reflex. He was adult enough to recognize that it was just lingering college-age 'don't trap me' stuff, not his present reality. Job, home, excellent woman. It was all good. It was perfectly acceptable, now that he'd nixed the 'not at work' prohibition, to start in with a real relationship. His life had room for that. So if holding Serena felt far more momentous than long nights with Kim or Erica or any of those casual dates he'd spent time with over the past couple of years, that was fine. That was good, even. Didn't he and Kim break it off, after all, because it was always too casual, and neither of them could figure out what compelled them to be together anymore? So, Serena was compelling. Besides, he'd been ignoring his attraction to her since his first day at Lanigan, thanks to whatever bullshit professional ethics he'd thought applied, so it shouldn't bug him that it was so intense between them.

Right, then. On to the farmers market.

"So you and Jorge talked more last night?" Serena asked as they turned into a lot where the produce was set out on various folding tables and blankets. She steered him towards a bee farmer whose soaps were her favorite.

"Yeah, I made him tell me all in exchange for a coffee."

"Why do I have trouble picturing Jorge of all people drinking coffee past dark?"

"Hey. Don't make assumptions," Dillon said, nudging her with his shoulder.

She grimaced, embarrassed to be falling for an Eddie characterization. "Sorry. I did take it for granted y'all'd gone out for more beers."

Dillon laughed. "Nope, Jorge had his limit—two beers—at Eddie's, so it was Starbucks instead. And, okay, it was decaf. But Jorge isn't quite as set in his ways as it sometimes appears."

Serena snorted, and hoped it wasn't as inelegant as it sounded to her ears.

"Hey, now." He picked up the lavender-beeswax soap she'd just set down, and sniffed. "Nice. You use this, right?"

"Are you trying to change the subject?" (Don't swoon, Serena, it's just a scent. A subtle scent, but there's no reason he couldn't have noticed it on her skin.)

"Nah, but it's hard to defend Jorge as much of a risk-taker."

"Yeah, apparently if he didn't have Bubba pushing him out of his comfort zone, Eddie would be more right about Jorge than any of us likes to admit," Serena said.

"Maybe," Dillon conceded, then set Serena's nerves to jumping again with a decidedly carnal smile. "Sorry I didn't stick around last night."

Probably that was just as well. She hadn't exactly been in the most prudent frame of mind. "It's fine." And then she was the one looking to change the subject, nervous about discussing what might have happened if they'd left Eddie's together. She settled for moving them on to the next booth.

Serena added some snow peas to her produce bag and asked the woman about the early rhubarb she saw off to the side. The stalks weren't particularly firm, though, so she passed. They bought drinks and sat on a bench near the street, shoulder to shoulder. She realized that since the initial awkwardness, they'd pretty much been touching all morning, and it had felt just fine. Her breathing was basically steady, her skin didn't feel flushed. Her hands weren't swollen. She nixed the idea of checking her chest for a rash, and figured that if her face had reddened up to an unwarranted degree, Dillon would have mentioned it. So whatever her body's problem was with getting too close to him seemed to be confined to work. It sure hadn't protested during that moment at Eddie's, or the one on the street, either.

She snapped herself back to the present, wondering if that present would presently contain kissing. "So is the farmers market all I promised? Are you glad I dragged you the blocks and blocks out of your way to visit?"

Dillon stared off at the passing traffic, eyes narrowed. Then he took a sip of his lemonade and grimaced. "It's chock full of vitamins and minerals, but would you mind if we find a table at Onion Creek for lunch and something more palatable to drink?"

She bumped his shoulder then stood. "Clearly, my work here is done. Lead on, O Future Ecowarrior friend of mine."

CHAPTER THIRTEEN

AFTER PANINIS AND ICED COFFEES at the restaurant that opened its parking lot to the local vendors every Saturday morning, Serena and Dillon set off towards her car, produce bags in hand.

"You're really going to use all that stuff, just for you?" Dillon asked as he compared the size of the shopping to the size of Serena. It hardly seemed possible.

"Are you angling for an invitation?"

He weighed the bags in his hands as she unlocked her trunk. "I'd hate to deprive you. You might just waste away to nothing." Damn if her smile didn't smack him in the gut. Once he'd stowed the cargo, he took her hand again. "How about this? I invite you to my place now, we can have coffee, sorry, tea for you, and if you think you can spare it, you can have me over for salad one of these evenings?" One of these nights. Tonight, perhaps. Every night, maybe. No rush, just as soon as humanly possible would be a fine time to get Serena alone and in private.

"That is very sly."

Uh-oh. Was he moving too fast?

But before he could back-pedal, she added, "I get a bit of flavored hot water from you, and you get a culinary masterpiece from me? People travel miles and miles for one of my salads."

What people? Men? Oh, hell no, was that jealousy? Just what he needed. Up the charm ante, quick. "I might have some cookies, too, if you want. If that tempts you to my place."

She hit the lock button on her car remote. "Consider me tempted."

Yes! "Right then. This way, Salad Queen." She laughed, he managed not to turn into a statue of lust, and when they set off again, he was rewarded for his patience when she took his hand. He'd been reaching for her all day, soothing the ache of not bedding her with the balm of a touch here, a shoulder bump there, as constant contact as he could manage in the midst of all the damn people everywhere. He ought to be grateful to the people, jostling them together, forcing them to share a tiny perch in the restaurant's waiting area, forcing him to not act like a barbarian in an empty wilderness, subduing his woman with kisses and touches designed to hopelessly bind her to him. He wasn't grateful to the people, but he did feel a surge of primal triumph that his sneaky plan to get her used to touching him all the time had worked. And now they were going to his place. His place, where the only people jostling together would be him and Serena. Roaring and beating his chest would be, sadly, out of place, so he settled for giving her hand a squeeze as they turned onto his street.

Serena's fingers felt slim and snug in Dillon's hand. It was a warmish day, but being palm to palm with him was nothing but comfortable. Comforting, even, which was weird. She hadn't known she was even in need of comfort, but there it was: this unprecedented feeling of protection and connection. As if their hands were made for each other. Not that she was getting fanciful or anything.

And for the record, she didn't think the fact that they both salted their ketchup before dipping their fries meant they were soul mates.

Fries just tasted best that way.

So all she was really looking at (and looking at) was a very well-built man who was easy to work with, appreciated basketball, liked to tease without being mean, was good to his friends, and knew a couple of basic culinary tricks. Dime a dozen. She could create an online dating profile tonight and find six or seven men just like him.

She glanced up at him again, and caught him watching her. "What?"

He laughed a little. "I was going to ask you the same. You got lost there for a second."

Shaking her head, she smiled. "It was nothing. Just remembering something I have to do when I get home." Or not. Odds were that those six or seven hypothetical men were all some version of Neanderthal or tool, and Dillon seemed remarkably flaw-free from where she was standing.

"Hmm. Are you in a rush?"

"Nope. I have time."

"Come on, then," he said, turning them up his walk. "Let's forage for those cookies."

She would forage, all right. Forage into his mouth. Launch an expedition across his chest. Burrow into his scent. She was under no illusions that either of them expected a civilized hot drink right about now. They were both holding themselves in check, vibrating. Once on the other side of that door, the game would change. Big time.

She paused on the landing, Dillon still a step below her. She felt his gaze move from her butt as she turned and looked at him. Even with the extra stair, he was still taller than she was. But they were much more eye to eye than usual, and chest to chest. Hip to hip. He was leaning into her. She was swaying towards him. Were there goddamn magnets sewn into their jeans? It almost made her uneasy, how much this pull towards him was stronger than anything Serena had felt before.

There was a slight question in his eyes. He was as tense with desire as she was, and wondering if she was going to back out now. Well, frankly, there might be a question in her eyes, too, giving him pause. Serena didn't want there to be any doubt between them, but when she came right down to it, this was big. 'Dillon was her friend' big. 'Dillon worked closely with her' big. 'Dillon was maybe as close as she'd ever gotten to her ideal man' big. The stakes were pretty damn high.

But then he had leaned forward enough to brush her breasts with his chest, and she gasped a sudden lungful of air. His palm hovered along her cheek and came to rest cradling her jaw. She felt every molecule bouncing between them, charged, alive. At this angle, his lips were able to easily trap her lower lip, suck it gently but firmly. His tongue swept into her mouth with delicate butterfly strokes, each one ratcheting her need up another notch. She hadn't even noticed her hands circling his waist, pulling his hips as firmly to hers as the stairs would allow.

Okay, big. Had she thought big? Huge.

Dillon could touch her as lightly as this, as tenderly as any Romeo had ever stroked his Juliet, but some things didn't lie, and one of those things—huge things—disturbed the molecules between them, proving that there was nothing tentative or doubting about that touch. He wanted her, and not in any idle way. Serena pulled away from the kiss, breathing hard, and met his intent cobalt gaze. The glint was back, the assurance, and the deeper feelings, too.

Their mouths had met in a shock of fire that so startled him he almost pulled back. But no, not going to happen, the pulling back.

One hand traced the outline of her ear. His other arm circled her waist and her hands were on his back, his neck, his ass. Serena was grabbing his ass! This was heaven. He was hallucinating about heaven, right here on the stairway to his front door. All that glitters is, indeed, gold.

The kiss was molten; her lips were so soft, but not tentative, no. Nothing reserved here, not from straight-forward Serena who always told it like it was. She kissed the same way, she spoke volumes with that kiss, so Dillon answered in kind. It couldn't be lost on her, with her body smack up against his—was he pulling her there? was she pulling him?—that just the touch of her tongue to his had given him an erection so strong that he'd once again almost lost hold of her. He could plummet backwards down the stairs with the propulsive shock. But instead the spark between them was fusing them together, tighter, closer; he curled his fingers into her and tasted the hot salt of her neck before finding her lips again. He was on fire and she was on fire and the fire was melting them into one creature, an insistent, hungry beast with no interest in being tamed.

This was not your everyday kiss. This was supersonic.

She practically raced him up the last steps, hands tugging his shirt loose from his waistband, desperate to get to the skin under the cotton, even as he unlocked both locks with trembling hands.

Alley-oop. They were in!

He shut them inside by pushing her up against the door, following with every inch of his tall lean frame. Coffee? Cookies? They didn't bother with the pretense. Or with words. Serena moaned and hummed a little, involuntary, ravenous, happy. Damn, there went her nipples again—but, no, it was okay! It was okay because right there, right where she needed and longed and yearned and ached, Dillon's body pressed against hers, soothed hers into submission. Not submission. Never submission. But joy, rightness, pleasure—his chest soothed hers with pleasure.

His legs caged hers, but she wasted no time pulling one loose so she could straddle his thigh. He yanked her hips up the length of his leg, then curved his hands around to fit them into the space he'd created between her butt and the door. She arched her back, pressing her pelvis—her dampening, aching pelvis—more firmly against the barriers of denim between them. She'd managed to get his shirt enough out of the way to finally, finally see, to feel those muscles roping up his sides. She traced his ribs back to his spine, then up across broad shoulders that were warmly alive under her palms.

His lips had moved down her neck, and at the same time his hands had moved up to cup her breasts. Thumbs and fingers gently pinched her nipples at the very moment that his teeth nipped the upper globe of her left breast. It sent a shudder directly to the apex of her thighs, where she hadn't stopped rocking herself against his leg. His cock sent an answering thrust against her hip. As her head dropped back against the door, she went for his fly with one hand and pulled down on her shirt with the other, trying to move it low enough for him to get to her breasts through the neckline before she died from not having his mouth and hands directly on her skin. Fortunately, Dillon was a very smart man, and a man of action. He reached through the vee of her neckline, freed a breast from the lace and underwire prison that had heretofore kept it from him, and paused to look at and touch each inch before lowering his lips to her tight lonely frantic nipple.

She was fumbling too much to deal with the button of his jeans, so she just reached into his waistband with seeking fingers. Yes! Right there, huge and hard, Dillon's cock, just waiting for her hand. He was so long she could rub her thumb across the broad head without any expedition after all. Her fingers traced the soft skin over the iron muscle, and he bucked against her, moaning.

Forcing open her eyes, Serena saw Dillon moving to free her other breast, felt his breath ragged and hot against her skin as he licked circles around her nipple, saw his teeth bared to take a gentle bite of her skin. Saw the bite mark pink against her pale flesh, caught an almost minty whiff of his dark hair as it brushed her collarbone, and barely noticed the red circles growing across her chest. Her eyes closed again. Her breath was shallow, his moans were hoarse, her lungs were aching, her skin was red?

Red?

She scooted away from him, braced her arms against his chest to give herself room. Serena tossed her head back and forth, trying to gasp down some oxygen, wheezing. She couldn't get a breath. Her heart was pounding. Was she shaking from passion or because she was about to collapse?

Dillon had pulled back, was holding her shoulders. "Serena, shit, I'm sorry. I'm rushing you? I'm sorry. I thought—Serena?" He stroked back her hair, but she still couldn't talk. She shook her head. "Shh. Don't. It's okay, let's sit."

He tried to pull her to a blue sofa just past the entryway. She shook her head again. Opened her mouth, shut it, rubbed her eyes. Her chest refused to rise; no air could move past the vise of her throat. He talked more, but it made no sense. Shaking her head one last time, she groped for the doorknob and let herself out.

Better. A little breath. Down to the landing now. Better. She clung to the rail, managed a few more shallow breaths. The door opened above her, but she didn't even turn to look at him. Just shook her head again, and stumbled off as fast as her lungs would allow.

CHAPTER FOURTEEN

Gone?

The hell?

He wouldn't chase after her. She clearly didn't want that. Didn't even look when she hightailed it out of his place. Didn't respond to him calling her. He may be confused, but he wasn't an idiot. The message was clear: Serena didn't want him.

He didn't slam the door. He had better control than that. Not that much of a barbarian after all. Yes, okay, he kicked the sofa a little brutally. Maisy jumped up howling at him for it, damn her calico hide. He ignored her and sank to the floor, leaning against the door he'd just gotten so happy with when it helped sandwich Serena to his body.

This made no sense, was the thing. She'd led the way to this door, obviously aware that her ass was swaying enticingly in front of him all the way. She'd raked nails through his scalp, which still tingled. She'd helped get those stunning breasts into his hands. She'd half ripped his shirt off. She'd stroked—better not think about that.

No sense at all.

Sighing, he dug his cell out from his pocket. Typed: "I don't know what happened, but let me know if you're okay. I'm sorry if I upset you. Give me a call." Thought about it. Got rid of the middle sentence. Hit send. Waited. It was half an hour before she replied, "I'm okay." Nothing else. No call.

Well, that was just fucking fantastic.

Serena sat in her car, the antihistamines she normally kept in her glove box cradled in her lap. She dug under the passenger seat until she found a water bottle and chugged it, hoping the liquid would help her body distribute the medicine to her vital organs sooner. She sat. She counted her breaths, which helped her believe she was still breathing. So that was good. Her eyes stopped itching, which is how she noticed that she was breathing just fine on her own, which meant she could finally take a deep breath and slump back against the headrest.

She'd never had an attack like that. Not from getting close to someone. It had to be Dillon—she'd been losing her breath when she got close to him and him alone. No one else had ever made her feel this way, given her such an intense and instant physical reaction. Unfortunately, the reaction wasn't just dampness in her nether region—it was also a closed up throat and a rash.

But not all the time, so it had to be psychosomatic. Which, she had to face facts, she pretty much knew already. She'd worked closely with him at first without getting hives, but once she started thinking about him sexually, she broke out. And then, she supposed, she got used to whatever level of intimacy they'd reached, but if it went further, her body freaked out. Talk about a flight or fight response—her body was screaming 'run' in no uncertain terms. She hadn't had an attack that bad since she was eight and her dad tried to get her to spend the night at her new stepmom's house. She'd been supposed to share a bunk bed with

Alice's bossy five-year-old twins, but just going near their shag-carpeted room full of every stuffed bear ever made had resulted in her first trip to the ER. After that, even though Alice cleared out a little storage area off the dining room for her and even let her pick the paint color, she avoided their house whenever she could talk her way out of it. And especially avoided the twins, who might have eventually grown out of their creepy non-verbal way of stopping her from doing every activity she instigated, but not by the time Dad had that second divorce under his belt.

Dillon wasn't a ruthless, petty kindergartener, though, and she didn't grasp why his hands on her breasts made her chest stop taking in air. In a dangerous rather than a sexy way.

So, Option A: go back to hand-holding and happy hour, but no tongue. Option B: avoid Dillon completely. Option C: take drugs twenty-four/seven and get to maybe see what was playing peekaboo in his jeans. Her breath hitched and she backpedaled right quick. Option C didn't seem to be on the table. Or on the bed.

Or against the door.

She groaned. It had been so, so good. His mouth had been so firm and so playful. His hands had a sixth sense about giving and taking. His body had been tight with sexual tension, muscled in all the excellent places, smooth under her hands and in perfect rhythm as they moved together. The only thing wrong with that embrace was that it wasn't still happening. Now that her rash and lungs were under control, her body was throwing a tantrum and a pity party all at once, because she was in this car. Alone.

"Well, why'd you go and be allergic to Dillon, then?" she groused right back at it. Just what every woman needed: a full out battle between her subconscious and her libido. And her subconscious employed guerrilla tactics.

It would likely be his message buzzing in her pocket. "Not a euphemism, sadly," she muttered as she slipped out the phone and read the screen. Was she okay? What did he think, she ran off because she'd been repulsed by him? He wasn't an idiot, he had to know she wasn't okay. She was furious and freaked and fantastically horny, so she just typed back that she was fine, and cranked up the radio so she could get home without thinking anything else.

CHAPTER FIFTEEN

RACHEL CALLED AT JUST THE WRONG TIME. Serena was parked outside Hakeem, staring at it as if she was able to project herself out of the car and into a life within its walls. An ordered life, the whole of it set out neatly, her own stuff in her own house and her days filled with her own pursuits. Art, food, friends. Semi-annual weekends with her half-brother. That's all she needed.

Definitely all she needed.

Though her breathing was just about back to normal, her mood was still grumpy and still freaked, and it took next to no prying on Rachel's part to get the whole story out of her.

"You know what it probably is?" she asked, when she'd heard it all.

"Do tell."

"He's probably, like, a serial killer or something."

"Rachel!" Serena shook her head. "Dillon is not a serial killer."

"Ha, got you to laugh."

"Thanks."

"Bet I'm right though. Bet he's secretly one of those really really creepy guys, you know, 'he was always so quiet' and then they find the S&M cage in the basement?"

Serena paused in the middle of restarting her car. "We live at sea level. No one here has a basement."

"Forty-three feet above sea level, Serena."

"Thank you, Wikipedia. The point still stands."

"As does mine. Something about this guy has, like, triggered your fear reflex, something you can't put your finger on, and your instincts are kicking in to warn you."

"That makes no sense. I've known him for weeks now, I've seen his resume, and he's perfectly normal. And why would my fear reflex kick in at work, where I'm perfectly safe?" And, she wondered, why would my sex reflex kick in at the same time?

"We can't control our instincts, Serena. That's why they're instincts. It's our job to heed their warnings."

"You really think it could be something like that?"

Rachel made sympathy noises. "I know you don't like it, but, well, honestly? Do you have a better explanation?"

She sighed and put the car in drive. "Not currently."

"Okay, then. Until you do, you stay away from him. Or risk ending up chained up in his garage."

"Nice image."

"He does have a garage, doesn't he?"

She sighed again. "Yes."

"Well, then."

She'd barely gotten her laundry sorted when the doorbell rang. Gillian gave her a finger wave through the peephole. She stepped in and hugged Serena in the same motion. "Heya! Rachel's right behind me. She's got to ease Hannah out of her car seat.

Fortunately it's nap time, so she was able to tell me all about the Dillon and his basement sex dungeon on the way over."

"Gill—"

"I know, she explained, no basement. Natalie had to show single family homes in Montrose all afternoon, but she says to tell you you're just afraid of commitment and to get over yourself and jump the guy already."

"Well, that's nice."

"Yep," said Gillian, dropping her bag on the coffee table. "I'm more moderate, as you know." Serena nodded, almost sincerely. "So I say just heavy petting for now, plus, let us meet him and then we'll tell you what to do."

"Oh, laundry day, fun," Rachel whispered, nudging the door back open with her shoulder and heading straight for the bedroom. "Make Hannah a pillow fort and I'll get her down."

Outnumbered and evicted by a one-year-old, Serena sent Gillian to the kitchen for the pitcher of sage iced tea she'd brewed that morning, switched off her music, and stashed her laundry basket by the front door. She'd planned to be efficient all afternoon, cleaning and packing and taking a walk in the park to enjoy the bright afternoon. But Serena wanted nothing more than to curl up in the dark and brood over what had happened at Dillon's that afternoon.

Or relive it. The good parts.

And imagine what could have come next.

But Rachel bundled Hannah into the room just then ("She's not in the mood to nap more") and Gillian pushed aside the table to make room on the floor for baby and toys. Serena glanced through the bedroom door at the pillows Rachel had left jumbled on her bed, and willed herself to leave it and pay attention to her friends. Gill was intent on her campaign to persuade Rachel to let her spike the iced tea. "You know you want it."

"Yeah, well you know I'm nursing. So."

"She's one now! You said you were only freaking nursing her for a year."

"What I said, and thanks for cursing in front of my baby by the way, is that I would nurse her for at least her first year. The American Academy of Pediatrics...."

"Right, so 'freaking' is a curse word now?"

"Serena, I sent you that link about infant language development, right?"

"Serena, I sent you that link about the longevity of maternal friendships being a good foundation for the next generation, right?"

"Okay, time out." Serena made a 't' of her hands, which stopped both Gillian and Rachel in their tracks. Because they were laughing at her.

"Um, Serena?" Gill got out.

"What?" She was not in the mood for this.

"It's supposed to be a capital 'T.'" Rachel demonstrated as best she could with Hannah curled up in her lap. Then she gasped—actually gasped!—and covered Hannah's eyes when Serena showed her the only hand signal she knew by rote.

"Oh, calm down, Mama Bear," Gillian said, handing her an unadulterated tea and popping Hannah into her own arms. "It's not like she said 'freaking.' Probably Hannah Banana here doesn't even have the fine motor skills to point properly, never mind give Auntie Serena the finger. Do you, Smoochums?" She helped Hannah clap her hands a couple of times before manipulating her fingers into various signals. Rachel growled a little, but to be fair, Hannah really did seem uninterested in even the most basic of gestures. "Show Auntie Serena how awesome your walking is," Gillian said. She stood the toddler on the floor and pointed her towards the kitchen where Serena stood, smirking at Gillian's tendency to get completely riled up by Rachel's motherhood-induced dictates. But Gill had been more smitten by Hannah than any of them—well, except Rachel—and went out of her way to hang out with them as often as possible.

Not that the baby wasn't perfectly adorable. She had Rachel's giant blue eyes, and Sergei's Mediterranean skin and dark curly hair. Although Sergei had turned out to be a rat-bastard who'd left

Rachel with sporadic child support and an ex-mother-in-law who sent lacy black dresses too big or too small every two months like the most steampunk clockwork ever, at least he'd given the child good genes.

Hannah stumble-stepped her way across the rug towards her, grinning a giant proud baby grin. Serena stooped and caught her up, handing her a wooden spoon. And then preemptively defended herself against both her friends. "It's unbleached wood, so don't worry about it."

"She'll get a splinter from chewing on it."

"She will not get a splinter."

"It's got a chokable diameter."

"Fine," Serena did not snap. Snapping would be snappish, and they were just concerned for the baby; that was sane. She took the spoon away, and put Hannah down to make her own way back to Mama and Aunt Gillian. There were chores to be done, and Serena hadn't asked for their company to begin with.

She wrapped and boxed the platters set out on her counter and ignored the tension in her shoulders and the tickling on her nape that assured her that her friends were engaged in non-verbal communication about her attitude. Well, tried to ignore it.

"Serena," Rachel sing-songed. "Oh, Serena Colby!"

"Serena," Gillian harmonized, badly, with Rachel's chant.

Serena rolled her head on her neck, expelled a quick gust of air, and closed up the box. Behind her, Gillian added the shaking of ice cubes in her glass to the cacophonous rendition of Serena's name. Finally Serena sighed and turned around. "Y'all need to stop it."

"Stop what?" Rachel pretended innocence. "We're just enjoying the day with our sweet pal Serena."

"Stop singing my name. My name is not a song. Also, y'all are bad singers."

Rachel laughed. "I knew it would bug you. Now you'd better sit and drink this tea before we start again." She took the tea glass from Gillian, thrust it into Serena's hands, and pulled her down onto a chair.

"You've gotten a lot bossier since you had the baby, you know."

"Stop blaming Hannah for your problems. As far as I can tell, everything is this Dillon's fault. And what the hell with the not telling us about him before now?"

"What the hell with you cursing in front of your impressionable child?" Serena retorted. "Besides, I've told y'all about Dillon."

"Oh, sure," Gill said, nudging her under the table with her sandaled foot. "Dillon is a person. Dillon likes basketball. Dillon met a deadline with minutes to spare. Boring."

"He's not boring," she grumbled.

Rachel pounced. "No, he's terrifying. He makes you break out into a sweat, and not in a good way. You had an obligation to tell us what a monster he is before now."

"What, like you told us about Sergei and the bullying and that BS of his about Hannah's sleep schedule?" He'd been adamant that the colicky two-month-old should go into her crib at seven each evening, not to be touched again until seven in the morning. It was not a pretty time for any of them.

"Hey!" Gillian outright kicked her shin then. "Ix-nay on that astard-bay, Serena. Rachel got out, and we are proud of her, and we don't blame her for how it all went down."

"Oh, God, sorry, Rachel."

Rachel had her head buried in Hannah's riot of curls. "It's okay."

"Rach—seriously. I'm sorry."

She rested her head atop the baby's and met Serena's eyes. "I know, Serena. It's not like I haven't second-guessed myself a billion times already. Second-billion-guessed. But don't you get it? That's why I want you to pay attention to your instincts with Dillon. I justified stuff you'd never believe with Sergei. Because he was charming every time he went too far. Because he explained himself, even if I replay those explanations now and see how much he was just manipulating me. Because I knew his behavior was bad enough that I wanted to hide it from you three, from my folks, from myself even, but I still wouldn't face the fact that if I wanted to hide his crap from you it meant it wasn't crap I should be willing to live with." She released her tight hold on her daughter and set her back on the rug to toddle around some more. "You think I'm kidding about Dillon, but I'm honestly not. It's the *Gift of Fear* thing, okay? You've heard of this? It's about honoring your gut reactions and the physical signals your body sends when something's not right. You know, the creepy neighbor whose house you never wanted to walk past when you were ten, or the friend of a friend who asks you out but there's something you just can't put your finger on telling you not to accept? Dillon is clearly that guy for you. I'm not saying he can't be okay as a co-worker or even a work buddy, but if you're reacting like that to him—hives, for God's sake!—then you clearly need to not be alone with him."

"Much less in his house when no one knows where you are and you have your tongue down his throat," added Gillian.

"Much less that," Rachel nodded.

"But he's not like that."

"Not like what?"

"Not a jerk, not a bully. He's nice—he's extraordinarily nice, actually. Everyone on the team likes him. He's even been the peacemaker when a couple of the guys have had problems with each other."

Rachel shook her head. "There's nothing to say he can't be nice and also a bully or a pervert. People have different facets. Are you telling me you didn't think Sergei was nice when you met him? Don't you think his friends thought he was the absolute bee's bloody knees, the charismatic one they all listened to? He still is, for all I know, and I'm sure they've all listened to all kinds of crap about how evil I am, keeping Hannah away unfairly, I don't know what-all. I don't want to know. I don't need to. But I bet it's happening, and I bet as Hannah gets older she'll hear it directly from him, and from Yia Yia Depy, and I'll be navigating those waters forever."

Gillian and Serena both reached out to stroke Rachel's arm, give her hand a squeeze.

"Okay, okay, you're right to warn me. I do hear you. And you know I appreciate what you're saying."

"Do you?"

"Rachel. Yes. I do. I admit I'm not convinced that's what is happening with Dillon—don't scold!—but I'm not discounting it out of hand, not by a long shot."

Gillian nodded at her. "Good girl. See, Rachel, she's listening."

"But only to appease me."

Serena threw up her hands. "That's not true! I can't figure out why my lungs seized up today, and so far yours is the most valid option. But honestly, guys, I have met that guy you were talking about—remember Mike, in college, I think it was junior year? And this is different. That was more like goosebumps and a kind of cramping stomach. I've never had that with Dillon. Even when we first met, when he started at Lanigan, all I thought was how gorgeous he was. Young, but yummy."

Serena trailed off, remembering. Remembering how their first eye contact had been a punch in the gut. How, several times as they'd gotten to know each other over the work days, she'd felt a brief shiver across her skin when he'd walked into a room without her seeing him. She'd put all that down to an attraction she had no plans to investigate, but had she been wrong? Was it this fear-gut thing Rachel was talking about?

But no. Dillon was no Mike or Sergei. Not that she'd ever told Rachel, but her friend's ex-husband had indeed given her an uneasy feeling when they'd met. Long before Rachel's pretty blue eyes had grown shadowed and her skin wan, Serena had suspected that the man wasn't nearly what Rachel was cracking him up to be. True, she hadn't known the extent of the problem, or how far Rachel had sublimated herself to him, but the divorce had come as no surprise.

She squeezed Rachel's hand again and turned to look at the good that had come from the marriage. Single parenting an active toddler was a lot to handle, but Hannah was a sweetheart.

Usually.

When she wasn't pulling Serena's thyme plant up by the roots and crunching it in her tiny fists before dropping it from the flower pot to the floor.

Gillian got there first. "Oh, Smoochums, oh, no!" She scooped her up and pried the last stem out of her hand, brushing bits of dirt from her cheeks and shirt.

"What is it? What did my baby eat? Call Poison Control!" Rachel joined the fussing, grabbing a bottle of hand sanitizer and container of baby wipes from her diaper bag.

"It's okay, it's just thyme. You don't need that." Serena took the sanitizer from Rachel. "They make hand sanitizer from thyme. Well, the natural people do. You should get some; you don't want to keep rubbing alcohol on Hannah's skin. Thyme is a good mouthwash, too," she laughed stopping Gillian from wiping too ferociously at the baby's mouth. "She couldn't have picked a better plant to rip up."

They all turned to look at the leaves scattered across the floor.

"Is it ruined?" Rachel asked.

"No, I don't think so. Don't worry." She gave the wriggly Hannah a hug. "You, little Green Thumb, are a quick mover these days. Remind me to have you over when I'm planting at my new house, you'll have a blast."

Hannah giggled, but Rachel was still fretting over the dirt and possible ingestion. "I'd better call the nurse practitioner. Here, Gillian, would you take her in and change her? Thanks."

Gill stacked the pitcher of sweating tea and the empty glasses on a tray before lifting baby and diaper bag to her other hip and carrying all towards the kitchen and bathroom area of Serena's scummy-butt apartment.

"I'll never understand how she does that," muttered Rachel, scrolling through her contact list for the off-hours number of her pediatrician.

"Too many years of waiting tables," Serena replied, then, with a sigh, fetched her broom and dustpan to take care of the mess. It wasn't like the thyme wouldn't grow back; it was a pretty hardy varietal. And she'd be moving all of her herb and veggie pots out of her one sunny window to spread across the entire width of her patio soon. And Hannah was just being Hannah, and none of them had stopped her in time, which was the grown-ups' job.

But between Rachel's lecture and Hannah's destruction, Serena was more than ready to be alone in her empty apartment, the floor plan to Hakeem spread across her little table and sketch pad open beside her, planning layouts and making lists and listening to her music and not hardly at all thinking about Dillon's chest or arms or back or butt or anything else that would disturb her peace.

CHAPTER SIXTEEN

When Shannon answered the door, Toby screeching and back-arching in her arms, Dillon cracked his first smile since his walk with Serena to his house the day before. Little guy was all red in the face, but Shannon was cool as a cucumber and managed to kiss him, pass the baby to him, take the casserole from his arm, and call over her shoulder to Justin at the same time.

"Is it cousin Annie's chicken and stuffing?"

"No, it's my chicken and stuffing. It's better. Hey, Justin," he added, giving his brother-in-law a half-hug, half-shoulder bump. "Maisy is on the porch there behind me. Her stuff, too." Juggling the box and bowls and carrier and baking dish while trying to ring the doorbell had been a challenge, but it didn't hold a candle to the frustration of Saturday's door-related escapade.

His smile had gone awry, but he flat-out laughed when Shannon shoved the casserole into Justin's chest and dropped to the ground outside the front door, actually cooing. "Ohhh, Maisy-kittie, come here, baby, Mama's missed you!" She had the carrier inside and unlatched in seconds. Dillon was impressed—it had taken him a good fifteen minutes to get Maisy in there and the door locked. No matter how often he told the darn cat that she was on her way home, she wouldn't cooperate. He'd almost overcooked the chicken, before figuring out that if he put some of the casserole in the carrier, Maisy would stay put. Sure, it made a bit of a mess, but Shannon had a surfeit of baby wipes at home now.

"Yo, Tobias," Dillon spoke low into his nephew's ear. "Your mom's gone nuts over a creature with fur and a tail. You'd best to stop that crying and start meowing if you want to compete." Though to be fair to the little bundle, he'd pretty much quieted as Dillon stood there bouncing him up and down on his shoulder.

Justin returned from the kitchen. "Hey, take a burp cloth. He's spat all down your shoulder." He grabbed a square of fabric from the stack of laundry on the back of the sofa and wiped at Dillon's t-shirt.

"Oh, Dill, sorry. Want something of Justin's?" Shannon finally noticed something other than the kitten. "Hey, look at Toby, he's loving on his uncle! Oh, he just looks so happy. Justin, grab the camera!"

Justin steered him to the den. "Quick, sit down in here. All she does is gurgle over things now, and I have a feeling you're next."

"No, sit in the brown chair, Toby looks so sweet in his yellow romper against the brown chair. Zoom in close, honey, get their heads together. Oh, my baby and my baby brother. Look, their eyebrows are just the same! Maisy-kittie, have you ever seen the like?"

Apparently the kitten had seen enough of the like to be disinterested now. She sauntered off to re-explore her home and figure out the many intriguing things that had changed in her absence. She would be in for quite a surprise when she got to the bedroom and found a bassinet in front of her favorite sunny window.

"Thanks again for taking the cat, Dillon," Justin said.

"She was no problem. Glad to help."

"Remember when Shannon was seven months along and saw the kitten adoptions and I told her maybe getting a kitten when we were about to have a baby wasn't the easiest idea?"

Dillon didn't answer, just let the new baby smell and the new parents' babble wash over him for a couple of minutes, content. Not that they needed his input—Shannon and Justin had a well-established ritual of talking to each other through comments to him, a habit that had started when they were newly dating and Dillon and Shannon had been orphaned by a reckless driver.

He'd been sixteen—his mom just three weeks before had taken him to the DMV for his license—and Shannon was twenty-one. She'd moved out of her apartment near UCLA so he could stay in the house and finish high school. She'd also scaled back on her heavy hours at college. Dad always called her the Imprudent Student, but after the funeral she spent ages with her advisors working out a plan that had her graduating from college the same month that Dillon finished high school. The new five year plan gave her a chance to turn her minor into a second major, but it also allowed her to be home with her brother in the mornings and most evenings.

Justin had been a rock. He and Shannon had only been on three or four dates before the crash, but they'd been good ones. Intense enough to keep him coming out to the suburbs and willing to do whatever he could to help them both adjust to this new life. His parents ran a financial services firm, and he'd made free with their expertise to help Shannon, and later Dillon, work out what needed to happen with the estate and set up budgets and plans to get them both through college.

He'd also gotten Dillon to start talking again. Shannon couldn't do it. She tried, and she tried, and she tried, but the more she pried and commented and broached topics, the more he curled inward. He'd known it wasn't truly fair. He knew her life had also gone to hell, and that she was no more wanting to suddenly be *in loco parentis* than he was wanting to be anyone's life-changing responsibility. But he just couldn't speak to her constantly kind and concerned face.

Justin didn't have a trick to get him magically communicating again. He simply tried one strategy after another, not giving up. When sports talk failed, he moved on to music. Dillon ignored that, too, and cooking, and girls, and, despite the research Justin had done to come up with something to say, sci-fi. (Justin was strictly non-fiction.) He took Dillon and Shannon surfing, to movies, and hiking in the hills. Of course, he was pretty intently pursuing Shannon at the same time—not that she needed much pursuit—but his efforts for Dillon were genuine.

And then one day he'd mentioned to Dillon that Shannon was so glued to her books that she could go hours without making eye contact with him. And Dillon had told him about an infamous Thanksgiving dinner when Shannon was in AP-level World History. Their folks had moved her to the foot of the table just so she could spread out her notebook and texts while the relatives passed yams around her.

"Uncle Bob just about blew a gasket. Respect for elders, honoring of customs, appreciation for food that has been set before you, on and on. Meanwhile, I was, I guess, ten or so? And so jealous. Mom told me no way could I bring my *Star Wars* book to the table, and she just wouldn't believe I had to do a history report about it the next week. But it says 'a long time ago' right there in the intro!" At the sound of Dillon's laughter, Shannon's head had jerked up from her chapter on post-Industrial farming techniques in the American South, and stared unblinking at Justin long enough for him to wink cheekily at her.

It was a breaking dam for Dillon. His school therapist Ms. Blodgett—it turned out that having suddenly dying parents buys a kid a lot of time with the school therapist—claimed that seeing Justin and Shannon move into a relationship phase that removed any first-blush blinders gave Dillon the confidence to feel as if he was once again under the stable, loving care of two good adults. Dillon thought it was realizing that Justin loved Shannon enough to find her irritating sides endearing. It meant that Shannon's happiness was no longer fully dependent on Dillon's happiness, which took a hell of a lot of pressure off him.

Looking back now, a dozen years later and with Shannon and Justin's firstborn son cradled in his arms, Dillon gave a little credence to Ms. Blodgett. The years that he'd stayed in LA while Shannon and Justin moved to Houston had been good for letting their relationship grow up, so they didn't treat him as a responsibility so much anymore. Not that they wouldn't do anything for him—and vice-versa—but he was able now to do what he wanted without looking for their permission. They were his best friends, not his guardians.

But he was glad they had Toby—and Maisy—so Shannon especially could channel all of her caretaker tendencies somewhere besides him.

"This baby of yours is the toast of my office, you know," he told them.

"Well, of course he is. Look at him! Oh, he fell asleep, you can't see his big eyes now. When he wakes up remind me to take a picture of the two of us with him—you'll do that, Justin? And find the tripod, we need to get one with all four of us."

"Magnolia, too, she makes Eddie forward all of the pics to her. I think they're about ready to start a family."

"How's Eddie feel about that?" Justin asked.

"Cocky. How else?"

"Typical."

"Yep. Oh, I didn't tell you, Jorge got engaged."

"And what joke did Eddie make about that? And did it make Jorge clam up again?" Justin asked. Justin was more incisive with each passing year.

"If you ever give up banking, you should become a therapist," Dillon told him.

"He's going to start an advice column in the quarterly newsletter," Shannon said, settling down on the sofa beside her husband. "Isn't this weird? I think it's the first time since he was born that we've been awake and neither of us have been holding him."

They took the opportunity to smooch, and Dillon looked down at the baby. He was something else. Huge for a newborn, yes, but still such a tiny and mighty force. He did have the Hamilton family eyebrows—straight from Dillon's dad, the original Tobias. He hoped Toby would grow up with his grandfather's sense of humor, too, and his mom's capacity for love, and his dad's patient dedication. And, eventually, his Uncle Dillon's way with the ladies.

Or not.

He used to think he was a reasonably attractive and decent guy to date. Women had approached him, even back in college, and he'd had girlfriends fairly consistency for much of his life. He was tall, he had pretty eyes—he'd been told so, anyway. No one had ever told him his kisses were so repulsive that they had to leave the room immediately. Or flat-out fled without a word. "I'm fine." What the hell, seriously? A two word text, and twenty-four hours later, still nothing else?

It was so unlike the Serena he'd thought he knew. They'd texted and emailed outside of work pretty often—more often than he'd realized until this unwarranted silence over the past day; whenever the Rockets played, and sometimes just for no reason. Not to mention all the back-and-forth at work, and the after-hours things the group did. And worse than the lack of follow-up communication was the fact of her running off to start with. In the middle of—well, of everything. Leaving him hurting with lust, fine. He was mature enough to handle wanting a woman but not being able to have her. Hell, that had been standard operating procedure with Serena since his interview at Lanigan, when he'd idiotically asked her out and been rejected.

But there was more to her than the body that called to his, the smile that socked him in the gut, and the face he felt he could sculpt, he knew it so intensely. Serena was a siren, yes, but also, she was a solid and sympathetic soul. So what had he done that was so egregious that she was running from him? No way—no way—had that kiss not been consensual. And even if he'd gone too far for her, had been too intimate (but how could he have been too intimate for her, when he could remember with burning ferocity each moment of her fingers upon his cock). No, no matter how he parsed it, her running off and her goddamn two word text were way off, reaction-wise.

He sighed and cuddled his nephew closer. Well, he could just dedicate himself to being a great uncle, and maybe one day when he was old and all alone, he could buy a house next door to Tobias and at least his nephew would stick by his side. Best to start him a college fund soon; he'd buy the kid's affection, if he had to.

"What's that look for?" Shannon asked him.

"What look?"

"That mopey look. You look like when you spent a week at surf camp and still couldn't stand on the board."

"Thanks for that memory."

"Poor Dill," Shannon told Justin, "he was so damned determined, but no matter what the instructor dude —"

"Kev."

"Right, Kev the Kool. No matter what Kool Kev showed him, he'd lose his balance as soon as he got one foot under him. By the end of the week, the other kids were calling him 'Wax Off.' I had to pick him up, part of my newly-licensed responsibilities, and he would just slam himself into the car every afternoon. If I had the radio on, he'd shut it off. If I had it off, he'd turn it on full volume. It was all I could do to keep a straight face."

"I was eleven."

"And a total klutz."

"Shut up."

"Okay, no more trips down memory lane. As long as you tell me what's going on with you now."

"Nothing."

Justin laughed. "Want me to turn the radio up?"

"No."

"Come on, it could wake the baby, then he could scream a little, that might help set the mood."

Dillon stood up. "Come on, Toby. Let's go get some chicken." He looked down at the little placid face, the one with his and his dad's eyebrows, and felt a lurching wave of love surge through his gut. "You're my guy, you know that? You get me. We're gonna grow old together, 'kay?"

"Oh, Dill." Shannon looked stricken.

"Dillon," Justin began, then hesitated. "Hey, man, come here. Sit. Shannon will get us all our dinner." He shot her one of those married-people-communicating looks that Dillon normally found amusing, but was irritated by at the moment. Nevertheless, he let Justin pull him down on the sofa beside him, shifting the limp deadweight of snoozing Toby up against his collarbone. The soft baby smell was more soothing than he'd have liked to admit.

"So. Girl trouble?" Justin asked.

Dillon just snorted.

"Come on, you're hardly subtle. Someone's bugging you—who, and is she an idiot, or what?"

"It's not a big deal."

"Which is why you're stealing my son? Who, for the record, is my guy, not yours. What you're holding right there against your chest is the man who will change my diapers in fifty years."

"Shannon can do that."

"Shannon barely changes Toby's diapers now, and he's the completely compelling fruit of her womb, who's only burdened us with a couple hundred of them so far. I don't see her attitude towards them changing when it's her crotchety old husband who's incontinent."

"Hire a nurse, then. Toby will be hanging with me."

"Have your own kids."

"Right. Cause the potential mothers are lining up on my damn doorstep."

Justin reached over and plucked Toby away with no by-your-leave. As if he just had the right to touch his nose to the button nose of his sleeping son. As if seeing their identical wispy blond hair head-to-head was a necessary reminder that Toby belonged with Justin, not him. It wasn't like he wanted to raise the kid himself. But what was wrong with being the cool uncle, the one the kid turned to for adventure and advice? It wasn't so much to ask, and Justin had everything. Wife, son, cat, home, happiness. He was just a selfish bastard, apparently.

"Dillon. I love you. Now get your head out of your ass and tell me what's bugging you. Or who."

"It's nothing."

"Right. Believable. Never mind, then."

Dillon studied Justin, this man who'd stepped in so crucially when he was a lost and angry teen. Who'd fathered the incomparable Tobias, and named him after Dillon and Shannon's dad. Who was looking at him like he would be happy to sic Shannon on him if he didn't come clean.

And so he confessed. Not quite everything. But the attraction to Serena that he had back-burnered for so long. The moments of late when he's allowed himself to move towards instead of away from her—the Rockets game, Eddie's, the farmers market. "And we went back to my place, I thought with—well, with a certain agenda in mind. But as soon as we got inside, right in the middle of...of a kiss, she bailed."

"Bailed?"

"Left. Ran off. Not a backward glance."

"Jesus. Was she—I mean, did you do anything?"

"'Anything'?" What the hell did Justin take him for?

"No, not that. You know what I mean—say something she might have thought was weird, or, like, bit her?"

"Bit her?"

Justin shook his head. "This is an embarrassing conversation. When you were seventeen I just snuck a box of condoms into your desk drawer and we never had to talk at all."

"That was you? Thank God. All this time I thought it was Shannon."

"Well, she told me to."

"Christ."

"It was no picnic, but at least I didn't put any thought into whether you were a considerate lover or not."

"Fuck off."

"Hey! Baby ears!"

"Toby doesn't exactly care if I curse yet."

"Watch it, or you're going to be subject to the swear jar, too."

Dillon snorted. "Okay, when I hear the two of you go an hour without cursing, I'll consider it. But to answer your not-quite-stated but probably offensive question, no, I can't think of a damn thing I did that would make Serena take off like a bat out of hell."

"And has she said anything about it? Have you asked her?"

"Well, no. I texted her."

"Classy."

"She. Ran. Away. I think if she wanted to hear my voice she wouldn't have done that. Besides, I asked in the text what the problem was."

"And she answered?"

"Yeah. After like, an hour. 'I'm fine.' That's all she wrote."

Justin gave a low whistle. He was very good at low whistles—could draw them out for ages, and finish with a nice melodramatic warble. It was a skill Dillon had always envied. "Sounds like you're better off." At Dillon's derisive look, he added, "No, really. I know you said things had simmered for a while there, and I won't pretend we haven't wondered, from the way you've talked about her."

"You've what?"

"Never mind, just that whatever you've thought might be between the two of you until now, it looks like you're mistaken. Or maybe she really is hot for you but has some deep psychological issues preventing her from attaining intimacy."

"There you go with your advice column again."

"The bank has no idea what a resource they have in me. The point is, actions speak louder than, well, not words in this case, but suppositions. She took a hike, and hasn't tried to explain herself or apologize. That's not a situation that screams out for you to pursue it. So, you have two choices."

"Yeah? What are they?"

"You can take Toby off for a diaper change and forget entirely about Serena, or you can change his diaper and ask her to explain herself, and then forget about her."

Dillon stood and reached for his stretchy-curly waking warm bundle of a nephew, giving Justin's shoulder a squeeze on his way past him towards the nursery. Talking it out had, kind of, relaxed his heart about it all.

But getting to the point where he entirely forgot about Serena wasn't going to be a smooth road, no matter how simple his brother-in-law made it sound.

CHAPTER SEVENTEEN

SERENA STRETCHED AND ROLLED OVER to glare at the clock. 7:22, as always. Her internal alarm had dragged her away from a very pleasant dream. A dream in which being up close and personal with Dillon had no adverse reactions whatsoever, except for the residual throbbing at her core. Groaning, she rose and switched on the morning news to keep her company through her morning routine. After dressing in a new cinnamon-orange top and her most comfy khakis, Serena gathered some parsley and chives from the pots in her one sunny window, chopping them to add to her omelet before brewing her first cup of tea.

She certainly wasn't admitting to herself that she'd dressed up for a typical Monday workday. Sure, she'd blown out her hair so the waves fell smoothly down her back, and applied the cosmetic counter makeup she'd stress shopped for on Sunday, but really, so what? And yes, the top was new, but she was due for some new clothes now that the weather was warming up. She wasn't thinking at all about the axe-murderer whose door she'd nearly orgasmed against when she picked out the pretty gold sandals.

Because if she thought about him, she'd have to figure out what had happened. And so far, despite Rachel and Gillian's advice, despite the mind-clearing yoga class, and despite whatever strange things her brain had thrown at her on Saturday and Sunday nights, she was no closer to an answer. So she'd made the decision to just not think about him. Simple, really.

Of course, it would help if he wasn't standing at the end of the hall, looking at her. Inscrutable. Gorgeous. Sexy. But silent and unreadable. She was flushing up again, she could feel it, and she caught herself running her hands over her suddenly itchy neck in search of hives. Damn. Fortunately Janice picked an opportune time to pass between the two of them, and collared Serena. They headed towards the warehouse door.

"Looking good today, Toots."

"Thanks. Likewise, I'm sure."

"Right. Brand new Levis, what could be more exciting?"

"Hang on, you went shopping? You never go shopping."

Janice flushed. Interesting! Serena nudged her shoulder in a 'give it up' gesture, and finally Janice mumbled something about needing new workout gear anyway.

"You also didn't answer my calls."

"You called?"

"Don't play innocent. I know a woman with tales to tell when I see one."

Janice rolled her eyes. "Fine. Smoothie Shack for lunch?"

"We aren't allowed to go get tamales instead?"

"Tamales? Toots, when have you ever seen me eat tamales?"

"Well, you're missing out. You can order the black bean tacos instead." Serena glanced over her shoulder, relieved to see that Dillon hadn't appeared behind them. With or without a *Psycho*-style knife poised to stab. Damn Rachel and her fear reflexes anyhow—this was weird enough without a potential criminal record thrown into the mix. And the only reflex she'd felt when seeing him again had been to rush towards him. She'd been able to suppress it, but only thanks to Janice's timely intervention.

Serena was beginning to foresee a large number of problems cropping up in her workdays to come. Fantastic.

As if on cue, her phone trilled with the ring tone she'd assigned to all of her coworkers. Swallowing a lump, she drew it out of her pocket, and saw with relief it was just her boss.

"Anica's calling. Catch you later—noon?"

"Noon," Janice agreed, and slipped into the warehouse.

Serena answered the call, then groaned a little when Anica asked her to bring her workflow projections and the nearly finished layouts for two web ads by her office as soon as possible. It could only mean more work landing on her plate, and odds were good that the new tasks would involve working with Dillon. It wasn't like Serena hadn't known when she'd been so excited— so freakishly giddy!—about the farmers market date that if things didn't go well between them it might get awkward. But she'd never even considered the sudden desperate need for antihistamines and a throat so closed she could barely draw in air, much less make polite excuses prior to her headlong departure. And how exactly do you go about telling your coworker, "Sorry we didn't have sex, but I seem to be allergic to you, so could you keep your distance, please?" It didn't help that most of what her brain had thrown into her dreams the past two nights were blatant fantasies about Dillon. Beyond blatant. Inflammatory. Who knew her subconscious had this much steamy stuff lurking within?

Well, best to leave that for another time. She managed to skirt the regular path to her office—past Dillon's—by detouring through the break room, and barely glanced at her in-box while she gathered everything for Anica. No message from Dillon. Well, why should there be? And she was ignoring him anyway.

Well, she'd been ignoring him. Until she practically stepped on his toes as she left her office.

"Oh. Um. Hi." (Good lord, that was smooth! Way to start off assured, Serena.)

"Morning."

Why did he have to look so good? Why did she have the itch to smooth the slightly scruffy black hair falling over his eyes? Why did his eyes have to be the blue of deep mountain pools, and why couldn't she read anything in them? She was sure her own face was giving all kinds of things away.

"I—good morning. Anica called me in, I have to get over there."

He nodded slowly. It failed to look like agreement of any sort.

"So I'll see you later, okay?"

There was a flash in his eye now. Anger? Anticipation? Hurt? Lust? It was gone too quickly. He spoke quietly. "Will you have lunch with me?"

"Oh, um. Sorry. Janice and I—we have to talk about something."

The next nod was definitely not agreement. "Right, then," Dillon said, and turned away. Serena watched his stride as he left. Quick. Shoulders set. She sighed. That hadn't gone well. Understatement of the day—it had been tense and awkward and she was as red as a beet. Rather than chase him down to explain that lunch with Janice had nothing to do with him, she squared her own shoulders, took a couple of reassuringly deep breaths, and headed to Anica's office.

It felt like days that she was closeted with the boss, getting a crash course in scheduling, budgeting, sourcing, bidding, and about seven hundred other things that Serena had probably forgotten before she'd finished writing them down. Most likely it was only hours, not days, since she was in the lobby to meet Janice at noon.

"You been dragged backwards through a barbed wire fence, Toots?"

"Just about. And I'm not sure, but I think I have about a dozen more fences before Anica is through with me."

"Ha. No wonder Dillon told Eddie he'd better get used to being shut out of An's office and not knowing what's happening.

Eddie was bull-mad about it, pacing up and down the hall and glaring at the door. Was Anica training you to take over Eddie's job or something?"

Serena blinked away her hurt at Dillon's cynicism. "No, but I am apparently destined for great things."

"Toots! I guessed as much. What'd she say?"

"Oh, it's all still vague at this point. I'm being evaluated, and how I deal with the Atkinson job will prove my worth. Or lack of worth."

"No chance of that."

"Well, you're nice to say so. But Anica keeps it all close to her chest, so how this gets played out might not be so easy to read. Honestly, I could really use the official promotion, and the raise— well, mostly the raise. And the mortgage it'll allow me to get."

They chatted Anica strategy until after their lunches were ordered. As Operations Manager, Janice had worked on a more equal footing with Anica than Serena ever had. She was able to give her a little guidance about pet peeves and some of the higher-echelon Lanigan workings.

"But none of that tells me what happened about Ricky."

"He's gone."

"Gone? What, fired?" When Janice nodded, not meeting her eyes, Serena asked, "Isn't that good? What happened?"

Janice sighed and stirred her iced tea. "I went to Miguel like we said."

"Okay. And?"

"When I told him the dyke comment, he first of all said some boilerplate about Lanigan not discriminating on the basis of sexual orientation."

"The hell?"

Janice looked briefly heavenward, then leaned back to let the waitress deposit their lunch platters in front of them. "Yep. I mean, he was pretty furious about what Ricky said, I'll give him that. More steamed than those tamales, you know? I'm not sure Ricky escaped his termination intact. Not that I object. Know what that vulture shit did after lunch on Friday?"

"He said something else? You're kidding."

"No, but I had to call him to offload a couple of pallets that had just come in, and when he got to the dock, he got down from the forklift and pumped his hips a couple of times at me, dumbass tongue wagging the whole time. I mean, not if he were Johnny Depp would that action be sexy, you know?"

"Aw, sweets. I'm going to sneak into Emily's office after lunch and find his address, okay? You can come with me when I go flatten his tiny nads."

"You're too kind," Janice smiled. "I think Miguel already knows his address. And a couple of the guys on the floor were giving me these upright stances and serious nods after Ricky was shown the door, so I'm not sure, but...."

"Maybe Ricky already had a bad weekend? Serves him right, if so. Here, try this tamale, it's the spinach one. To die for, right?"

"Mmm. I can feel the fat warming my tummy now."

"Oh, you'll just spin class it off later on. Come on, tell me what else Miguel said. Not just the anti-discrimination stuff, right?"

Janice shook her head. "Nope, he buzzed Emily and told her to get Ricky's termination paperwork together, fired for cause, and guess what?"

"Hm?"

"He told her about the dyke thing and I had to sign a statement after all."

"Good."

"Well, it's not what I was looking for. But Miguel was—I guess 'considerate' is the word. I don't think it'll change much of anything. People talk so progressive until Little Missy puts on steel-toe shoes, and suddenly there are manly lines not to cross. But at least Miguel sets a good example for the rest of the warehouse."

"I told you he'd handle it right."

"Thanks, Toots, that's always a classy comment."

Serena grinned. "Nyah-nyah-nyah. But wait a minute. Does Miguel think you're gay?"

Janice blushed. "I don't know."

"Janice," she drew out her friend's name, intrigued. "Do you have a reason Miguel needs to not think you're gay?"

"What does it matter if he does or not? We're just coworkers."

Serena tried to hide her wince. It wasn't so long ago that she'd pretended to a similar level of equanimity about Dillon. "Okay, sure, it's not like it affects your job. But are you telling me the new jeans and the haircut are purely coincidental?"

"Asked the woman with a brand-new top and, if I'm not mistaken, a shade of lipstick never before seen upon her very guilty face?"

"Okay fine, you were just shopping. Time for new clothes. Happens to everyone." Serena scooped some more salsa onto her tamales and carefully distributed it across the entire surface.

"Toots, you are easier to read than my first primer."

"Don't know what you're talking about. And did Miguel notice your hair?"

"Changing the subject, that'll work. No, he did not notice my hair. Or how excellently these jeans hug my firm ass, either. Not so as he mentioned, and not that he would mention, on the heels of firing someone for harassment."

"Do you want him to notice?"

"More importantly, who do you want to notice the extremely flirty ruffle on your cute little bodice, Serena? Can't be Jorge, he's Bubba's guy through and through. Can't be Eddie, he's a dubiously married man. Philip is probably twice your age. That leaves Johnnie or, and I know you are impressed with my powers of deduction, the sexy-as-sin Dillon."

"How do you know it's not Miguel?" Serena asked, then realized she'd given too much away with just that question. "Or anyone at work? Maybe I met someone at yoga."

"Please, after the last guy, with the dream journal? I don't think so."

"Or anyone at all. How do you know I'm not just trying to please myself?"

"Right, Toots. I will believe that of you, and you of me, and we will have a harmonious little life in fairyland."

"Which is where you should be, since you're gay and all."

"I'm pretty sure Ricky thought you were my girlfriend, so you can come live under the toadstool next door to mine."

Serena laughed. "Deal."

Janice, bless her, didn't mention Dillon again. Or Johnnie, who was one step away from the frat house he'd lived in fifteen years earlier, so if Janice thought the cute shirt was for his benefit she was really reaching.

Of course, the cute shirt wasn't for Dillon, either. She just liked it. A woman was allowed to enjoy her wardrobe without everyone seeking ulterior motives all the time.

Except Janice looked damn good in those jeans, and Serena had to wonder just how much their new clothes were giving away about both of their ulterior motives.

That was his smile.

He wasn't even aware he'd cataloged Serena's smiles. Or that he had laid claim to any of them as his particular possession. But she was standing there in the lobby, shaking hands with some silly ass with gray hair and wrinkles everywhere, relaxed and happy as you please, and giving him Dillon's smile. The one that meant he'd said something to please or entertain her. The one that told him she liked being with him. The one that had always quickened his pulse a little, even when they were in the middle of a meeting and it was totally inappropriate.

Maybe it had been inappropriate every time, no matter the circumstances. Because if he'd been reading anything into that smile, and she was just as likely to give it to a cretin like the one who finally took his talons off of her and left, Dillon was clearly a fool.

And of course the smile disappeared double-time as soon as she saw Dillon looking at her. Not unlike the way she herself had disappeared double-time on Saturday. He could practically feel her searching the lobby for an exit that would allow her to continue avoiding him. Well, not this time, he thought grimly as he approached her.

It wasn't that she took a step back when he was close. But he could tell that she wanted to. He interrupted the half-formed excuse on her unsmiling lips. "Come outside with me for a minute."

"I. Anica and I," Serena started.

"Have been meeting all day and will probably meet all night, sure, whatever. You took time out to cuddle up to the old man there, you can give me five minutes, too."

At that point, Serena literally did search for exits, but with Dillon deliberately crowding her space, she couldn't come up with an escape plan. She did mutter something about the guy being an accountant not a teddy bear, but let him lead her to the door. He didn't touch her, though. As much as he wanted to, he didn't even reach for her arm to guide her. The last time he'd touched her, after all—well, first she'd torn at her shirt to get him closer to her breasts. Then she'd bolted.

Once clear of the door and any prying eyes or ears within the building, Dillon just looked at Serena. She looked good. Gorgeous. Composed. But with widened eyes that belied her calm façade, so at least he knew she hadn't forgotten what had happened. Whether she could explain it or not was another matter.

"So."

She fidgeted, then squared her shoulders. "So."

"You left." He instantly wanted to revoke his words, to go for a less direct approach. While most of him wanted to confront Serena, compel an explanation from her, and give no quarter, an ungovernable part of him begged him to slow down and give her a chance. To accept whatever feeble excuse she gave—dead phone, broken modem, dead relative, broken bone. His own mind had come up with a hundred reasons for her leaving, and for her dodging of him afterwards. All that reckless part of him wanted was for her to offer up any half-hearted excuse that he could whole-heartedly embrace so that they could move past Saturday and see what might happen next.

But, no, he'd gone for the confrontation. So it served him right that she said, "I left. I'm sorry I didn't say goodbye."

No excuse at all. No apology for the lack of an explanation. His eyes narrowed as he determined to pin her down. "That's what you're sorry for? Only for not waving as you ran down my steps? What about avoiding me for the past forty-nine hours? What about a pretty clear indication that we could have some sort of relationship, and then you leaving without a word? What about a two-word text then radio silence? What about kissing —"

She broke in, flushed and furious. "Relationship? Dillon, who said anything about a relationship? Did I say it? I think I'd remember. You didn't either. I never gave you any reason to believe we were headed to the altar here, did I? No I did not. For your information, I'm not looking for a husband, so maybe you could lay off and give me some space to figure this all out for a minute or two?"

He clenched his jaw, drew a hissing great breath in through his nose, and didn't move. If he moved, he'd open his mouth. If he opened his mouth, no one in the building behind him would miss the fact that he was pissed. Royally, royally pissed.

His utter silence apparently gave her a chance to replay her own words—they were certainly echoing relentlessly through his mind. At any rate, her eyes widened, her honey skin paled, and her mouth worked for a quiet moment.

"Oh, God, Dillon, that's not what I meant. Shit. I can't—I just don't know why...." 'Why' what, he wondered. But didn't ask. He still wasn't moving. "Don't listen to me, Dillon. I won't listen to Rachel, and you don't listen to me, and we'll remember that we're friends and if we're friends then whatever is happening with my breathing isn't panic—it's something but I don't know what but we can take it slow, taking it slow worked fine, and then I'll figure this out. Okay? Is that okay?"

But he was galvanized—'friends' was all she had to say to get him moving after all. Friends. It was clear enough, as brush-offs went. One did not suckle one's friend's breasts. One's friends did not tantalize one's erection. Friendship was not carnal.

Never mind that friends, real friends, explain when they behave inexplicably. Or at least apologize. No, Serena was not his friend. And she clearly didn't want more. So he would remove himself from her orbit and she could befriend the ancient accountant with his vintage abacus or whatever. It was, after all, the friendly thing to do when one's friend is hell-bent on avoiding one's company. Only polite to comply.

So he walked away.

Serena watched the stiffest neck she'd ever seen, retreating from her at speed. Just walking away without a word. So, that's how that felt. No wonder he was mad.

What had she just said? Talking about weddings? Where had that even come from? And who was she kidding, she didn't want a relationship? Last time she checked, people only shaved before trips to the farmers market when they wanted—well, okay, often just sex. But more than friendship, at any rate. And she'd gone full-tilt into the encounter—the kiss, the more—with Dillon. No rewriting history, Serena.

No, the problem wasn't her stance on relationships. The problem was the fact that she was irresistibly drawn to a man who, for her, was literally breath-taking. So her task was to figure out why this particular man had the power to both inflame her and sicken her. Why had his going from nice coworker to hunk of sensual delights caused her to subconsciously freak out?

And maybe once she understood that, she could explain it to Dillon in a way that didn't make him stare through her and turn away.

CHAPTER EIGHTEEN

SERENA HAD BEEN SAVING, in addition to money, her vacation days. After another few excruciating days at Lanigan, wrapping up MediCost with far more terse back-and-forth messages between her and Dillon than she'd have liked, she was as happy to be getting away from him and the office as she was to be signing the lease for Hakeem and moving out of the scummy-butt apartment.

No. Not as happy. Dillon was just a fly—no, a gnat—in the ointment of her life, and Hakeem the Dream House was momentous. The culmination of a decade of adult life. The fulfillment of all her childhood wishes.

Dillon was nothing compared to all that.

So Serena didn't consider him at all on her first vacation day, when she was finishing packing up her apartment.

Or on her second vacation day, when she met the seller's brokers to go over the final paperwork and hand over a giant portion of her savings account.

Or on her third vacation day, when Serena covered patches of her new walls with the hues that were the finalists in her great room color debate.

Or on her fourth vacation day, when returning to Hakeem after a long day spent cleaning out the scummy-butt apartment, she walked through each of her new, mostly empty rooms and noticed that one of the blues she'd picked for her possible bedroom color exactly matched Dillon's eyes.

And certainly not on her fifth vacation day, when she was done refinishing the hardwoods and took a little time to just sit and stare at their gleam and congratulate herself.

It was the weekend by then, actually, with another week ahead of vacation and not one single thought of Dillon ever crossing her mind. She focused instead on her empty stomach and her empty fridge, and talked herself into heading out for a few grocery-store essentials. She was too tired to go out, too reluctant to leave her butter-gold living room, her sage dining room, her superbly orange office. But she was too hungry to subsist on tea and the last of her oatmeal. And vacation day or not, sore from cleaning or not, her internal alarm would have her up at 7:22 exactly, like always. She needed the fuel to keep checking things off her to-do list, so she forced herself to shop.

It was full dark by the time Serena pulled back onto her street, which maybe accounted for how she got halfway up her neighbor's drive before realizing she'd made a wrong turn. When her headlights finally caught the paint rollers drying on her carport walls and the pile of colorfully spattered thrift-store sheets she'd used as tarps, it was ridiculously relieving.

She was home.

As she fumbled the lock open and patted the wall for the switch, Serena tried to downgrade her hurricane of emotions to a mere tropical storm of clashing unease and pleasure. The lights played across her freshly refinished floors and vibrant walls. The new furniture would arrive in the morning, but already the spaces were beginning to feel a little less vast and empty. She was wiped out from her hours of painting, and a tad bleary as she located a glass from a box on the kitchen counter. But something about pouring herself a glass of water from the pitcher in her fridge gave her goofy goosebumps. Her very own fridge. Clean and white against the warm cinnamon walls, energy efficient, and like her stomach, no longer empty.

Humming a little, she set to unpacking and rinsing the dishes from the box on her counter. For years she'd dreamed of a kitchen overflowing with spice hues, and as soon as Natalie'd led her into the room she'd visualized the perfect cinnamon color to bring out the sandy tones in the granite and the warmth of the walnut cabinets. It was one more Hakeem the Dream point: the kitchen was perfect for the nutmeg, paprika, and sometimes espresso hued crockery she'd been collecting from yard sales and discount shelves for a couple of years. Finally she had the room to unpack and rediscover them all. She stacked her tangerine Fiestaware in the dish drainer alongside a handful of melamine plates with a swirl of burnt orange and asparagus and her big ceramic mustard-seed platter, and stuffed all the packing material back into the box.

She made a circuit of the doors. Her back door, with its growing pile of cardboard to be broken down for recycling. Her patio door, the snug enclosure of her garden already inspiring her next big project. Her front door. All locked up, lights off in the rooms she'd spent so much time picking colors for and painting. Since taking possession, Serena had become an expert spackler and sander, as proficient with using paint tape as if she'd studied it instead of graphic design. So even as she made her way through the dark, empty rooms to the air mattress in her perfectly Maya azul bedroom, she could feel the colors surrounding her, buoying her up, celebrating everything she'd so far put into the house that had become, at last, her very own home.

And if falling asleep felt the tiniest bit lonely, the mental images of the floor plans she'd sketched, the herb pots she would balance for aesthetics and optimal growth, and the gold Marrakech rug she would soon spread across her hardwoods reassured her that this house would end up as her haven from any and all troubles the world chose to throw her way.

Dribble twice. Crouch then spring, releasing the ball. Swish. Catch the free throw, move in for a layup. Shoot. Slide across the chalked half-court. Shoot for three points.

Miss.

Dillon caught up the ball and paced the length of his driveway, breathing fast. He'd been out in the increasingly warm March day for an hour, at first just idly shooting from inside the paint, but pushing himself harder and harder as he got into the zone.

Muscle memory returned to him, and he settled into familiar patterns. The drills his father had set him, back when the backboard was only six feet off the ground and Dillon considerably shorter. For years, practically day in and day out, Dad would send him out to the driveway before dinner to drill and Shannon would grumble because she had to set the table. Never mind that Dillon had to clear the dishes while Shannon escaped back to her books.

Shannon. What a know-it-all.

He missed another three-pointer.

Shannon had called. Justin, the rat, had of course told her everything about the aborted date with Serena, and Shannon had called to commiserate. Treating him like a little boy who needed soothing, playing the grown-up and wise big sister to the hilt, and then starting in with the dramatic sighing. "I just keep hoping you two will find a way to talk, Dill. The things you said about her, I really thought she might be The One, you know? That my baby bro might finally settle down and get his Happily Ever After. I just want you to have that so much."

The One. As if that was a thing, to start with. Sure, she and Justin had bonded early and fast, and more power to them. But not everyone was destined for Happily Ever After with their sweetheart and their baby and their cat and all. Relationships took work, and couples were flawed—well, excepting Justin and

Shannon—and it wasn't like there was just one person out there who could mind-meld with him and make his life complete. Make him not be alone. Enable him to stop searching for happiness everywhere and just live with it, secure beside him, day in and day out.

Dillon yanked off his t-shirt and used it to wipe his brow, stalking to water bottle he'd left beside his garage door. His life was perfectly fine. Happiness was overrated.

And Shannon wasn't as much a know-it-all as she liked to think.

Serena's parents had divorced when she was seven. Okay, fine, it happened. She wasn't going to let herself be scarred for life by an event twenty-three years earlier. But the thing was, she'd really really liked her bedroom in her mom and dad's house. It had a window seat with secret storage for her treasures *de jour*, and wallpaper with fluffy rabbits on a field of bright green that exactly matched the green on her pink and green plaid comforter. It was a happy room, and some of her earliest memories took place in it.

After the divorce, they sold the house. She'd lived in a lot of places since then—her dad's four remarriages and her mom's three ensured that—but it wasn't until her junior year at UT that she'd found herself in another truly happy room. The apartment she and her three roommates shared was a bit of a dive, but they'd made it their own and it was a cozy, relaxed place for them to share, rarely tainted by conflict or uncertainty.

After living in that dive for a couple of years, they'd graduated and taken various paths, but had all ended up in Houston. And Serena loved seeing them regularly, but for years had never felt adequately able to welcome them into a space of her own. Ten days in her house—days spent considering the furniture and accessories from every angle, optimizing the layout of her kitchen and office, and using her favorite set of markers to cross completed items off the to-do lists she'd spread across the dining table—and Serena was feeling decidedly welcoming. It was with a certain amount of trepidation but a heck of a lot of pride that she opened Hakeem's door to Rachel, Natalie, and Gillian.

Natalie, of course, was her realtor, so she'd seen the house several times, but not since closing. "Oh, Serena! The colors. Look at your floors, they turned out great. You did such a beautiful job with it all." She gave Serena a giant hug and a bouquet of wildflowers. "Aren't you glad I made you get it? Aren't I the best friend ever?"

Serena laughed and agreed, at least until Rachel pointed out that Natalie had gotten a commission out of the deal, "And I actually paid for a babysitter for tonight. Which makes me the best friend." Which she was, although Natalie and Gillian weren't far behind. She took them all on the grand tour, the spring in her step getting springier as the *oohs* and *ahhs* piled up. As she stood on the back patio with them, surrounded by her pots of herbs and in sight of the hibiscus bushes she'd settled against each post of the pergola, Serena's heart hitched just a tad. No more bunny wallpaper, no more student digs where the ants never fully cleared out of the kitchen, but just as much a place where she was surrounded by happy. And she owned it. Well, she almost owned it, but the new feeling of permanence and security was a treasure she didn't need a window seat storage area to keep handy.

"To home," Gillian toasted, after they'd seated themselves around the farmhouse table Serena had found, on clearance even, in the furniture warehouse Natalie had pointed her towards. Having one of her best friends as her realtor had been a boon on so many levels.

Except for when that realtor friend got just a little too pushy about her romantic agendas. "And to filling that home with a man," Natalie said, grinning.

"Hey, now. Unless you're willing to share your Chris, you have to admit the good ones are all taken," Serena said, leaning forward to re-center her table runner, which Gill had knocked askew.

"We don't all want to share Chris," added Rachel, then at Natalie's questioning look: "Not that Chris isn't awesome. You know I love Chris. Platonically. Even Hannah loves Chris, and she doesn't love men very much." A more suspicious toddler than Rachel's Hannah would be hard to find.

"She loves Sergei the Idiot," Serena pointed out, before she could remember to bite her tongue.

"Well, Serena, I can hardly stop her from loving her father. Yia Yia Depy bribes her into it."

"Poor Rachel," Serena said, and poured her more pinot. She encouraged the latest annoying-ex-mother-in-law tale, both to atone for bringing up Sergei and to divert Natalie's one-track mind.

But it wasn't long before Natalie was pointing out again that, now that Serena had a place to call her own, she should search for a guy to bring back to it. "Someone who doesn't turn you into a walking histamine, though, so you can get laid without having to go to the ER after."

"Funny. Besides, I've given up on anything happening with Dillon. I haven't been thinking about him at all." Not at all. No remembering his jokes or his stunning blue eyes. Never reliving his hands on her body, his tongue setting trails of fire across her skin. His strong hard thigh wedged against her bucking crotch and his strong hard shaft straining his jeans.

After the briefest of silences, Rachel started laughing, and it wasn't long before they were all three cracking up. Serena opened her eyes and cleared her throat. "Shut up."

But a smile settled deep inside her. She looked at her three best friends since college, gathered at her table, celebrating this milestone with her. She had them, and she had Hakeem the Dream Bungalow, and she had her good job. She was perfectly happy, settled, grand. There just wasn't any reason to complicate all that by adding in a relationship, Natalie's domesticating tendencies be damned.

CHAPTER NINETEEN

SERENA TOOK SOME TIME TO WALK each room of her little house before heading out for her first day back at work. The muted morning light gave a subtle glow to her paint colors, and she especially enjoyed the east-facing windows in the living room. Her buttery walls became a little more golden, the grain of the wood floors that much more defined. She itched to grab a sketchpad and play with a new configuration of the sofa and chairs, to give herself a place to sit over her morning cup of tea while admiring the view of her patio and the highlighted walls, but work awaited. Her commute was far from the worst-case scenario she'd hedged against, which meant a truly decent parking space and plenty of time to chair-dance to the radio before she headed in.

It all bolstered her, giving her a cloak of imperturbability as she prepared to face Dillon for the first time in weeks.

"So tomorrow Jorge will get a few more location shots for Houston Green." Anica wrapped up the team meeting. "Anything else?"

"Is Dillon really turning twenty-one this week? We should take him for lunchtime tequila shots to celebrate," Eddie said, grinning to beat the band. Of course. Dillon had been foolish to hope that the day could pass unremarked, especially by Eddie. Dillon had never been much for birthdays, but those first few 'celebrations' Shannon and Justin had tried to throw for him after his parents had died had been excruciating. He'd entered college frankly relieved to be in the company of people who would only know his birth date if he chose to tell them. He'd just never counted on the perfidy of office birthday parties.

When he didn't speak up, Anica answered. "Yes, Wednesday is Dillon's birthday. Come by Conference A at three for cake. It's on the calendar." She paused and smiled at him. "Not his twenty-first. No shots. Which I know none of you would do during the work day anyway, right, Eddie?"

"Never," smirked Eddie with a wink that drew probably a third of the laughter he'd hoped for.

Dillon caught himself glancing in Serena's direction again, and looked away before she could give him one of those looks of hers. They'd not managed to talk since she came back from her house-moving vacation, but she certainly had her eyes on him every time he put his eyes on her. Which was well and good, but Dillon was no longer in the business of non-verbal communication with her. If she had something to say, she would have to flat-out say it, because body language between them had failed. Epically. Cosmically. Supernovas. Black holes. Beyond the final frontier of failure. From now on he would remember to take her actual words as her message to him.

Unfortunately there was nothing to take him out of the office for the rest of the week. That meant four and a half more days of unavoidable meetings, hallway encounters, email exchanges, and, of course, the celebration of his twenty-seven happy years on earth. Silver lining? Young Toby's sleep schedule meant the sombrero-wearing extravaganza at the Lupe's Tortillas near Shannon and Justin's house was postponed indefinitely. Or at least until a more sedate Saturday brunch, but it was better than nothing.

Janice paused on her way out of the conference room. "Hey, Toots, why do you keep tousling those pretty locks of yours? Are you seeing how far the scruffy look can take the young copywriter of today?"

Dillon assessed her sidelong, but she didn't seem to be hiding a deeper meaning. So maybe Serena hadn't told everyone about their farmers market encounter. At least, not Janice. There was still her mysterious Rachel reference to figure out. Not that he was in the business of figuring anything out. He'd asked for an explanation, and been denied one, and he wasn't Dirk Gently. If Serena wanted him to understand why she did or said anything, she was going to have to do better than dropping clues via coded messages from their friends.

God, he really needed to stop thinking about her.

"Janice, I've wondered something. Why do you call everyone 'Toots'? Male and female, right?"

"Do I look sexist? Why would I give a different honey-pie nickname to people of a different gender? That's appalling."

He was surprised by the light laugh she got out of him. "Okay. I'll give you that. But why a honey-pie nickname at all?" And what on earth was a honey-pie nickname to start with? Something Texan, he supposed.

"Oh, Honey Pie! A gal has got to have a nickname for people. At least, a gal who works half the time with the ever-changing warehouse gang and the other half the time with a whole rolodex worth of vendors and customers. If we still used rolodexes. So I call everyone 'Toots' and they know it's me on the phone. If I'm consistent, they don't wonder if I just forgot their name or what."

"So you can't remember names, is what you're saying."

"Actually, I'm better at it than you'd expect. Or than I'd expect, at least. But it charms the customers and disarms the loading dock, so I stick with it." She nudged his shoulder. "You're not answering my question about your hair, Toots."

He caught himself rubbing at his forehead again, and stuck his hands in his jacket pockets. "Dandruff," he smiled down at her, and headed back to his office.

Serena drafted three or four different emails and one train-wreck of a text to Dillon before giving up on written communication between them. He was the writer. She could draw him an apology picture, she supposed, but it seemed a little off base. She'd tried it, once, when she was testing that she'd set the drawing table up at the right angle in her home office. Not because of Dillon, specifically, but she'd had to draw something and it was the first thing that came to mind. All she really wanted to say was that she didn't want him to hate her, and that she was sure he wasn't really dangerous. No matter what the articles Rachel crowded her in-box with said. Rachel and Gill had told Natalie the whole story, of course, and Natalie had tapped into some realtor-accessible database to find that not only did Dillon have no criminal record in Texas or California, but he also had pretty decent credit and only owed $22,000 on his townhouse. It was way more than she'd been comfortable with her friends snooping into on her behalf, even if it did calm Rachel's fervor a little. "He's never been caught, anyway," Rachel conceded.

Serena had lingered at the end of the day Monday but chickened out and hurried to her car when she heard him walking out with Eddie after work.

She wasn't trying, exactly, to hide that she and Dillon had personal things to say, but Eddie's presence sure wouldn't lay any soft groundwork for Serena to explain that she was allergic to Dillon. To give her a chance to, oh, go to a shrink to find out what was wrong with her, so they could go back to kissing. Or more. Or less, even. But leaving things as they were was clearly not a good idea. Ignoring and avoiding him hadn't worked. Trying to maintain an appropriate work distance hadn't worked. Shifting uncomfortably every time they were in the same room was definitely not working. He wasn't taking the habitual chair next to hers. He wasn't watching her doodle silly things in the margins of their meeting notes and jotting down captions to her cartoons on his own copy. Their eyes weren't meeting with an unstated smirk whenever Johnnie started a sentence with 'Bro' or 'Dude.'

Serena was lonely. Janice was bolstering her when she could— when she wasn't chit-chatting with Dillon so they were both leaving her behind. And as a modern independent woman who'd prided herself on building a life of self-sufficiency, Serena shouldn't care so much if she had a work buddy or not. Or so she told herself. But apparently she counted rather heavily on Dillon's company. Thanks to several days of chastising herself whenever she thought of him, she knew he was on her mind with alarming frequency. For work, for friendship, for fantasizing. Sometimes for all three bundled into one erotic office-based imagining that she sure as hell hoped no one but her could read in her thoughts. It only added to all the damn blushing she was doing whenever he caught her glancing at him. Since she could no longer tell if the blush was the start of a rash or not, she was keeping herself doped up with antihistamines. As with her other allergies, just thinking about the hives made her neck itch, so every other moment she was near Dillon, Serena was rubbing under her collar and focusing on deep breaths. It must have made her quite the strange sight.

Everything was going in circles in her mind, which prompted her to do the unexpected: she called her mom on the way home, and invited her over. At the very least, her mom had lots of relationship experience and had seen Serena in hives over the years.

Everything was in good shape at Hakeem, which didn't stop Serena from nudging each chair into alignment and adjusting the curtains and lamps for optimal afternoon viewing. When the bell rang, Serena finished a round of deep cleansing breaths before opening the door. "Hi, Mom." She leaned forward to kiss her rouged cheek before standing back to gesture her in. "Was the traffic okay coming over?"

Becky Lofthouse-Colby-Russo squeezed her arm on the way past and wasted no time before setting off to explore the house. "Well, Serena, it's quite lovely," she said, as her daughter trailed her from the living areas down the hallway. "I suppose you can redo the paint if that orange gets to be too much, but be sure to use a base coat first. Maybe with a blue tint, in case the color bleeds through."

"I know about base coats, Mom," Serena said, instead of saying that she'd never repaint her office, because it was her favorite color and it was uplifting every time she went in there.

"Oh, I do like this," Becky said, stopping in actual admiration in the middle of the bedroom. She did a slow three-sixty, nodding, and turned to Serena. "This room has a great energy to it. Very affirming. You should be proud of this room."

"I am. I'm proud of the whole house. I'm glad you were free to come see it. Do you want some tea?" She led the way back to the kitchen, where her mom carefully pulled herself onto one of the stools at the counter. "I have sun tea, or I can brew hot."

They settled in with their drinks, and Becky gave her all her updates, the majority of which were about Zane's three kids. Regina and Rufus were excelling in college, apparently, and Ridley's wife—Becky's face brightened considerably as she relayed this news—was going to have a kid. "I'll finally be a grandmother! And just in time for Thanksgiving. It's wrong to wish for the baby to come early, but I think a birthday so close to the holiday is tough on a child, don't you? Zane said I could wish for one week early, but nothing more, in case it's bad karma."

Serena remembered about the calming breaths, and didn't comment on the "finally" part, or mention that she would really be a stepgrandmother, which wasn't exactly the same thing. She even said she'd call Ridley to say congratulations, but Becky told her not to, because it was still early days. "They're only telling family for now, just in case."

So it wasn't very easy for Serena to focus on the memory of the two of them in her early teens, her mom telling her things about not crying over spilt milk when a guy she'd crushed on had started a very public relationship with the girl who sat next to her in geometry. Still, she did it, and concentrated on telling Becky about some of the favorite things she'd found while shopping for the house, and a story about Rachel and baby Hannah, and the promotion waiting for her in the wings.

"Well, that's excellent, Serena, about time you got your due. You've been there for a decade."

"Just under four years, actually." A decade ago she'd still been in college.

"Really? Are you sure?" Becky sipped her tea. "Well, I guess I can't keep up. It's hard enough to stay on top of your current address. Maybe that will change now that you have this house. A mortgage really settles a person down, I was telling Ridley and Neera that the other day. Zane and I said we'd help them with a down payment, of course. We want them to live close, if they can manage it, to make all that baby minding easier on us old folks, but you know Neera," she sighed, not giving Serena a chance to point out that she'd only met her stepsister-in-law maybe three times, "she's set on this school district thing, has charts about demographics and graduation rates for practically the whole west side of town."

If she bit her tongue for just a minute or two, her mom could talk on and she wouldn't have to think too hard about everything being said. Down payments and babysitting and the obviously frequent contact with people who'd been essentially out of Becky and Zane's house for at least a few years. She was an adult now, and theoretically just as responsible as Becky for the dynamic between them. No amount of yogic breath control worked, though, and in the end she resorted to going to the fridge to pull out some fruit and cheese for them to munch on before she was ready to calmly head the conversation in another direction.

"So, Mom, I haven't told you about the date I had."

It was a little amusing how quickly Becky became focused. Her face actually rearranged somehow—maybe her eyes weren't as widely open and her smile was a little easier?—and she looked more like the Mom of old days. Serena reached for a few grapes and reminded herself that she had called Mom up to invite her over because she actually wanted something from her, and that theoretically mothers liked it when their kids turned to them for advice.

"Well," she said a little slowly. "It's actually a little complicated. I was wondering if I could get your opinion."

"He's married, isn't he?" Becky asked, eyes wide again. But without the smile.

"No! I wouldn't." Serena blew out a gust of air. "After the way I grew up? Really, Mom? I can't even believe that's the first thing you think of. When Dad left you for Alice—hell, even when he left Elaine for Tennessee—how can you not remember all the times you told me what a betrayal it was for a woman to sleep with a married man? Trust me, it was very well drummed into my little head. I even managed to decide it was horrible for a man to sleep with a married woman. So just so you know, even though you never said it, I applied the lesson equally across gender lines."

Serena stopped ranting and narrowed her eyes at her mom. "And by the way, given how you moved directly from Samuel's house to Zane's, don't think I've never suspected cheating on your part." Well. She'd been holding that one in for nine years. Not that she felt better that it was out in the open.

Becky stood up. "Well, I'm sorry, Serena, that I'm such a bad and suspicious mother. Obviously you can't really be looking for anything but some validation from me, since I'm of low moral character and not fit to have an opinion about your life."

"Mom. Come on, that's not what I mean."

"I'll accept that as if it was an apology." She made a show of looking at the dainty gold watch on her wrist. "I should be heading out, Serena. Zane is cooking tonight, and I don't want to be late. Maybe next time you call you could invite us both over, offer to make us dinner perhaps? He would be honored if you started to think of him as a member of your family, after all this time."

And they were back to the same ground as always. "I do think of him like that. Didn't I send him a birthday card?" She took in her mom's tense mouth and added, as sincerely as she could muster, "I'd love to have you both over for dinner sometime. That sounds delightful."

Becky bestowed an approving smile on her, but still headed towards the door. "Here, I brought this for housewarming," she said, pulling a small package out of her handbag. "It's a smudge stick. White sage, of course. Be sure to put it out in some salt when you're done cleansing the house." Becky leaned in for a kiss, leaving a faint coolness on her cheek as she retreated. "Goodbye, Serena."

Chapter Twenty

WELL, HIS DAY HADN'T STARTED with a fart cushion in his desk chair, he could say that for it. Dillon was not otherwise finding a lot to celebrate. But he was playing nice. Justin had called the night before for a quiet chat while Shannon nursed Tobias to sleep. He'd be irritatingly logical and practical when Dillon confessed what a balls-up he'd made of asking Serena for an explanation, and grumbled about how awkward Lanigan had been since Serena had returned and their mutual silence had grown more palpably strained. So Dillon had had to agree to be non-judgmental and calm and to ask her again.

"You're not so stupid you think you can leave it like this, are you?" Justin had asked.

"You're a real supportive guy, has anyone ever told you that?"

"I think they put it in my yearbook. Are you going to ask her nicely?"

"She's not acting nice."

"Which is always a good excuse for your own bad behavior, of course."

"So turn the other cheek is your advice?"

"No, be a better person is my advice. Look, you've told us a thousand nice things about Serena since the day you met her. What you're describing doesn't sound like the same woman you've talked about all this time."

"I don't know why you keep insisting I talk about her all the time."

"And we always thought when the two of you got together it would be, you know, an easy kind of relationship. So we're a little surprised by this whole thing."

"It has occurred to you that I don't want you talking about my love life with my big sister, hasn't it? And what do you mean 'when' Serena and I got together?"

But Justin had just laughed, and then Shannon had come on the line to tell him she was sure Tobias had smiled, even though the books said he was too young yet for smiling, but a mama knows what a mama knows and she knew a smile when she saw it.

He knew he'd be grilled again soon enough, so he was making an effort—and it was effort, no doubt about it—to be not only civil but also nominally open to a real conversation with Serena.

But not, of all days, on his friggin' birthday.

Three rolled around soon enough—Eddie had taken him to lunch, but without shots. As usual, one-on-one with Eddie was a different experience than Eddie in a group. His overkill practical jokester persona faded considerably when his audience was reduced, and Eddie was merely genial as they ordered their burgers. Justin had armchair-diagnosed Eddie with a social insecurity that led to the class clown antics when in groups. And Dillon, keeping this in mind, saw it in action often enough. Only when Eddie was at home with Magnolia was he able to be the same carefree, funny—but not cruel—guy that Dillon knew from their lunches and one-on-one time on the basketball court. He thought Eddie might know it about himself, too, at least a little bit. Or that Magnolia did. It explained Eddie's bribing people with beer can chicken or Mags's peanut butter cake for the third Friday of the month cookouts at his place; when he got the work gang onto his own turf, he could finally shine in a group setting.

Dillon caught himself staring at the salt shaker as he held it over his glob of ketchup. Perversely, he salted the fries instead of the sauce, and decided not to add that to the list of things he was analyzing. It was his damn birthday, after all, and he was allowed to at least get through it without worrying about people who'd turned their backs on him.

But not without being subjected to a conference room party, it seemed. He'd made one attempt to get out of it by bringing a concern about the Galveston B&B proposal to Anica's attention, but she'd just rolled her eyes at him and told him he could deal with it in the morning. So to the slaughter he went, lamb-like.

There were balloons. All colors. No streamers, at least, which gratified him. At Ida's birthday celebration the previous week, whoever had hung the streamers had been a good foot shorter than he was. Or very bad at extension. Something, because he'd managed to knock about half of them over just by walking from one part of the room to the other, which had amused everyone to no end. Johnnie had given him about a dozen high-fives.

Everyone was there. Well, everyone from the offices—the warehouse gang didn't bother with the office birthdays. Ms. Lanigan handed him the card, and Janice's still-surprising clear bright soprano led the singing, and he smiled nicely, for all the world as if he was actually enjoying the attention. He read the card aloud, dutifully. "Happy B-D," "Feliz Cumpleanos," "Hey! Let's Get Hammered!" and "Have a great year," all with vaguely decipherable scrawls. That last one was signed, "Serena Colby." With her last name, yet. How many fucking Serenas did Serena think Dillon knew?

The day was shaping up to rival the surprise party Shannon had thrown for his seventeenth. Because what does a high school guy like more than a surprise party with, like, his seventh-grade lab partner and who knows who all showing up? It was the first birthday since their folks had died, so he got the theory that Shannon was operating under—distraction and whatever—but it failed. He'd thought about just going out for food with the team after their next game as a token celebration, but Shannon had invited all of them and another random twenty people over instead. The dark house, the "Happy Birthday!" banner, the shouts and laughter and camera flashes—a complete horror of a party. And unlike when he was a teenager, he no longer thought walking out of the room was an option, so he just had to stand there and act like all his coworkers' exclamation marks on his birthday card meant the world to him.

Anica was pushing him towards the knife on the table. Oh, and the cake. Why did the honoree always have to cut the cake and pass it out? Shouldn't someone serve him so he could retreat to a corner and an undisturbed sugar high? But, no. He sliced, he dished, he repeatedly wiped the whipped cream off his increasingly sticky fingers.

"None for me, thanks," he heard Serena tell whoever was passing out the plates. Dillon glanced up.

"Watching your weight?" Johnnie asked Serena, handing the slice to Anica instead. "Cause your bod is almost as sculpted as Janice's, you know. Don't get too scrawny."

She shook her head. "No, but thanks? Oh, wait, I forgot—I don't thank people for objectifying me."

"Ditto," said Janice from her spot to Dillon's left. "Give me another slice of cake, will you, Toots?"

He turned to her long enough to comply, but kept his ear on Johnnie and Serena.

"Well, excuse me. Didn't mean to hit a nerve. I was only complimenting you."

"Johnnie, you have so many fine qualities. Please don't make me focus on the negative ones."

"And what does that mean?"

"I think," put in wrinkly grey Neil from accounting, "that Serena prefers to be treated as a coworker instead of a party girl."

"I think," said Serena, "that even what you call party girls are due for respect no matter how much you might admire their physical forms."

Emily from HR almost-casually wandered over at that point to draw Johnnie away for a little talk. Good old Emily from HR. But Neil was leaning into Serena again, and from his expression, was murmuring apologies in her ear. She shook her head a little and shrugged and then gave him that smile again. Damn her.

And then Neil tried to give her a bite of his cake. Off the plastic fork covered with all his old-man germs. To her credit, Serena recoiled a little.

"I can't."

"Sorry. I didn't mean to be too forward," Neil said, and Eddie, no fool to the dynamic, laughed.

"On top of which I have better things to do today than go to the ER," Serena snapped, moving away—at last—from Neil.

"ER?" Janice asked, then looked from her plate to Serena. "Oh, Toots, I forgot! I should have gotten him a different cake. It's just—he said that's what he always has."

"It's fine. I'm fine without cake. Do we need to all be staring at me at this moment?" Serena asked, glancing around the room and blushing.

"What's the problem?" Eddie asked.

"It is not a big deal. Relax, everyone. I'm just allergic to strawberries."

And then everyone was looking from Serena to Dillon's strawberry shortcake and back at Serena. And asking questions, the same questions Dillon wasn't quite articulating: since when, how do you mean, allergic, what happens if she eats a strawberry? Dillon set his own cake down, untouched, and wiped once again at his sticky fingers.

"It's not that big a deal, seriously," Serena protested again. "I just get hives and my throat swells closed if I eat one, so I don't eat them. There are plenty of delicious things in the world besides strawberries, it's not the end of the world that I can't eat them."

"But—hospital?" Neil asked.

"Well, a whole strawberry would send me into anaphylactic shock. I would need an ephedrine injection. But I keep an epi-pen in my car, actually, so I wouldn't have to go to the ER. I was exaggerating."

"Unless we didn't know what was happening and then we'd call an ambulance," Dillon said. How had they'd hung out and gone to the farmers market without covering this basic ground?

"Janice knows."

"She double-checks every dang time that I didn't give her the wrong smoothie," Janice said. "Liza over at the Smoothie Shack got a special 'no strawberries' stamp to put on her cup but I still have to taste-test hers each time to be sure."

"See, it's not a problem. I've been living with this my whole life, I know how to avoid the things, no matter how sneaky chefs get." Serena nodded at what was left of the strawberry shortcake on the conference table. "And that's easy to stay away from."

"So you're not watching your weight?" Johnnie asked before Emily from HR could stop him.

"Of course she's not," Neil said. Dillon didn't like the appraising look the old guy gave Serena's body. She didn't object, though, so what did he know.

"So, are you allergic to anything else? What happens if you eat cherries?" Johnnie raised an eyebrow behind his steel-rimmed glasses. "Bananas?"

Serena chose not to give him the cold shoulder. She just traded a glance with Janice and said, "No, I'm not allergic to other foods. Just strawberries."

"And cats," Janice added.

"Well, I could probably eat cats. If I wanted," Serena laughed. "I just can't be in the same room as one."

Philip shared some story about his wife and bees, and Anica complained about pollen counts, and Johnnie mentioned pussies before Emily from HR could drag him out of the room, but Dillon heeded very little of it. His focus had narrowed entirely upon Serena. Serena, who was allergic to cats. Serena, who'd held his hand on the street but run away shortly after entering the same house as Maisy. Serena, who'd said—he thought back, and yes, she had—something about panic and breathing along with that 'let's be friends' line that had been such a low blow. Serena was allergic to cats.

Well, if that didn't just beat all.

CHAPTER TWENTY-ONE

Serena beat a hasty retreat from the Strawberry Interrogation Room and packed up her notes on the website revamp for a small hotel in Galveston. What was the point of decent weather and the ability to work with pens and paper if she couldn't run from all her problems and sit on her patio once in a while?

A fresh pitcher of iced tea and a few deep cleansing breaths later, she curled up on her comfy new deck chair and sketched a while, singing along to her favorite work time playlist. She'd invited Rachel and little Hannah over for dinner, so the crock pot spaghetti sauce had been bubbling away all day and her whole world felt homey and comforting. As long as she ignored any parts of that world that had to do with her love life. Damn Dillon and his birthday and his eyes and his stares and his lips and his judgments and his strawberries!

Just like that, her patio peace was shattered, and she stalked into the kitchen to stare at the veggies she was going to toss into a salad when Rachel arrived. And thought of Dillon teasing her at the farmers market. She moved to her living area and noticed the shipping envelope containing *The Wit and Wisdom of Charles Barkley,* which she'd ordered after Dillon'd confessed his young hero-worship for the player that night at Frijoles. It had been waiting for her when she'd gone to hand over her scummy-butt apartment keys to her landlady. She hadn't known what to do with it, so she'd left it on one of her new shelves. It refused to just fade into the background and leave her unplagued with thoughts of Dillon.

Was no part of her home safe? She threw herself onto her bed and glanced at the clock. Still an hour until her guests arrived. She could use it to toddler-proof the place—impossible task though that seemed to be around the energetic Hannah—or she could do something different.

Serena did have the fleeting thought, as she closed her eyes and ran her palm slowly across her breast, that writhing in her bed while remembering every electric contact Dillon had made with her skin was just going to spread his presence to every room in her little house. It was too late though. Her nipples had contracted, and she felt his tongue circling them. Her other hand traced her stomach and remembered tracing his lightly muscled abs both through his shirt, and again over his skin once she'd ripped his shirt out of his waistband. Waistband. Oh, yes, the waistband, and what waited beneath his. Straddling those long basketball player's legs of his. Serena reached. She circled. She tensed, and tensed, and tensed. And tensed. Remembering, reliving. Reliving but with a different result—not rash and closed throat, no, but skin flushed with passion, breathing short in ecstatic pants. The right conclusion to that electric air between them. Tension, such gorgeous tension, and finally, yes, finally and finally release.

Damn.

Serena sank into her pillow, relieved of only part of her frustration. The air had sung between them. Just looking at him had turned her on beyond all reason. And it still did. But she couldn't touch him. And she couldn't just deal with it by touching herself. What the hell was she going to do?

Over dinner Rachel repeated her secret murderer theory while Serena wondered how she'd forgotten about those once cute images of babies covered in spaghetti, sauce flung everywhere, that were all over card shops and the internet.

"Okay, but that's not helping, Rachel. Because he's just not dangerous. There's something going on, but it's, like, psychosomatic, okay? All about me and some, I don't know, repression I have from my parents' divorces or whatever."

"So now you're afraid of intimacy? Even though you were practically living with Joey a year ago?"

"I thought we had a pact never to mention him again!"

"No, just his ratty hair. I'm allowed to say he existed."

"Hmph."

"Well, he did. And a lot of the time, the two of you existed under the same roof."

"But there was never any danger of my spending the rest of my life with Joey."

Rachel stopped plucking spaghetti off of Hannah's portable baby chair. "The rest of your life? Serena, you can't spend the rest of your life with Dillon. He has a sex dungeon!"

"Aren't you afraid your innocent daughter will start repeating some of the shit you say?"

"Oh, if she says 'sex dungeon' it'll just sound like 'six dozen' and we'll claim we were buying lots of eggs."

"Best mom in the world award."

"Damn straight. But when did Dillon turn into a forever guy?" Rachel looked at her steadily, then grinned. "Of course, the rest of your life will be awfully short, what with him planning to murder you and dump your body in the bayou and all."

"Rachel!" Serena laughed, but she was relieved. It was the first time Rachel had really backed off on the fear thing. And it wasn't that she hadn't given it some serious thought, but Serena'd eventually discounted her friend's theory. She did have gut feelings that she trusted, but until recently, nothing she'd felt from Dillon had been at all uneasy or threatening. And she didn't think he'd suddenly gone from being a likable sci-fi geek with no dancing skills to being scary. It was something wrong with her.

"You know what Natalie thinks, right?"

Serena handed Hannah a frozen fruit bar and shook her head.

"I can't believe she hasn't called you about it. She has this super-elaborate theory about how often you had to move as a kid, bouncing between your mom and dad and all their houses." Serena had counted once; she'd had a dozen different bedrooms growing up. "I guess she knew you thought Dillon was a forever guy, cause her theory is that now that you have your own home, your own space, you are protective of it. So you're allergic to letting him in to your space."

"Trust a realtor to think like that." And little did Natalie know how thoroughly Dillon had already invaded her home, even though he'd never been there.

"Well, sure, but she could be on to something, right? Face it, Serena, you breaking out into hives when he's around is a pretty effective way to create some distance between you two."

"Oh, I'd noticed that," Serena said wryly. "Trust me, I'd noticed. He has, too, as a matter of fact, though I don't think he knows about the hives."

"What do you mean he doesn't know? What have you told him?"

Serena looked away and mumbled, "Nothing."

"Oh, I know you didn't just say 'nothing,' Serena Colby. You work together every day. Haven't you talked about what happened yet?"

Serena focused on Hannah's babble, indulging in a quick session of peek-a-boo, before admitting that she'd laid into Dillon about uttering the word 'relationship' and never explained about her physical reaction to their physical interaction. Rachel was a tad too relentless in pointing out that she'd handled it badly—as if Serena was unaware of that!—and to cap it off, said, "Well, I don't blame him if he's pissed at you now. If you're going to get into his pants again like you so clearly want, you'd better figure out how to make this right."

All in all, Serena decided she liked it better when Rachel'd thought Dillon was into bondage.

Dillon handed Janice the coffee pot to wash out and bit back each and every question he kept not asking about Serena and her allergies. Justin had told him to consider everything he knew about Serena, not just her one reaction. But had Justin ever considered that how someone acted in a crisis showed their true selves? Not that he knew what was so 911 about making out against his front door, but clearly Serena had felt some urgency surrounding it. And not the same urgency he had, because if she had been on the same page as him, they'd have ended up naked together and happy. Yes, sure, the allergy to Maisy. Maybe that had propelled her out the door in the first place. But what had made her keep going? What had made her ignore his advances, yell at him about marriage, and give him the 'let's be friends' brushoff?

If she'd told him she was allergic to cats, he would have been happy to move the party to her place instead. Or anywhere, really. He wasn't picky. Just unbelievably frustrated and far too unsure of his footing.

"What's the deal with Serena and cats?"

Janice grinned her Puck grin, and Dillon wondered just how red the tips of his ears were and just how abrupt his blurted question sounded.

"You got a cat, do you, Toots?"

"No." But he slid over to the fridge to dig out his lunch. He wasn't hungry, but he also wasn't about to meet Janice's eyes.

"Sounds to me like there're some queries burning holes in your gullet."

"Nope."

"Well, since you've no need to know, I won't bother telling you about how she was hospitalized a couple times as a kid with her allergies, or how it took her parents months to figure it all out, since they were divorced already, just passing her back and forth without bothering to share any information about her attacks. Or how one stepmother had cats and refused to get rid of them so Serena had to get her dad to meet in a neutral location if she was going to see him. One time she tried to spend the night there, all doped up on antihistamines—that accounted for another hospital visit. But you don't want to know anything about what that would mean to a kid whose parents were constantly negotiating over whose turn it was to take her off the other's hands. So I won't tell you any little bit about it."

Dillon had edged closer as Janice rambled on, drawn by her story and the images it evoked. Poor Serena. Damn. He sighed. "Thanks, Toots."

Janice refilled her mug, raised an eyebrow at Dillon, and said, "Don't call me Toots," as she headed out the door.

Bad enough allergies to mean the hospital, Dillon mused again as he sat at his desk eating a late and solitary lunch later that afternoon. That ought to make him a little more secure. Although he was frankly sick of himself, thanks to the number of times he'd replayed the lunchroom scene and parsed out its meaning.

Fact: Serena had debilitating allergies.

Fact: She still ran off and wouldn't talk to him about it.

Fact: She didn't know about Maisy.

Fact: She also went around feeling allergic but never mentioned a problem to him.

Fact: Janice made sure he knew that the allergies were emotional and not just physical problems for Serena.

Theory: That was probably her way of warning him. Janice knew something was up between Dillon and Serena. Or suspected it. She was a good enough friend that she wouldn't have told Dillon any of Serena's secrets if she thought he was a failure of a date. So....

Fact: Janice didn't know about the grope-and-run.

Scary theory: Serena had run shortly after what he had thought was positive skin-on-skin contact with his cock. Had she run because she'd thought something had been wrong there? But, no. Maisy. He was reduced to being comforted about his manhood thanks to a two pound kitten. Depressing.

Fact: The grope-and-run was not because he didn't have a damn fine cock. But Janice still didn't know about it.

Fact: Janice and Serena were good friends.

Fact: Good friends would tell if there was important news on the dating scene. Size of erection information optional. Hopefully.

Fact, reasserted: Serena didn't know about Maisy.

Theory: Having her breath cut off mid-grope without knowing why had freaked Serena out, so she'd run, and since she was freaked out she didn't tell Janice. Even though it was important news on Serena's dating scene. But Janice had picked up on enough to make her take shots across Dillon's bows in hopes of riling him up.

Fact: It had worked. Damnit.

Dillon rubbed his hands down his face and tried to clear his head. Belatedly, he remembered the mustard on his sandwich and grabbed a couple of tissues to swipe at his nose, glancing at the door to make sure no one had seen.

"Idiot," he mumbled, then balled up all of his trash and shot it into the can across the room. "Two points." At least he had this one skill to give him a petty amount of pleasure in life.

When it came down to it, he was thinking about Serena all the damn time, and not resolving a thing. He needed to tell her about the cat. Basically, he was shooting himself in the foot by holding on to her two-word text and friends speech instead of explaining about cat-sitting and making her face the tension between them.

He opened the birthday email from his sister and smiled. He had an idea that would put the ball—and the facts—in her court.

CHAPTER TWENTY-TWO

SPRING HAD GIVEN WAY ENTIRELY to the middle of March, and a muggy hot morning blasted Serena in the face as she stepped onto her patio the next morning. Her mint stood up valiantly to the weather, but the basil and parsley were complaining, so she took a few extra moments to water them, humming along to the eighties hits coming through her sound system. Getting the herbs happy and pausing for a little dance break had eaten into her prep time, and she almost skipped her habitual morning check of her email.

Rachel with a picture of Hannah in the latest monstrosity from Yia Yia Depy. The usual spam. A schedule update from her yoga gym, she could deal with that later. And one from Dillon, send late the evening before.

It was a group message—Jorge, Eddie, Magnolia, Janice, and Serena. Subject: "Birthday Cuteness." Well, that would be about his nephew. Serena doubted Dillon had used the word 'cute' more than twice in his life before Toby was born, but it popped up frequently about the infant. She admonished herself for scratching. The hives only showed up when they were in the same room—she'd tested herself back before Eddie's cookout. Voice and text messages from Dillon couldn't cause her reaction, so this itching was purely psychosomatic. Still, it was annoying, and she was late, so she was a little surprised to realize her mouse had opened the message before her mind told it to.

"Thanks all for the celebration yesterday. Sis put off our family meal until the weekend to fit the baby schedule, but she couldn't let the day pass without a memento, so she posed Toby and Maisy for me. Cute, right? It seems Maisy is settling in well to life with a baby, and doesn't miss hanging out with me at all. I guess my cat-sitting days are over. Good news for my jackets, though my place is awfully quiet now that she's gone."

And there was the blue-eyed boy looking displeased with the party hat perched on his blonde tuft, next to a calico kitten batting at the tassels that sproinged from the top of the baby's hat.

Serena slumped back in her breakfast-room chair and stared at the screen. Cat sitting? At his place? She hadn't seen one, but it must have been there. He'd told her on Saturday that he was going to his sister's house on Sunday, so he'd probably returned the creature then. Well, fuck a duck. This explained a lot—this undoubtedly explained everything—and now...now! Oh, this meant very good things for her body. No more breathlessness, not of the bad kind, anyway.

She sat up and hit 'forward' to send the photo to Gill, Rachel, and Natalie. Subject: "CAT! HE HAD A CAT!" No need for more—they'd get it immediately. Time for some chair dancing while she grinned at the adorable little Toby and his beastly kitten. Dillon had had a cat! Serena bubbled over with relief.

As she brushed her teeth she looked over the outfit she'd chosen. It was fine for basic work attire, but that was no longer her top dressing agenda of the day. So she changed her slacks for a dark denim A-line skirt, and switched to the dangly earrings that brushed her neck when she wore her hair caught loosely up. Singing to a bit of Van Halen, she grinned at her reflection in the full-length mirror in her bedroom, and hurried off to work.

Clearly he'd figured it out himself, she thought on her way in. So the photo and message had to be directed at her. She was mulling that over when her cell rang. "What are you wearing?" Natalie demanded.

"Morning to you, too," she answered, removing one of the dangly earrings so she could hold the phone to her ear. "Hang on, I'm exiting." Once she was on the feeder road she gave Natalie the rundown.

"Lose the earrings."

"I love these earrings. They're hot."

"Right. Lose them."

"But why?" Serena whined, then winced. Whining was not a good indicator of an in-charge woman with a handle on her emotions.

"Serena, listen to me. I am over the moon about this cat, goodness knows I didn't want to hear anything more about basements from Rachel. Basements. I know she's not a native Texan, but when has she ever seen a basement in her life?"

"I think they have basements in Colorado."

"I don't care if they do or not. She's been to seventy of my open houses, she knows about no Houston basements."

"Okay, and we all appreciate the free wine and cheese, but why can't I wear my earrings?"

Natalie tsked at her. Tsked! "Get a grip, Serena. You can't wear your flirty 'have sex with me on this conference table' earrings because answer me this—how did Dillon find out you were allergic to cats?"

"At his birthday party. He had strawberry shortcake. It came up."

"Uh-huh. And what day was that?"

"Wednesday."

"And what day is today?"

"Friday," she sighed, again, a little poutily. Dang.

"Right. So, he's known for two days—two days, Serena—and he dealt with it by emailing a bunch of you a picture?"

"It's a cute picture."

"Do I care that it's a cute picture? No, I don't. I care that he chose this passive-aggressive journey of silence and indirect semaphore to get his message across."

Serena pulled into the parking lot at Lanigan, noted that she was already seven minutes late, and tried to be fair. "I didn't tell him why I ran from him after the farmers market. I just left, Nat, and if I'd told him I was allergic to him we could have figured it out sooner."

"Well, you didn't. And that's a shame. Didn't help that Rachel was filling your head with all kinds of nonsense at that point, but never mind. What matters is how he should behave, not some scorecard of whose turn it is to act like an idiot. You can't move forward with this guy unless you're both open and honest with each other. If he's really into you, and really respects you, then the moment he found out his nephew's kitten caused you to break out into giant disgusting pustules, he should have pulled you aside and said, 'Hey, Serena, I think if we go back behind the dumpster and make out like randy teenagers we'd be able to get to second base without sending you to the hospital.' But he didn't. He emailed— let me look at this again—yes, five people, only one of whom is hot for him, and without even a postscript to tell you that he'd be waiting naked in the boardroom during the coffee break should you want to drop by."

"Wow. Nice imagery."

"I spend all day describing kitchens that haven't been updated for forty-two years as 'quaint' with 'vintage touches.' Sometimes I have to break out of the rut. Now lose the come-hither earrings until he's earned them."

Serena had no intention of obeying, so she just said she had to rush off—which was true enough. But sly Natalie had either gotten to her on a subconscious level or just delayed her enough to throw Serena off her normally organized game. As soon as the elevator doors closed and Serena glimpsed herself in the brushed chrome walls, she groaned. She'd left the earring she'd removed to take Natalie's call sitting in the cup holder in her car. Marveling over her friend's powers of mind control, she stashed the other earring in her bag and headed into her office for the day.

It wasn't long before she saw him. She'd suspected it wouldn't be. Of course, she didn't have her 'come hither' earrings, and Eddie had him cornered going over something probably work related, so she had no idea how to convey to Dillon that she was on the same page as him. Or, that she thought she was. She opened her mouth two or three times, trying to formulate an even half-coherent sentence. "Your kitten gave me hives," seemed out of place, as did, "Care to come over tonight?" or "Does my inability to breathe around fur relegate me to the unfuckable column in your little black book?" It got to the point that even anti-sensitive-man Eddie was giving her funny looks, so she just mustered up as much of a smile as she could and fled.

She ended up turning practically into Janice's arms. "Toots, you have to come for smoothies with me today. I need you," Janice muttered, and if Serena hadn't known better she'd have thought the way Janice placed her body was a deliberate attempt to keep her from making eye contact with Dillon.

"I...."

"I mean it, Toots. I won't even make you jog."

"Will you let me drive there?"

Janice scoffed. "As if." She glanced down at Serena's cute heeled sandals. "You have runners in your office, right?"

Serena grudgingly admitted that she did, and they all headed into the ten o'clock meeting.

She tried to sit beside Dillon. There was an open seat there and everything. And it was on his left, which was the perfect situation for her to draw her right-handed doodles and him to add his left-handed captions on her notepad. But before she could grab the chair, Anica gestured her over to sit at the head of the table beside her. Oh, right, promotion. Authority. Moving up the corporate ladder—or the corporate table, in this case. More important than her sex life, at least while she was actually at work.

Janice took the chair by Dillon, and Serena did not trust the glint in her eye. She got a brief moment to half-smile at Dillon before Anica leaned in to check with her about scheduling. Meanwhile, Johnnie was leaning back in his own chair, the better to take in the way Serena's skirt rode up her thigh. Tugging it down only drew attention, so she gave up.

It was energizing to take the lead on the Blue Capri B&B account, and Serena noted with no little pleasure the way Eddie's head bounced back and forth between her and Anica while he explained the parameters of what the hotel owner wanted. Plus, she'd dreamed up a really luscious agate and Blue Grotto color palette that worked beautifully with the fonts she'd provisionally picked out for their rebranding. She was buzzed by the work, and the undercurrents that she sensed when Anica deferred to her. It was a clear signpost about Serena's future role at Lanigan. She held back a ferocious smile when Eddie saluted her with his water bottle, but she was sure everyone could see it in her eyes.

Of course, it also meant that when most of the others— including Dillon—filed out after the general part of the meeting, she stayed behind with Anica and Janice and Eddie and Miguel. Johnnie, the other graphic designer, hung back for a few moments with clear hopes that Anica would give him a 'stay here' nod, but finally trailed out after the others. Poor Johnnie, Serena thought smugly. Then she caught herself and gave herself a little lecture about humility and everyone having their role to play and all sorts of other stuff her mom's second husband, Erik, had quoted from his business management books over dinner for several months in a row. The day Erik had graduated from his part-time MBA program had been a blessed one in their home. Of course, so had the day he and Mom had separated and they'd moved out.

Erik: incredibly nice, incredibly boring. Not a bad way for Mom to get over the toxicity of her marriage to Dad, but not close to being, as Rachel would say, her 'forever guy.' Neither had her next husband, Samuel, been, though at least that had more legs on it. She'd not liked Samuel as much as she'd liked Erik, though, and only pretended to be shocked, her second year of college, when her mom had totally dumped Samuel to move in with Zane and his three teenagers. Well, the three kids part had been weird. Was still weird. Seeing all the Facebook posts of Mom with Ridley and Regina and Rufus, her big proud grin at graduations and dancing with Ridley at his wedding—his wedding! the kid was barely into his twenties, but whatever. She felt a little bad about missing his wedding reception, but didn't honestly think she'd been missed. She hardly knew Zane or the Three Rs. Unlike, apparently, her mom, who seemed to have found her place in life. Erik probably had a corp-speak quote to apply to that, too.

When they'd been living with Erik, Serena had been eleven or twelve, and she'd cared a hell of a lot about whether or not Kent Penny had stood next to her in the lunch line or taken the seat behind her on the bus. Sometimes she even got off at his stop and followed Kent to the turn-off for his street before she went on home. They never talked, but Serena knew to the inch how close he came when they passed each other. She'd more than doubled her age since then, and was once again obsessing over seating arrangements and banal quotes about effective workplace motivation. Maybe if she'd gotten up the nerve to talk to Kent before the divorce and subsequent move to yet another school, Serena would be a little more evolved on the relationship scale now.

She wished she had on the earrings, though.

CHAPTER TWENTY-THREE

DILLON FELT AS ANTSY AS HE HAD back in fifth grade the day his dad was going to pick him up to go to an early screening of a new *Star Trek* movie. He'd never admit it to anyone, but he'd rewritten that email with the cat news three or four times. Okay, six times. He'd been a communications major. With honors, even. Good lord. It had taken him a ridiculous amount of time to perfect, and he didn't end up sending it by the end of the work day, which had been his plan. His little fantasy involved her getting the email, realizing about her allergy to Maisy, and showing up in his office ready to pick up where they'd left off. Well, maybe not actually pick back up in his office. Or, okay, in his office—his fantasy included everyone else leaving on the dot of five except the two of them, so their floor would be empty. And he had a door on his office and everything.

But, alas, he'd spent so long redrafting the message that it had gone out after everyone had gone home. He'd been forced to spend the evening forcing himself not to wonder if she would check her email from home. Magnolia and Eddie had seen it— Mags had sent him a reply about how Eddie was reconsidering using Dillon's genetic material for their own child. And Eddie had followed with a contradictory, and fairly rude, reply. They'd gone back and forth a few times before an impatient Dillon had replied to them both that maybe they should just go have sex already and leave him out of the foreplay.

But with all of that activity—all of those moments when his phone had beeped that he had an incoming email—nothing had been from Serena. He'd finally gone to bed, resigned to her not knocking on his door. But he had left the light on over his front steps, just in case.

So he'd shown up to work in one of the new shirts he'd bought to ensure that no trace of Maisy lingered about him. It was about time he sent his jacket in for dry cleaning anyway, though despite the warmer weather he felt a little exposed without it. He'd spent as much time in the hallway near Serena's office as he could as nine o'clock approached, not precisely stalking her. She might not see the email until she got to her desk, and he wanted her to see it before they talked. Dillon's mouth tightened as he remembered the frustration of lingering in the hall when Serena was five, then ten minutes late.

A few minutes before the morning meeting, he'd left his desk to try again, and at first he'd been glad when Eddie had waylaid him just outside Serena's door.

"Hey, Dillon, look. About the stuff with Magnolia?"

"Not interested in hearing about your sex life," he'd answered, but with a smile. Eddie and Magnolia were both such big personalities, but they suited each other really well. They each knew when to pull back from being the dominant one, and that was as far as he was going to go with analyzing their relationship, now that the specter of their bedroom had been raised.

"Naw, it's more than your virgin ears could handle. But Magnolia made me swear to apologize to you."

"Not a virgin, man."

"Sure, sure, keep saying it, it'll turn true."

Dillon shook his head. "You are so full of it. Your wife makes you say sorry? Very manly."

"Hey, I am a man of the new millennium. I can do what Magnolia says and still be the alpha stud she fell for."

"Sure you can."

"Yeah, well, she told me to take you to lunch today."

"You told her we already go to lunch every Friday, right?"

"Well," Eddie scratched the back of his neck. "She probably knows that. Anyway, I'm supposed to buy."

Dillon started to beg off, weird as that would be given that they did eat together every Friday that Eddie wasn't having a lunch meeting with a client. Serena came out of her office just then, and words died in his dry mouth. She'd surely checked her email? He met her eyes, and she didn't look away. She didn't say anything, but Eddie was going on and on and on. Dillon glanced back at him and nodded a little, probably agreeing to some lunch scheme or another, and then Janice managed to get Serena turned away from him. Damn her.

"Come on, then," Eddie said, leading him into the conference room. "And send a text to Magnolia, will you? She's all embarrassed now."

"No problem." He typed her a couple of lines, all the while watching Serena move into the room. Anica pulled her away from him, then Janice took the seat beside him and leaned forward, blocking his view. He could see behind her, though, and did not miss even a little bit of the way Johnnie eyed Serena's legs in Dillon's favorite blue skirt. Only her orange plaid skirt topped that one in his ranking of Serena's sexy skirts.

She hadn't responded to his email. He checked his phone again. Nope, no reply. But she hadn't run from him, either. She'd even brushed right up against his chair on the way into the production meeting. Dillon counted that as a triumph, and despite the fact that Eddie dragged him off for Chinese food and he got involved in a monster of an afternoon conference call that tied him to his desk past the point of sanity, the anticipation of more triumph sustained him for most of the day.

"Mango papaya today, Liza," Serena told the Smoothie Shack girl.

"Ditto, and put protein powder in them both," Janice ordered. At Serena's curled lip she said, "You have to balance your intake of nutrients. We've talked about this."

"Can't I just eat a cheese stick when we get back to the office?"

"No, you cannot. Besides, if, as I suspect, Toots, you are going to shortly be engaging in aerobic activity, your muscles will thank me."

Liza gave her an arch look and Serena blushed. "Janice!"

"Do tell," Liza said, handing Janice her change.

"Do not tell. I mean, there's nothing to tell!"

Janice laughed. "And hens have teeth and frogs have fangs."

"I believe her. Also, I have this bridge on sale, direct from London, are you interested?"

"You two are absolutely hilarious." Serena categorically did not stomp on her way to the table in the corner.

Janice followed after leaning in to whisper something to Liza, who giggled.

"Whatever she said, she's lying!" Serena called over to her, but Liza had turned on the blender and gave her a cheeky 'can't hear you' gesture.

"Toots."

"I don't know what you think you know."

"What I *know* know? Know for sure? Nothing. I'll tell you what I've seen with my own two eyes, though."

And then she paused long enough that Serena had to give in and ask, "What?"

"I know that Dillon was pumping me for info about your allergies. I know that Johnnie was memorizing the curves of your thighs during the meeting today. I know that Dillon glared at him until Johnnie looked away. And," she glanced up then shifted over so that Liza could sit down beside her as she delivered their smoothies, "I know that you're allergic to cats and Dillon just got rid of a cat."

"Hmmmm!" Liza raised her eyebrows. "Dillon I know about, but who exactly is Johnnie?"

"Frat boy idiot at work," Serena said.

"Well, that answers that question. I didn't think he was your type."

"He talks too much," Serena told Liza, "and he thinks he's more charming than he really is."

"So we can discount him. That leaves Dillon."

Serena didn't answer.

"Liza's right, Toots. That leaves Dillon."

"Didn't Emily give you guys a lecture about workplace relationships after all that stuff with Ricky?"

"It was about harassment and the one for the offices is in a couple of weeks, so look forward to that. Anyway, she said there aren't any rules about dating coworkers."

It was really Janice's bright red ears that gave her away. "She said this during the harassment training? Or...in a separate conversation?"

Janice sipped her smoothie until Liza nudged her. "Okay, I asked her, just, you know. Theoretically. Not because I'm interested in anyone."

Liza laughed, "Oh, sure."

"And maybe I was just asking to clear things up so Serena and Dillon can start holding hands in public."

"You are such an altruist."

"You are avoiding the topic, Toots. I get that there's nothing going on between you and Johnnie, but there is clearly some vibe between you and Dillon. He is pitching woo at you all the time, and my question is, are you two playing ball, or what?"

"That," Liza said, reluctantly getting up to help the customers who'd just walked in, "is one seriously messed up metaphor. And just because I'm missing all the details doesn't mean you don't have to fill me in later."

"Yes, ma'am," Janice replied, and turned back to Serena. "Spill."

So Serena had admitted that she and Dillon had been skirting around the edges of a relationship, and that she'd been confused by the hives and shortness of breath when they'd gotten close.

"But that's what you're always like when you're around cats."

"But Dillon didn't have a cat! At least, I didn't think he did. I never imagined he'd get one without telling me." And wasn't that interesting, she mused. How many other coworkers, besides Janice, would she expect to hear that type of domestic information from? "Looking back, I know it was stupid. I should have figured I was allergic to something around him, not to Dillon himself. But, well, I'd get short of breath a little when I just heard his voice, too. And sometimes flushed, too." She trailed off, too embarrassed to meet Janice's sparkling eyes.

Her friend took a little bit of pity on her. "Hey, it's not such an inexplicable mistake. And it's kind of not the point, too."

"It's not?"

"No way. I'm far more interested in the fact that you've been sneaking off together behind my back."

"Oh, God, don't ever let Eddie know about those basketball tickets! Swear it."

Janice laughed. "What a disaster that would be. No worries, Toots, that cat stays in the bag. But the fact remains that you and Dillon have been enjoying a little one-on-one time and you both seem pretty interested in enjoying a lot more of it. Am I right?"

"Well...I mean, yes. Yes, I'm interested." Serena looked out the window for a bit, trying to find a way to articulate all of the swirling thoughts she had. "I think he must be, too. I think that was the reason for his email yesterday."

"Ya think?" Janice was very good at sarcastic when she wanted to be.

"Yeah. To tell me about it so I'd know why I'd had to get out of his place so fast. So I'm pretty sure we'll be getting together or, you know, seeing each other more, whatever."

"Toots!"

"Janice, don't. I mean, the reason I didn't tell you any of this before...."

"And don't think you're out of the hot water yet."

"I have reasons! I don't want this to be a thing, an awkward thing, for everyone at work. I mean, hardly anything's happened yet, and you and Eddie are both already giving us looks."

"I think Jorge suspects, too."

Serena groaned.

"And maybe Anica."

"What? Anica? No. No way. Why would Anica know anything? There's barely anything to know yet!"

"'Yet.' I like that. I knew you two would be getting your groove on."

"Janice. What about Anica?"

"Oh, calm down, Toots. I'm not for sure. But she's given you two a bit of a look a couple of times. And there's something about the way she always attaches him to you—it's always 'Serena and Dillon and Jorge,' never 'Serena and Jorge and Dillon' or whoever."

Serena ran a few conversations back through her head and realized Janice was right. Maybe. "But no one knows anything for sure. And if we start, like, dating for real. Well, just imagine."

Janice waggled her eyebrows.

"No, seriously. Stop that. I'm talking about everyone going out for drinks, or staring at us in the lunchroom, all that stuff."

"Not to mention you giving him orders now."

Serena blanched a little. "Not to mention that. This promotion—this maybe promotion with no real parameters, which by the way is a bullshit kind of thing for Anica to be doing—anyway, it doesn't help make things less weird with us."

"Poor Anica. She has no idea how to share her power."

"Yes, I pity her so." Serena sighed. "I wish she'd either make it official or keep it more under wraps for now."

"Hmm."

Serena gave Janice a sharp look. "What's that supposed to mean?"

"Oh, you know. Just that you're basically saying the same thing about Dillon. Keep everything under wraps until it's all official. Has it occurred to you, Toots, that you're just a little obsessed over having things official and defined?"

"What's wrong with wanting definition? Do you think the way Anica's handling it is the best way?"

Janice stood and took their trash to the bin. "No, but is it the worst way? You're getting some leadership experience. You're getting everyone used to the idea that you've got more authority. It might make an official transition easier, when that happens."

From behind the blenders, Liza gave Janice a 'call me' signal and waved as they headed out the door for the return to Lanigan. Serena expelled a deep breath and let Janice pull her into a light jog. "Okay, so, I'll let Anica be wishy-washy, but can you please, pretty please with sugar on top, not let anything slip about me and Dillon until I know what's really going on?"

Janice rolled her eyes. "Toots. You know I don't eat sugar."

CHAPTER TWENTY-FOUR

SERENA DROPPED EVERYTHING ON HER entry-way bench when she got home and, snatching up the envelope with Dillon's book, headed to her office. She grinned as she docked her iPod and opened the top door in her supply cabinet. Perfect—fine mesh netting, spray starch, a roll of string. She rummaged a little more and came up with a blue bucket and some matching heavy paper stock, and set about fashioning a new handle that made the bucket look like an oversized teacup. Or mostly like one. She wrote 'tea' on the pail, just to be sure, then set it aside to play with the net.

Spreading it out across her blade-scored worktable, she measured and cut and starched and reinforced with cardboard and whipstitched the netting until she'd created a tea-bag shaped container for the Barkley book. Her final touch was, of course, to find a Sir Charles saying ("You can't fake hustle. You either have to be into the game or not") and print it on the blank side of a page from a Scandinavian design book she'd been slowly denuding over the past few months. She clipped the corners of the tag and attached it to the end of the string she'd hung from the mesh bag.

She'd just set the bag inside the cup and stood back to admire her creation when the doorbell rang.

Dillon was practically tapping his foot in frustration while he waited for Serena to answer the door. Her car was in the carport, so he knew she was home. Or probably home. Sometimes people in this overheated city walked places. But probably she was home. Just as he'd been, just sitting around checking for messages every ten minutes and debating whether to call. Okay, every five minutes. But for fuck's sake, he'd sent her the picture of Tobias and the kitten, and she hadn't said a damn thing to him. Oh, sure, a smile here and there, maybe a few looks that might mean something. But that was no indication that she was ready to talk. Or have sex. So finally he'd pulled up her change-of-address email and mapped a route to her place.

Her house suited her, at least from the outside. At least, it suited the Serena he thought he knew. If anyone had asked him to speculate about where Serena would hang her hat, he'd have easily imagined this little bungalow with peach brick and tangerine shutters. The sunset-colored hibiscus plants anchoring the small but colorful flower beds fit her sense of style and bright, appealing personality. The whole place was welcoming but not ostentatious, and it seemed to exude the warmth and openness Dillon had always associated with Serena.

Until she'd gotten freaked by a kitten and spent weeks barely uttering a word to him.

He knocked again—maybe a little firmly. Maybe almost pounding on the pale wood of the door, until he saw movement through the beveled glass of the window and attempted to get a grip. At least it looked like she was home. And alone.

He fixed a hopefully-friendly look over his tense jaw and when Serena opened the door said, inanely, "Hi."

Serena was an idiot.

She was just staring at Dillon. Dillon, in his new cerulean shirt, which echoed his eyes in the sunlight. Dillon, whose eyes, now that he was shadowed by her front porch, were deepest cobalt but still blazed intently at her.

Dillon, who had just shown up on her doorstep.

She finally remembered how to talk. "Hi."

If that could be defined as talking.

"Hi," he repeated, then stood there some more. Finally he glanced over her shoulder, as if scoping out her house, then back at her. "This is a new shirt."

She blinked. "I can see that."

He looked down at his chest, where the fold lines from the shirt being wrapped around cardboard were still visible, despite them having had a full day of gravity and motion to help them disappear. He nodded, then fished a small box out of his messenger bag. "I also got you some allergy medication, in case there are any traces of Maisy on my shoes, or something."

Serena just melted. He was looking at her so straightforwardly, but there was the hint of caution in his eyes. And he'd gone shopping to ensure she was safe to breathe around him. And there he was, at her front door, just being himself. She was such a goner, it wasn't even funny.

Inhaling deeply, she stepped back. "I got you something, too," she said as she gestured him into her home.

He ducked a little as he came under the threshold. A tall man's habit; she'd noticed him doing that before. It seemed a little reverential in this case. The first time he'd been on her turf. Serena could practically feel the air molecules inside stretching around Dillon, rearranging to accommodate his presence in her front hall. Her hyper-awareness tripped her up a little, made her shy.

Made her babble. "I was going to call you. To see if you were busy this weekend. I was just finishing this up, this present for you. I mean, for your birthday, so it's late, but. Well. Oh, this is the living room. There's the dining room through there, the kitchen. Wait here a minute, I'll get your gift. Or do you want to see my office? No, never mind, it's a mess. Sit there, I'll be right back." Almost shoving him towards the sofa, Serena retreated to the office.

She leaned against the worktable a moment, staring unfocused at the neat row of framed prints lining the wall above her desk. With a quick shake of her head and a breath to prove that she was still able to, well, to breathe, Serena told herself to get a grip and go back to Dillon. So she picked up the giant blue teacup and sedately headed back.

Dillon sank a little into the soft fabric of Serena's sofa. Her living room was colorful but not over-bright. He sensed that she'd put a lot of thought into choosing her paint colors, her furniture, her accessories. Not that that was surprising—her office was the most appealing room at Lanigan, even though she had the same mass-produced desk and credenza and chair as everyone else. Now that he was ensconced into this external representation of Serena's entire vibe, he kind of got why Shannon had been so exasperated when they'd furniture-shopped for his townhouse. He stood by his vintage posters of the *Millennium Falcon* and, of course, the one and only NCC-1701 herself, the USS *Enterprise*. Otherwise, his walls matched his floors and his chairs were comfortable, so he'd never had a complaint about his space before. Serena, though— and where was she anyway?—Serena had created a room where he could instantly imagine spending a ton of time relaxing with her. Watching a ball game. Talking. Hanging out with friends. Hanging on to her hand. Touching her, being with her, and where the hell was she right now?

Before he could go snooping around her house looking for her, Serena emerged from the hallway off the dining room, hands behind her back. Dillon forgot his impatience at the sight of her—and not just because holding her arms that way did extremely nice stretchy things to the front of her shirt. If she was nude in his arms, and he pinned her wrists behind her, he could seriously feast for hours on her upthrust pink areolas, her arching breasts, opened wide to his gaze, his touch, his mouth.

His mouth was dry, and as Serena walked towards him, Dillon lifted his eyes slowly from her chest, past her inviting collarbone and throat, the curve of her jaw skimmed by her fall of hair, and her glossy lips. Her lips, which were parted as if waiting for him to meet them with his. To press, to lick, to exchange tongue for tongue as their mouths explored each other, the first of many mutual explorations.

He landed at last on the soft grey of her eyes. Probably his own face held too much of his raw lust, his desire to get past the last weeks of questions and uncertainty, his determination to subdue whatever it was about her that had made her run away and give in to their pull towards each other. In some ways he knew her better than he had before they'd laughed in the farmers market together, before she'd exposed herself for him against his front door, before she'd avoided him rather than face the fallout of her escape. In theory, it should all make it easy enough for them to move forward, now that they both knew why she'd run. But despite that, he was now less easy with her than he'd been even when trying to pry an apology out of her after seeing her with the gristly accountant.

If his expression worried her, she didn't let on. Her eyes didn't hide from his, but met them steadily, slightly tilted up under cheeks that lifted in a wry smile.

"Happy birthday," she said, and brought her hidden gift forward.

Dillon stood and walked to her, making a conscious decision not to mention that his birthday was two days before, with all its implied 'when you wouldn't be in the same room with me.' Instead, he looked from her slight blush down to the creation she was presenting to him. It was a smallish blue bucket, but she'd transformed it into a coffee cup. Or, he modified as he read it, a tea cup, complete with oversized tea bag that held something tissue-wrapped inside it.

An unguarded laugh escaped him as he caught hold of the colorful tag and read the little saying on it. He shot her a quick glance, remembering teasing her about her making her own tea bags. Well, she'd done it for real this time, whatever she normally did with all the herbs and vegetables she grew.

"What is it? I don't want to undo all your work," he said, pulling out the faux tea bag.

"No, go ahead."

"You're sure?"

But she nodded, so he ripped a little at the mesh until it gave way enough for him to pull the book out from its enclosure.

"Hey! Sir Charles!" Dillon turned the slim volume over, grinning outright now. "My hero, you know." She nodded again, and he was caught by the light in her eyes. "You remembered. Thank you, Serena. This is great."

She cleared her throat a little. "What it says on the card? To be in the game or get out?"

It was his turn to nod. She was a little fidgety and that meant a little nervous. All at once his mouth was dry again. He was trapped by her uncertain gaze.

"I want to be in the game. With you. That's—that's why I picked that particular piece of Barkley's wisdom." She laughed. "There was so very much to choose from. But trash-talking Larry Byrd didn't really have the right tone for this occasion."

Dillon set the gift and packaging down on her coffee table and took the final steps to bring him to Serena. Such a small step, but a giant leap. There was Houston, rubbing off on him again.

Houston, where he could stand inches from this beautiful woman, meet her clear bright gaze, and tell her his biggest truth.

"I want that, too."

And for the first time in way, way too long, Dillon reached out a hand and touched Serena.

CHAPTER TWENTY-FIVE

Serena could barely believe her own words. She'd blurted them without planning them out at all. And she'd been rambling like an idiot, too. Disconcerting, confusing, irritatingly compelling man!

But he seemed to like her present. He appreciated the packaging. He'd been pretty mad before, but he'd still shown up on her threshold today, which meant forgiveness, right? And here he was. In her living room. Touching her.

She melted into his hand as it cupped her face. And her own hand cupped his jaw in return—slightly bristly from the scruffy 'haven't shaved in a day or two' look he sometimes wore, but square and firm beneath the beard, and moving so willingly towards her own.

And the kiss. It was magnets, colliding. Dillon's hand moved up into her hair, one finger tracing the outline of her ear, skimming past the 'come hither' earrings she'd put back on, thinking of him, as he pulled her closer. As she pulled him closer. She stretched her body up, leaning into and up him to wrap around his shoulders and bring his face to hers. Every individual muscle in his lips sent separate questing little shock waves through her nervous system, and every individual nerve she possessed ended in fire between her legs.

His teeth caught her bottom lip and tugged, opening her mouth to the pursuing entry of his tongue. He moaned—or was she moaning?—as their tongues tangled, as they tasted each other again, anew, at last.

Serena was light-headed, everything about her floating and fusing to everything about Dillon. There was nothing separating them but his new blue shirt, her recklessly chosen skirt, a few millimeters of woven cotton thread. Their hunger and their pleasure simmered in what air their bodies allowed between them.

The kiss went on.

He pulled her closer still—how was that possible?—and slowed, and deepened, and slowed some more. She might have moaned again, she really couldn't say. She couldn't say anything— words escaped her even as their mouths achingly, reluctantly, sweetly pulled apart and his forehead came to rest on hers.

"Serena."

A million pounds of effort, but she got her eyes open. His were all she could see, and all she could see was unguarded blue depths, those pools into which she'd dreamed of diving, clear and achingly beautiful.

"Hi," she said, and he tightened his hold on her.

"Serena."

She reached up to his black hair, amazed by its coarse thickness, amazed to be stroking it, her fingers memorizing the texture. "Would you like to stay for dinner?"

His eyes wrinkled up at the corners a little. "I was hoping you'd ask."

"Well, you're in luck." They disentangled, just a little, and she glanced toward the kitchen. "I'm not sure what I have, though."

He reached out a long arm and snatched up his messenger bag. "I brought a couple of things."

She was surprised. "You did?"

"I told you, I was hoping to eat with you. Rude to invite myself without bringing something along."

Serena felt almost dangerously touched by that. This man, as much as she thought their months of working together had familiarized her with him, was still someone she couldn't always predict. But when he threw her, it seemed, it was always to the good. Give or take a kitten. She wrapped an arm around his waist and steered them towards the kitchen. "Okay, great. Let's see what we can cobble together."

She pulled down a couple of her Fiesta-ware plates while he unloaded grapes, a salami, and a petite baguette onto the counter, then a cheese spread and a bottle of wine. His tone was mischievous when he said, "I didn't get any veggies."

She smiled back and slid her small salad bowl and a couple of tomatoes towards the cutting board. "Now you'll see why I brag on my salads. Oh, and I infused some excellent basil and thyme olive oil last week, it should be just about perfect now." Turning from the fridge, lettuce in hand, she caught his expression. "Do not laugh at me. My infused olive oils make the most kick-ass salad dressing you'll ever taste, buddy. People tell me I should start a franchise. Anyway, you've tried them before, at Eddie's."

"At burger night?"

"Yes, at burger night. I bring a salad practically every month."

"Well," he trailed off, abashed.

"Are you serious? You didn't eat my salad?"

"It's burger night. Burgers. Beer. Chips and salsa. That's a very complete meal right there."

She grimaced. "Does anyone eat it? I mean, Magnolia asks me to bring it, so I do. Are we the only ones who have any?"

Dillon moved closer to her and wrapped his arm around her shoulder. Kissed her temple, which was way more comforting than she'd have expected, if she'd ever thought about anyone kissing her temple before. "Janice ate nothing but salad and a burger with no bun. Jorge had salad. I'm glad I finally get to find out why your salads are the world-famous creations I've heard so much about."

"You heard about them from me."

"And I trust your good taste, so there's no problem."

"Flatterer."

"Hungry flatterer. What else can we add here?"

She surveyed the spread he'd brought. With her salad it wasn't a bad meal, considering he'd been limited by the size and lack of refrigeration of his messenger bag. She retrieved a jar of olives and some locally raised grass-fed roast beef slices from her fridge and added them to his platter.

"Do you want to eat in here or out in my garden?"

"Oh, I have to see this famous garden of yours. Al fresco, please, so I can fully appreciate the flavors from your own labors."

"Now you're making fun of me again," she said, but she pointed the way, humming along with the 'Best of Summer' playlist that had shuffled up on her iPod.

Dillon complimented her salad, probably sincerely, and she raised her eyebrows at the first taste of the spicy wine, and the evening had cooled enough to make sitting under her twinkle-light-strung pergola very pleasant. There were even a few chirping crickets off in the distance as it got darker, and more intimate.

Three or four times as they ate and laughed and, frequently, touched, Serena tried to come up with the right thing to say about the past week since she returned to work. But really, Dillon hadn't brought it up, and she didn't want to ruin this amazing feeling between them. And again, she reminded herself, he was here. He'd come over, and brought antihistamines. Surely that meant it didn't need mentioning?

"Hey, how did you find my house?"

He stopped popping grapes into his mouth. "I followed the smell of the—what was it? Basil? Yep, I just sniffed you out."

"Ha, ha."

"You sent that change-of-address email to everyone."

"You saved that?"

He gave her a half-smile and shrugged. "You don't mind, do you?"

"Did I slam the door in your face?"

"Not this time."

Oh, shit. She'd walked into that one. And the humor had vanished off his face. He was a little wary, but he didn't retract, didn't give her a way out. She had to move forward.

"Dillon, listen. Well, first of all, thank you for figuring out about the kitten. I'm so glad—relieved—to know what was the matter."

He nodded, but still didn't speak.

"So you had the kitten since the baby was born?"

He nodded again, and while he was tracing the outline of his fork on the tabletop, his gaze didn't waver.

"Which makes sense. He must have gotten all over your clothes or something, because that next Monday in the elevator was the first time I couldn't breathe around you. My throat kept closing up, or I'd get hives, or both. And that Saturday, it was both, and so fast, and I didn't know what was happening, and I was so sick. I had to get into the clear air immediately." Serena watched him, but he wasn't talking. She was rubbing at her neck where the hives used to pop up, and forced herself to stop. "I keep medications in my car, so I could only think about getting to them, and it takes a while for them to kick in. I was just sitting there in my car, feeling like an idiot. Kind of like I am now." He didn't even crack a smile. Serena took a deep breath and kept going. "And you're going to think this part is stupid, but remember all I knew was this was a serious problem, as much as I was, well, yearning for you, every time we got close I had this reaction. And the closer we got, the worse it got. I was getting all these mixed signals from my body. So Rachel—my best friend from UT—she told me it was an instinct response and my subconscious was sending me a danger signal that my lust—oh crap, I can't believe I just called it lust." Serena tried to figure out what he was thinking, but it was an impossible proposition. She really needed him to talk to her. "I'm sorry. I let Rachel's theories get to me, even though I told her she was wrong. I mean, I knew she was wrong. I knew you didn't have a sex dungeon or anything."

"What?"

He speaks! One word, but still. Serena was relieved, and just a little too amused by his astonishment. "A sex dungeon. Or attic, or garage. No basements in Houston. That was her theory—that you might be super nice to work with, but that my, oh, I think it was my neocortex? Something like that, that my neocortex had figured out about your sex dungeon and was keeping me from getting intimate with you."

"A sex dungeon."

"It was a working theory."

"You didn't have anything to counter with?"

"I told you—attic. No basements. You can't imagine how adamant our friend Natalie was about the whole basement issue."

His eyes narrowed. "Exactly how many people did you tell about my sex dungeon, anyway?"

"Attic. I didn't mean to tell anyone, but Rachel just caught me at a bad moment, and she told the others."

"Others?"

"Natalie—she's a realtor, she found me this place—and Gillian. That's all, I swear."

"Well. I don't know what to say. I seem to have a bit of a reputation. Do you know where I can get a dungeon? Can Natalie help me with that?"

Oh yes, oh yes, oh yes—he was smiling. A real smile, and his posture had relaxed, and he was leaning towards her again. Bliss and thanks to the gods above. She ducked her head to hide her triumph, and batted her eyelids at him. "So, am I forgiven?"

CHAPTER TWENTY-SIX

ONE PART OF DILLON still wanted to pursue the fact that Serena hadn't just talked to him about the hives, but the part of him that pictured her sitting in her car trying to breathe, and the part of him that was all too happy to be entertained by her ridiculous theory combined forces with the insistent part of him twitching in his pants to override any reservations.

"She," he said.

"She who?" A little frown crossed Serena's face.

"Maisy the cat. You called her 'he.' She slept on my jacket every chance she got. On my usual messenger bag, too—the one I brought here I pulled from the back of a closet, so it should be safe for you."

Something extra-gorgeous happened with Serena's face then, the way she was looking at him. Happy shining pleasure in the soft glow from the lantern she'd set on the table between them. Dillon glanced around the back yard. It was secluded, surrounded by the arms of her house and a high wood fence, and though he'd joked about it, he really could smell some herbs from the pots surrounding them.

"Which one is basil, anyway?" he asked, standing and offering a hand to help her up. She led him to the darker side of the patio and bent slightly to pluck a few leaves from a plant.

"This one is sweet basil. Try it."

He sniffed the leaves then nibbled. Not bad.

"And here's some lemon basil, which I love to put in stir fries, that sort of thing."

It was a lot sweeter than the smell would have led him to believe. "Mmm," he said, and held one of the leaves up to her lips. She caught it with her teeth, and closed her mouth around his finger and thumb just for a moment. Slowly he drew a line along her eyebrow with his damp fingertip, and Serena shivered a little and moved closer to him.

"I have some mints over here," she said softly, and he followed, pressing his front to her back as much as possible, as they walked to the back of the garden where a slightly raised bed covered in a sprawl of low plants was visible in the dim light. Serena sat on the timber edging and reached towards the back. "This one is spearmint."

He sat beside her and opened his mouth, allowing her to put the leaf directly on his tongue. The tang was refreshing and he picked a few leaves of his own, crushing them slightly in his palm to release a sharp sweet scent into the air.

"This?" he asked, since the one he held was shaped differently from the one he'd tasted.

She leaned forward for a whiff. "That's regular peppermint. Good in teas, ice cream, and toothpaste."

"Or on its own," he added, placing a few leaves in her palm. She joined him in eating the mint, and in answer to his unspoken command or prayers, Serena leaned forward for a kiss.

Under the minty freshness she tasted of red wine, and heat, and desire. If any minuscule shred of Dillon was holding onto reservations about moving forward with Serena, this kiss defeated all resistance. He was colonized by his need for her, and he reached for what he wanted.

Within seconds, Serena was in his arms, and he'd scooted them both back so he was sitting in the mint and leaning against the fence. She shifted to stretch across his lap, and while one arm remained wrapped around her back, anchoring her warm softness to his grateful chest, his other hand moved down to settle her legs more securely. Not incidentally, that pressed her hip against his ecstatic crotch. His fingers found the hem of that blue skirt of hers, and it was only natural for him to slip underneath the barrier to her bare legs. God, how many times had he watched her walk across a room in this skirt and imagined reaching under it just like this?

Serena was unbuttoning his shirt and kept leaving his mouth to kiss his neck, his shoulder—oh Christ, she bit his shoulder and his hand was on her thigh and he was no longer of this world. She returned her kisses to his mouth, his jaw. Dillon breathed into her ear, nipping the lobe as she rasped her lower lip along his beard. And her hands. She'd shoved his shirt wide and was stroking his spine with a couple of fingernails while her free hand palmed his nipple and explored the hair that trailed down to his waistband.

"Oh, God, Serena," Dillon breathed when his hand climbed her smooth thigh to the lace of her panties. She moaned in response, opening her legs enough to trap his wrist between thigh and skirt. His palm pressed into her skin, feeling the muscles flex and tremble as his fingers explored the lace as far as this bliss of an imprisonment would allow him. He feathered light kisses down the column of her neck. Nuzzling aside her hair, Dillon slipped her shoulder free of sleeve and bra strap and dedicated himself to the exposed skin, which tasted of honey in this moonlight. With each breath she was pressing her breasts into him, and he let his tongue trail along her clavicle to burrow down to the rise and fall of her chest.

Head bent, unwilling to move his hand from her thigh to assist in the effort to get at her breast, Dillon used the palm at her back to press Serena upwards and his teeth to draw the top of her shirt downwards, and there—yes, there he was, mouth hovering above satin covered breast. Serena's breath was coming rapidly now, and she pulled herself up on his shoulders to press the taut nipple into his mouth. Dillon didn't hold back, sucking it and savoring the tight peak and drawing away enough to breathe heated air over the wet cloth and her moans and her grip on his shoulders and her hip in his lap and her writhing freed his wrist to move further up her thigh to fully palm her ass and trace the lace to the damp cotton between her legs and dear God almighty this was another planet he was on now, because nowhere on Earth could hold an encounter this intense.

Serena's mind reeled and gasped and rose and fell and she filled every sense with Dillon, his mint smell and spice taste and the feel of his coarse chest hair and the sound of his breath hitching as he bent his dark head to her breast. It was her favorite sexy orange bra, but she'd trade a million rubies to have it gone this instant. And then she realized there was no reason it couldn't be, and with an effort, pushed herself back.

Rather than fall out of his arms, she straddled him so she could lift her shirt over her head. Before she could remove the bra, Dillon reached behind her and captured her wrists. He brought her hands down behind her to anchor between his thighs and, with a private little smile, flicked his thumbs way too lightly against her aching nipples.

Her pelvis jerked involuntarily forward, seeking the pressure and friction that he was denying her breasts. Fortunately her pelvis was well placed, and as she grasped his thighs with her trapped hands, he met her thrust that proved his own pelvis had an agenda. It was too dark now for her to see much where their legs were joined, but she could feel the leaping hardness of his erection beneath his khakis. Unlike the jeans he'd worn before, these were thin and accommodating enough to give her aching, aching crotch something definitive to rub against.

Dillon squeezed her breasts briefly, firmly, then almost roughly yanked the cups down, leaving her free and open and exposed to the night air, and to him. His mouth devoured along whatever trail his hands blazed, and it was so so much, but not nearly enough. Serena took back her hands so she could rip the bra off, then leverage her pelvis more perfectly against his shaft. Her hands danced from his biceps to his shoulders to his hair to his chest to his sides to his nipples to his face. He took one of her fingers in his mouth and sucked hard while his hands encased each breast with a hold that felt like the most natural enclosure her breasts had ever found.

Reluctantly, eagerly, driven, he moved his palms downward, tracing her ribcage and her stomach before going to the rucked up hem of her skirt. "I changed my mind," he murmured, running his fingers lightly over the tops of her thighs to the apex where her wet mound moved restlessly in an attempt to get past the barriers to his full, hard erection.

She was half-raising herself up to allow his hands to roam more freely, but she sank abruptly at his words. "What?" Where was her bra? Her shirt?

"I thought your orange plaid skirt was my favorite. But I've changed my mind. Now this one is."

Oh God, she just had to kiss him. Leaning forward pressed her chest to his, and that was such a sweet thing that she wrapped her arms around his neck to ensure it would happen for as long as humanly possible. And she went back to raising herself up, and he didn't disappoint. His palm found her wet mound and he pressed his fingers flat against her and she moaned, she moaned his name, she just moaned. Then his other hand slipped under her panties from behind and with one strong finger he stroked her entrance. Serena rose higher, firmly held between his hands, and took a breast in one hand while angling the other one to his tongue.

She pinched her nipple and he suckled the other and he stroked her cleft and she rode his fingers and he growled and she groaned and he moved to lightly bite her finger and she released that breast to his focus and she pulled her fingers through his hair and he flicked the nub of her clitoris and he rubbed and he flicked and she sank down to bury the two fingers he'd worked into her and she rose again, arching forward, to reach her hands behind her. Breasts thrust forward into his face, pelvis sandwiched between his clever palms, her hands found his cock and stroked and stroked and traced and cupped as she dropped her head back, moaning, panting. Dillon and Dillon's thumb and Dillon's tongue and Dillon holding her and moaning with her and drawing her breast tightly into his mouth while he drove his fingers inside of her and pressing his thumb firmly against her clit as she thrust her clit wildly against his thumb and came with a cry of desperate passion.

Dillon had never smelled anything headier than the mingled mint and dew of Serena coming in her garden, or licked anything smoother than the silk of her breasts, neck, and then lips as his mouth blazed yet another trail across her skin. She nudged his hands away so she could lower his fly and release an erection that was all too eager to replace his fingers inside her as she rubbed her swollen cleft along his length. He may have been this hard and desperate at some other point in his life, but he doubted it. He sure as hell didn't have enough blood to his brain to allow him to think back and figure it out.

Serena's thumb circled the head of his cock and he bucked forward, groaning out her name. Her face was radiant under the moon, and the gentle light picked out the curves of her breasts and thighs, the dark tips of her furrowed nipples. Dillon's only desire in the universe was to stay where he was, stroked by Serena's wet and open vagina while her breasts swayed before him and her hand cupped his balls. On the other hand, his only desire in the universe was to spend an hour or three thrusting into her.

"We should go inside," she said, her tone a relaxed and seductive toy he wanted to play with forever. "Inside is where I keep the condoms."

He grinned cockily. "I keep mine in my pocket. At least, tonight I do."

"Hmmm," she said, regarding him through narrowed, teasing eyes. "And is that where you want to keep them now?"

His laugh was low and intimate. "No. Not even close." Much as he didn't want to let go of her glorious breast, he lifted up his hip long enough to dig the foil packet out. "Serena," he said, but didn't have any follow up words. He just handed her the condom, and she rolled to the side long enough to remove her panties and for him to lower his pants, and then she was back atop him, wearing nothing but the skirt hiked up her waist. The cheeks of her ass peeked below the hem and he compulsively stroked them, their smooth round curves leading directly to the still wet and now entirely bared to him entrance to her vagina. The light curls around her clit were damp and he bracketed her hips so he could lift her higher and blow into them, just a little, just lightly. And oh, God, but she smelled hot and ready for him. And her hands were on his cock.

She hadn't put the condom on yet. She was tracing his length slowly with one fingernail, and his hands gripped her sides to stop himself from dropping her directly onto his shaft without preamble. He needed to be inside her, but God, she was circling the head again, rubbing moisture over the tip, and even if he didn't know from the way her hips were pulsing under his palms, he could sense the damp and heat that meant she was ready for him.

He tried to let her play, but it was no good. He finally leaned forward and bit her nipple, and she jerked convulsively, and he growled with eagerness, and she wasted no more time. She rolled the condom on and followed her hands with her body. Dillon angled up his legs and put his arms under her knees, pulling her chest to his as he thrust upwards. He sat forward, opening her legs wider on either side of his shoulders, and caught her mouth with his. She held his head to her and their tongues and teeth and lips and breath and moans met and traded places. They explored each other inside out and Dillon was buried in her warmth and was able to thrust to his heart's content.

They kissed, and Serena's arms went around him, and he grasped her ass and pumped into her as he rocked her to his rhythm. Her hair fell over his shoulders and they moved together, finding a pace together that had her panting and pulsing higher and higher, repeating, "Dillon, Dillon, Dillon, Dillon," in a plea that he was thrilled to answer with deeper thrusts and just enough space between them to slip his hand around and rub her clit lightly with the base of his thumb. She dug her fingers into his back and nodded, rocking, taking every inch of him into her and pulsing, pulsing into another orgasm that squeezed his cock tight, so tightly, again and squeezed again until with a loud moan of his own, Dillon joined her, coming and coming and holding Serena to him, a perfect fit inside and out.

CHAPTER TWENTY-SEVEN

EVENTUALLY THEY ROLLED OUT of the mint bed and brushed each other off and gathered their clothes and headed inside. Squinting against the indoor lighting, Serena pointed Dillon towards the bathroom then laughed as he walked that way. The butt of his khakis looked, well, like those of someone who'd been rolling around in plants.

He turned, eyebrows up. "Something funny?"

She shook her head. "You may want to retire those pants after this."

Swiveling around to look he grinned back at her. "Aw, that's nothing. I think there are about a million splinters in my shirt from that fence."

Her eyes widened. "Are you okay?"

"None the worse for the wear. Anyway, if any got through the fabric your hands probably brushed them away."

She was still inspecting her palms when he poked his head out of the bathroom and said, "But perhaps you could shower with me, scrub my back, just to be sure?"

Serena watched his widening grin and had a quick-fire review of moments from the past several hours. Dillon on her doorstep, handing over a box of antihistamines. Dillon grinning as he flipped through the Charles Barkley book. Dillon pulling grapes and salami out of his cat-hair-free messenger bag. Dillon pouring her a glass of wine and complimenting her garden. Dillon tasting basil from her palm. Dillon pausing on the brink of her first orgasm to joke about her wardrobe. Dillon gazing searingly into her face as she sheathed his cock inside her. And now Dillon leering suggestively despite the bedraggled shirt and woodsy debris in his hair.

She was really, really, really glad that she wasn't allergic to him.

As intense as the garden sex had been, Dillon was pretty happy with this, too. Jostling for room in Serena's little tub-shower, ducking his head so it would fit under the spray while she rubbed the leaves from his hair. Running a soapy washcloth over her body, and she doing the same to him. They didn't fuck in the shower—not this time, but Dillon was making plans for later—but he got to see her fully nude, to touch her everywhere, to slip and slide and laugh and hold her.

"You still taste minty," he told her, licking into her mouth while she brushed her wet hair back from her forehead.

"Mmm. You, too."

"Maybe I don't need my toothbrush after all," he said, wrapping his arm more securely around her waist.

She started back a little and looked at him. "Your toothbrush?"

"Yeah. When I was getting the groceries, I got the condoms, too, and a toothbrush." He wiped water from his eyes and tried to gauge her expression. "I was just hoping, not presuming."

She smiled, but didn't relax. "I know."

"I'm not inviting myself to stay over."

She only hesitated for a second before she said, "No, you should stay over. I'd like you to stay over." And she kissed him. Lightly, but she did say it, she did kiss him. So he was probably imagining her resistance. Or reading her wrong, maybe it was just surprise. And frankly, he'd felt more abashed and conspicuous putting the toothbrush in his shopping cart than he had with the condoms. So he got her being surprised, if that's what she was.

"Serena?"

"Yep?"

"Are your sheets made of natural organic fibers?"

His question took down her guard, at least. She squinted her eyes a little at him. "What if I said they weren't?"

"That," he said, turning her and pulling her so that her slick wet backside was snugged into his thighs and he could soap-stroke her breasts, "would not be acceptable. I can't sleep on cotton that has been in contact with pesticides." He bent his mouth to her ear, her neck. Her shoulder. She backed against him and he growled.

"You're in luck."

"Mmm?"

"My sheets?"

"Mmm?"

"They're unbleached, too."

Dillon nipped the vein pulsing in her neck, lightly pinching her nipples, and wondered how long the smell of Serena's lavender honey soap would linger on his own skin, and if it meant he would spend every moment until his next shower at least half-aroused. He would just have to make sure he spent as much of that time as possible naked, next to her.

He did that guy thing, Serena thought as she watched Dillon sleep the soundest sleep ever. He'd managed to dispose of the condom and wash up a little after they'd made out again, but he was asleep almost as soon as he was back in bed. At least he didn't snore, and laying there all spooned and wrapped up and snug in her, yes, organic bedding was a fine feeling indeed. But Serena's mind was a little active yet, and she rolled over to her back to watch Dillon's sleeping face while her thoughts chased around.

It was dark, and his hair and beard meant most of Dillon was shadow and darker shadow. She could pick out the angle of his cheekbone, the plane of his forehead sloping straight to his brow, echoed by the straight slope of his nose. His lips, relaxed in sleep, still gently curved and Serena resisted the temptation to reach out and trace the lower one. No doubt about it, he was about the most comfortable guy to spend the night with she'd ever met. It took months of dating Joey before the post-coital snuggle felt this relaxing and just plain right. Of course, his sheets were not only not organic, they weren't even cotton.

She had a frowning suspicion that if Dillon's sheets weren't cotton, he would rush out and replace them, and she tried to sort out why that made her uneasy. She was all for promoting natural fibers, of course. But as charmed as she'd been by the antihistamines and the new shirt, there was something on the verge of off-putting about the toothbrush. She couldn't put her finger on it, but when he'd mentioned the toothbrush her stomach had twisted up a little. He'd shown up without asking, yes, but she'd been about to call him. He'd brought the food, sure, but that was mannerly and romantic. It was all part of what she'd sort of imagined as the road map for the evening. Seeing him, eating together, talking out the cat allergy thing. Touching and kissing. And more. Yes, her road map had definitely included the 'more' part, which is why she knew for sure where her condoms were after the move. In case. In the happy, happy case. And it had been—oh, so truly been—a happy case.

In her road map, though, there wasn't an extra toothbrush in her toothbrush holder. It was out of place.

Dillon, though. He was so so sexy-sweet. And an amazing lover. But they already saw each other at work all the time, and she suspected they'd be seeing plenty of each other on their off hours now. Oh, yes, there was a lot of him she was looking forward to seeing, she mused, no longer resisting the urge to touch the dark arch of his brow, his smooth soft lip. It wasn't impossible that she would fall for this man. She was honest enough to admit to that. But she had to face up to a worry, too, that he was going from zero to sixty in the blink of an eye. From not speaking for days, to bringing over a toothbrush. And she wanted to proceed with caution. They were already friends. They had great chemistry. They were coworkers. No, correction—she was kind of his boss. Or on the verge of being his superior, in some arenas. If he went full steam ahead, he threatened to drag her onto a runaway train—the Dillon Express, where everything in her world was hitched to everything about his world. No stops for Serena's friends, Serena's hobbies, Serena's time to just be her self-reliant self. It would be a train wreck.

And now she was going to have bad dreams about locomotives. She mentally rolled her eyes at herself, and reminded herself that all she had to do was apply the brakes when he got too intense. If he got too intense. No need to borrow trouble. Still, having identified what was niggling at her about Dillon helped her relax. She sank into the mattress beside him, wrapping one hand around the bulge of his forearm where it was draped over her chest, and drifted off to sleep.

CHAPTER TWENTY-EIGHT

SERENA STRETCHED AS SHE WOKE, and as she arched her back she brushed against Dillon's warm, naked body. He was propped on an elbow, and his eyes were fixed on the sheet that covered her chest. She followed his gaze and noted that the more he gazed, the more prominently her nipples peaked under the cotton. Then— wicked grin in place—he reached over her to dip a forefinger into the glass of water on her bedside table. He tapped a few cold drops onto each peak, then he blew on them. Anticipatory moisture flooded Serena's vulva, and she tried to squirm, but Dillon had pinned the sheet on either side of her with his forearms, so she couldn't even reach for herself to solve the problems he wasn't solving fast enough for her.

She could, however, reach for him, and she made damn sure he stopped his silent teasing and got to work satisfying her. He pulled the sheet out from the bottom of the bed so he could keep her torso pinned but still slide his cock—and cock was the right word this morning, he was being so cocky about being so agonizingly slow—slide every hard inch ever so gradually into her. Serena couldn't move her body and Dillon's hands held down her shoulders and upper arms, but she had enough agility left to take her breasts and press them together and up until they were free from the sheet. Then she could readily squeeze them together and hold them tight for Dillon to devour with lips and tongue. And if he tried to be too cagey, too deliberate when she wanted abandon, she could thumb her nipples her own self, Dillon be damned.

And lo and behold if her taking action like that didn't motivate him away from whatever sadistic pleasure he was getting from driving her crazy with his molasses speed, because suddenly he was pounding, not sliding. And suddenly she was trapped and immobile again but it did not matter because his grip was on her breasts and his tongue was roughly tasting each nipple in turn, in rhythm with his thrusts, and she could give up any need for self-control and mastery over her own limbs as she rose into an orgasm that pulsed with each lick-thrust and pulsed and pulsed again as Dillon's final thrusts broke the rhythm and he, too, came and came.

And the light filtering through her curtains was bright enough to see each sweat-glistened muscle on his torso, and Serena smiled.

"Good morning," she said, fruitlessly smoothing back the hair that fell over his eyes. She had the answer to a long-held question: he didn't need gel or comb to get that sexily scruffy look each day. His nearly black hair did it all on its own.

"Well, howdy, as you Texans say."

"Listen, buddy, if you have any cowgirl fantasies we'll have to have a talk."

"Not willing to yee-hah for me? After I promised you a guided tour of my sex dungeon and everything?"

She could eat his smile for breakfast every day, it was that delicious. And nutritious, her sated soul reminded her. "No, I'm willing. I just don't have a Stetson, so I'd have to go shopping."

He planted a smacking kiss on her lips and hauled them both up to sit against her headboard. "I do admire your forethought and practicality in all things kinky. It's a side of you I'd never have guessed at."

"You thought I'd be slap-dash about it?"

He considered. "No. I suppose I didn't dare to picture it one way or another. Too dangerous to my self-control at work to spend much time thinking about you in the bedroom."

"Or garden."

He laughed and pulled her closer. "Especially in the garden. When time travel is a reality, remind me not to go back to the Dillon of January and tell him about the mint, okay? It would entirely ruin his ability to work."

Serena rested her head against the lovely strong plane of his shoulder. "When it's a reality?"

"Don't mock me."

"I wouldn't dare. You'd chain me in the dungeon. And I'd have to wait for time travel to become a reality—somehow I take it this will happen in my lifetime? And travel back to free myself."

"What makes you think you'd want to free yourself?"

She glanced up into his bright blue eyes, practically the same shade as the wall behind his head despite her earlier determination to veer away from that compelling hue. "You make a fine point." He kissed her again, so she kissed him again, then giggled when her stomach growled.

"You want some eggs or something? They're free range."

"I'd expect nothing less," he laughed, and glanced at the alarm clock. "Maybe just coffee, though. My sister and Justin arranged brunch for my birthday in just over an hour. It's a buffet, so I want to go hungry."

"Wow. You are such a boy."

"Man."

She stroked his thigh and agreed, wholeheartedly. "Man."

Dillon used the spare bath and came back to watch her brushing out her hair. He was wearing the mint-pressed khakis but a clean shirt.

"You packed clothes, too?" Serena rubbed at the back of her neck after she pulled her hair up into a knot at the nape. She reminded herself that it didn't itch, and lowered her hand.

"Just a clean shirt and boxers. I told you, I was hopeful. But listen, I can't go to brunch in these." He wiped at a green mark on his thigh. "Well, I could, but Shannon would ask questions."

"Somehow I think you're right." She walked him to the kitchen, hand in hand. "Also, I don't have coffee. I could make you tea, though?"

"Does it have caffeine?"

"I can offer you either black or green tea in addition to a wide selection of herbals and tisanes."

"You are wonderful, you know that? But also, I'm glad you're not a vegetarian."

"I was for a while."

"Of course you were."

She nudged his upper arm. "Hey, be nice. It's far better for the planet."

"I know, I know. But I'm unrepentant. Besides, this place has a great carving station."

"What place?"

"The brunch place."

"But even if I was a vegetarian still I wouldn't mind if you ate meat." She pulled out tea mugs. "Especially if it was local and grass-fed and supported a small farmer."

"Well, you should at least try their bacon, no matter where the pig grew up. When you're ready, we can just swing by my place and I'll run in to change, then you can see what I mean."

Serena froze and stared at Dillon. He was leaning against the kitchen counter, reading the box of breakfast blend tea, and appeared to be perfectly relaxed and calm and not even some time-travel version of himself. The same guy she'd only spent one night with, and he wanted her to go to his family birthday brunch?

She hadn't answered, and he finally looked up at her. "We should take your car, though, since Maisy was in mine. I'll get it detailed or something, do you think that will take care of it?"

"Uh, yes, I—well, probably it wouldn't matter. Unless she was curled up on the passenger seat."

"No, she was in her carrier on the floor."

"So that's not the problem."

He put down the box and straightened. "There's a problem?"

"No. Not a problem," she moved over to kiss him. Same amount of stubble, even, so definitely not a time-travel version of Dillon. "You want me to go to brunch with you?"

"God, sorry, I shouldn't have assumed you were free. Do you have plans?"

She shook her head. "No plans. But, Dillon, your sister is taking you out for your birthday. That's not something I should go to."

"I'll text her, I'm sure she wouldn't mind. They'd like to meet you at last."

Serena was working hard to keep her face placid. "At last?"

A little flush spread across Dillon's cheekbones and Serena couldn't resist touching him. Again. Some more. "Apparently I talk about you a lot. So when I took the cat back to them, Justin— that's my brother-in-law, I've told you that?" She nodded. He spoke often of his family, and Serena wasn't unhappy, but was distinctly freaked out, to find that he talked to them of her in return. "Yeah, so Justin said that they'd been wondering when you and I were going to get together."

Her eyes widened. "Wow."

"My thoughts exactly."

"But wait a minute. You talked to them on the Sunday?"

Dillon nodded.

"After the—well, before we knew about the cat thing?"

He nodded again.

"So...what did you tell them about me?"

Dillon turned so he could wrap his arms lightly around Serena's waist. "I said you were sexy and I wanted you to be my sexy lover and, of course, I wanted to sex you up in my sex cave."

"Attic."

"Right, no basements, because your realtor won't allow it."

"Right."

"But I don't think 'sex attic' sounds as good. It has a touch of Rochester, yes, but also a little taste of decaying grandmothers, which is just not sexy."

Once again, Dillon had taken the light teasing path away from her impulse to freak out. So maybe he got that he was going fast, or maybe he had a well-tuned sense about when he was about to presume too much. Either way, Serena was glad. She'd far rather joke and stay in his embrace than get serious and put space between them. Of course, if he would just proceed with a little more caution to begin with, give them a chance to see what was happening before dragging her off to meet the relatives, that would be even better.

Dillon wasn't a fan of the tea, but gamely took a few sips before packing up his bag. Serena walked him to the door. He was kicking himself about the brunch thing, but he wasn't going to let the rest of the weekend go by without seeing her.

"You busy tonight?"

She shook her head, but still looked a little wary. On the other hand, her hand was on his ass, so she was bound to be a little willing.

"Can I take you to dinner?"

"Sure. Thanks."

He didn't want his relief to show in his smile, but he was sure it did. "I'll pick you up around seven?"

She had a yoga class that didn't end until six, though, so they pushed it back a little. He wasn't going to suggest any changes to her routine, not on purpose, anyway. Apparently Serena wasn't as comfortable with spontaneity in her daily life as she was in bed. Garden bed or mattress bed, either one. He grinned at her and leaned down for another kiss.

"Dillon?"

"Yeah?" It was going to be hard to leave her doorway if he couldn't make himself stop touching her.

Smiling, she tugged lightly on the strap of his messenger bag. "Bring the toothbrush back tonight."

Oh, it was going to be hard, indeed, he thought, as he took in Serena's sun-dappled face and raised a brow. "I already left it here." Nine hours and counting until he got to touch her again.

Hot damn.

Serena's idiot grin faded as she closed the door and headed into her bathroom to check. Yep. There, in one of the mason jars she'd decorated with gem-hued acrylics and wired to the wall beside her over-sink mirror, her bright red toothbrush nestled up against his plain white one. She sighed and walked out, rubbing her neck again. On the one hand, she was shaken up by his presumption. On the other, well, it would be churlish and not very self-serving to pitch a hissy about it, when it was an indication that she was going to be licking his naked torso by the end of the day. And one thing those button-downs he always wore hid was the fact that Dillon's naked torso was delicious.

Lost in thought, Serena almost jumped out of her skin when her cell rang. She'd dropped it on her entry bench with everything else in her rush to start crafting the package for Dillon's present after work yesterday, and hadn't thought about it since.

It was Natalie. "Yo," Serena said. Chirped, really. But maybe Natalie wouldn't comment on it—she wasn't a cynic like Gillian.

"Well, I guess I know why you haven't called back."

Serena pulled back the phone and looked at the list of missed calls while she hedged. "Don't know what you're talking about." All three of them had called around seven yesterday, and Natalie twice since then.

"You wore the earrings, is what I'm talking about. That 'yo' was the 'yo' of a woman whose come-hither was heeded."

"Did y'all get together last night or something?"

"Haven't checked your email, either, I see. This makes something like twenty hours that you've been ignoring us. We could all be hospitalized or something, and where would you be? In bed with the Cat Man is where."

"Is anyone hospitalized?"

"Not this time."

"Because I have a landline, too, you know. You could always call it in an emergency."

"Listen to little Miss Misdirection. What was the sex like?"

"Superb."

Natalie was grim. "I knew it."

"Is there a reason that's bad news? And I didn't wear the earrings at work. He just came over and we had dinner and then he stayed the night. No earrings necessary." Though the skirt probably hadn't hurt. She bit her lip and wondered if she should wear the orange skirt tonight.

"Smug. Nice. Did you call him on the photo thing?"

"We talked some stuff out."

"Including how he was a passive-aggressive coward?"

"Natalie, look, there's no need for that. We're not negotiating a contract here, we're just sleeping together. Dating. We talked about what happened, and then we made sweet, sweet love, and now he's visiting his sister and I'm considering a nap before we go out again tonight. Be happy for me."

Natalie's tone softened just a tiny bit. "Okay, I'm happy. Even though you're the only one of us having sex now, I'm happy for you."

"Hang on, what? What happened to Chris?"

"Chris moved."

"What do you mean, Chris moved? How could he move? Where? Why?"

Natalie sighed. "Yeah, there's no good answer to that. I went by yesterday so we could catch an early movie, and the place was empty. Cleaned out. Nada. So I called his cell, and it was disconnected. So I went home, and there was a note in my mailbox."

Serena had to sit down. Chris had been nothing if not predictable, or at least as predictable as his flight schedule would allow. Gillian tended to be snippy and call him 'safe,' but Natalie had been so content with him. "What did it say?"

"Oh," Natalie sighed, "essentially, that he was sorry for the short notice, but he had to disappear, and he hoped I had a nice life."

"You're shitting me."

"I wish. So that's why we got together last night."

"Natalie, I'm so sorry. This is crazy. It doesn't fit."

"Yeah, well, Gill promised to make me a voodoo doll and arrange a ritual burning of the crap he left in my house, so that'll be fun."

Serena laughed. "Count me in. What did Rachel say?"

"Rachel's theory is that the child support enforcement people caught up with him."

"Chris has kids?"

"Not that I know about. But, and I don't know if you've ever noticed this, a lot of Rachel's theories can be traced directly to her situation with Sergei."

"You don't say."

"Shocker, I know. Hey, now that Chris bailed, can I take up smoking again?"

"Not if you want to spend any time around me."

"You'll be too busy with your sweet, sweet lover to care."

"Oh, Natalie. I'm really sorry about all this. I'm sorry I missed the bitch session last night, and I'm especially sorry about Chris. I mean, I hope he's not in danger or anything, but even if he is, this is no way to treat you."

"Yeah. Well."

"Do you want to get together? I can cancel dinner with Dillon."

Another big sigh. "No. Have your dinner-which-is-code-for-more-sex. I have an open house all afternoon and two more tomorrow. Maybe I'll sell something and go buy a gorgeous handbag to celebrate."

"Okay, call me if you change your mind. I promise to pick up."

"As long as you're not in the middle of anything naughty."

"Me?" Serena thought of her new neighbors, and hoped no one else was outside last night. "Nonsense."

Natalie barked out a laugh that was only a little bitter. "Okay, that's enough from you."

After Serena disconnected the call, she went through voice mail and email for a bit and washed up everything from the previous night's dinner. She wasn't normally one to leave crumbs lying around, but Dillon had been quite the distraction. Fortunately her mint plants were practically indestructible, and seemed none the worse for wear. She snagged some peppermint to add to her water bottle, and just about got goose bumps when she crushed the leaves, releasing the scent.

She took the water and a small plate of munchies into her office so she could burn a CD for Natalie of ass-kicking empowered woman songs, and spent a happy hour collaging a cover for the jewel case. Jeanne d'Arc, Elizabeth Cady Stanton, Queen Victoria, Harriet Tubman, Marie Curie, and Aretha Franklin all boogied together with Boudica and Natalie herself. It was a little goofy, sure, but not as goofy as a voodoo doll, and if it lifted Natalie's spirits, then she'd done her job. She would drop it at her house before yoga.

But first, she needed to store up some stamina for the night ahead. It was time for a nap.

CHAPTER TWENTY-NINE

"TOBIAS, BABY-DUDE, come here," Dillon said, snugging the wide-awake and wide-eyed little guy to him before leaning down for hugs from Justin and Shannon.

"We've been supplanted," Justin told his wife.

"You bet you have. I told you how all my hopes and dreams for the future are pinned on this guy," Dillon said, but his expression must have given him away.

"Why do I think you've considered alternate retirement plans?"

"My lips are sealed."

"Right," Shannon said, then turned to direct the host in the complicated logistics of placing them so that they were far enough from the crowds but close enough to the buffet, and how to set the chair that Toby's carrier would rest on. The men stood back and watched.

"First time out with him?"

Justin nodded.

"He's okay around all these people, though, right?"

Justin shrugged. "I thought it was a little early for public outings, but Shannon insisted. She says you love this place, plus they have your precious shortcake, and even her baby's well-being seems to take back seat to her baby brother's well-being."

Dillon groaned. "I know you're kidding, but that is way too close to the bone. Shades of the dismal days." Granted, those were mostly dismal because their parents had just died. Poor Shannon had been the one dealing with most of the interminable fallout—guardianship of him, transfer of ownership for the house and other inheritances to a trust, plus the settlement from the truck driver's insurance company. The paperwork for that, and everything the courts required to prosecute the guy. Rearranging her school schedule and getting out of her lease so she could live at home with him. She'd barely gotten into her twenties, and she never complained about any of it. And through it all, all she ever asked of him was for him to see the therapist and to, just occasionally, be happy.

It was about the hardest thing she could have asked of him.

That was the thing with that god-awful surprise party. She hadn't wanted him to mope about his first birthday without their parents, so she'd gone all out on the bash. And he'd been so clammed up for so long that it wasn't like she could've known he no longer got along with his seventh-grade lab partner. Or with lots of people, really. Being the local orphan hadn't been the kind of notoriety that he craved, and definitely not on his damn birthday, everyone full of sympathy and fake elaborate good wishes until he'd sought refuge behind the garage to get away from it all.

Justin had found him out there. He didn't scold or anything. He just told Dillon that Shannon had spent hours trying to perfect their mom's pineapple upside-down cake. After she'd thrown out two failed attempts, Justin had persuaded her to stop, but she was sure it would ruin Dillon's birthday, not having his favorite cake. Since Dillon wasn't a total asshole, he'd followed Justin back inside, and when Shannon brought out the strawberry shortcake, he'd made like it was his new favorite. They'd had it every year since.

Justin squeezed his arm. "Hey. It's okay. She still worries sometimes, but I think most of the time she never thinks of you at all."

"Thanks. That makes me feel a million times better," Dillon laughed. The funny thing was, it kind of did. Shannon deserved a life where she could think only about herself. Where she could revel in the love and security of Justin and Toby and the cat, and go days without making a decision more momentous than what flavor yogurt to buy.

Dillon reached an arm around Justin and just held him a minute. Some days he forgot to thank the universe for sending a man like this to Shannon—and to him—when they so desperately needed him.

Justin seemed to understand his train of thought. He reached up and kissed Dillon's cheek. "Gah. You need to shave."

"Serena didn't mind." Still half-stuck down memory lane, he hadn't thought before answering.

Justin plucked Tobias from his arms, locked him into the carrier, and told Shannon all sing-song and superior, "Dillon has a girlfriend. Told you he would."

"No!"

"Yes! They were making kissy-kissy face, and she likes it when he doesn't shave."

"Shut up."

"Okay, sure. No problem. You tell us everything, and I won't say a word," Justin replied, grinning across the table at him.

Shannon leaned in to hear every word, and no matter how many times he disappeared to the omelet station and the carving station and every other station where there was a line to keep him away from their prying, they managed to drag a good bit of info out of him before the brunch was over. He even offered to change Toby at one point, but Justin shook his head and went himself, while Shannon pinned him in place with her best big sister look.

"So you really like this woman?" she asked with a smile that said she knew what the answer was.

He gave up—there was no hope of holding anything back from her. Especially given how fondly he looked back over the past several hours with Serena. "She's amazing," he said. "I want you to meet her. I mean, I asked her to come here today, but that was too fast, I know."

"Dillon!"

"I know. I said I know. But, Shan. You'll love her."

"But you invited her to brunch?"

"I didn't think you'd mind."

She wrinkled her nose at him. "It's not that I mind. I wouldn't mind, I'd like to meet her. But you don't just spring 'birthday brunch with my family' on someone you just met."

"I met her in January."

"You know what I mean. Just got together with, romantically."

"Well, she offered me breakfast. It seemed like it would be rude to just say 'no' instead of inviting her to eat with me."

Shannon just looked at him. Finally Dillon admitted, "Okay, that's not why. I mean, it might have been part of it, but, yeah, I just wanted her to be with me more. To meet you guys. Let's face it, she's going to meet you eventually."

"I'm sure she will, sweetie, but you can't just drag her off to meet us the first morning you're together. I mean, ease up a little. Next you'll be making reservations at a drive-up Vegas chapel."

"Hey, I'm not you."

She threw her napkin at him. "My wedding was not at a drive-through."

"Not for lack of trying," Justin said, returning with a tidy Toby.

"I make one little suggestion about wedding planning and he holds it over my head forever," Shannon said, but she was planting a kiss on Justin's hand as he squeezed her shoulder in passing.

Dillon watched them fondly. Shannon and Justin just plain fit together. Even as much as they'd had to go through when they first started dating, they'd always fit. Wanting what they had didn't seem, to him, to be too much to look for in life.

Chapter Thirty

"You shaved!"

Dillon rubbed his jaw. "I hope you don't mind."

She kissed the smooth skin, nuzzled a little. "Hmm, no. It's nice. I just wasn't expecting it. Come in."

"Wow. Speaking of nice," Dillon snagged Serena's waist and pulled her hips to him. "You wore my favorite skirt."

And she was glad, seeing his reaction. "I thought it was your second-favorite now."

"Changed my mind."

"Fickle. Just when you think you know a guy." She was having trouble moving her palms off his face. He must have shaved moments before coming over, it was that baby smooth. "So, where are you taking me?"

It was a new Italian place on Washington. "I can't explain why that area is bustling in this economy, but as long as it is, we may as well enjoy," he said, holding his car door open for her. "Plus, I looked at their website. They grow a lot of their own veggies. I thought you'd like that."

Serena had taken her pills before he came over, in case he was out of new shirts, or the cat had shed more than she'd expected in his car. But he wore a crisp white button-down—not new, but fresh from the cleaners—and he'd put a cautionary towel down on the seat and foot well. If this kept up, she was going to rethink her reservations about his overeagerness thing.

They'd shared 'how did it go today' type stories in the car, and for a moment after they were seated at the window table Dillon had reserved, Serena was tense. It took her a moment to figure out why: she didn't actually know what to talk about next. She'd been conversing with Dillon for months. They didn't need to exchange any of that 'just getting to know you' chit-chat. She didn't want to talk about the night—or morning—they'd just spent together. Too many pitfalls, and she wanted to stay a lot closer to the surface. They'd already covered the hours they'd been apart. The future was another danger zone she would only approach with caution. So basically she had no road map; just another transportation-themed analysis of what was bothering her about her relationship with Dillon.

She scanned the menu, and was saved.

"But this is awful!"

His head jerked up from the wine list. "What's awful?"

"This," she showed him her menu. "It's got a dozen spelling and grammar errors in the About Us paragraph, and there are at least four—no, look, five—different fonts in the descriptions."

He looked at his own menu, which was of course identical. "Only ten errors in the About Us. But they bury the lede and don't say anything about that vegetable garden." Dillon shrugged. "It's a shame. They have a good backstory, but who's going to read all that about the location to get to it?"

Serena was still counting typestyles. "They switch to Franklin Gothic, of all things, for the desserts. Did someone literally cut and paste this?"

The waitress knew all about the specials, but wasn't expecting to be quizzed on the menu design. She offered to send a manager over after she got their order in. "If you're ready to order?" she added, a little pointedly.

"Poor gal didn't really expect to deal with the likes of us," Serena said after they were alone again.

Dillon raised an eyebrow at her. "Us?"

"Okay, me. I know. But did you see their logo?" She pulled a small pad of paper and a couple of colored pens out of her bag. "Way off balance, and a stereotype, to boot. Not a good inspiration. This place is so nice, too." She glanced up from her sketch to smile at him. "Thank you for inviting me out, for bringing me here."

"Well, as long as you're enjoying yourself," said Dillon, and pulled out his phone to show here the restaurant's website logo. "They do it differently here, see?"

Serena studied it and flipped to a new page of her notepad. "That's better. But if they did this, see, but imagine it in a kind of saffron and basil color scheme? More Tuscany that way, and still Italian without being pizza parlor about it all."

By the time the appetizers were out, she'd pressed her card and a couple of sketches into the manager's hands. To give him credit, he agreed about the logo and just shook his head grimly when Dillon asked about the text. As so often was the case with these things, there was an owner's relative somewhere in the works. The old 'I can do it just as good but cheaper' argument. Serena pointed out that she could create templates that would make for easy menu updating both in print and online, and their new buddy Dante was pulling up a chair before he realized that Serena and Dillon were out for romance, not business. He was very sweet about it, not that she in particular minded. The third wheel (more transportation!) actually smoothed the path to easy conversation, even after he left. Plus, they got free dessert and liqueur.

"Well, Eddie is going to be a pain in the ass," Dillon told her.

"I know." Serena was quite self-satisfied. "But I'm sure he'll think of things to sell them on. Anyway, Dante's boss may be harder to convince."

"Still. Very boss-like there. You're going to be great at this new job."

She sighed. "Well, thanks. I sure wish Anica would make it official."

"Then I can start 'yes ma'am'-ing you in the hallway."

"Just don't do it in bed," she laughed, then blushed. "Have you ever noticed my tendency to blurt out whatever's in my head?"

"I prefer to think of it as your refreshing honesty. I like that you're straight-forward."

Then she blushed again, because although he didn't say it, she heard the 'usually' at the end of that statement. Pitfalls! Veer away!

"I'm sorry I'm talking shop so much. And I didn't mean to turn dinner into a sales pitch. You picked this lovely place, and it's delicious, and I should have let the menu problems slide."

"They were pretty egregious, though."

"Right?"

He smiled and offered her the bread basket. "Well, we need to talk about it anyway."

"About those fonts?"

"No, not about those fonts, funny girl. Work."

Serena closed her eyes a second, swallowing. So much for avoiding pitfalls. "Okay," she slowly, reluctantly asked, like she didn't already know what he meant. "What about work?"

He assessed her for a minute, but gave in graciously enough to her faux-innocence. "So no saluting you in the hallways, we agreed about that. No matter how much authority you have over me." He put on a thoughtful expression. "How does you being in authority at work go with my sex dungeon? Is it better, because we have a role reversal?"

"I always heard it's actually the submissive one who has the power, because they're the ones allowed to use the safe word and stop everything."

"Okay, now I know you're trying to change the subject, right? But just because I'm not going to let you distract me now doesn't mean we're not going to revisit that topic in a while. I have to find out what your sources are. And more interestingly, why you have sources."

"Need to know, buddy, sorry."

"Oh, I need to know. Don't doubt that for a minute." He squinted at her as if he had to put a whole new puzzle together. Serena tried to hide her ridiculous burst of giggles. "Right. We'll get back to that. What we have to agree on is how we play the relationship at work. I don't want to hide it, just so you know."

Of course he didn't. Not that Serena did, exactly. But she didn't want to send out an email to everyone in their domain, either. "Well," she said, "from what I got from Emily after—well, that's a different incident, nothing to do with us. Point being, I have recent info only third-hand from HR that there aren't any rules against workplace relationships. There's not even a disclosure requirement."

"So everyone could be getting it on behind closed doors and no one would need to be told about it?"

"I'm getting concerned about the number of times you've mentioned having sex at Lanigan. We are not going to be having sex at Lanigan."

He smoldered at her a little. God, he was charming. "I never thought we would. Doesn't mean I haven't thought about it. And I'll continue to think about it. Just so you know. Matter of fact, every time you've worn a skirt to work for the past, oh, ever?"

She nodded warily.

"I've made plans about the best place to get private with you so I could scootch it up. Inch by inch. Usually with my hands, mind you, but sometimes —"

"Dillon!"

He switched from devil to angel. "Serena?"

"You aren't allowed to have fantasies about me at work."

"Too bad."

"But." She didn't know what to say.

"Every. Single. Skirt. For months. Did you think the favorite, second favorite thing was something I decided casually? I have a whole ranking system. Ease of access is just one of the primary considerations.”

Serena buried her face in her hands and peered at him between her fingers. Okay, yes, she’d had some serious, detailed workplace fantasies about him, too. But that was mostly research. And—months? Months? “Months?”

“Months.”

“Oh.”

Dillon reached across the table and moved her hands aside, stroking her cheek lightly for a moment. “Serena. You know I’ve been interested in you for a while. Well, I wanted you from day one, but it’s been about more than the sex, too. Especially the more I got to know you. For a long, long time I just set it aside and told myself it wasn’t right, because we had to work together. But it was never easy, setting it aside. And never felt right—not like this feels right.”

“Dillon, I’m not....”

“Let me finish? Because I waited, Serena. And then you sent me signals. And I knew I wasn’t alone in this, and I was really, really happy. Despite all of the cat stuff that drove me crazy there for a bit, I threw out the caution, the barriers I created, and I’m not putting them back. There’s something real between us, and I’m going to find out what it is.”

And he was quiet, and waited. And she didn’t know what to say.

Dillon held his breath, realized he was holding his breath, and forced himself to breathe. It probably wasn’t the years later that it felt before Serena picked his hand up and pressed her cheek into his palm. He expelled a quick lungful of air, relieved.

She kissed the base of his thumb, then the center of his hand. “I’m happy, too. You know I’m happy, right?”

That little half-smile of hers was Dillon's third favorite. He returned it. "I'd hoped so."

"I am. And not just because of the sex, for the record. Are you keeping records? You seem to have a few too many lists and charts for my liking."

"You'll get used to it."

"That's comforting." She gave him a wry nose wrinkle. "But, Dillon, can we just go slow a little?"

And there it was. The payoff for his rash brunch invitation. His inward sigh fought with his inward wince and the battle made him clear his throat.

She rushed on, "I don't mean we should stop, or anything, of course. I like being with you. I like this whole romantic dinner thing; this is really perfect to me. I'm just worried some. I don't want to mess anything up with you, so I hope I can say this right. But the thing is, Dillon, I'm just—this is such a new thing for us. And we work together, we work great together. And I liked you so much, before."

He smirked at that.

She laughed. "I still like you. A lot. So much," she said softly, tilting her head and taking hold of his forearm. "So I want to preserve all of that. These things are really important to me. And I want to move on with you, with us, and I want to have lot of time together. In your dungeon, and out."

Dillon grinned back at her. "Sounds good so far."

"Right, to me, too. So that's why I want us to be careful. Cautious. Not to hide anything at work, not from Janice and Jorge, nothing like that. But for us, for you and for me, to just go a little slowly with all this. Make sure that we don't lose what we have already, that Dillon and Serena the friends, Dillon and Serena the coworkers, don't get buried under Dillon and Serena the," she searched for a moment, "the King and Queen of the Attic of Whips."

"I don't care what your friend Natalie says, it's a dungeon not an attic."

"Well, garage, maybe. But no basements, she's very firm on that point. Poor Natalie."

"Why is Natalie poor?"

"Long story short, she got dumped yesterday."

"Poor Natalie."

"And she's so upset. Not that I blame her. But it was a blow, and she lost her equilibrium. And I don't want to get so caught up in us that if something happens I'll fall apart like that."

Dillon's eyes narrowed and he almost had to physically restrain himself from retorting with any number of unhelpful things. While he wasn't enamored of the idea of starting a relationship with contingency plans about when it ended, he recognized that Serena was speaking from an honest place. No matter how badly she put everything. Natalie's ex probably wasn't helping her frame of mind. He reminded himself, too, that he'd never gotten into a relationship with someone he was friends with before—not since the usual low-stakes high school stuff, where everyone dated in a big circle, so your girlfriend one season was your friend's friend's girlfriend the next, while you were paired up with your buddy's sister. He'd never worked with a girlfriend, either, and trying to entice her into sex on the conference table while they were on deadline was a sure was to add stress to their fledgling relationship. So Serena had a point, however ill phrased.

Just so long as she didn't think going slow entailed him spending the night under his own roof, was all.

"Okay, so we don't have to start by planning for disasters, you know that, right?" He was channeling all of those Communications Major skills to say the things he wanted in a way she would hear. "Right. Good. But you're right that we've got...complications that other couples don't have from the start. And we'll be careful about those."

Serena was with him so far. He squeezed her hand. She squeezed back.

"You're way too fun to hang out with and our group is way too solid to endanger any of that," he said. And now that she was reassured that they were on the same page, time to poke some holes in her theories. "But the truth is, Serena, that I really, really like you. Really. And last night…. Well. Last night, this morning, that was all worlds above my fantasies. Yes, I've had fantasies. Long, detailed fantasies. And you, Serena, surpassed them all. It's possible that you've ruined me for all other women," he added as lightly as he could, because there was no need to make her run screaming from the restaurant.

"Dillon," she breathed, but didn't go on.

"So I'll be careful, yes. We'll put off moving in together at least for a week or two, and we won't crawl under desks to service each other when we should be in meetings." He surprised a laugh out of her with that one. Good. His voice leveled out as he finished. "But I won't hide from you, and I don't want you to hide from me. I've always admired your honesty, so I want to give the same to you. As far as I'm concerned, this is the start of something. Something that might end up big. And going slow is bearable. I can go slow. I can't just stop, though. Not even if it meant countless nights like last night. And," he wiggled his eyebrows at her, "like tonight will be."

She was smiling silently at him, quiet but visibly relaxed, when Dante descended with tiramisu and gelato. Even better, she raised not a single objection to his coming in (and in, and coming) when they got back to her house.

CHAPTER THIRTY-ONE

FOR A WEEK, they went at Serena's speed.

Slow.

Dillon discovered he had almost enough Texan in him to lasso his impatience and pen it in while they avoided eye contact, much less physical contact, at Lanigan. Only because, mid-week, she visited his place, where they cautiously tested the air. His cleaning crew had done a stellar job, and once he had her naked and writhing on the sofa where Maisy once napped, he didn't begrudge a cent of the expense.

She made fun of his spaceship posters, though, so he had to teach her a lesson or two about interstellar exploration up against his wall. Undeterred, she moved on to making fun of the solar system place mats on his kitchen table and his bookcase full of second-hand sci-fi. And of his pod-shaped swivel chair, but that didn't work out so well, so she settled for learning her next lesson in his bed.

They came up with separate excuses about skipping Eddie and Magnolia's third Friday cookout, slipping away from Lanigan and meeting at her place, only leaving for a foray to the farmers market the whole weekend.

And then his patience was really rewarded, because Serena suggested an off-schedule Monday happy hour to let their friends in on their relationship. He'd picked up on her nonverbal cues pretty thoroughly by then, so Dillon knew this was her way of telling him she was ready to dive in to their relationship.

He was too distracted to shave properly, so he let the stubble alone, and spent the time instead debating whether to bring a bag with his toothbrush and razor and a change of clothes to the office. But she might want to spend the night at his place instead, so in the end he left it. He could always swing by when their plans were firm.

Speaking of firm. He texted Serena asking which skirt she was wearing, just to rile her up. Only fair to make her squirm, since the one thing not slow about their relationship was how fast he got hard with her. And how she liked it fast, and hard. And slow. Achingly slow. He would use the stubble on Serena, rasp his way up her thighs, soothe the burn with his mouth while he discovered what was under whichever skirt she wore.

Before he left for work, he stuck a condom in his wallet.

Just in case she was wearing one of his favorite skirts.

Serena replied to Dillon's morning text while sitting in the parking lot, checking her appearance in the little visor mirror and mentally running over The Plan.

After breakfast turned to brunch then to lunch over the course of a long lazy Sunday morning, she'd sent Dillon on his way so she could do all the weekend things. Laundry and groceries and mopping the floors. Tying back the little snow pea vines that were already sprouting up all over her trellis. Napping. And she'd banished the idiot grin quite a few times in the process, though each time she then caught herself singing along with her 'Back in the Saddle' extended playlist.

Still, Serena had managed to come up with The Plan. Taking into account his determination to be up front about their status seemed only fair. Besides, it was increasingly difficult to hide it from Janice, or anyone really. So she'd floated the idea of drinks with Janice and Eddie and Jorge after work, which Dillon had quickly approved of. Too quickly? No, didn't matter, he was in with The Plan. And as long as he knew drinks were on the horizon, he would surely be okay with the rest of The Plan. That part she hadn't quite explicated to him, but it wasn't so bad. It was just that they'd be friendly, like usual, and do their jobs, like usual, and maybe have lunch together, which wasn't that usual. And not touch or hug or kiss or play footsie or make eyes at each other or any of those things that weren't exactly usual between coworkers. Not at Lanigan. As far as the mutual touching was concerned, out to lunch was okay, traveling together to a job site was okay, after work was great, and at home was amazing.

Serena took a fortifying breath and reminded herself that Dillon had been fine with going slow. She probably didn't even need to tell him about The Plan. Or if she did, she probably—no, definitely—didn't need to refer to it as The Plan.

It was time to go to work.

By the time they all hit Mudlark's and settled in with a pitcher and a bowl of nuts, Serena wasn't much thinking straight. Oh, not because of The Plan. All of that had gone great. Dillon had been quite gentlemanly, and if she hadn't known better she'd have thought he'd somehow accessed the notes on her phone where she'd, maybe not so wisely, laid it all out. She'd have to delete that.

The problem was Anica. Or herself. Or some sort of intersection between the two of them. She didn't know where the wires had been crossed, because Anica had said quite clearly that Serena was to step up on hospitality and tourism jobs. And if Houston Green didn't fit in that category, she didn't know what did. And even leaving out any issues of power and authority and whether she should have been able to get the feedback directly from the client, Serena's proposed logo was brilliant. It kicked ass, and she knew it. Anica had to know it, too. But if she's stood up for it to the Houston Green people, Serena sure hadn't heard it. Or even heard about it. Instead all Serena got was a barely sensible critique and nothing concrete regarding another direction.

So screw that. Anica must be either testing her or throwing her to the wolves, which amounted to the same thing in practice but varied widely in intent. Trouble was, should she fight Anica to preserve her logo first, or lobby for a clearer definition of her role on this account? Both needed doing. But if this was a deliberate attempt on Anica's part to test Serena's power position, she should go after definition first. If it was instead one of those frustrating times when Anica let pandering to the client overrule her employee's experience about the direction of the job, she should go after her logo's integrity first.

Noticing her distracted sigh, Dillon reached for Serena's hand across the table. "Hey, something wrong?"

Well, that was a warm feeling. Serena smiled gratefully. "I don't know. Well, that's not true—I know something's wrong. Anica's being a tool about my HouGreen logo, which is completely unwarranted. I just don't know if she's dumping on me to see me fight back or if she doesn't know what they want so she's throwing the confusion my way."

Dillon squeezed her hand. "Rough one. What does your gut say?"

She shook her head. "My gut? Is divided. Which frankly is bad for my digestion."

Eddie laughed. Dillon blinked a little, like he'd forgotten their friends were sitting right next to them, and released her hand. She moved it back to her lap and added, "I'm pretty sure it's more to do with her own lack of direction but if I go in guns blazing about the logo and instead she's looking for me to be more assertive about overall issues, she'll ding me on the promotion. I don't think this is one of her little tests, but knowing Anica—well, I just can't be sure."

"I don't suppose you could just ask her which one?" Dillon suggested, but Janice and Eddie shook their heads as quickly as Serena did.

"If she's testing Serena," Janice said, "the last thing Serena should do is mention it."

Eddie nodded in agreement.

Dillon shrugged. "Okay, then, what I said before. Go with your gut. You know the logo is good, and unless she tells you exactly why it's not good, or suitable, whatever, then act the same way you would if there was no promotion in the picture. Pretend it was me in this situation. I'd stand up for my work. Maybe standing up for it would help my future at Lanigan, maybe it wouldn't, but if I knew the work was solid, standing up for it would only show me to good advantage in the end, right?"

Serena closed her mouth double-time. It had temporarily escaped her brain that if—when—she got the full promotion, she would be on the same level as Eddie and Janice, leaving Dillon a ladder-rung below. Maybe she should cool it with the analysis of the best way to achieve her promotion, in case Dillon felt slighted? But, no, then she would be doing some throwback Quiet Little Woman bullshit. She'd gotten this opportunity through her damn good and hard work, and if Dillon, or Jorge for that matter, both of whom were younger, and had less seniority at Lanigan, were bothered by her success, screw them. Dillon should be happy to talk this kind of thing through with her. He said go with her gut, and her gut said not to censor herself. If that was a problem for him, he could just get over it.

She met his clear, friendly gaze and softened a little. It didn't seem, right at that moment, like he had any problems with her at all. Well, then. Good.

"If it helps at all," Eddie said, pulling her gaze away, "I can tell you that Kenzi and Goldman both sent emails this afternoon, and they clearly hadn't collaborated on their responses. They may not have spoken to each other at all. Or read the same bid request to start with, for that matter."

"Really?"

"Really."

Dillon's foot found hers, nudged closer. Their calves intertwined, and Serena smiled. Things were looking better already.

"Thanks, Eddie. That helps a lot." She smiled and refilled her glass, then offered the pitcher round. When Dillon took it from her, he squeezed her hand again.

"Toots?"

Serena looked over at Janice. "Yeah?"

Janice just arched her skinny eyebrows and gazed at her.

"What?"

Dillon laughed. "I have a feeling Janice is alluding to us."

"Us?"

Now his eyebrow raised, too, and something in his expression made Serena blush fiercely.

"Toots! And other Toots! Well, well, well. This is a new scent on the wind."

Serena pulled her eyes off Dillon to take in Janice's smirk. "So, Dillon and I wanted to tell you guys." She faltered. Tell them what? They were dating? A couple? Together? You'd think that somewhere in The Plan would be some sort of definition she could pull out at times like this, but, nope. She'd failed to include that little detail.

Dillon spoke up. "We're seeing each other."

"A lot of each other?" Janice asked, all mock-innocence.

"Hush, you," Serena said, though her blush spoke for itself.

She glanced over at the guys to see how they were taking the news, and tried not to let her heart sink any at Eddie's fairly stunned expression. Jorge was smiling quietly, but Eddie looked gobsmacked. Was it really so unlikely? She was only a few years older than Dillon, and according to her Pros/Cons list, they had a good amount in common.

But then Eddie turned to Dillon. "I didn't think you'd ever go for it. Hang on, I have to send a text to Mags. Damn, I owe her a foot rub now, she was sure you'd get your ass in gear."

"You guys had a bet on us?"

"Hell, yeah. I'll bet Mags on anything. When I win, I get," he glanced up at Serena and Janice, then leered at Dillon, "and when she wins, she gets a foot rub. And she likes my foot rubs. A lot. So she expresses her appreciation. I bet that woman about the sun rising in the east if she wants."

Dillon snorted, but just rolled his eyes.

As Eddie put the phone back in his pocket he added, "But I thought I had this one in the bag. 'It's been weeks,' I told her. 'All he's gonna do is moon over her. Ain't never going to make a move.' But Mags said no, said she had a sixth sense about it. She said that's why you skipped out on burgers on Friday, both of you. And damned if she wasn't right. Good for you, man."

Dillon's head was down as he made himself busy picking the pecans from the nut bowl, barely looking at her, but the tips of his ears were red. Serena was torn between a slightly smug pleasure and a hint of alarm that Eddie and Magnolia had been speculating about them.

Janice pressed for details, some of which Serena shared over the next round, until she was interrupted by Eddie's sing-song, "Serena and Dillon/sitting in a tree/K-I-S-S-I-N-G!" Luckily, Dillon shoved into his shoulder to stop him before it got any worse.

"I just got a text from your wife."

"Yeah?"

"Yeah?" Serena chimed in.

He flashed her a quick grin before reading aloud. "'Does this mean I have to look elsewhere for my Baby Daddy? Be happy, but if you change your mind, you know where to find me.'"

Jorge laughed.

Eddie scowled and snatched the phone from Dillon, grumbling as he read, "You can find her in my bed, that's where you can find her. Except you can't find her there, cause I won't let you look."

"I'm not looking, man."

Eddie's fingers kept flying over the keyboard, heedless.

"Hey, Eddie," Dillon said. He reached for Serena's hand, didn't let go this time. "I'm done looking. I've found."

Dillon lifted a hand in farewell as Jorge, Eddie, and Janice headed off to their respective homes a bit later. That had been fun. Eddie was such a dumbass, really, but Magnolia and he fit together in an unexpected and rather sweet way. It made Eddie's boorishness bearable. He drained his beer and suggested to Serena that they grab some dinner.

She smiled easily at him. "There's a decent Thai place a few blocks from me. I could call in an order and we could get it and eat at my house."

Dillon stood, offering a hand to Serena as she slid out of the booth and into his arms. "I love Thai. How about if I stop at my place, grab a nice bottle of white I have there?"

"And?"

"And, if you don't mind, I could grab a change of clothes, too?" He watched her expression as he made the suggestion. She was a little more skittish than he'd anticipated. Still worried about moving too fast, whatever that really meant. Not like he was packing up his townhouse and putting her address on his driver's license. It seemed normal to him that they'd spend nights together, getting to know this side of their relationship. And the sex was mind-bending. It was only sensible to have as much mind-bending sex as possible.

Serena seemed to agree, anyway, leaning her torso into his, wrapping her arms over his shoulders in a way that did quite excellent things to the press of her breasts against his chest. "Dinner and a sleepover sounds great. You like peanut sauce?"

"Love it."

"Satay? Lab gai? What kind of curry?"

"Perfect. Green curry. And basil rice if they have it."

They walked out to the parking lot, Serena calling in their choices. "It'll be ready in twenty minutes," she said, pausing by her car door. "But it takes less than fifteen to get there."

The woman was amazing. "Oh, we can't have you getting bored. Come here. I'll try to entertain you for at least seven minutes."

She laughed. He loved that low chuckle. He didn't hear it in public very often, so that made it special for him. "Seven minutes in heaven. How very junior high."

"When I get that wine we can play spin the bottle."

"When we get to my bedroom we can play doctor."

He nuzzled the sweet spot below her ear. "I like the way you think."

"Make a good plan and stick with it, I always say."

So that's what they did.

CHAPTER THIRTY-TWO

SERENA WOKE UP HUMMING. It didn't take her long to identify what had stimulated her, and she rolled over to pull herself up tight against Dillon's long frame. He groaned a little and peered at the clock.

"What time do you call this?"

"7:22. Also known as getting up time."

He pulled her head down onto his shoulder and covered his eyes with the other arm. "Getting up time is 8:30."

"Being at work time is nine."

"Yep. Ten minutes to shower and dress, ten to eat an apple and find my crap, ten minutes to drive. Therefore, 8:30."

Serena sat up and took in his rumpled, groggy face. It was clear that he wasn't even joking much. It was pretty damn cute how disgruntled he was. "Okay, your way might work. For you. I don't have any apples, though, so after I'm dressed I'm going to enjoy a cup of tea while I make an omelet with a few fresh herbs, which I will eat while catching the news and checking my email."

Dillon just made a throat noise that could have meant he was impressed with her energy but had no plans to join her, or could have meant he was going back to sleep for an hour and thought she was simply insane. Serena laughed.

"You could try it my way, just this once. You might like it."

He hmmmmed again.

"All right. I'll tell you what. I'm getting up now." She matched actions to words, setting his roving hand firmly aside, "And if you change your mind, I'll be in the shower for the next little bit. Warm, naked, wet, and soapy. But it's your call!"

She was almost out of the shower before he joined her, but that was okay. They had time. Still, it didn't escape her notice that Dillon was rather slumped and monosyllabic as he sat at her kitchen island turning an orange over and over in one hand while she put her electric kettle on and rinsed some fresh-snipped chives. So he wasn't a morning person. Over the weekend it hadn't been an issue—they'd slept in, enjoyed being in bed in the morning, had no schedules to meet. But work was work, work had a start time, and Serena liked to feel fully inhabited in herself before stepping through the doors at Lanigan.

Well, The Plan didn't particularly call for them spending work mornings together. It didn't prohibit it either, but clearly this was something she should consider adding. The morning sex was nice, maybe a little lazy on his part, but was the tiptoeing afterwards worth it? The grimace he hadn't hidden by the time she looked around from putting the morning news show on loud enough to hear over her stove vent made her feel she was violating his mental space.

In case she was being too critical about the fact that he was, after all, disrupting her morning routine as much as she was disrupting his, Serena found a fond smile to send Dillon's way and lifted two mugs off her cup hooks.

"Tea?"

"Eh?"

"Do you want some tea? I have—well, you saw. A hundred flavors."

"Oh, right. I forgot." Dillon headed back to the bedroom, socked feet sliding across the hardwoods.

"Huh." Serena set down his mug and made her own tea, then took a spatula from a paint can on her island. She'd etched two clean paint cans with a swirly abstract pattern that echoed the florals of her curtains. One held a variety of kitchen utensils—spoons, tongs, spatulas, masher—and the other a selection of pens and markers. She kept a couple sizes of sketchpads in one slot of the plate rack, and loved to perch on her cane stool in the afternoons, sipping at a warm mug of licorice tea and drawing. Maybe she should have made time for that over the weekend. Maybe then she wouldn't be so antsy about Dillon's morning moodiness.

He returned, half-lifting a familiar looking jar of coffee crystals at her. She wondered briefly if Joey had ever found his own stash of the stuff, but then dismissed thoughts of her ex and focused on what her present guy was saying. "I'm not normally an instant coffee person, but I read some reviews about this stuff and figured it would be worth a try. You don't even have a coffeemaker, right?" He wrapped himself around her and rested his head on her shoulder as she shook her head, bemused.

"I've heard that's a good brand, actually. And it's fair trade."

"Well, then, it should fit right in if I leave it here. If you don't mind. I should have thought to get apples, too."

Apples? Plural apples?

But he was kissing her neck, and apparently he hadn't thought to pack his razor, either. His stubble scraped her nape and she shivered back into his hold, tension seeping away with each graze of his lips against her shoulders. Maybe she'd been getting a little tetchy herself. Too inflexible about her routine. The Plan could go un-amended, for now.

Finally, to-go mugs in hand, they headed out to their cars, and it didn't even seem that they'd be late. If the beastly light at Shepherd cooperated, anyway. But instead of heading for the curb and his own vehicle, Dillon stopped at her passenger door. When she didn't thumb the remote to unlock his side, he shot her a quizzical half-smile.

"Serena?"

"Dillon?"

"I just know how you'd love to impress the Houston Green people by telling them about your carpool program."

He was serious. It was a joke, but he was serious—he was planning on leaving his car at her place. Which was definitely not part of The Plan. Serena made a point of blinking so as not to be staring incredulous at his seriously expectant expression. She glanced away, then back.

"I'm sure it would be the one thing to tip the scales and make them embrace my logo for the stunning piece of art that it is, but I can't. This afternoon I have to head out to Katy for a meeting, and there's no telling how long it'll take me to navigate I-10 in rush hour. I don't want you to be stranded in the Lanigan parking lot."

"I could just work late."

Serena sure as hell hoped that her cheeks weren't as flushed as they felt. It was a return to the days of the kitten plague. "Natalie and them were going to get plastered tonight. In honor of her freedom from the jerk. Rachel got a sitter for Hannah and everything. So I'll probably be going straight to them from the meeting anyway."

Dillon hid whatever he was thinking and gave a light shrug. "Well, when you have to change the HouGreen logo again, don't blame me, that's all."

He was walking to his car, but turned back to her when she said his name. Even though she'd said it pretty quiet, like a timid-ass mouse or something, which made her mad.

"You're around for lunch?"

"It's Tuesday." Tuesday was his basketball game.

"Oh, right. I forgot."

"But," he lifted his mouth into a half-grin. "Phillip hasn't complained about his knees for days now, so I'm sure he can manage to fill in for me. Maybe tacos? Noon okay?"

Serena set her stuff in the front seat of her car and caught up to him on her lawn. "Tacos is great." Her arms were beginning to feel most at home in the world when they were wrapped around his waist. Her lips, for that matter, had few places they liked better than upon his. "Tacos is perfect."

So despite the luck with the Shepherd light, they were both late to work after all.

CHAPTER THIRTY-THREE

LEFT TO HIS OWN DEVICES, Dillon met Jorge for a coffee after work. As Jorge dumped a calorie-free sweetener into his half-caf latte, Dillon suppressed a grin thinking about Serena's pegging their friend for a no-caffeine-after-dark kind of guy. Though based on her early-to-rise energy, Dillon wondered if Serena ever stayed up too late on a chemical buzz, herself.

Jorge filled him in on the lunchtime game, which had, as usual, ended with the office team slaughtered by the warehouse team. Dillon knew Eddie would have had plenty to say about that, but Jorge didn't report any of the slights. And when Dillon switched topics to wedding plans, Jorge just smiled a little and shrugged. "Bubba's in charge of all that. I'm just supposed to pick our photographer."

Dillon scrutinized his friend. He'd figured Jorge's shyness was a big part of what had put him behind a camera to start with, and as the tension with Eddie proved, he wasn't the greatest at navigating relationships. Dillon had thought about setting up a double-date, but Jorge was so private he'd never brought Bubba to the office. He floated the idea anyway.

Jorge shook his head a little, but smiling. "Are you already looking for ways to escape Serena's clutches?"

"Clutch City, baby." It was one of Houston's nicknames, after a couple of back-to-back NBA championships in the nineties. Good times.

"Well, it's about time you two hooked up. Enjoy it while it lasts."

Dillon clinked his coffee cup against Jorge's in thanks, but couldn't stop himself from asking, "Why 'while it lasts?' It's—I mean, it's early days, but it's going great." He wasn't going to admit to how often he'd been thinking of her just in the few hours since noon. As she'd dropped him off at the office after lunch, she'd said she would text when she was leaving the meeting in Katy. He resisted checking his phone. It was on vibrate. He'd feel it.

"Sure, Serena's a good time. She's a one of my favorite people to hang out with."

Well, that was true for Dillon as well. "So, why?"

Jorge shifted again, this time angling towards him some. "I'm not saying anything bad. Serena is a lot of fun, and I've seen you being interested in her for a while...."

"Everyone keeps saying that," Dillon grumbled.

"Is it untrue?"

"No."

"That's why, then. So, you're together, and that's great. You'll enjoy it while it lasts."

"Okay, I am. We are. But you're saying it like it's doomed to not last. Why can't it last?"

Jorge looked steadily at him. Being shy and awkward in group situations hadn't only meant he gravitated towards his camera. Not participating had also given him a lot of time to watch others interact. A knot in his gut had Dillon worrying that Jorge had noticed something that he'd never paid attention to, himself. Dillon sighed. "Just spit it out."

Jorge nodded, hesitated another moment, then asked, "You love that nephew baby, right?"

"Right. Of course. He's the greatest lump of joy ever. What does that have to do with Serena? The kitten's out of the picture."

"Not the cat. Well, a little bit the cat. You had that cat for, what, a couple of weeks? Making her allergic the whole time?"

Dillon nodded.

"But that whole time, she's swollen with a rash, and she never says a word to you?"

Dillon shook his head.

"Even though—well, we all saw your chemistry. And the way you were eyeing each other at Eddie and Magnolia's place last month. Did you know Janice moved over when y'all came out so she would be sitting between the two of you? We could hardly stop from laughing when you saw you couldn't sit next to Serena."

"Damn."

"Well, it was obvious. Not just on your part, either. But the thing is, even though we could all see that Serena and you were into each other, and you honestly couldn't have been putting out stronger signals, bro. She had to know. But the allergy, and instead of talking to you, trying to figure anything out, what did she do? The easy thing, and avoid you."

"But come on," Dillon argued, ignoring the twinge again and these all-too-clear echoes of his own thoughts, "it's not like she knew what the problem was, or even that the feelings were mutual. Why not be cautious?"

Jorge nodded. "Okay. Cautious. If you're sure that it was caution. I don't mean to make you mad. I just think, you know, you want little Toby to have some cousins someday, even someday soon. You're a settling down kind of guy. And I know Serena's great at the easy thing, the fun thing. You guys should enjoy that. But if y'all get to the hard work, future plans, making accommodations for each other phase, well. I hope you do, and I hope she's more of an in it for the long haul kind of person than I thought."

Dillon didn't know what to say. Not that he felt like unclenching his jaw to say anything.

"I'm sorry. None of my business. Not to mention I'm probably wrong."

Dillon nodded, not meeting Jorge's eyes.

"And you're having a great time, right?"

He nodded again.

"And even if she was a good-times-only type before you came along, well, everyone has that phase. And then they grow up, meet someone worth working for. Why shouldn't that be you?"

And another nod. Dillon sighed and forced a smile. "I'm hella worth it, man. We're good together. Even if you were right, I'm worth it."

Jorge rolled his eyes. "Ego much?"

"I speak only the truth."

"Sure, sure. In that case, did you hear anything more about the location shots for the B&B?"

"They think the ones they had made a decade ago for their original website will work."

"You're shitting me."

"Truth. I'm all about the truth," Dillon laughed, relaxing his jaw and his shoulders. With luck and a little more joking around, maybe his stomach would settle down soon, as well.

"Okay, fess up. What's with the emergency deployment?" Rachel asked, setting the bottles of wine on Natalie's coffee table.

"This is not an emergency deployment," Serena said.

Rachel raised her eyebrow.

"It's not."

"Your message said, and I quote, 'Can we all meet at Natalie's tonight?' And you didn't explain why."

"I wanted to finally have that bonfire of Chris's junk."

"Uh-huh."

"I want to have the bonfire!" Gill added, bringing in a platter with veggies and hummus. "Can we have the bonfire tonight?" she asked Natalie.

"I haven't gathered all his crap up yet," Natalie admitted. "But I'll play Serena's 'boys are dumb-dumb-heads' CD if you want. It's most excellent."

Serena grinned. "See?"

"Proves nothing," Rachel countered. "This has something to do with the new guy."

Serena tried to hide in her glass of wine, but Rachel, on the scent, was not going to give up. Serena loved her, and was grateful she'd agreed to leave Hannah with her neighbor for a couple of hours so they could all get together, but sometimes Rachel's guarded negativity was daunting.

"Okay, okay. It's just—it's nothing. I do want to have the bonfire. Well, when you're ready," she said, turning to Natalie. "Did you run a criminal check on Chris?"

"You're changing the subject," Gillian pointed out.

"What's more important? My maybe-too-fast romantic life or Chris turning out to be in witness protection?"

Natalie laughed a little. "I hadn't considered that one. But I don't think that's it. I ran another background check on him, but nothing's changed. A couple of parking tickets outstanding, nothing funny financially, nada to explain this."

"What about the landlord?" Gill asked. "Did she call you back?"

"She said the rent was paid through May, but she'd call if she needed help marketing it when it was out of contract."

Gillian whistled. "See, paying his rent two months in advance seems like the Chris we know. Frankly, the parking tickets surprise me, just because they're unpaid. Did you use the voodoo doll?"

"No, but thanks. And thanks for this music, Serena, and for getting us together. Even if you clearly have an ulterior motive." Natalie's eyes were sadder than Serena liked. Serena pulled her into a hug, and then laughed.

"I know what we need!"

The others looked at her, expectant.

"Remember when Dad and your mom were about to divorce? We made those fortune tellers to tell us who the perfect men for us would be." Serena turned to Gill and Rachel, "We didn't want to grow up to be like them—well, especially me, since that was already Dad's third divorce and my mom was fighting with my soon-to-be-first-ex-stepdad every time I walked in her door. Natalie showed me how to make a Forever Man chart and we used it so we would know when we were looking at the Real Thing."

Rachel shook her head. "You two give me such hope, as a single mom."

"Oh, you know Hannah's way better off than I am," Serena said. "Even, dare I say it, Sergei is a more stable parent than I ever had."

Rachel just snorted, though Gillian nodded. "It's true. And sartorial choices aside, Yia Yia Depy is really a stellar grandmother."

"She beguiled you with her baklava."

"A baklava-baking grandmother is a stellar grandmother."

"Fine, fine, whatever. I'm somewhat lucky to have her in Hannah's life. But her son is another matter entirely. Now, what are these fortune charts? Sounds like I could use one myself."

"Ditto," Gillian said lightly. Rachel shot her a look, but didn't pursue it. Gill had dates, and second dates, and third dates. And then she would be alone for a couple of months, before starting on the same brief cycle again.

"Okay, get me some paper and a couple of dice," Serena said, reaching for the pack of Prismacolor markers she always carried in her purse.

"You know I just made the whole thing up to cheer you up back then?" Natalie asked, standing anyway to get some paper from her printer.

"And I loved you like a sister for it," Serena said, not entirely honestly. She and Natalie had been stepsisters for barely more than a year when they were about twelve. At that point, between both her parents's remarriages, Serena had already chalked up six transient bedrooms. Even having a stepsister so close to her own age whose mom was scrupulously fair about allowances and new school clothes wasn't enough to overcome Serena's reserve by the time Dad had married Elaine and presented Natalie as the sister she'd never had. (He conveniently forgot that one of the Evil Steptwins from his first remarriage had been a girl. Though perhaps Satan-spawn didn't really have genders.)

"Don't mock. I totally got to trade on having had a mysterious fortune-telling ex-sister well into high school after that Forever Man game," Natalie said, grinning one of her few real grins of the night. Serena barely remembered the classmates Natalie sometimes brought up, although she'd spent most of that year living in Elaine and Natalie's house. It was zoned to a better middle school than was her stepdad Erik's house. She actually had far more memories of Erik than of Elaine. Serena smiled, thinking of him. Poor doomed Erik, who, when he wasn't at business school or fighting with her mom, was always willing to sit with her through a Rockets game, explaining zone defense and pick and roll. He'd insisted that Serena's mom wait until after a long-planned trip to the Summit to see the Rockets defeat the Phoenix during the Western Conference Semifinals before announcing that particular divorce. Not that she'd been either fooled or surprised, but he still ranked as a favorite among her various stepparents.

Natalie's mom, on the other hand, seemed relieved to be rid of her once that marriage had dissolved. They'd all lost touch after Serena and her dad had moved out, but in her second year at UT, there Natalie had been in Serena's marketing seminar. It took a little while for Serena to think back and place her, though she'd apologized with the excuse that she'd had, at that point, six stepparents and one half-brother to her credit. Serena met Elaine again at graduation a couple of years later, and didn't in the least credit her pretense of not remembering Serena. Elaine had never remarried, making Serena the only stepchild she'd ever had. Elaine had unbent in the decade or so since then, but it was still never quite easy when the two met.

And people wondered why Serena was cautious about relationships.

"Okay," she said, taking the copy paper from Natalie and sketching a quick grid. "We fill each column with traits we might be looking for. Then we roll the dice for each column and whatever we get, that's the detail on our own personal perfect mate." She took the markers and wrote 'HAIR' at the top of the first column, then began applying various shades in the boxes below it. "So if you roll a three," she tapped the third row down, "you're looking for a brunette, and can ignore all others."

"Better add bald in there," Rachel said, peering over her shoulder. "Our pool of applicants is getting older each year."

"And maybe purple or green, something dyed," Gillian added, laughing. "Because we're all still young at heart."

"No toupees, I beg of you. I have my standards," Natalie said.

Serena nodded, "Agreed." She finished the hair and moved to the next column, 'EYES,' and drew a quick series of eyeballs down the page. If she lingered a little, perfecting the blue eyes, no one noticed.

"What else? Height?"

"No," Serena said, "I think we assumed he would be tall and handsome regardless. It had occupation, right, Natalie?"

Natalie rolled a pair of dice onto the coffee table and picked up her wine. "Right, jobs, and I think number of siblings, and how much money he made, and of course, what kind of car he had."

"We were very, very deep young women."

"Well, you can substitute the money one with—well, how about what pets he has?" Gillian said with a little glint in her eye.

"You're a funny person."

"She is," Rachel said. "Can you draw pictures for how overbearing his mother might be once you have kids?"

"No need," Natalie said. "These guys will be our perfect mates. That means they'll be all the mother-in-law buffer we need."

"Put in how he is in bed," Gillian offered.

"Um...I kind of hope that's not an issue," Rachel said.

Serena held up a quick staying palm. "It's okay, I got this." She wrote 'SEXYTIMES' at the top of the last column, and filled the row with pictures of a fire, an angel, a rainbow, a lightning bolt, a rocket ship, and a tiger.

"Bravo!" Rachel applauded. "I want three rolls for that column."

"Okay, me first," Natalie said. "Let's see who I can replace the amazing disappearing Chris with." A few rolls later, she nodded, satisfied with her pet-free, black-haired, black-eyed, sports-car driving tiger of a banker.

"I know three guys like that," Gillian offered, "but not one of them has five siblings."

"Are you sure?" Natalie asked. "Check around. I'm forgetting what Chris looks like already. Rowr!"

Rachel and Serena exchanged pleased glances. It was as cheerful as Natalie had yet been about Chris. "My turn!" Rachel grinned, reaching for the die. "Isn't Sergei going to be surprised when Hannah has a new—let's see—brown-headed, green-eyed papa who...what is that?" She tapped the picture of an apple in the first space.

"It's an apple. For the teacher. Or a farmer. Or a grocer. It's versatile," Serena explained. The dollar sign for Natalie's banker was versatile, too, but if she wanted a banker, so be it.

"Or a cider distiller?" Rachel asked ominously.

Too late, Serena remembered that Sergei's newest job was with a brewpub that made, among other things, its own cider. And he had green eyes.

"Never mind, there are plenty of other things the apple could mean," Gillian assured her, keeping the peace for once. "William Tell, Johnny Appleseed, mayor of New York."

Rachel harumphed, but kept rolling. Serena hoped Sergei hadn't recently bought an SUV or a snake, either one.

Gillian's perfect man was a bald, hamster-owning, ball-playing, angel lover, which was an image that befuddled them all. And Serena scored the blue eyes and the pencil that could easily mean copywriter, while commenting, "Oops, a dog owner with a motorcycle? Not Dillon, then, alas."

"Why do you look a little relieved?" Rachel asked, suspicious as always.

"I'm not relieved."

"You are, a little."

"She's relieved about the pencil," Gillian said.

"And the rocket ship," Natalie smirked.

"Hey, hands off Dillon's rocket ship," Serena said. "That baby's all mine."

"So why are you tossing dice with us instead of blasting off to the moon tonight, then?" Rachel asked. Serena shook her head. Her fortune teller hadn't been the total distraction she'd hoped for after all.

"I told you, I wanted to burn Chris's old t-shirts."

"Sure, because an effigy is totally as much fun as blast off. Look, I have to go get Hannah from Mary Lynn's in about thirteen minutes, so enough with the evasions, Serena, what's the problem?"

Serena sighed. "You are relentless."

"One of the many reasons you love me. Spill."

"It's not a big deal. And I really did want to see you all. But he spent the night last night, and this morning made one of those not-really-a-joke jokes about carpooling to work. So, I claimed I was going to be getting drunk with you tonight and not available for any more rocket ship fun times today."

"Today?" Gillian jumped in. "Any more *today*?"

Serena really hoped she wasn't blushing as much as her warm cheeks suggested. She bit her lip. "I was late for work, and you guys know how I hate being late for work. I figured this way I'd make it to work on time tomorrow. So I said about drinks, and then I had to fix the lie, because blah blah whatever you're going to tell me about communication, Gillian, and don't pretend you weren't, so thanks all of you for getting sloshed on short notice." She clinked her wine glass against the other three before draining it. "See, not a big deal."

"Sure, for those of us having rocket ship fun times every morning," Rachel agreed. "Oh, wait, that's only you. And you did lie. And I am happy to be a party to it, because now I know about Gill's bald ballplayer, but remember that whatever speech Gill is about to give you after I leave is right, you are starting something new here and starting out with the little lies doesn't exactly spell happily ever after for you two."

"Wait, who said anything about happily ever after?"

Natalie reached for her wrist and squeezed it. "You want happily ever after, remember? That's why we call it a Forever Man game. That's why we got you a house with room for a spouse and even a baby?"

"Even if I do—and that is not why I got my house, for the record—it doesn't mean I want him moving in after the second weekend together."

"So tell him that," Gillian said. "Go on, Rachel, we've got this," she added, accepting her kiss as Rachel made the good-bye rounds. "Dillon sounds like a reasonable guy. Tell him you don't want him to move too fast, enjoy the whole spaceship thing, and when he gets a dog, make sure it's trained to stay off your furniture, because if it sheds on your upholstery you're going to be irritated."

Serena knew they were right. She'd even tried to protect herself by talking to Dillon about going too fast when they were at the Italian place. And she didn't need Gillian's lecture about open communication to know that she'd handled that morning badly. She helped herself to more crudités and sank into Natalie's plush sofa. "Fine. I'll go with the dang flow and not get my back up about his pacing. Besides, have I mentioned that I could have rolled every number for that Sexytimes column and not been exaggerating?"

"Go, Rocket Man," Natalie said. "You're a lucky woman."

"Your tiger is out there, Natalie. I know he is. I'll help you find him," Gillian said. "And if you end up with a client who needs space for his giant hamster habitat in his new home, give me a call, will you?"

Serena pulled them both close beside her on the sofa and dropped her head back, smiling to the core. "Whatever else you want to say about me, at least I have the best friends ever."

CHAPTER THIRTY-FOUR

"DID YOU SEE THIS?" Dillon stood in Serena's office door, a printout thrust towards her. Her heart jumped a bit, which she attributed to surprise at seeing him so suddenly (so gorgeously; the bristle was back, the hair was mussed, the blue ocean eyes were just a little narrowed) in her office door. It was the first time she'd seen him in a couple of days, and they'd only been able to spend one night together the previous weekend, and damn but she'd been thinking about him a lot. She wondered if his mouth would taste of apples and coffee, then stopped herself and reached for the paper he held.

Wednesday, April 1, 9:07 AM
From: Emily Wright
To: Dillon Hamilton, Serena Colby
CC: Anica Sands
Re: Workplace Relationships
Hello, Dillon and Serena,

It has come to my attention that the two of you may have a personal relationship that goes beyond the parameters of mere friendship.

In accordance with the workplace harassment seminar you both attended on Monday, March 30, and due to Serena's position of authority over Dillon, it is my duty to inform you that Dillon is required to provide a written statement about his subservience to Serena and affirming that he has entered into this relationship of his own accord and not because he was coerced in any way. In addition, Serena must provide a written statement guaranteeing that she will not use her working authority over others to promote or favor Dillon due to any personal, as opposed to professional, accomplishments he may have engaged in with her.

Please provide these statements to me by lunchtime today via return email.

Thank you,
Emily Wright
Head of Human Resources
Lanigan Printing and Advertising

Serena scanned, reread, turned to her own computer to see the same message there, then looked across at Dillon, who'd sat in her guest chair.

"I don't remember anything along those lines from her seminar," he said.

"No." Serena thought it over, and also remembered the conversation with Janice over smoothies. "There's definitely no rule against dating. Definitely. But is there some sort of disclosure rule we didn't know about?"

Dillon shrugged. "I don't remember anything like that."

She looked back at her screen, double-clicking to open the full message in front of her. And then she saw it. "Come here," she gestured, then when he was leaning over her (a whiff of soap, and one of coffee), right clicked on Emily's name to open the address properties. "He changed his outgoing name, but not his reply-to address."

It was Eddie. Dillon closed his eyes and muttered, "Idiot," before moving back a little to perch on the edge of her desk. Serena felt deliciously trapped between his body and the wall, and swiveled so her shoulder met his leg. "It's even April Fool's Day, and I didn't suspect him for a second." He ran a hand through his hair then let it rest on the edge of the desk over hers.

She grinned. "So now we'd better reply."

He grinned back.

In the end, she wrote that her outside relationship with Dillon showed that he worked very well in group situations and that he had an admirable attention to detail, but that she'd known about those qualities before they'd begun their "intensely personal" relationship and it would not therefore be the reason she was recommending he be the one to accompany her on an overnight trip to the Blue Capri B&B instead of Eddie from Sales, who, yes, got the account to start with, but who wouldn't be nearly so good at pleasing the customer, if her experience was anything to go by.

Dillon's reply was, "I've been engaged in a long-standing affair with a superior's wife for months now, and we are hoping to have a child together soon. Since this is likely to hurt my standing with management, I started a relationship with Serena to balance out my chances of advancement. She's not coercing me, but I am willing to use whatever HR language you can provide to ensure that this all works out in my favor."

He hit 'send' on his phone, and Serena did on her desktop, and they sat back and waited for Eddie's explosion.

"So. Galveston?"

Serena nodded. "I do need to do a site visit. And it would make so very much sense if I was there for the breakfast part of their bed and breakfast."

"Not to mention the bed part."

"Well, I want to be thorough."

"Sure. You're very dedicated."

"Gotta show Anica how capable I am of directing the entire course of the project."

"Eddie would just get in the way of that. Whereas I could be inspired by the décor, the atmosphere, the location. My copy would be so evocative, so winning. Blue Capri would be impressed."

"And here at Lanigan Printing and Advertising," Serena said, taking a furtive moment to lay her cheek against his thigh and look up at him, "our mission is to impress our clients."

Dillon inhaled deeply, but didn't banter back, caught up in gazing into her grey eyes, noting the way her breath stirred the air against his trousers. The easiest thing in the universe would be to shift over a little, arrange it so he straddled her, that mouth of hers breathing on his inner thigh. Higher. Sweet glossy peach lips opening for him, tongue darting forward.

Serena licked her lips and he moaned softly. She closed her eyes briefly and reluctantly—it was reluctantly, wasn't it?—lifted her head away from the hard tense muscle of his leg. She looked at his thigh, followed the line up to the bulge of his crotch, which jumped visibly as she gazed. She smiled. His moan was a little less soft.

"Well, I'm going to get a hell of a lot done today," he muttered, standing up.

"Same here, Rocket Man," she grumbled back.

Double-take. "You—who? Rocket Man?"

"Never mind. Irrelevant. Lunch?"

Dillon moved back to the safety of her office door. "Lunch. Definitely lunch." With a fierce grin that probably told her too much of the wolfish desires he had for lunchtime, he headed back to his own desk. There was a stickie note from Eddie on his monitor. "Dumbass." Dillon laughed, made a two-point shot with it, and tried to get through a few items on his to-do list without thinking about Serena and his cock.

The next days were smooth. Friendly. Fun. Funny. They caught a Rockets-Lakers game on Dillon's big screen TV, and by special request Serena wore her #34 jersey. Sometime in the final quarter she lost her bra. Dillon figured he could close his eyes at any moment for the rest of his life and picture the globes of her breasts glimpsed through the armholes, her nipples puckering beneath the thin polyester mesh as she sat beside him, his right arm hooked over her shoulder. Then moving, her barely-clad backside nestled against his crotch, his hands roaming her thighs, stomach, chest. His chin over her shoulder, drawing his gaze away from the fast breaks on the screen to memorize the peaks getting tighter and tighter as they were abraded by the fabric. The Lakers were playing rough, but by then they were, too. Maybe Serena caught a few moments as he held her hips, lifting her then pulling her gorgeous ass back as he thrust into her, her hands braced on his knees and her back arched and her toes pointed to the floor and she rode him and he stretched his legs apart to further open her up to his full hard length as maybe people cheered LA's win from the sound system but all he could hear was his heart pounding in the rhythm of her name over and over and over.

There were other nights, at her place, at his. Out with friends. Yes, even carpooling, and the first time she suggested it Dillon felt a tiny moment of triumph he tried hard not to show. Of course she noticed, but she just laughed and admitted what he'd already guessed: that first morning, she'd invented plans with her friends because she was a little freaked by how fast they'd been moving.

They were still moving fast. Well, not fast for him, but he suspected fast for her.

She was handling it, though. No more instructions about not racing ahead of her pace. An expectation that they'd have lunch together unless one of them was off-site or sweating with coworkers. A weekend of indoctrination during which she actually sat through hours of Ridley Scott movies with him, although she refused any *Star Trek* movies with the wrong-headed notion that she already knew through cultural osmosis everything she'd ever need to know about it, or *Star Wars* either.

"Come on, that can't be true. These are vast worlds and complex franchises we're talking about here."

"Uh-huh."

"Rich backstories. Narrative arcs that stretch over decades. A hierarchy of excellence. You can't know everything. Which Star Fleet Captain is the best?"

"Jon-Luc Picard. Because Kirk is a sexist and Janeway—well, I can't remember why not Janeway. But I know there is a Janeway, so there."

"Picard likes Shakespeare."

"Another good reason he's the best. Make it so."

Dillon whistled. "You've never watched any of it?"

She shrugged. "Never say never. I must have seen a bit in the dorms, or at least parodies on *The Simpsons*, but no, I never watched the shows. I would recognize either a Jedi or a Vulcan if I saw one on the street, and also whatever kind of creatures those little fuzzy Chewbaccas are, so I'm good."

"Just when I thought you were too good to be true," Dillon laughed. "I come to find out that you can't tell a Wookie from an Ewok. This is seriously depressing."

She stole a handful of his fries. "Don't put me on a pedestal, Rocket Man. I'll just fall off and skin my knee."

"I'll kiss it better. You're never going to tell me why you call me that, are you?"

"Because you like science fiction, of course."

"So, it's an insult?"

Serena's look was not entirely appropriate for their public setting. "Nope."

He arched an eyebrow at her, but she just turned her attention to the window boxes outside the restaurant. "It looks like it'll be a good year for bluebonnets."

"Oh, that reminds me. It's Tobias's second-month birthday this week."

"Bluebonnets remind you of your nephew?"

"Well, his eyes are awesomely blue, you'll see when you meet him."

"Chip off the old block," she said, studying his own blue eyes for a happy moment. "But why the wildflowers?"

"On Saturday, if the weather's still good, they're wanting to drive out to Washington County to get a picture of the baby in the fields." There were several grassy roadside areas and pastures along the freeway from Houston to the Texas Hill Country that were regularly seeded with the state flower. People flocked to them with their spring-dressed kids to pose in the picturesque expanses of blue and green, and since Justin had decided a passel of new camera equipment was vital to his role as Toby's father, he wasn't going to let anything so iconic pass him by. "I said I'd go with so I can take some family photos, and we're going to stop at Big Daddy's BBQ for lunch. Do you want to come?"

It was a brief pause. Hardly noticeable, if he hadn't seen her fork freeze midair. Damn. He pretended not to see, and she pretended to take a little long to swallow her bite of salad, and he just waited for her answer.

"Saturday?"

"Yep," he aimed for casual. "Toby's been napping late mornings, so the idea is to set off around ten, ten-thirty, let him sleep in the car. Shannon's trying to get the whole routine of getting out of the house down, but her timing is still imprecise."

Serena nodded. "I can imagine. Rachel said the other day how amazing it was to take Hannah out to dinner with only the items she already had in her purse. Of course, her purse is a bottomless pit of crackers and toy cars and wipes, but it was still a triumph."

"I'll tell Justin and Shannon there's still hope. Or you can. What do you say, are you up for a good sliced brisket sandwich and some baby blues?"

"It sounds like I'd be crowding them. All of us in the car together, and they've never met me. I can just go to the farmers market and meet you at your place afterwards. I'll make you one of my famous salads."

Don't push, Dillon cautioned himself. "They offered. They want to meet you. But if you'd rather not, it's no problem. You'd be missing some amazing barbecue, though, just so you know."

After a moment, Serena squared her shoulders, and nodded. "Make it so."

CHAPTER THIRTY-FIVE

Serena changed clothes more times than she had the night they'd gone out for their first dinner. Bloody bloody ridiculous—she was who she was, and if Dillon's family didn't like her, no well-matched accessories were going to make it better. Besides, if they didn't like her, they could go jump in a lake. Well, not the baby. He was allowed to dislike her all he wanted.

She paused, two white t-shirts in her hands. What if the baby disliked her? She put back the silk tee and pulled on the cotton one with the scalloped edge. If he spat up on her after a furious spate of crying because she exuded some sort of anti-Toby vibes, at least she could wash it.

Once again, she tried to talk herself into feeling that this whole 'meet the family' thing wasn't happening too soon. It helped if she timed their relationship from the night at Eddie's, instead of after the kitten revelation. Kitten! She diverted to her medicine cabinet to take an antihistamine, just in case its dander was on the car seat or anything.

She called Natalie for moral support.

"First of all, they'll love you. Second of all, the baby is no judge of character. Third of all, I thought these guys were his friends as much as his family, right?"

"Right," Serena admitted.

"So it's the same as us meeting Dillon, which, by the way, you need to arrange. And fourth of all, I'm in the middle of showing a house and I can hear them coming back downstairs, so relax, go have fun, and don't call me again."

"Oops."

"Yeah, yeah. Love you. Relax. Bye."

Natalie hung up before Serena could properly apologize, so she typed out a quick text and took a deep cleansing breath. Wildflowers and roadside barbecue. Nothing to stress over. No need to jump half out of her skin when Dillon rang the doorbell.

"Hey, lovely," he said, scruffy in the best way with jeans and a French blue t-shirt that made his eyes practically glow. "Ready?"

Wow. Just the sight of him was insanely calming. This was an interesting development. She leaned in for a quick—maybe not all that quick—kiss, and headed out to the SUV where his family awaited them.

Okay, Serena admitted to herself, Justin and Shannon and even baby Tobias were great. They'd offered her the front seat, Shannon taking the entirely understandable stance that she wasn't going to be able to stare at Toby's every movement during this first long car ride of his life if she wasn't next to him, and Dillon promising that if it was too cramped for his long legs, he'd kick the back of her seat the whole way in retaliation. Justin was a bit of a hottie, all broad and California in a way that Dillon and his sister weren't, despite them all having grown up there. She could picture him, or at least a slightly younger version of him, playing beach volleyball. Shannon was more like Dillon—lean, with strong features and even darker hair than his.

"So Toby is one of those spitting-image-of-his-dad kind of babies, then?" she asked, half-turning to address both parents as Justin put the car onto the freeway out of town.

"Justin thinks his eyes will stay bluer, like mine, but a lot of infants have blue eyes. If they go brown, I'll hardly be able to tell his baby pics from Justin's."

"Hey, I didn't come out that big. That's on you Hamiltons."

"I was only nine pounds. Dillon was the hefty one."

"Yo," Dillon said. "I was adorable. Just because I weighed as much at six as you did at eleven is no reason to call me names."

Serena laughed. "Oh, I hope there are pictures."

"There are," Shannon promised. "Play your cards right, because I've got them all."

Dillon reached across Toby to tug at his sister's hair. "You are not allowed to show my baby pictures to my girlfriend. You shouldn't even still have them. Why isn't that one of the boxes you left behind when I took over your townhouse?"

Girlfriend?

Okay. Girlfriend. There was no reason for that to be a bad word. It even made sense. Dillon was her boyfriend. Hey, y'all, this is my boyfriend, Dillon. Don't call him Rocket Man to his face or I'll eviscerate you. Sure. That sounded okay. Serena forced herself to relax and engage with the conversation. Justin launched into a long and sinful story about the machinations of a co-worker that seemed almost too calculated to relax her and ease the potential awkwardness of a longish car ride with strangers. Dillon had said his brother-in-law's emotional intelligence was off the charts, so maybe Serena was watching for it, but she was still impressed. And grateful.

Toby wriggle-fussed a little as they approached the first group of cars pulled to the verge. Families moved *en masse* towards the biggest clumps of the bright blue flowers.

"It's a little crowded here," Justin said. "Want me to go on a bit further?"

"He's going to wake in five minutes."

"Okay, but further, or stop?"

Serena looked back at Shannon. She wasn't looking up from the baby at all. Justin had tensed up his shoulders. She'd seen it before: every decision about what to do with every minute of a newborn's life was vital to some parents.

"We just passed Hempstead, right?" she asked. Justin nodded. "Jorge told me there's a field near Chappell Hill, probably not fifteen minutes from here. There's a big section of bluebonnets, and another part with mixed wildflowers—Indian paintbrush, blanketflowers, buttercups. Do you think Toby will be okay that far?"

Justin waited, silent. Shannon studied her son; Serena and Dillon studied Shannon. They were already past anywhere reasonable to stop, so Serena guessed the answer, but was almost as relieved as Justin seemed to be when she said that Jorge's field sounded perfect.

"He took his fiancé out there for a photo shoot last week. They're kind of precious. And I'm sure Toby will look even better, since he's the cutest baby in the world."

"I like this woman," Shannon said.

"Agreed," Justin agreed. "Where do I go?"

"Turn right on FM 1155. There's a traffic light so you can't miss it. Then it's just past the Chamber of Commerce but before the historic hotel on Main Street."

Justin almost giggled. "You Texans are so damn adorable."

"Y'all sure are, little lady," Dillon drawled from behind her.

Serena whipped around to give Dillon a pointed look, and caught Shannon pinching his ear. He grimaced and slumped a little, jamming his knees into the back of her chair. "Fine, fine, no accent. You've made your point."

"Mockery is a low form of humor, little brother," Shannon sang in a soothing voice, head bent over Toby's car seat. Dillon instantly leaned over the baby and began humming softly, which took the knees out of Serena's back, fortunately.

When the faint wailing started, Justin's shoulders tensed up noticeably. His eyes were on the rearview as much as the road in front of him, and Serena wondered why these people weren't just taking the baby to one of the patches of wildflowers growing in a city park instead. But Rachel and other mom friends of hers had taught her well not to question parent logic, and, besides, they were almost there.

"That's Chappell Hill," she pointed. Justin breathed a sigh of a relief, which did little to ease the fussy-baby tension bearing down on all of them. Serena employed her deep yoga breaths in a silly attempt to spread calm throughout the car. She'd have laughed aloud at herself if she weren't worried it would upset the baby, and, therefore, every adult member of his family.

"Turn here," she said quietly. "That's the one. Looks like there's parking past that gate." The field was every bit as photogenic as promised. Large swathes of bluebonnets, a few lone oaks dotted around, and a white split-rail fence enclosing it all for the full countryside effect. And there were only three other cars parked by its side.

Justin whooshed out a lungful as he put the car in park. Shannon was already unbuckling the infant carrier straps, and when everyone else got out of the SUV, she was settling Tobias on her breast.

"He likes a snack when he wakes up," Justin told her. He opened the back hatch to set up a changing station.

"Let's take a walk," Dillon said, grabbing her hand. "Kiddo snacks for twenty minutes at least."

Serena smiled and off they went.

It was a perfect day. Seven fluffy clouds in an otherwise expansive blue sky, temperate, and that something fresh and green in the air that didn't really happen in the middle of a city, Houston Green and its campaign notwithstanding. Serena's honey-lavender scent fit right in with everything else soothing to his senses: the faint breeze, her cool hand in his, and the colors of the flowers.

On the ride up, Shannon had given him her big-sister look of approval behind Serena's back, not that he was surprised. And Justin liked her because he liked her. Well, not because Dillon liked her, precisely, but because he approved of the way Dillon was about Serena. He'd made up his mind when Dillon had asked to bring Serena along today.

"She'd be up for hours hanging out with a baby and your sister?" he'd asked.

"I think so. I'll ask her. I just wanted to clear it with you guys first."

"Dillon, if you want her there, I want her there. You—well, you want us to meet her, and I'm glad. Good for you." Justin had a way about him. Toby had lucked out in the paternal department. Maternal, too, of course, but Dillon had known Shannon all his life. He couldn't read Justin the same way, and didn't know where everything was coming from. That slight uncertainty meant Dillon was often watching Justin for his reaction, and when it was positive, Dillon felt it.

"What do you think of them?" he asked Serena now. "They like you. Is it too much for you? Do you need me to find the one taxi this town has and send you back to Houston to escape us all?"

She laughed. "Somehow, I'm not so sure Chappell Hill has even the one taxi. I could always hitchhike if I get desperate. Plenty of guys in ball caps and pickup trucks passing by."

"Not a chance I'm giving you up to one of those guys. I guess you're stuck with me."

She halted, pulling their clasped hands around so he was circling her waist. Her other arm smoothed across his chest as she leaned into him. "Well, I'd best to make the best of it then, Boyfriend Dillon."

Uh-oh. He eyed her. He'd slipped that in while she was facing forward, so he couldn't see her reaction. It had been deliberate. Dillon was trying to not count her tiny hesitations and delayed reactions when he talked about their relationship, or plans, or being public together. Saying 'girlfriend' when she wasn't facing him gave her the time to adjust unobserved.

But she'd just called him 'boyfriend,' and her tone was teasing rather than displeased, and Dillon pressed her closer.

"Okay, Girlfriend Serena, what is your version of making the best of it?"

In answer, her fingers raked into his hair and their lips met and the sun was shining and birds were twittering and all was right with the world.

Walking back, Serena kept looking at the flowers, enchanted. She'd done the photos in bluebonnets thing a few times over her thirty years. Not too often with her mom, but periodically with her dad and whichever wife he had at the time.

"Dad and Flan brought us out every year after Jonas was born," she told Dillon.

"Flan?"

"Fran! Fran. Jonas's mom is Fran. I can't believe I still do that—bad holdover from a bad joke. Mom and I found her a little...uninspiring."

He snatched up her hand and kissed it. "Clearly. Now I'm worried about what you call me behind my back. Chillin'? Willin'? I am willing, you know."

"Stop leering. I was a teenager. It was practically the law that I give my steps insulting nicknames." Poor Flan. She was the only one Serena still saw regularly, since she made a point to get together with her young half-brother every few months. She wondered if Jonas was still dragged out here every spring now that he was a teenager. She wondered if Fran still had some of those old photos of them on display—her sullen college-age self holding the squirming toddler still long enough for an in-focus shot, or the earlier one when she'd allowed Fran to color-coordinate them and she held baby Jonas upright and an opportune butterfly had helped Dad catch their delighted smiles. Probably Fran kept that one up, at least.

Dillon was running her hand down his torso. "Want to see how willing I am?"

"Your sister is right there," she protested, although, really, they were a ways away still. "Besides, they have to be insulting nicknames. Like if I switched the 'i' for a 'u' or something."

Narrow-eyed, he tugged her to him. "You're going to pay for that."

"It was just an example."

"Right," he drew out the word, clearly contemplating retaliation. Serena scrambled for a diversion, and, even though she felt the tiniest bit silly, pulled the digital out of her bag.

"Hey, go lean against that fence post," she directed. She'd only half-planned to take photos of him, but he was beautiful in the setting, and all these memories were getting to her some. He caught her gist right away, but instead of censure his eyes lit up, pleased. And why shouldn't they? Nothing wrong with a girlfriend taking a picture of her gorgeous boyfriend. His soft blue shirt and jeans delineated all of the muscles she adored, the hues playing tag with the blues of the sky and blooms. The white fence was a strong line in her frame, and he was smiling just a perfect half-smile as he regarded her steadily. The breeze kicked up a notch, ruffling his dark hair, and Serena nearly forgot to hit the shutter button, he was so beguiling standing there.

"Now you," Dillon surprised her, approaching fast while she was still studying the image on her screen.

"I refuse to fuss with my hair like a girly-girl," she said, surrendering the camera, "but wait until I touch up my lip gloss. It feels like it all disappeared."

Dillon bared predatory teeth and snatched a kiss before she could get the gloss on. "I like the color your lips are now. They're the same shade as your nipples when I've been kissing them."

Dear lord, where was that breeze when she needed it? She shot a quick glance towards the SUV, but they were still well out of range of his family. Defiantly she used the gloss, and smoothed back her hair as she walked to the fence. She hitched herself up onto the highest rail, pulled a half-turned, leaning back pose that sent her breasts skyward. Dillon shook his head at her grin and took a couple of quick shots as he stalked towards her.

"Are you trying to get us rolling around in this field?"

"I'm sure that wouldn't scar the baby for life or anything."

He grabbed her off the fence and plastered her body to his, holding out the camera at arm's length. "Smile, funny girl."

She kissed him instead, but he took the photo regardless.

"It's a damn good thing I didn't pack condoms for a day trip with my sister," Dillon growled into her ear, making her both shiver and giggle. "If I had half a chance to get you alone right now I would be indulging in some very bad behavior."

It was wisest, all things considered, not to mention the contents of her purse.

CHAPTER THIRTY-SIX

"YOU NEVER ANSWERED MY QUESTION," Dillon said later, as they waved off Shannon's family and went into his townhouse.

They'd managed to behave like sensible, mature adults for the rest of the afternoon. Toby had been relatively cooperative about the photos, and once Justin's fancy lenses were in play, they'd gotten lots of shots of various groupings. Mostly Toby with one or several adults, but a few of Dillon and Serena together (behaving maturely and sensibly), and even the two of them with the baby. That had felt strange, to say the least, but Justin had been so matter-of-fact about it that Serena had just dropped to the blanket and leaned up against Dillon's knee as instructed. Still, she was glad he'd forgotten the tripod and been unable to take a photo of all five of them. The server at the barbecue joint had obliged with a group shot, but that didn't feel as intimate, somehow.

"What question?"

He pushed her flat against his door, an echo of that allergic kiss but one which made her breathless for such better reasons.

"Do," he nibbled at her neck, "you like," he slid his leg between hers and rocked his thigh at her apex, "my family?" his hands were pulling her breasts from the silk cups of her bra.

Dropping her head against the door, panting, scraping nails up his rib cage as she wrest the shirt off his back, Serena hummed her approval. "I didn't get that taxi, did I?" His chest was right there, slightly salty, ready for her teeth to lay claim to his pecs, and the jeans weren't going to be a barrier for long. "I didn't even pull the condoms out of my bag, that's how much I enjoyed their company."

He groaned. "How dare you?"

"Anticipation, Rocket Man. I don't know if you noticed," she got both of their jeans unbuttoned, her shirt lifted over her head, "but I am really, really ready for you." She stopped the aggressive riding of his thigh long enough to allow him to shove his hand into her panties, his long fingers finding the slick proof while he sucked her always-wanton, eager nipple deep into his mouth. Now she was moaning. She got his jeans lowered, and his erection fit into her hand as if they were made for each other. Yanking her bra off, she shoved him to perch on the back of his sofa.

There it was, the full unfettered length of him, pulsing gently as she gazed. Dillon's hands were circling her waist, but she resisted, bending forward so that she could rub the moist tip of his cock against the aching underside of her breast. She sank lower, pressing her breasts together to make a valley into which he thrust, unhesitating, the head coming closer and closer to her mouth as she lowered her chin to take in the sight of his erection and her taut nipples and her hands on her breasts and his hands covering them.

She licked the head of his shaft as he bucked against her, then arched and threw back her head to give him a clear view, and his eyes burned, the blue of a storm and a raging sea. Dillon chanted her name and hung on as she knelt and licked and circled and sucked. He'd managed to kick off a leg of his jeans and he spread his legs wide, giving her plenty of access to his hard muscled, smooth skinned, fever-hot erection.

She took her time, then didn't, then taunted him by backing off again. "Serena," he moaned, and the tenor of that moan she knew now, knew intimately, and she sucked hard one more time, never letting go of the base of his cock. Then she licked, just the tip, once, twice as he breathed hard and she was breathing hard, too, because his tension was exciting. So exciting. Straightening, arching again, she brought him back to her chest and they both watched her breasts bouncing while she pumped his thick hard erection, and with a final cry of her name, Dillon came over her breasts. She held him, stroked him as the fluid traveled up and out, coating her hand so she could spread it to her nipples which peaked even more tightly in the cool wet air.

"Serena," Dillon whispered again, the only thing he'd said for ages now, a dozen variations of her name on his lips. His lips, which grazed the top of her head, then lower, lower, as he shifted off the back of the sofa and joined her on the floor, barely past the entry way of his home, but a thousand miles from the first time they'd been there together. Her heart tugged at the way he said her name. It was a little scary, that tug.

"See how well I can manage without a condom?" she asked, smugly, and he growled her name again, and proceeded to show her what he could manage, for his part.

Later, post-condom and stretched across his bed, they lay staring at the ceiling, hands idly wandering up and down each other's arms. Serena traced circles on the inside of his wrist while he proposed various solutions to the problem of dinner when there was no food in the house.

"I'm not super hungry after that brisket."

"No, well. You didn't even finish your potato salad."

"And you didn't even finish your half of the pecan pie."

"I was afraid you'd impale me."

"Impaling is your job."

"Funny girl."

"Funny woman, thank you very much."

"Ma'am, yes, ma'am."

"You can't call me a girl when I'm older than you."

"You can call me a boy."

"Mention C-3PO one more time and I will."

"Hey, you got his name right!" He pulled her hand to his lips and kissed the back, then turned it over and kissed her palm. "And if I get to call you my girlfriend, I also get to call you my girl. Funny girl is but a short leap from there."

"Look before you leap, there, kid." She opened her eyes and propped herself up on her elbows. "This generation gap of ours is beginning to show."

"You're three years older than me."

"I'm a hippie's child. You're a total product of the eighties. It's a significant cultural shift."

"Next you'll be blaming me for Reaganomics."

"You're the one always going on about *Star Wars.*"

"Oh, funny, funny, funny girl."

Serena had no choice but to brain him with a pillow. He inexpertly fended it off, but she somehow still ended up with his long torso pinning her to the bed. Again. It turned out that cheese and crackers and staying in was a perfectly workable plan for the evening meal.

On Sunday, Dillon drove Serena back to her house, but she demurred when he hinted about plans for that day. Keeping his resignation at bay, he contented himself with a few final kisses and headed off to restock his fridge. It gave him some time to take Shannon and Justin's 'Toby is asleep, now we can focus on talking' call, at least.

"She's so nice, hon, I couldn't be happier for you," Shannon started.

"Pretty, too," Justin chimed in. Damn speakerphones.

"Superficial much?" That was Shannon, not as chirpy.

"I only have eyes for my gorgeous wife. Did you hear that guy at Big Daddy's whistle when you came in? He said no way had you just had a baby."

"Sexist pig."

"You like it anyway, and you know it."

Dillon sighed. "You two need me for this conversation?"

"Dunno," Justin said. "You going to tell me what she said about us?"

"Inveterate gossip."

"I am a student of human nature, my friend, and as such I collect impressions to piece together the greater whole."

"The greater asshole."

"That was a cheap shot," Shannon said, "and nonsense to boot. What did she say about us?"

"Serena liked you guys a lot. Of course, she didn't see this side of you. I'm sure she'll change her mind once I fill her in, start giving you the cold shoulder."

"Hey. Be nice. I had a baby two months ago and I'm shedding hormones left and right. The littlest thing could send me down the rabbit hole."

"I love you, Shannon," Dillon and Justin both said at the same time.

She laughed. "Couple of idiots."

"Idiots who love you. Okay, here's the full scoop. Serena thinks Toby is gorgeous, of course, and I suspect she thinks Justin is, too, but she didn't come right out and say it. Fortunately. Gross. She said Justin was funny and could tell why he was so good with people, and that Shannon was amazingly on top of things for being such a new mom, and smart, and beautiful, and strong, and loving, and the best person she'd ever met, hands down."

"I'm going to hang up on you now."

"Well, don't be such gossips. Obviously she liked you guys, who wouldn't? And she was impressed with your organization. Have you uploaded the photos yet?"

Justin was happily diverted by talking about his camera angles and Dillon let him ramble on a bit before plunging in with his own question.

"What did you really think of Serena?"

"We told you," Shannon started.

"Yes, nice, pretty," Dillon mocked. "She's got a lot more to her than that."

"We guessed as much when we almost had to send out a search party for you when Toby was done nursing," Shannon said. She did nothing to hide the smirk in her voice.

"Really, big sis? You want to actually discuss my sex life?"

"God no, don't be disgusting."

"Okay, good, because I would hate to remind you that I was only sixteen and you and Justin were far from subtle about disappearing into Mom and Dad's shower together."

"Stop it. I do not want to discuss your sex life, I promise. I'm happy to pretend that you're still a virgin."

Dillon laughed. "Okay, I'll pretend the same about you, despite Tobias looking a tiny bit like Justin."

"Fine. Sex is off the table."

"Wait, not quite," Justin put in.

"Dude," Dillon started at the same time as Shannon clearly slapped at his chest on the other end of the line.

"No, stop it. Not that. Dillon. And I don't want details. I just want to say this. I get that you two have chemistry—we all get that you two have chemistry, horndog—but I just want you to remember that no matter how long you've known Serena, you've only been dating for a few weeks. Just be careful not to confuse that chemistry with deeper feelings. You want to stay smart."

Dillon took a slow, deep breath. No point yelling at Justin when he was only saying what Serena herself had said. Never mind that he was being as careful as he could be not to push her. "Okay thanks, I hear you. No proposal, not this week, at least."

"Proposal?" Shannon gasped.

"No proposal. I said no proposal."

"But—sweetie, you're not even thinking about that, are you?"

"Why wouldn't I be interested in it? I mean, someday. Why date her if I'm not serious? You said you liked her. You said she could be The One."

"Of course we like her," Justin put in, and Dillon could practically see the warning look he was giving Shannon. "She's smart and nice and very easy-going, to spend the day with us like that. And pretty, of course. You've picked a good one, dude, and we hope to get to know her better as the months progress."

"Right. That's right," Shannon said.

Dillon took his time responding. "Okay. Good then. Thanks."

"Don't think we don't like her," Shannon said, more earnest now.

"I don't. Thanks. Look, guys, I've got to go put these groceries away, I'll talk to you soon. Kiss Toby for me."

"Right. Bye, dude."

"We love you, Dillon," Shannon said.

"Love you, too. Thanks. Bye." Dillon sat for a moment, thinking over the conversation. He knew Shannon's voice almost too well. Never mind that she'd been way younger than he was now, still in college and recently not only orphaned but stuck with guardianship of her teenage brother when she and Justin fused at the hip, never to budge again. She was still warning him about moving too fast, and Serena was warning him about moving too fast, and given half a chance, Justin and Jorge and probably friggin' Emily from HR would warn him about moving too fast. It was frankly pissing him off more than a little that he apparently couldn't be trusted to know his own mind and his own heart and to know how to navigate his own love life.

If he wanted to fall in love with Serena Colby, no one, not even Serena herself, was allowed to stop him.

Chapter Thirty-Seven

"You are so full of bull honkey," Janice said, *sotto voce*, never mind that they were in the middle of Monday's production meeting.

Serena narrowed her eyes at her.

"All he did was walk past the door and your head popped up like a prairie dog to track him," Janice whispered. "Do not tell me this is casual."

Serena deliberately looked away from the door—which, okay, maybe she had been keeping an eye out, but she hadn't seen Dillon since he'd dropped her at home the morning before—and from Janice's impudent smirk. Anica was finishing her rundown of the work in progress and it was just about time for Serena's update on Blue Capri.

Right. Meeting mode. She passed out a project workplan, highlighting the areas of immediate importance. "They promised a firm decision on the colors by early next week, so you'll be able to get the cardstock order in pretty soon. I know some of these are long lead times, but they understand that. They're focused on the copy—you can see from their current site and brochure," she tapped page two of her workplan, "Mrs. Kirby has sort of the opposite of a way with words. Dillon and I will go down next week so he can work up some room and breakfast descriptions and I can talk her through a few design options." Serena went on about tie-ins to other historic homes and community events, steadfastly ignoring the way Janice nudged her knee under the table. She texted Dillon once she was secluded in her office again.

MONDAY 2:48 PM: If you see Janice smirking at you, tell her to stuff it.
Meeting?
Y. She's on about the B&B trip. Practically waggled her eyebrows at me in front of A & them.
Want me to take her down?
Nice. You're such a boy.

TUESDAY 9:08 AM: On for lunch today?
It's Tues.
?
Tuesday
Oh. You have to go play with your balls, right.
Funny girl
Don't start with me. Save all that aggro for Miguel
Pretty sure we'll beat them this time.
No comment.
Funny, funny girl.

TUESDAY 3:00 PM: **Guess who's the best point guard at Lanigan?**
You don't say?
I don't say. The words will never pass my lips. If it gets back to Ida, I'm dead, and if I'm dead, you're dead, funny girl.
You'd better have some good ideas to ensure my silence, then.
…What say I show you my attic tonight?

WEDNESDAY 11:44 AM: Janice is making me jog at lunch today.
Didn't you tell her you got enough cardio last night?
Funny man. No. I told her it was getting too hot out for lunch runs.
Hey, can I borrow your car at lunch then?
You better not be getting burritos without me, boyfriend.
On my sacred honor, no. ;)
Is that a winky face? You're winky facing me?
Just a typo.
You can have the car then. Janice is here. Keys in the middle drawer. Where are you going?
Found this place on Westheimer with organic sheets
Oh
Is that okay?

WEDNESDAY 12:55 PM: **You there? You okay about the sheets?**
Yeah! Buy local!
I did. There wasn't a whiff of corporate about the place
Good then.

WEDNESDAY 4:02 PM: I'm working late
I've got stuff to do, no rush
You can go on home
We drove in. I take your car home, then what's you plan?
Sorry forgot.
We carpooled every day this week
I know
I'll wait until you're ready then
Thx
Don't you even want to know what color sheets I got?

THURSDAY 3:19 PM: We should stay at mine tonight
I'm out of shirts at yours—let's stay at mine

No. I have to make the salad for Eddie's tmrw, need to stay at
mine.
Plus that way you can avoid my organic sheets longer
Don't be weird. I'm not avoiding.
Weird?
Whatever. Don't you have that aubergine shirt in the closet?
Is that the dark purple-looking one?
Y
It's smoky from Natalie's Chris burning
Well we'll do laundry then
Had to happen sometime
Domesticity?
Domestic bliss, baby.
Funny man.

Between Johnnie's puerile jokes, Eddie's obvious nudge-nudge
wink-winks at the sight of Dillon and Serena arriving together, and
the fact that Jorge had declined his invitation to show up, Dillon
found Eddie's back patio less than engaging at burger night.
Serena clearly had no time for anyone other than Magnolia, not
that he could blame her. Even Mags was having trouble
containing Eddie in the midst of this particular group of yahoos.
Eddie and Johnnie failed to bring the best out of one another.
Which, okay, is probably why Jorge had bailed.

When Serena finally gathered up a couple of empties and
headed inside to get more beer, Dillon didn't even try to hide that
he rose to follow her.

Dropping the bottles into recycling, Dillon cornered Serena up
against the kitchen counter. "You know, I have this one huge
regret in life."

"Yeah? What's that then?" she smiled wide, grey eyes sparking
as they held his.

"Last time we were in here, I didn't kiss the hell out of you."

"Last time we were in here, I was allergic to you."

"I still wanted to kiss the hell out of you. Besides, I cured you
of that."

Serena's hands traced patterns up and down Dillon's spine as he leaned in closer to her. "Ah-choo."

"Funny girl."

"Funny woman."

"Right, funny Mrs. Robinson. Stop making jokes and kiss the hell out of me, please, ma'am."

"You are on thin ice, buddy."

"Mmmm. Ice. Don't give me ideas," Dillon said, leaning towards the cooler for a moment before Serena laughed and tugged him upright and damn if she didn't kiss the hell out of him at least twice before Eddie came looking for them to offer up a heated defense of his beer can chicken.

For once, Dillon was the first one awake on Saturday morning. He rolled up onto an elbow to look at the light playing with Serena's face as she slept. One thing about being at the house instead of his townhouse, the mornings came with bird chirps, and no matter what time the neighbors got going, the rumble of their garage doors never penetrated his sleeping brain. Plus she had an eastern exposure window, which may have had something to do with her early to rise habits, but it let a golden light in through the wood slats of the blinds that did some pretty captivating things to the strands of her glossy brown hair.

Dillon smiled softly, then broke into a grin at his mushiness. He did balance his thoughts about Serena's beauty and the depth of their connection with ones about how fucking hot she was and a bit of chest-beating posturing that his ability to satisfy her was a mark of his extreme manliness. All in an entirely post-feminist way, of course.

He decided to let her sleep, no matter how his cock twitched at the thought of tracing the paths of the slatted sun down her torso. They'd talked of hitting the farmers market later on and he wanted to try finishing up a freelance project first. If the edits on a geophysical services company's annual report was more enticing than waking Serena with a dozen kisses or so, Dillon thought, he'd clearly gone mad. But editing first meant more hours hand-in-hand looking at vegetables, so his less and less latent romantic side would be happy.

After putting the kettle on to boil for coffee and her tea when she woke up, Dillon pulled his laptop from his messenger bag and looked around the kitchen. Serena always sat at the breakfast bar, but from the living room window he could watch the leaves fluttering in the wind like the neo-poet he was clearly turning into. Also he could see the front porch railing where she'd once perched, daringly opening her thighs to let him see up her skirt with the neighbors none the wiser, so it was manly, too.

Still grinning, Dillon moved a little table from beside the sofa over to the window and set up his laptop, then grabbed a dining chair along with his coffee. He was a good fifteen pages into the document by the time Serena came in, her freshly showered lavender scent overpowering the remains of his coffee.

"Morning, gorgeous," he turned to her. "You slept for ages. I must have tired you out while sating my raging lust for you."

"Hi," she said, but quietly, and she didn't bend down for a kiss. "What are you up to?"

"Editing this Schwartz Geo thing. Super fascinating, but I was hoping to get it out of the way before we go to the market. I can leave it until later if you're ready now. Just let me grab a shower."

"No, no rush."

But she pulled away from the arm he'd hooked around her waist, and Dillon still hadn't gotten a kiss. He turned to look at her, and found her looking around the room. "What's up?"

"You could do that in the kitchen. Or the dining table."

"I like it here. I like the view."

"But the kitchen is all set up for working at the island. Those stools are really comfortable."

"I know they are. But I wanted to sit by the window." Something about the conversation was screwy. "Is it not okay if I sit in the living room?"

"No, sure, if you want. The sofa, or that chair," Serena nodded her chin at a Victorian-style armchair she'd covered with a Pop Art inspired print. "You can see outside from that chair."

"Serena." She didn't look at him until Dillon said her name again. "Hey, Serena, as far as I can tell, you're telling me to sit anywhere but where I am. Is that right?"

She tried a smile that didn't quite convince him. "I just like my furniture to stay where I put it."

"Well, unless it's *Beauty and the Beast* furniture, or you have poltergeists, I'm guessing that's not really a problem." Levity didn't even begin to lighten her mood, which in turn tightened the muscles between his shoulder blades.

"No, but you moved it."

"It's not forever. Look, let's go to the market and when we get back, you can make me one of those infamous salads and I'll finish this editing and then put the furniture back." Not that he couldn't finish it now, given half an hour and the end of this odd discussion, but her pulling back made him want to push in return.

"Couldn't you just move it back now? And work at the dining table later?"

"Couldn't I just leave it where it is for a few more hours?" he countered. Okay, it was getting inane, a battle of wills when no one had called for one, but come on. He hadn't broken anything. It would take two minutes to put it all back where it started, and she'd never know he'd been in the room.

Which maybe was too much the point.

"Serena, what is the real problem here? I'm honestly trying to figure it out. This isn't really about furniture, is it?"

"I just like things to look the way I put them. What's wrong with that? There are perfectly good places to set up your laptop with the layout how I had it."

"But I'll put it all back this afternoon. I'm not trying to move my grandmother's big oak desk into your living room. I just want to type for an hour or so while admiring your yard."

"But that's not where things go. I'm sorry, look, Dillon, I'm not explaining it well, but it really matters to me that everything is a certain way. I know it's idiotic, or you think it is, but I just—I need it like that. So could you please put the table and chair back and work in the kitchen?" Serena could barely look at him. Or maybe it was that she could barely look away from the offending table.

He tried to control his tone. "I'm sure I'm not getting some deeper meaning here that I should, but the thing is, I don't want to work in the kitchen. I want to work here. I want to leave the computer right there while we go shopping then come back and have it still be there, and put it all back when I'm done. I get that the floor plan is important to you for whatever reason, but ultimately it's not going to change. Can't you just leave it for now?"

Serena looked torn, but she didn't waver. Dillon was beginning to feel aliens writhing in his gut. The damn blueprints in her head, the physical ones and those to do with her vision of their relationship. She either didn't know what to say or was opting to keep her words to herself.

"Fine," he said, and no longer worried about his tone. "I get it. The temporary accommodation of your boyfriend, his comfort for a few scant hours, that's not as important as your floor plan. Your idea of how the house should look is more essential than what I want. Well, Serena, that's just fine. No words necessary. Message received."

Dillon strode halfway to the kitchen, then turned and walked back to grab his coffee cup so he could put it in the sink. God forbid he be a rude houseguest, since guest status was clearly all he would ever be allowed to claim.

She hadn't budged.

"Dillon, wait. No. Don't...it's not what you're saying. I just— I'm having trouble explaining. I have rules, that's all. About my house, about how I like it. I put a lot into making it this way, and I mean, listen, it's not just you. I don't like anything changed. Even Hannah knows not to move things around at Aunt Serena's house."

He just stared at her. "Hannah? Hannah who is, what, one? Two? Serena, I'm not a toddler. You're supposed to make rules like that for toddlers, they're incapable of reason. But I have news for you, in case all the fucking hadn't clued you in. I'm an adult. *We* are adults. We're capable of having—supposed to be capable of having—a conversation. A conversation, which implies the ability to see things from each other's point of view. To consider what each other want, and even to want to...." Dillon slumped his shoulders on a rush of breath. "To want, Serena, to accommodate each other's point of view. At least, that's what I think a conversation should be, especially between people who love each other."

Serena's breath rushed in as fast as Dillon's had expelled. "Did we say that?"

Dillon's frustration warred with a sad chill. He kept his gaze locked on Serena's as he shook his head. "No. No. We did not." Then he dropped his eyes down, the burl of the hardwoods sharp after a couple of blinks. "Okay, maybe I'm reading too much into everything. I thought we were in accord. I thought you'd seen the way it was for me, and felt the same. But maybe I'm the only one in this conversation. I'm the one following your rules, buying cruelty-free shampoo, sleeping whichever place you choose, doing it all your way." He looked up again, met her silent eyes, took in the lean of her torso away from his. "But your way just doesn't include falling in love, does it? It sure as hell doesn't include opening up your house to me, much less opening your heart. If I fit in the edges, if I don't disrupt anything and follow your lead, we're okay."

He shot a quick glance at Serena's perfectly still face. It gave him no answers, so he went on. "You said it was so easy to be with me, Serena, but did you wonder why? Did you think how I was working my ass off to make it easy for you? Did you think how I saw how skittish you were about all of this, you with your plans and rules, and maybe think how I'm working damn hard to show you that it's not as scary as you think for us to be together, to look at a future maybe? A future when I might—God, Serena," Dillon stopped himself. He closed his eyes, and shut up, and shut down. He knew damn well this next part wasn't included in Serena's vision of things, and pretty much knew how that was going to go over.

He shook his head and said it anyway. "A future where I might want a table by your window, Serena?" he asked quietly. "Had you thought of that?"

Deliberately, Dillon picked up the chair and returned it to the dining room, putting it perfectly in line with the others at her table. Serena hadn't moved from her spot in the living room, so he skirted her silent form before shoving his laptop in the messenger bag he'd dropped on her sofa earlier, and walked to the door.

He turned, looking at her for a few moments before sighing. From the beginning, she hadn't moved. "I'll see you at work," Dillon said, picking his keys out of the bowl on the hall table. He walked out, leaving the little side table exactly where he'd left it next to the window.

CHAPTER THIRTY-EIGHT

SHE WAS CRYING. Standing upright in the middle of her living room, soundless, but the tears kept escaping down her cheeks. Which was stupid, crying, that wasn't going to fix anything.

What kind of asshole tells her he loves her and then just walks out? It was ridiculous. He wouldn't listen to her explanation about the furniture, which, let's not forget, he moved without asking or apologizing or moving it back when she asked. And then he said he loved her. And then he proved that he was just trying to manipulate her by walking out, because if he really loved her, he wouldn't go around accusing her of not letting him into her heart or whatever, he would stick around to talk about it.

Serena wiped the tears and forced them to stop falling. Stupid to cry when he was a jerk. Had he seriously just left? She went to the window to confirm, and yes, his car was gone. Fine, then, he could just get on with his life and she'd get on with hers. When he calmed down and apologized for walking out, for moving her stuff, then they'd talk. Probably he'd call within an hour anyway, or just show up that evening to watch the playoff game. Well, maybe she wouldn't even be around. She had a life to get on with, too. She went to the kitchen to make her solitary breakfast, free from his teasing about her not-at-all-too-elaborate preparations, thanks very much. If she wanted to harvest some sage and mint for a batch of sun tea, that was entirely her right, and he shouldn't have anything to say about it.

Except she didn't want to get near the mint bed just at the moment.

Fine, hot tea would suit her just as well. Serena went to the stovetop and lifted the kettle, only to find that it was still hot and filled with enough water for her tea. And she knew Dillon had done it deliberately, thinking of her while she slept. Suddenly she didn't feel like making anything, and sat slowly on the island stool. Her back was to the living room, but she'd swear she could feel the out-of-place side table like a physical ache. The table, and the man no longer sitting at it. It was all messed up. Serena gave in to her tears.

And even after zombie-ing out for at least an hour, Dillon hadn't called or come back over.

The Rockets won. She was curled on her side of the sofa for the whole game, watching the Trail Blazer fans becoming more dejected by the quarter, and never before had she felt such empathy for the other side.

Natalie had agreed to clear her schedule for a Sunday brunch in honor of her thirtieth birthday, even turning an afternoon open house over to an associate so she wouldn't have to rush off. It was a hard-won victory, and Serena, Gillian, and Rachel had taken it in turns to ensure she didn't reneg at the last minute.

After a very long and not terribly restful night, Serena did her best to put her party face on. She'd kept her phone next to her all night, but Dillon never called, never texted, nothing. An email had binged into her inbox after two in the morning, and Serena had the phone in her hand pressing the email icon practically before she'd opened her eyes. Stupid spam. And no matter how many times she'd hit refresh, nothing came in from Dillon. She'd almost hurled the thing across the room at that point, but if she had, she knew she'd be getting up to retrieve it after ten minutes, and she had to try to sleep some. Even though she couldn't get comfortable. And his pillow smelled like him.

It wasn't like this was the first time they'd slept apart since they'd started dating.

It was just that she wasn't sure when they'd sleep together again.

Now she was going to this brunch, and she was going to pretend that the reason Dillon wasn't with her was that she'd chosen to not bring him in deference to Natalie's still broken heart. Unless he showed up unannounced. He did know about it. But Serena figured that was as likely as Chris showing up— Natalie's mysteriously disappearing ex had known about it, too, but after a month of total radio silence, it was beyond improbable that the guy would reemerge with a birthday card, ready to party.

"See you at work," she muttered to herself while she fastened the necklace Natalie had given her for her own thirtieth. "Not if I see you first, buddy." How could he have gone twenty-four hours without contacting her at all? Not exactly her definition of a man in love.

Not that she wanted him to be in love with her.

Fine, let him go off-radar. Knowing Dillon, he was thinking about the things he'd said and how he hadn't been willing to listen to her and how he'd dropped that ridiculous bombshell and then walked out. By Monday he'd be embarrassed and apologetic, and Serena would make sure he knew how childish he'd been before she forgave him. That's what she got for dating a younger man.

And on her way out to brunch, she barely glanced at the empty space under the window and didn't picture him sitting there for more than a second or two.

"Hey, sweetie," Rachel kissed her hello and let Serena lift Hannah from her hip. "Where's Rocket Man?"

"Halfway to the moon, I suppose," Serena smiled as brightly as possible. "I didn't want to bum Natalie out."

"Oh, she'd be fine," Rachel said. "Is he busy with something else? Give him a call. We have twenty minutes before everyone shows up."

"Twenty? Crap, I'm later than I expected. Oh, sorry," she added, belatedly trapping Hannah's ears between her shoulder and her spare hand. "I mean, darn it. I meant to be here earlier to help you unload. Did you already get it all inside?"

"No, I have a couple more trips. You hang in here with my little Banana Monkey and Gill and I will get the rest. Call Dillon." He'd finally met them all when Natalie had held the ritual burning of Chris's possessions in Serena's back yard, to make it easier to transfer the ashes to her compost pile. "May as well feed it to the worms while we're at it," she'd said, which had certainly pleased Gillian's more vicious tendencies. Dillon had made himself scarce after pouring wine for everyone, so he'd passed muster, but they all still called him Rocket Man more often than not.

Serena nodded noncommittally at Rachel and turned to the first box of decorations. "What do you say, Hannah Banana? Shall we put some of these pretties on the tables for Aunt Natalie's party? Here, you take these flowers," she gave her a few rose petals, "and I'll take these ones, and we can put them all around." Together they distributed the blush and yellow petals until the first guest arrived.

Of course it was Natalie's mother Elaine. "I wanted to be sure you girls didn't need my help with anything. It looks very pretty. I guess you got on just fine without me," she said, only a little stilted.

"Lovely to see you, Elaine," Gillian said smoothly. "Did I tell you what Natalie said when we planned this brunch? About how you always put so much work into her birthdays when she was a child, that it was so special that you got to just attend and have fun for once instead of having to be in charge? Let's put your purse over here, at the head table next to Natalie's spot."

Rachel rolled her eyes at Serena under cover of turning to check on Hannah, and Serena let out a little grin. Fortunately a couple of Natalie's coworkers showed up then, allowing Serena to escape the forced pleasantries with Elaine while she greeted them and showed off the photo montages of Natalie she'd compiled. Serena had tapped Gillian to be the one to get Natalie's childhood photos from Elaine, but the half-dozen shots of Serena and Natalie at twelve that Elaine had included had likely been an olive branch of sorts. At the very least it was in line with Elaine's determination to be scrupulously, if ostentatiously, fair at all times.

Either way, it had been nice to see those photos. Over the years of her friendship with Natalie, Serena had reconstructed a lot of those months of stepsisterhood, thanks to Natalie's more vivid memories. Her dad wasn't great at hanging on to photos of his kids, and it wasn't the first time she'd turned to a former stepmother for pictures of herself at an earlier age. It was nice to anchor the specific carpets and windows and sofas of Natalie's mom's house in her memories.

Dillon had laughed at the pictures, especially the one of her and Natalie on the first day of school, pretending to fight over which of the matching backpacks was their own. Serena had that one in the same frame as one of the two of them in college, on either side of the cute dork of a boy that neither had admitted they'd both liked.

Serena checked her phone again—nothing—and stashed it hastily as Natalie arrived to cheers and hugs and laughter. Rachel tried to corner her when she caught Serena looking for messages again ten minutes later, but she hedged by cooing over Hannah, which was always enough to get Rachel off the track of whatever pessimistic thing she was thinking.

The brunch was an unqualified success. And Natalie introduced her mollified mom to everyone as the main reason for her success and strength, which didn't stop Elaine from speechifying: "I just have to thank you three for making such a special event for my dear daughter. It's so nice that she has friends like you, willing to do all the work her family is used to doing." Serena even succumbed to Elaine's hug. It was only when she half-turned to exchange a glance with a tall dark-haired guy out of her peripheral vision and realized that, of course, he wasn't Dillon, that she felt something akin to wishing she had her own mommy there, instead of this frequently bitter and always unbending former stepmother.

As it was a day for ex-steps, and she still hadn't heard from Dillon, she called Fran after brunch. They determined that yes, there was some random PG movie that Jonas would consent to seeing with his ancient half-sister. Serena had an hour or so to kill, but she didn't give in to the impulse to go by her place to see if Dillon had shown up. Or to his place to see if he wanted to go with her to the mystical-quest-laden flick. Even though it was a fantasy adventure and bound to be a lot more fun for him than for her. She was doing it for Jonas, because the kid deserved to know his sister even if she was an old lady and probably way too boring to spend much time with. At least he should feel free to text her and maybe get a little spoiled by her. Just enough for some bragging rights with his friends. She wasn't going to buy him booze or porn or anything, but at some point in his life as a teenage boy there had to be something cool about having an adult sister. When he figured out what that was, Serena planned to be in close enough contact with him to allow him to ask for it. Dillon's stories about Justin treating him like an adult instead of a grouchy monosyllabic newbie orphan had impressed that much on her, at least.

And damn her twice over for every three seconds thinking about Dillon. It was like an addiction, or an infection, the way he wouldn't get out of her head. She wanted to tell him about Elaine, and sound him out for things to discuss with Jonas, and sit in the sunshine with him.

Except she didn't.

She wanted to do all of that without reference to him. She didn't want to have wanted him to taste the restaurant's egg strata. So he'd have loved it, so what? He could go get egg strata any damn time he wanted, he didn't need her to find the best damn egg strata in the city on his behalf.

And the fact that she'd bought the restaurant's cookbook didn't mean she was planning to make it for him, either. Just as soon as he apologized. And as soon as she forgave him.

She happened to like egg strata in her own right, and Dillon had nothing to do with it.

CHAPTER THIRTY-NINE

MONDAY PARKING LOT: Dillon's car, but no sign of Dillon.

Monday production meeting: no sighting through the doorway.

Monday lunchtime: no sighting in the lunchroom or out by the basketball net. Not that she went out there on purpose to look. It was just on the way to her car and she'd decided she wanted to go out for tacos instead of eating the salad she'd brought. Noted: his car, unmoved in the parking lot.

Monday right after lunch: overheard rumor that Dillon was over with Philip's group working on some revisions to one of their projects.

Monday mid-afternoon: Almost half an hour spent composing an email about meeting for drinks after work. Should have been the easiest thing in the world, except Dillon still owed her an apology, and no way was she going to word it so that he would think it meant she was apologizing to him. She went back and forth several times before unclicking the 'read request' box.

Monday at five till five: still no sighting, and no reply. Third double-check that the message actually was sent. He was such a child. Pouting? Really? The silent treatment? Honestly? Well, she wasn't going to go chasing him. She'd made an overture, taken the first step, built a bridge. All he had to do was respond, and then they could talk about his overreactions and his running away after dropping ridiculous bombshells and all of the things he'd stirred up. She was the mature one, and perfectly willing to engage in a dialogue to resolve their issues. It wasn't like she was going to abandon ship at the first sign of a problem like some people. Gillian had accused her of that a few years ago with a guy who'd pulled a stupid amount of passive-aggressive BS. Gill had told Serena that she was running away instead of calling him on it and seeing if there was something to salvage. And maybe she'd been right. Serena was younger then. Kind of like Dillon now. Didn't change the fact that that guy had been too much of a tool anyway, but Serena had listened to Gill, had learned. She was too smart to do the same thing now, not when Dillon had so many other good qualities. Gillian would have nothing to reproach her about, if Serena told her about all of this. Which she only hadn't done because she was sure it would all be sorted out soon.

Monday at ten past five, on her way to her car: incoming email chime on her phone. Serena was dignified, so instead of grabbing her phone right away she waited until she was sitting in her car.

It wasn't even from him. She turned to glare over at Dillon's car, which was sitting innocently a few spaces away, as if it had nothing to do with not showing up at her house since Saturday morning. Unfortunately, its owner caught the force of her glare as he approached his car's passenger side. Dillon stopped almost comically mid-stride, then went ahead and beeped open his doors. Serena could feel her eyes widen like an idiot as he opened the door, but regained her composure somewhat when he turned away only long enough to sling his bag into the passenger seat. By the time he'd slammed the door and walked towards her, she was positively neutral.

Dillon was mad.

Serena had clearly been avoiding him all day. He'd gotten to work early, hoping to catch her in the parking lot, but she hadn't even glanced his way when she pulled in seconds before nine. She'd managed to be behind closed doors all morning, and when he went looking for her at lunchtime, Janice said (all too damn innocently for his tastes) that she'd gone to the fridge and stared at her salad—her salad, which was right next to his own lunch bag—before saying something about tacos and leaving. Only the curt email about going to Frijoles indicated that she knew he was alive. And then she hustled out to her car without waiting for him to stop by her office, as had become their habit. Or maybe it was just his habit. His going out of his way for her, again. His putting himself in her orbit, playing by her rules, obeying her directives. Avoiding him all day, then asking him to go to a crowded happy hour where, like as not, other people from Lanigan would also be grabbing drinks and nachos?

Well, maybe it was past damn time for him to have some rules, too.

"No," Dillon told her when she lowered her window.

"Excuse me?" Oh, she looked haughty. He wasn't swayed.

"No, I won't go for drinks with half our coworkers. You've been avoiding me all day, you haven't called, nothing. I love you, Serena, but I'm not going to let you take me for granted like that. I'm going home now. You are more than welcome to join me. Ball's in your court, but the game can only go on for so long."

She hadn't answered, and wasn't doing anything more than narrowing her eyes at her steering wheel, so Dillon carried through with his resolve, and walked away.

Monday, quarter past five: Sighted, Dillon yelling at her about love, middle of the parking lot. Definitely Johnnie and Emily overheard, maybe Colleen, too. And okay, probably he wouldn't classify it as yelling. She'd heard him yelling—at games; at Eddie once during a whole Jorge, Sr. prank; that time he slammed his fingers in the car door. But his "I love you, Serena," wasn't in subtle tones, and the hell did he mean, she'd been avoiding him all day? He was the one who'd been in hiding, the one who'd walked out because she expected a little common courtesy in her own home.

The one who walked away from her again just now.

Serena concentrated hard on drawing a deep calming breath, especially after she found herself rubbing irritably at her neck. Right where the rash from the cat used to show up. Maybe that had been prescience rather than farce after all—maybe she should have taken the hint and just stayed away from Dillon from the beginning.

With a sigh, Serena put her car into drive and followed as Dillon turned out of the parking lot, towards his home.

CHAPTER FORTY

"FOR THE RECORD, I THOUGHT you were the one avoiding me," Serena said when they met at his front door. "I just wanted to see you, and thought maybe Frijoles would be a neutral location. I wasn't trying to put you off by suggesting it." She hoped her face was calm and her voice not as pleading as it sounded to her ears. She had no need to plead. She wasn't the one who'd walked out, she reminded herself.

Dillon let them in without comment and went about his after-work routine of shedding and putting away things. Serena had slipped out of her shoes and headed into his kitchen to get them drinks before she pulled up short with the realization that she, too, had an after-work routine at his place. Since when had they even been together long enough for her to develop routines? She put the beers back in the fridge and walked back to the living room.

Dillon looked up from the shelves crammed full of the sci-fi paperbacks he picked up at used bookstores every chance he got. He glanced briefly at her hands but didn't comment about her lack of beverages. "Do you want to sit down?"

So formal. Okay, then. She slipped past the sofa and took his 'Ikea version of futuristic' arm chair instead. Dillon gave her a hint of a sardonic look, but just tensed his jaw and sat right down in his usual spot.

Serena resisted the urge to sit on her too-fiddly hands and met Dillon's eyes. "I wasn't avoiding you," she repeated.

"So you said."

"Okay, so we're clear. I looked for you, and I checked for messages from you, and you were the one who disappeared."

Dillon shook his head. "Okay, look, I didn't disappear. We just missed each other. It happens, and I'm not going to go back and parse every second to figure it out. It's not even relevant."

Oh, he got to decide what was relevant now, did he? Interesting. So much for her using her own brain. Serena supposed she could just turn over all of the thinking to the man in this relationship, as she was clearly not competent to know her own mind or what was important to her own happiness.

"I suppose you'd like to tell me what is relevant? If it's not too difficult for me to comprehend, of course."

"Oh, come on, Serena, you know that's not what I mean."

"Do I? Well, of course, if you say so. You are the judge of what I know and what I need to know and what is important. Do you have a list of the topics I should consider, Dillon, or should I just wait for you to introduce them one by one? I don't want to get confused or anything."

"Great. Great, fantastic, you're being very reasonable and rational. This is just how I hoped we could talk," Dillon snapped.

"Oh, dear. Am I doing it wrong? I must have misplaced my Girlfriend's Guidelines for Proper Conversational Etiquette, my deepest apologies."

"No, no, my apologies. I violated Serena's Relationship Rules by being honest about my feelings and what I want. We can't have that. Everything has to go according to your plan, no matter what, and I dared to forget that the worst thing in your world would be you changing the tiniest bit to make room for me in your life."

Dillon stood up and paced back to the bookshelf then spun to face her.

Serena ignored whatever the pressure in her chest was encouraging her to do in the way of protesting or smoothing things out, and sat straighter in the chair. If he wanted to accuse her of things, she'd just sit and listen and let him have his say. That's what she was there for, apparently, but certainly not to concede any points or give any ground. She reminded herself that he still hadn't apologized for walking out on Saturday, or in the parking lot, either, and raised her chin to look straight at him.

"I never said anything about rules or plans." Which might not have been strictly true. "I never said we couldn't make changes for each other." That was true. She was sure of that. "I just asked you to put my furniture back, and you reacted by getting emotional and storming out and not talking to me for two days. I had to make excuses for you at Natalie's birthday yesterday, and her mom was just smirking at me, I could feel it, but I did it anyway, because apparently I am that person, now, who covers for her boyfriend's immature behavior by lying to her best friends."

He winced, which was something.

"So if it's allowed to be talked about, can you maybe clarify what the hell you meant by disappearing?"

He was back to glaring. "I told you, I didn't disappear."

"Not today. Well, today, in the parking lot, actually, yes," Serena found herself advancing on him, without realizing she'd stood up. "It was the same thing. You got mad, spouted some emotional stuff, and drove off without giving me a chance to reply. That's bullshit, Dillon, you can't just drop a bomb like that and storm off and act like I'm the one who is behaving badly. It's not fair and it's not mature and it's not what we said we were about. We were about having fun and being friends and fireworks and not rushing it and then you went and," Serena stopped and turned away. She wouldn't—would not—mention the love thing.

She tried to focus on the pod-like chair, to lighten her mood by imagining Dillon pretending to command a spaceship as he sat in it playing video games. All she could picture was his face breaking into laughter when they'd tried to figure out the logistics of making love in that chair, so she shut down her imagination, reminded herself that Dillon was behaving like a petulant child, and swiveled to face him again. "You changed the rules."

"So, you admit there are rules," he said, flat and quiet.

She threw up her hands. "Not like a rule book. But you can't agree that we're on one path and then suddenly say we're on another path and get mad when I don't agree."

"I'm not mad that you don't agree, Serena. You want to know why I'm mad? It's not because of the table, either. You think it's because of the table, but you want to know why? It's because you think that you're the only one who can have ideas about our relationship. It's because you think that there's one path that's just sex and friendship and an entirely separate path that's deeper, that's love and making a future, yes, a future—no, let me say it," Dillon shook his head fast when she started to speak, and went on in his low relentless tone, "a deliberate future, a place we go together, a place where you, apparently, don't want to go.

"But those paths, Serena? They aren't two different paths. The first one leads directly to the second one, and maybe I rushed ahead of you a little, but you know what? You're not as far behind me as you think. You know I love you. You know exactly how that happened, because you have been right there with me every step of the way on this path, Serena, you know you have. And you can pretend that I'm violating some grand idea of yours about our relationship, but all it really is, all it comes down to as far as I can tell, is that I know I've been heading to this part of the path all along, and you're trying to pretend that you're not. So refuse to face your feelings if you have to, Serena, but don't you dare stop me from feeling my own." He shook his head again. "Just don't you even try."

CHAPTER FORTY-ONE

DILLON SANK BACK DOWN on his sofa, dropping his head into his hands. He swore to himself he wouldn't let her see that his arms were trembling. He heard her move, and knew it was too much to hope that she'd sit down beside him. Sure enough, when he looked up she was perched on the coffee table, way down at the end furthest from him.

At least her voice had lost the sarcastic edge, when she finally spoke. "I never tried to deny your feelings."

After a moment's consideration, he sighed. "I suppose you didn't, no."

"That doesn't mean I agree with you," she said.

What could he do but try to laugh? "No, I got that."

She echoed his sigh. "Look, I will think about what you said. But I'm mad, too, Dillon. I'm mad that you're not willing to give me time to adjust. I'm mad that you keep pushing then walking away, like you just don't want to hear my response. If we weren't at your house right now, I don't even know if you'd have bothered to say all you did say, instead of leaving again after telling me I didn't know what the important things to talk about were."

"Don't go back there."

"Fine, right, okay. You didn't mean to say that. But that's my point. You're mad and you're saying, well, some volatile things, and then you're walking away. I shouldn't have to follow you or provoke you or corner you in your den to get you to talk this stuff out."

He couldn't help but glance at his front door, and might have stopped himself from muttering, "Speaking of walking away." But he didn't.

Serena's whole torso twitched as if prodded. "That was a different time for us. I thought we'd dealt with it."

"Yeah, maybe. Maybe not, though. Maybe I'm still not all that fine with the way you ran off and didn't tell me why, not until I figured it out on my own. Sure, yeah, I understand it now, but face it, Serena, your gut reaction there wasn't exactly about communication and honesty, was it?"

She glanced at the door herself. "I suppose you can read it that way."

"Well, tell me how else I'm supposed to read it then! So far when things have come up between us, you've either gone all ostrich on me or come up with a seventeen point plan to keep me in my place. So don't accuse me of walking away, if you're not willing to face the same truth about yourself. That's not fair."

"It's not? And you're not suddenly sitting on the edge of the sofa because your instincts are telling you to run right now?"

Dillon made a show of settling against the back of the sofa. It wasn't like she could see his heart racing with adrenaline. He rolled his shoulders back and blew out a long breath. After a moment's consideration, he asked, "Are you telling me you want to talk about my loving you?"

Now Serena was the one on the balls of her feet, about to stand. She gritted her teeth and glanced away before answering. "No. Not right now." Surprising him, she shifted onto the sofa and briefly, lightly squeezed his forearm. "I will say thank you. It's nice to hear, no matter what you think I think. But I'm still too—

too full of feelings, negative feelings. I need to have some time to adjust. And I need you to not push me."

"So you accept that I love you?"

"I," she paused, too long for Dillon's taste, "I do accept that you think you do. And I know you have a point about the paths—well, the one path. But you know why I'm, a slow walker or whatever, with the steps—the stepparents. And there's too much to—it's too much, right now. Not when I'm mad, and you're mad, and I'm not sure what I want. I think it's better if we talk about it some other time."

Dillon just looked at her. Her eyes, darker than usual, maybe a result of the unusual circles beneath them. The tilt of her tense jaw. She'd worn her hair tightly clipped up, in the style he'd always privately called The Sergeant for its fierce and purposeful air. He was looking at a losing battle. He just wished he knew if it was going to be one of many, or the loss that would allow him to regroup and eventually win the war.

"Do you want me to stay for dinner?" Serena asked him after a moment. She wasn't sure if they were in the middle of a fight still, or done. There was sure as hell no vibe of make-up sex in the air, so she supposed that was the answer.

"You're really done talking about all this for now?"

"Are you?" she asked.

"Question with a question. With a question." He rolled his shoulders and stood up, then pulled her to her feet. His hands were dry and warm and an anchor around hers, and she wanted, she really wanted, to leave them there.

But he let go.

"I think, for tonight, maybe you should just leave."

Serena closed her eyes a moment to absorb that. She knew the fact that it felt like he'd swept her legs out from under her would be a significant one in her calculations. She knew that what she wanted, but would not ask, was for Dillon to say, "Let's just order in and watch a movie and have a quiet night," so she could be assured that those quiet nights weren't out of reach for her now. But she also knew that if he hadn't said he loved her, they wouldn't have lost those quiet nights to start with, and the hard knob of anger she still nurtured about that wasn't even close to dissolving.

So she didn't take his hands back.

With a small smile, she nodded and hoped her face didn't reveal any devastation. Any desperation. Any regret. Any fury.

He walked her to his door, his cursed front door, and held it open while she slipped on her shoes. Dillon did reach, briefly, to her shoulder as Serena leaned in to kiss him goodbye, but he dropped it as soon as she moved back. So what could she do but leave?

"Lunch tomorrow?" she asked.

"It's Tuesday."

"Right. Basketball, right."

"I'll see you, though."

"Sure. See you." Serena looked into the familiar blue of his eyes, the black hair that had strayed towards his eyebrows. She leaned in for another kiss, her lips abraded just slightly on the afternoon bristle of his cheek. "Good night, then."

"Night, Serena."

By the time she'd gotten to her car at his curb, he'd gone inside and closed the door.

CHAPTER FORTY-TWO

SERENA SPENT SERIOUS TIME ranting on the drive home, startling the boy at the drive through window when she'd allowed herself some stress-junk for dinner. "Be better off just stopping all this right now."

"Excuse me, ma'am? I didn't get that?"

"I said I'm better off finding someone easier. Less invasive."

"I?" the speaker crackled a little. "I didn't get your order, ma'am, I'm sorry. Can you repeat?"

Serena reigned in her temper. Some. "Fries. Small fries. And a chocolate milkshake. Please."

She stopped at home just long enough to change into workout gear. She couldn't run with all that grease in her stomach, but twenty minutes of jogging pounded out the last of her rage. The long walk that followed was way introspective, which she blamed on her failure to bring the thought-obliterating iPod, but by the time she was in the shower she was calm. Very zen, very centered.

Also, she'd figured out why Dillon had triggered her most volatile switches. She didn't grow up within so many broken homes without learning a thing or two about emotional fear. Her college Psych 101 class had all been about Mom, Dad, and the phalanx of stepparents. Identifying her switches, though, didn't really do a damn thing to tell her what she wanted to do about it all. Knowing that she was terrified to really let him into her space—physical and emotional—didn't stop the panic.

And it wasn't all her. Dillon clearly had his own switches. Even if he could accept his part in their discord, would he change anything in the future? She couldn't move forward with him if he kept launching grenades and taking cover. If she wanted to move forward with him. If she wanted him to love her.

She spent all night tossing and turning on it, and hadn't come to a conclusion. Stupid fear. And every person was in every place whenever Serena left her office on Tuesday, and she began to feel like the universe's biggest idiot walking the halls. She wasn't trolling for private time with Dillon, not exactly, but it would have been nice to have a couple of minutes. Just to gauge his mood.

But then Dillon was walking towards her, and the lurch inside her wasn't just anxiety. It was longing, and attraction; had he purposely worn that bright ocean shirt he knew made her drool? It was trepidation and hope that he was looking for her, that he was lurching towards her, too.

And he gave her a smile.

And he kept walking.

Serena turned as Dillon passed her, only vaguely mollified to see him pulled into Conference B by Anica, who then ushered Philip inside and shut the door. It had not been a smile that said, "I miss you and wish we were alone right now." If she had to guess, to apply her increasingly vast knowledge of Dillon's smiles, it had said, "Hi, got to go, and no need to keep stalking the corridors, because today will not be the day we finally have sex under your desk."

Maybe if he'd let his shoulder brush hers as he passed. Maybe if his hand had reached out to quickly squeeze her arm. Maybe if he hadn't gone on without a word. Maybe then Serena wouldn't have felt they were lost on that damn path of his.

But none of those maybes had been true, so she took the hint and went back to her office, shut the door, and tried to focus on a layout.

Serena was surprised a couple of hours later by a light knock on the door. She looked up to find Janice and Anica regarding her with mischievous grins.

"What am I missing?"

"Lunch," Anica sing-songed.

"Are we having lunch?" Serena glanced at the clock on her monitor. Noon. "Give me a couple of minutes."

"Have you noticed how warm it is these days, Toots?"

Serena nodded, distracted by saving the file she'd been working on. "It's April, Janice. Of course it's hot."

Anica laughed. "Someone's a little dense today."

"Okay, what are you two talking about?" Serena replayed the conversation, but was still not getting it.

"Toots. What's today?"

"Tuesday."

"And what time is it?"

"Twelve, so?"

"So," Anica said, grinning wider now, "on Tuesday at lunchtime, a bunch of people play basketball in the back parking lot. And several of them are men. Attractive men. Including, if I may be so bold, your man. And in April, when it's nice and hot out, they tend to take their shirts off while they play."

"And while they play, they engage their sweat-glistened muscles, pursuing an endorphin high, moving fast, chests heaving, and arms and shoulders pumping like a kaleidoscope of lust for the happy viewer," Janice explained. "So, Toots, are you ready to grab your lunch and sit outside with us to eat it?"

Ideally, Serena's smile was up to the task. She didn't want to give anything away, and as she headed to the break room to grab yesterday's salad from the fridge, she tried to figure out what it would mean. What it would look like it meant, to him. She didn't want Dillon to think she was still chasing him around the company. Or that she was happy to sit and stare at his abs—no matter how much those abs whetted her appetite—as if nothing was going on between them. And if he thought she'd dragged the others out on her own initiative, well. He'd better not think that. But there was no way to tell him that she was there just so she could pretend all was well.

This was exactly why she'd come up with The Plan to start with, frankly. Not that she could point that out to him. Unless she wanted the drama on the court to be of an entirely different, personal nature.

There was nothing for it but to get on with it. Serena plastered on her 'happy and calm' countenance and joined her friends on the rolling plywood table that, when covered with a moderately dust-free shipping blanket, served double time as a bench. At least her group wasn't the only one out there. Emily, Inés, Pete, and a woman Serena didn't know were perched on their own makeshift bench. They'd taken the only decent shade, but maybe that would persuade Anica and Janice to throw in the towel early.

"You didn't!" Serena quick-turned on Janice after her friend let out a piercing wolf whistle. Janice wasn't the least abashed. Even the shrewd look from Anica, as she noticed that Miguel had stopped in his tracks to stare are them, didn't stop Janice's grin.

For her part, Serena was beyond glad to see Miguel's obvious reaction. Partially it was her anticipation about grilling Janice later. But she also saw Dillon notice the vibe between Janice and Miguel. If he picked up on that, he might not think she was dragging her pals out to watch him in all his half-clothed glory.

"Good lord, Janice, I had no idea," Anica said, shaking her head as the game got back underway.

"Aw, I'm just appreciating his ball-handling skills."

"Dirty," Serena coughed into her napkin. Anica laughed.

"Toots, don't you start on me. I see you eyeing a certain tall black-haired forward. Who, by the way, has superb shoulders."

"As his supervisor, I can't comment," put in Anica.

"As his girlfriend's girlfriend, I can totally comment. Or whistle, if you prefer. The boys like it when I whistle."

"Said the woman who just got done inspiring a sexual harassment training onslaught," Serena said.

"Do you suppose that's why Emily is here? Checking to be sure everyone's on his or her best behavior?"

Anica shook her head. "Emily is here because Pete is here. Pete is here because Jorge is there." She lifted her can of soda towards the hoop, where Jorge was knocking out a rebound attempt. Serena's gaze moved almost involuntarily past him to land on Dillon's bare back. Why had she not spent more time looking at his bare back? She knew the feel of those traps and lats moving under her hands, but seeing them working in concert together was like gaining a new sense. A revelation. And that just got Serena wondering when she'd touch them again, what it would be like to feel their movement with these new images in her head. Her irritatingly confounded head.

"Poor Pete. Someone should tell him Jorge is off the market," Anica said.

"Are you volunteering? Because it should be someone who's not Emily, in case he's a shoot-the-messenger kind of guy." Serena stared across at the spectators in the shade, glad to have a topic— any topic—other than Dillon and her tentative status as his girlfriend to discuss.

"Since workplace romances are a disaster—you and Toots excluded, I hope," Janice said, looking briefly at Serena before her eyes started tracking Miguel again, "it may as well be Emily, so she can start looking for someone not at Lanigan."

Serena turned to look at Janice over the top of her sunglasses, wondering if Janice was just picking up on whatever weird vibe Serena was sending out regarding Dillon, or if there was something else going on.

Janice read her mind and huffed out a breath. "Ignore me, Toots. I must be skipping too many workouts. It makes me all grumpy. You'd better be prepared for some lunchtime cardio tomorrow."

"Do you ever join the game?" Anica asked.

Janice laughed. "You've noticed I'm five foot nothing, right? Not much of a jump shot. Besides, I have a feeling they'd fight over me. The office would insist I belonged with the warehouse team, and the crew would claim my daily use of the computer made me part of the office team. And I do so hate to have men fight over me."

That did it. "You and I, cross-trainers and smoothies, tomorrow," Serena told her. She glanced belatedly at Anica. "Are you in?"

Anica shook her head. "No, but thanks. Not that I'm ever likely to go outdoors at lunchtime—without a good cause," she added, nodding at the teams, "but I also have an off-site tomorrow at eleven. I'd never make it back. Which reminds me, not that we're talking work on our lunch hour, but I need to meet with you tomorrow afternoon, be sure we're on the same page with Blue Capri."

Serena smiled her acknowledgement, but inside, she was lurching again. It wasn't that she hadn't realized she was only two days away from her Galveston overnight trip with Dillon. It was just that she'd never factored this awkwardness and unresolved hostility into the trip. Of course, if he had just stuck with The Plan, there wouldn't be any need for hostility, resolved or not.

Suddenly ogling Dillon's abs, no matter how surreptitiously, was no longer tenable. Serena tidied up the remains of her lunch and made excuses to Janice and Anica. She thought maybe Dillon would look over while she made her obvious pre-departure motions, but he was in the middle of a fast break. Even without the action, he probably wouldn't have noticed that she was heading inside. Which, she reminded herself, was fine. She'd gone down to keep Anica and, it seemed, more importantly, Janice company on a pretty, late spring day. The sun was shining, the flowers were blooming, not much pollen was in the air. Houston at its best.

The question was, could Serena say the same about herself?

Aggrieved, Dillon slammed shut the front door of his townhouse and headed to the kitchen for a beer. It ought to have been a good day. Anica had pulled him in to sort out one of Philip's screw-ups, so score one to him, and Philip had even been a little gracious about it. His team had only lost by a half-dozen points to Miguel's—he probably owed Janice a beer for that—except when he'd turned to exchange a knowing look with Serena, she'd been looking away. Then she'd walked out just before he'd dunked the ball, missing his best shot of the game. Why had she shown up to watch, if not to talk to him afterward? Or at least admire his manly form, hinting at a more private admiration session in his future?

That had been the real start of his downhill trajectory. The second shower stall in the warehouse changing room was broken, so they'd all had to wait on an annoyingly fastidious Jorge, making just about everyone late back from lunch. Serena had barely turned his way during the afternoon's team meeting, especially when talking about this supposedly romantic yet still work-related trip they had coming up. Compounding everything, Johnnie had spilled half his coffee down Dillon's shirt as they were leaving the conference room. And sure, it was an iced coffee, but the embarrassing thing was, he knew Serena really liked that shirt, and he didn't know how to get the coffee stain out. He'd had to call Shannon and ask. And here he was, after a lengthy search for the drain plug, soaking the thing in detergent water and wondering if he even had such a thing as rubbing alcohol in the house.

Not to mention that Shannon had used her sister-sense to pick up on his mood.

On cue, the doorbell rang, and he wasn't the least surprised to see his nephew goggling at him through the peephole. Well, that was cute enough to get him to crack a smile, and when Shannon pulled a bottle of rubbing alcohol out of the diaper bag, he laughed.

"Justin made me show up unannounced," she told him as she leaned in for a kiss.

"Like an ambush?"

"Exactly like an ambush. Here, take Toby," she added unnecessarily, since Dillon was in the process of snatching him away. "You didn't call back Saturday or answer his email Sunday. And judging by your tone today, it had nothing to do with you and Serena running off to the Bahamas together. So I protested that Serena might be here, or you might be there, but he just pointed out that Tobias—the doctor promised he's at the peak of his colic phase—what was I saying?"

Dillon hugged her. "He's not letting you rest much, huh? I think you were telling me that Justin voted it was your turn to drive in circles to keep him from going into full blown afternoon hysterics, so you may as well drive here as anything else."

With a weary sigh, Shannon nodded. "Yes. That. Poor Justin went back to work yesterday, and everyone's been on fire about some client, so I figured he could use the nap. Was it only a week ago I was bragging on what a perfect baby he was? Oh, hell, it could have been yesterday. I don't know what day it is anymore."

"He's still perfect. Aren't you, champ?" Dillon hugged the drowsy infant close and steered Shannon to the sofa. "Are you wiped out? Want to take a nap while I watch him? Or, I don't know, run errands? Shower?"

She shook her head. "What are you hinting at?"

"Nothing. I just always hear that cliché, new mom, no time even to shower. I have new shampoo, it smells like a rainforest or something."

"Hmmm."

"Yeah, yeah. Serena likes the organic stuff, you know. Cruelty free or whatever."

"And yet, she's not here using it. Or is she? Did I interrupt shower time? Is that why you're shirtless?"

"Ha ha. You know that's from the coffee. Damn Johnnie. I wouldn't mind so much if he was any good at drawing fouls."

"Why, is anyone on your team good at the free throw line?"

Dillon slumped back, hitching Toby closer. "No."

"Well then."

"Well then."

They were silent a few moments, contemplating the baby, who, miraculously for the time of day, was also quiet. After leaning over and planting her head on Dillon's shoulder, Shannon asked, "So?"

"So?"

"Do I need to call Justin over here or are you going to fess up on your own?"

"What makes you think Justin is conscious enough to answer the phone? You know he fell asleep before you pulled out of the driveway."

"I programed his cell to ring with a Toby shriek when it's me calling. He'd hear me. He wakes up like he's been cattle-prodded every time the little guy cries."

"Well, that's nice."

"It'd be nicer if he didn't start so violently that it feels like an earthquake hit our bed. It's impossible to sleep through."

"As if you're sleeping through the crying anyway."

"Whatever. Point is, I could have him over here in a flash, if you need interrogating. I'm trying to go easy on you, give you a chance to talk on your own. But if you won't, I've got the phone right here."

Dillon sighed. She'd do it, too, and then he'd be forced to give up more information than he wanted. Justin was uncanny enough with casual acquaintances, but with him and Shannon, he could figure them out from the most micro of micro expressions. Poor Tobias was never going to be able to hide a thing. That was going to be fun to watch as he grew up.

"There is honestly not much to tell. Serena and I—we're having some adjustment issues. You know how it is. Or maybe you don't. You and Justin just moved straight into high gear, huh?"

"It wasn't as smooth as all that."

"It wasn't?" That was news to him. Yes, he'd been sixteen and bereaved, but it had always seemed as if they'd clicked right away and kind of accepted from the start that they'd be together forever.

But she shook her head. "I promise, there were growing pains along the way. Not that I ever harbored much doubt, but still, he kind of steamrolled his way into the middle of my life—both our lives—and it was...tricky, sometimes."

Dillon tried to recast those days with this new light. It just didn't fit. At least, not regarding Shannon. Justin had definitely steamrolled him, but Dillon had been so shut down, so full of teen angst ratcheted up to an extreme, that a steamroller was what he'd needed. "Huh."

"Huh is right. I know you worship Justin, and of course the fact that you did worship him, back in those days, was one of the reasons I let myself fall in love with him. But he has faults, you know, and the steamroller thing ranks right up there."

"Shan?"

"Oh, stop. It's not an issue. We're as head over heels as the parents of a colic monster are capable of being."

"Don't call my guy a monster."

"He's my guy, and I'm frankly a little put out with him at the moment, for being so settled with you. I just know that the moment I put him back in the car he'll start screaming and not stop for an hour."

"God, poor Toby."

"Poor me."

"Poor Shannon. And Justin. And Toby."

"And poor Uncle Dillon. What's the fight about?"

She was relentless. All those years of living with Justin had only honed her big sister radar. Dillon searched for the words that were true, but not true enough to subject himself to a serious talk. "I guess I was a little too steamroller myself. She's pretty cautious, and even though it's been going great, she's scared, I guess, to look at the big picture."

"And you want to be big picture already."

"Look, Shannon, I know we've only been dating for a while...."

"Not even as long as Toby's been alive," she reminded him.

"Okay, no, not even that long. But for most of his life. And I think it can go for a lot longer." Dillon looked down at his nephew, who emitted one of those crazily content baby sighs and sank deeper into his arms. "For the rest of his life," he added quietly. "That's what I want. For the rest of my life."

Shannon tilted her head to the side to gaze at him. "Oh, Dill."

"I'm not crazy. And I've liked her for months, remember. The day we met. You two were telling me 'at last' when we first got together, so don't pretend you weren't expecting this."

Shannon squeezed Dillon's wrist and nodded. "Okay, yes, we knew you'd be falling for her, given half a chance. But maybe she's not falling for you?"

"She is."

"Don't sound so grim about it."

"Not grim. Sure. But she has these walls, you know? And every time I get too close to one, she has this look, and I end up backing way away. Which doesn't seem to help things."

"Have you considered looking for a gate?"

"A gate?"

"Extend your metaphor. Walls have gates. Find one, let yourself in. Or keep knocking until it's opened. Don't go sieging the walls and getting knocked back and returning to the same place. Definition of futility."

Toby started to wriggle, so Dillon stood up and began to walk him in circles around the room, and suddenly his words were being sung into the baby's ear. "So I drive my steamroller around and around, around and around, looking for a gate."

"I'm stealing that tune."

"And I drive that roller up to her door, her door, her door. For a knock one, two, three, knock one, two, three, knock, knock until she says hi." He dipped and swayed in tempo.

"This is going to be a bestseller on the infant charts."

"Little guy, your mama's kinda mean, mean, mean. Let's leave the room, I want to think, think, think."

"Stay. I want to hear the next verse."

"Little guy, your mama's really snide, snide, snide. But you and me, we can hide, hide, hide. Come on, come on with me." And with a grin over his shoulder, Dillon took Toby with him into the bedroom, where he rustled up a shirt. Of course, putting the baby on the bed so he could dress meant a heart-stopping moment of Toby gearing up for a scream session, but Dillon was quick. With maybe a second to go before the wailing started, he had Toby back up against his newly-clad shoulder, and kept up the low singing as they swayed around the room. "I confess I want Serena to be your aunt, aunt, aunt. But the way she is now I just can't, can't, can't. It looks like I have to ask her to change, change, change. And if that goes bad it'll be a shame, shame, shame." He did a half spin, which made Toby's arms flail, so Dillon tried to reign himself in. "Roll that steamroller on up to her gate, gate, gate," he crooned and swayed. "Get your mean mama off my back, back, back. Send you on home to your dad, dad, dad. Figure out how to make your uncle glad, glad, glad."

A few more nonsense minutes later, Dillon brought the zoned out Toby back to Shannon, who'd fallen asleep on the sofa. He threw a light blanket over her and kept the baby on his shoulder for another half-hour while single handedly rubbing out the coffee stain and heating up a couple of plates of leftovers for them to eat. By the time he'd seen them off, a little more rested and fed than before, Dillon felt perversely soothed himself. Nothing had been resolved, but fessing up to Shannon had been a necessary step.

All he had to do next was convince Serena that he would be patient, but would not be going away. And hope that Shannon was right about there being a gate somewhere that, eventually, would open up to him. Because if Serena thought he would back down from talk of love and involvement, she had another thing coming.

CHAPTER FORTY-THREE

"Awesome, you're finally here," Liza said as soon as they jogged into the Smoothie Shack on Wednesday afternoon. "How's your hot sex life?"

"Are you asking me or Janice?"

"Funny. You, of course. It's been forever since you guys came in. I was about to phone Lanigan myself to check up on you. You totally left me hanging."

Janice tapped the menu laminated to the service counter to indicate her usual order, then turned to Serena. "Yeah, Toots, how's the sex life?"

Oh, hell. Deflection time. "More to the point, how's yours? And do you think I'm not telling Liza—blueberry mango, Liza, thanks—about you making goo-goo eyes at Miguel yesterday?"

"Goo-goo eyes! Do go on."

"Well, since Janice sees a lot more of Miguel than I do, I can only imagine what's going on between them. Passing notes along with the work orders, probably, and a little hip bumping as they walk the production floor? I really wouldn't put anything past her."

"For someone who gets her panties in a twist about even holding Dillon's hand in front of coworkers after hours, you sure have a very vivid imagination."

"The question is, how close to true are these supposed imaginings of mine?"

Liza held up a shushing hand so she could run the blenders without missing any gossip. Once she'd shaken their orders into cups and stamped their frequent buyer cards, the three of them moved to the corner booth.

"Step back a minute. What is all this with Miguel? He's the head of the warehouse, right?"

Janice nodded, but her cheeks flamed and she didn't say a word. Interesting. Liza and Serena exchanged raised eyebrows, then just turned in unison and looked at her until she rolled her eyes at them.

"There's no hip bumping going on."

"Bumping boots?" Liza asked.

"You're hilarious. No bumping in the warehouse. Or note passing, or whatever other perverse thing you two can dream up, so no point in asking whatever you were about to ask, Toots."

"Well, something's happening to get you shouting catcalls at him in front of his subordinates."

"I was not shouting catcalls."

"Whistles during lunchtime basketball. Plus she said 'Good shot, Miguel' instead of calling him 'Toots,'" Serena explained to Liza.

"It was a good shot," Janice added.

"Nevertheless. And then she started drooling over my shirtless boyfriend, and I decided it was well past time to drag her here so you could drag the truth out of her," Serena told Liza, who grinned.

"I'm on the case. She'll have to fess up, or I'll 'accidentally' run out of the soy-based protein powder. It'll be all brown rice, all the time, around here."

"That's dirty pool," Janice protested.

"Well, you brought it on yourself. You may as well give in now before I start inventorying my amino acids incorrectly."

"There are other smoothie shops, you know."

"Are there? Are they within running distance of your office? Do they keep a monthly tab for you?"

Janice slumped. Slumped! It was as if her core muscles just gave out entirely. Serena was beginning to think this was pretty damn serious indeed. "Fine," she grumbled. "Miguel asked me out."

"Out out? Like a date?"

"No, like as opposed to inside. Of course like a date."

"Geez, sorry," Liza said. "I just—you haven't been on a date in months."

Janice stabbed the bottom of her cup with the straw. "I am aware of how long it's been since I've been on a date. Not all of us have hot boyfriends or the kind of breathy voice that makes guys flock to her smoothie shop even though most men wouldn't admit to a smoothie habit under torture."

"I just happen to have a substantial male clientele."

"And does the branch over by Greenway Plaza also happen to have a substantial male clientele?"

"I'm not aware of their demographics," Liza said as primly as her sultry voice would allow. She waved that aside. "The important thing here is, when did this happen, and what did you say, and have you already been out? In other words, I need details. Lots and lots and lots of details."

Janice tried to wriggle out a bit more, but even she knew it was hopeless. It turned out that Miguel had been friendlier and friendlier since the incident with Ricky the Jerk Forklift Driver, and Janice had found herself softening towards him, ever so gradually. And Friday after everyone had punched out, Miguel had shown up in Janice's office with a fully formed date plan to spring on her.

"Wait, so that's where you were instead of at Eddie's? Jeez, you left me practically in the middle of a frat party there. I hope it was worth it."

"You had Dillon, don't complain, Toots."

Serena put a lid on the stinging behind her eyes at Janice's offhand comment. She'd had him all right, that night. And the next morning, he'd moved her furniture and everything had changed. Another night without a word from him, another day so far without a moment together. Serena was sure they'd had more contact back when she was allergic to him. She remembered checking for hives and short breath several times a day, between phone calls and emails and face to face moments. Probably she still had a chart somewhere. If she compared it to a chart of contact from this week, she would feel too like a stockbroker the day after a crash.

Liza wasn't as easily distracted as Serena. "So he had a whole plan? And he just thought you'd drop everything and follow it?"

Janice nodded, stirring the dregs of her smoothie.

"And you dropped everything and followed it, huh?" Liza asked.

"The 'everything' in question was a night at Eddie's watching him light up his farts, apparently, so I'm not thinking it was much of a loss."

"Well?" Serena prompted, when Janice stopped there.

"Well, what?"

"Was it much of a loss? What was this plan? Did it involve bumping in any way?" Liza answered.

Janice shook her head, a reluctant smile playing across her face. "It was a disaster. Fart flames might have been preferable."

"Details!" Liza turned to Serena. "Haven't I explained how I need details?"

Serena confirmed that she had. "It can't have been that big a failure, if you're openly ogling him on the basketball half-court."

"I never said it was a failure. I just said it was a disaster." But no matter how Serena joined with Liza's pleas for more information, Janice was done talking about it. Apparently all she'd needed was a decent run and to drop a few hints to feel more in command of herself. Serena figured that as long as that was also enough to get Janice to stop bringing up Dillon's sex appeal, she would have to be content. Fortunately, Liza had a couple of stories about her own, often chaotic love life to tell, which kept Dillon off the radar.

On the way back to Lanigan, though, Janice said, "So, Toots, you and other Toots, off tomorrow on an all-expense paid romantic getaway. Way to go with getting the company to pay for your booty call."

"It's not like that."

"Of course it's not."

"Janice."

"Oh, relax, Toots. I'm teasing. And I'm not an idiot, you know. I can tell there's something up with you two."

Serena glanced away, unsure what to say. Janice had opened up some about Miguel, and she didn't want to be coy in return. But whatever was happening, Janice and Dillon were coworkers with a relationship independent of her. It wouldn't be fair to put his actions out there to be picked over.

"Relax, Toots, honestly. It can't be tragic or you'd find a way out of this Galveston trip. You don't have to go into it. I'm here if you want me to be here, though, you know? I'll just listen and give you the motherly advice your own mother is too busy doling out to the steps to give you."

Serena had a momentary vision, then, of her and her mom sitting at the scarred walnut table by the back door of the duplex the two of them had lived in for her early teen years, between Mom's marriages to Erik and Samuel. It was actually just five houses down from the duplex they'd lived in right after her parents had split up, and had a nearly-identical layout. Kind of a *Twilight Zone*-version of familiarity, being just the two of them again, but with her mom a lot less of an auto-pilot zombie. Even though Mom hadn't shied from sharing her righteous indignation about Erik, she'd managed to be pretty focused on Serena's own middle school and high school dramas. They'd ranted about stupid boys at that table, and her mom had sometimes managed to slip in suggestions that Serena deigned to hear. Occasionally she'd even admitted to Mom that her ideas had worked.

It must have been good practice for Mom for when she found herself stepmother to the Three Rs, who'd all been in high school when Zane became her third—and longest-lasting—stepfather. Not that she thought of him like that, since she'd been in her college when she got the wedding invitation. In her nicer moments, she even remembered not to act amazed that they'd been together for close to a decade already. If she ever had a truly, deeply nice moment, she'd go ahead and invite them to dinner as Becky had commanded. Serena let out a long, slow breath and bumped her hip against her friend's. "There. Send that to the rumor mill," she said, grateful she wasn't being pressured. "And the same goes for me—if you need an ear about Miguel or whatever, you've got it."

"Thanks, Toots. Thanks for the run today, too."

"Any old time. Except next month, when it gets unbearably hot, and for the three months after that."

"You're a pal."

Laughing, they headed through the lobby and up to Lanigan's offices. Serena felt lighter than she had for days.

Once again, Serena had strolled right past him at lunchtime without even a glance in his direction. Bailing for burritos on Monday, walking off at the game Tuesday, and now appearing— pretending?—not to notice him standing in front of the elevators while she and Janice chatted their way up the stairs. Dillon suppressed a growl. It was beginning to feel like a scorecard, and one that didn't bode well for his chances in the playoffs.

Before he got too annoyed, though, he hummed the "gate, gate, gate" song he'd invented for Tobias, and tied himself to his desk to finish up a few edits. He didn't want to call Serena out on her blow offs in the middle of work, since that was contrary to the knocking at the gate plan, and he would have her to himself for eighteen or twenty hours soon. If she thought she could keep him at arm's length during the overnight, she was an idiot. And Dillon didn't date idiots. Therefore, she knew good and well that the reckoning was fast approaching, and he'd vowed to himself to be the patient one. Patiently relentless. Serena would listen to him saying "I love you," if it was the last thing he did.

Before he had to resort to lullabies to calm down again, an email from the woman herself popped in: "Dillon, Mrs. Kirby is expecting us between 2:30 and 3:00 tomorrow. I thought we could head out after lunch, or eat it on the road, if you want? Also, I can swing by and pick you up in the morning, if you like, so we just have the one car and you don't have to leave yours in the L parking lot. Let me know if that works. S."

Well, that was better.

"My sister's gonna have to eat her words, words, words. Justin and his theories are absurd, absurd, absurd," he sang as he typed a quick reply, asking Serena to pick him up by a quarter till nine in the morning. He made it positive, and affectionate, but not pushy. Didn't suggest they spend the night together to make carpooling easier, but did tell her he'd pack the small bottle of her favorite co-op shampoo so she wouldn't have to bring her own. He was still humming when Eddie walked past his office.

"Somebody's cheerful," Eddie laughed. "Looking forward to your trip to lover's lane tomorrow? Are you two going to frolic in the sand, take a moonlit walk along the Seawall, share a plate of fresh oysters? Nudge, nudge, wink, wink."

"I've mentioned my deep appreciation for your clever wit, right?"

"No need, my friend, no need. It goes without saying."

Dillon tried to hide his impatience. Whatever peace the baby song had brought had fled as soon as Eddie had barked out in his 'most jovial guy in the room' laugh. Jokes in the office were no way to soothe Serena into accepting his love. As neutrally as he could, he said, "I've got a few things to wrap up before I can go anywhere. You want anything?"

"No, man, just passing through. Pay me no heed. Hey, I'm meeting with Serena and Anica in a minute. Want me to give her your love?"

"Oh, I think Anica knows how I feel about her."

"Man, you slay me. Catch you later." And with that, Eddie was gone, but Dillon wasn't able to shake off the disquiet he'd left behind him.

"Oysters," he muttered, and turned back to the edits with a sigh.

CHAPTER FORTY-FOUR

As she put everything together for the overnight, Serena noticed the smudge stick tucked in her jewelry drawer, and rolled her eyes. But she would almost definitely have Becky and Zane over someday, and it would be best if the thing showed some evidence of use by then. So, and not without putting on a meditative playlist first, she smudged.

The annoying thing was, as she walked through the living room carrying the smoking herbs in an abalone shell that normally nestled in her bookcase, she looked around her house through fresh, slightly stinging eyes and had an idea. She had to call on Natalie's know-how. And it would never come together if Gillian couldn't help out. But by the time she was done purifying every corner of the house, her idea had become a full-fledged Plan.

Dillon dug through his closet, searching for an overnight bag. He'd left his usual one at Serena's, which wouldn't have been a problem if she'd invited him over; the one he unearthed with the wonky zipper would just have to do. He'd kicked everything else back into place and was shutting the closet door on the mess when his cell rang.

"Yeah?"

Justin was clearly in his car. Probably driving to keep Toby from a colic fit. "Hey, can I come by?"

"Oh, is asking first the thing you guys do now? I thought you were a big proponent of the ambush."

"Dillon. Can I?"

As if he had to ask. "Of course. What's up?"

"Nothing."

"Everyone's okay? Toby?"

"Fine, he's fine. I'll be there in five."

Which meant Justin had been driving for a good quarter-hour already. Hopefully Toby wouldn't be too cranky about the ride stopping too soon, but hey, he had his Uncle Dillon to sing ridiculous songs if necessary. The packing could always be done later.

Except it was only Justin at the door.

Justin, and an overnight bag with a zipper that strained against its contents, but held together. Dillon just stood there, frozen, thinking inane thoughts about the relative merits of overnight bags, because taking in the ash under Justin's skin and his brother-in-law's inability to meet his eyes wasn't going so well for him.

"What are you doing?"

"Can I come in?"

Dillon looked at the bag again. "I don't know. Why don't you tell me what you're doing first?"

"Dillon. Let me in."

It took him another moment, but he stood back and waited for Justin to sit on the sofa before closing the door and joining him. But Justin still wasn't looking at him, or at anything, really—it was clear that the poster of the *Millennium Falcon* was nothing more than a blur in front of his face.

Dillon cleared his throat. "I think you'd better explain, Justin," he said, carefully, and far more calmly than he felt. In truth, there was a red blur thing happening with his own vision that was a little freaky.

When Justin turned towards him, it took a moment for his eyes to find and focus on Dillon's face. "Can I stay here?"

But Dillon was halfway to his kitchen before the question was out. Not that he wanted anything in there. He just needed to not be in the other room for a minute. Justin didn't wait for him to return, but his tone made it clear he knew it didn't make it much better when he followed and added, "Just for a couple of nights. I'll go home after work on Friday."

"I," Dillon stopped and tried again. "I need to know what's going on, man." He looked directly at him then, narrow eyed but as in control as he could get. "And I sure as fuck hope you can explain."

Justin nodded, and leaned against the counter, rubbing at his face. "I can. It's—look, Dillon, do you think I'd be coming here, to you, if it was something bad? Shannon said it was the best, the...." But Justin's voice cracked a little and trailed off.

"She knows you're here, then?"

Justin nodded.

"Did she? I mean, she's okay? Toby's okay?"

Justin nodded again, and hooked his hands behind his neck. "She suggested it."

It took Dillon a minute to think about that. She hadn't said anything weird when she'd dropped in the night before. He tried again, carefully. "Did she throw you out?"

Justin shook his head, though, so Dillon looked around the room like it might just tell him what's going on instead of him having to pry it out of Justin. His kitchen, though, kept secrets, so he eventually got a couple of beers and pointed Justin back towards the sofa.

"Just two nights?" he asked, after handing a longneck to Justin.

It was another few minutes before Justin started responding with words again. "Tonight and tomorrow. Then I'll go home for the weekend. Not just for the weekend, I mean. I'll go home, period. Forever."

"And she's okay with that?"

"With me being gone two nights, or coming back?" Justin asked, more than a little irony in his otherwise bleak voice.

"Both. I guess."

"Yeah. She's okay. She said." He sipped his beer and dropped his head back against the sofa. "It's not that bad, Dillon. Stop looking so frantic at me, will you?"

Ha. Like he was the freaked out one. Justin was the one whose knees were vibrating. Dillon could handle it, he was just worried about Shannon, like any brother would be. 'Not that bad,' his left nut. He'd packed a fucking bag and left. "So things were fine yesterday, right? Shannon didn't say anything, just that work was busy? You went back on Monday?"

He waited, but Justin was non-verbal again, barely nodding.

"And twenty-four hours later you're at my door." Now he was getting pissed at not being answered. "Justin, the fuck? Could you tell me what's up, or not?"

He was on his second beer before Justin started talking, still with his head back and eyes closed. "Ten weeks I was off, Dillon. I was due it. They know that. But whatever you've heard about first-quarter profits lately, it's not all that easy to step away from the bank for ten weeks at the moment. Or to step back in, with everyone covering their asses and looking for scapegoats at every turn. So it really isn't the time for me to be fucking up a corporate loan renewal for one of my biggest clients, you know? But I did." He opened one eye and closed it again wearily. "I sure as shit did."

Dillon reached out a hand to Justin's shoulder, rested it there a moment. "Sorry, man. Sorry it's been rough going back."

Justin stood then, more explosively than Dillon could have ever expected, practically vaulting over his coffee table. "You don't get it. God. Shan says the same thing—you Hamiltons are so alike sometimes. 'Sorry, hon,' she says, 'you'll get back into the swing,' she says, as if that's all it is, just a blip and everyone will shake their heads then shake hands and get on with it. But I can't. Fucking. Think right now. I'm on no sleep—none!—and she said ear plugs but ear plugs don't work, and every time he's down he's up again within minutes, and the colic was fine when I was at home. You know I do my share; we both walk that baby for hours and hours and hours and get him out of the house so the other can nap and I make all her meals and clean the kitchen and the cat box. I can do all of that. I *want* to do all of that. But I can't fucking do all of that and my job, too."

Dillon sat still as Justin paced. He wasn't sure what to say. Certainly nothing that Shannon hadn't probably already said.

Justin turned back then, arms akimbo and head down. "If I lose the job, Dillon, that's it. No one is hiring. No one. They can't fire me for paternity leave in the middle of a downturn, but they sure as shit can fire me if I lose a client like that. We don't have the savings to go more than a few months, maybe a year, without me working, not without breaking into our retirement, and forget about Toby's college fund. And what the fuck would we do then? Does it look like there's going to be some magical cure to everything and I can just go anywhere and get paid what we need? We barely finished with student loans, and now we have Toby, and I. Need. My. Job."

Dillon stepped towards him, just a half step. "Okay. I get it. Justin, fine, look, I get it. You need to sleep. Sit down. You can stay here, just sit down." He guided his brother-in-law to the sofa and stood back a moment, regarding him. "Look, can I call Shannon?"

Justin shook his head, then shrugged. "Toby might be asleep now, I don't know. I went home a little early from work and took him for a walk so she could nap for an hour, but he's going to eat again before long, and that sets him off again." He was rambling, clearly disassociated, so Dillon just pulled out his phone and texted his sister to call him when she was free, then went to rummage for some bedding he could put on the sofa. Fortunately he'd gotten the natural sheets for Serena, so it was easy to locate the non-organic set he'd taken off his bed. Which was a whole thing he didn't need to add to the mess in his brain at the moment.

Dillon sat on his bed, thinking. Or not thinking. Just, not being in the same room as Justin for a moment. Because okay, he didn't live with the colic. Or the job in the financial sector. But...Justin. He just up and left Shannon to deal with it. To deal with a fussy two-month-old baby overnight. Over two nights. So he could, what, catch forty winks and settle his boss's ruffled feathers? And he thought that was worth it. After only three days back at the bank, he was abandoning Shannon and Toby in favor of work.

And there he was, circled back to anger and betrayal again. Which made him feel guilty. Which made him mad.

He grabbed up the sheets and a pillow and took them to the living room. Justin hadn't moved, so, fine, he knew where the towels were and how to make up a sofa by himself. Dillon just dropped everything on the coffee table and went back to his bedroom.

It was a half-hour later, when Dillon had finished packing and was lying in bed rereading *Hitchhiker's Guide* in an attempt to cheer up, or at least momentarily stop brooding on every damn facet of his miserable life, that Justin entered his room. He didn't talk, though, and Dillon saw no reason to be the one asking questions all the time when Justin was the one who'd screwed up at life. Whatever his reasons were.

"You know I'm not doing this for the hell of it, right?"

Dillon lowered his book and shrugged.

"It's not a spur of the moment thing. Well, it is, of course, but it's not a light thing. I'm standing here aching to be with them. It kills me that I'm not there. I left Shannon's meals for her, you know? And folded all Toby's things. Made sure there were diapers and wipes. But I know none of that's the same as being with them."

Dillon propped himself higher against his headboard, nodded at the foot of the bed in case Justin wanted to sit.

He didn't. "I'm not going to stop taking care of them. Jesus, Dill, I've been taking care of Shannon—and of you for that matter—my entire adult life. You know that? I mean, do you really know that? Do you think about it? What it means? I couldn't even buy booze when we met. Think how long ago that was."

Words without thought hissed from Dillon. "I know how long ago it was, Justin. My parents were hit by a truck, remember? You were at the funeral? First time I meet you, I'm standing at the crematorium, as if there was anything of them left to burn, and I want to hold my sister's hand even though I'm too old for that shit, and I can't, because you were doing it, instead."

"Jesus."

Dillon gulped. Gulped again, then muttered, "Sorry."

"No. Jesus. No, it's okay." He started to back out of the room.

"Justin." He tried to say it properly. "I'm sorry. I didn't mean to say all that."

"Yeah. I know. I'm... I'll turn in now."

"I don't think that, it's not—it just came out."

Justin's smile was brief. A split-second smile. "I know. We're fine. I'm going to just get some sleep now."

If Dillon could have come up with something else to say, of a better way to apologize, he would have followed. Instead he slumped back on the bed, unfocused gaze locked on his book, listening to Justin's quiet settling down to sleep noises in the next room.

No amount of Marvin the Paranoid Android was diversion enough for him.

CHAPTER FORTY-FIVE

SO IT WAS THE BIG DAY. Serena woke unreasonably early, even for her, and no amount of yoga got her centered. She was jiggling her leg every time she sat down, wandering aimlessly every time she stood up. Even while going to shower, she stripped off half her workout clothes, went back to the kitchen for a glass of water, started up the shower, went back to the utility room for her laundry basket, stopped half-way back to the bathroom to change the playlist on her iPod, and found the room full of steam by the time she was finally naked. And then she forgot to shave, and had to hop back in for round two after she'd toweled her hair dry.

She quadruple-checked her overnight bag (condoms: packed; lingerie: not packed. She wasn't going to jinx it by being overconfident, but she was going to keep her fingers crossed.) She double-checked her portfolio, since that was easier to be sure about. They were going to rock Mrs. Kirby's world, between her designs and Dillon's provisional copy. Because they were a good team. And only a fool would interfere with good teamwork. Serena was not, she reminded herself, a fool.

She was maybe an idiot. She was definitely scared. But she was not a fool.

She squared her shoulders and headed off to pick Dillon up. Well, she had to stop mid-way to her car and go back for her purse, but as soon as she had it—oh, and her to-go cup of tea—she was on the way.

Thanks to Serena's training, Dillon was up in plenty of time to chat with Justin before he headed in to the bank. "You sleep okay there?"

"Yeah. It was fine, thanks."

So they were both being polite. Great. He sighed. "Well, I'm out of town tonight, so you can use the bed. I changed the sheets a couple of days ago."

"Thanks."

After setting the coffeemaker going, he cleared his throat. "I, um, talked to Shannon last night."

Justin perked up. "What time? Was Toby awake? Did he go down at all for her?"

"It was after eleven. You were out like a light. I guess you needed it," he offered with a brief smile. "She said not to disturb you. Toby was fine. She was nursing him, but said they'd both slept a couple of hours already."

"Good. Good." Justin scraped back a chair and sat heavily. "What else did she say?"

"That I was an asshole. Basically." Dillon laughed. "She's right, as always."

"You're not an ass."

"I'm a little bit of an ass, Justin."

"Well, you're a pain in the ass."

"This is what you're like when you get a good night's sleep? Nice. See if I let you keep my key."

"Dill. Look." Justin held up a hand to stop Dillon from interrupting. "No, seriously. I want you to hear me say this: I didn't mention taking care of you guys because it's a bad thing. I know I wasn't making a lot of sense last night. I was fucking tired, and stressed out. And scared. But I don't take care of Shannon and Toby, and sometimes you, if you're not being a pain in the ass, because you're some kind of albatross. You're my family and I love you and I take care of you because I take care of what I love. It matters to me."

"You think that's news?"

"It's not like I took pity on the orphans and feel like I can't ever, I don't know, go to the store again without checking to see if Shan needs something first."

"Like you've ever gone to the store without asking what she needs first."

"Well, I mean. I don't want to do every diaper. I'm not a selfless fool."

"You kind of are, though."

"Shut up." But Justin smiled a little.

"Why, so you can tell me that you only mentioned taking care of us to point out that it took an unusual combination of stressors to make you leave last night, and that you were actually taking care of Shan still by taking care of the big picture stuff like making sure you still have a job, and that she was the one who insisted you make it two nights instead of just one? Don't bother. She read me the riot act. Thank God Toby needed changing, or she'd still be yelling at me."

Justin didn't even pretend he wasn't crying. "I don't deserve them."

"Bullshit, man." Dillon leaned closer, spoke intently to him. "You guys are sick, how perfect you are together. And by the way, I'm taking Toby out for two hours after dinner every Wednesday night from now until he's over the colic, at least, to give you guys a break, and I'm an asshole for being so caught up in my sex life that I haven't offered to do so before now."

"Is that a direct quote?"

"More or less."

Justin laughed and swiped his cheeks. "All right, then. Best not to argue with her."

"I wouldn't dare. Coffee?"

He nodded. "Thanks. And about the funeral...."

This time Dillon cut him off. "Nope. Not going there. You're the one with all the insight, so you don't need me to tell you that I have issues about their deaths that pop up once in a while. I'm dealing with it."

Justin just rotated his coffee mug and looked at him.

"And I'm not in love with Serena because I'm in a hurry to rebuild my nuclear family. Shannon covered that, too. I'm in love with Serena because I am. Because of—well, her skirts." Justin raised his eyebrows, and Dillon grinned a moment. "And her smiles, and the cruelty-free linens she dries outside on a line. And the way she sees color everywhere, and cause she took the time to figure out that she likes Janeway better than Kirk, even though that's clearly the wrong opinion to have. And because she was scared to meet you guys, but did it anyway, because I asked, and she's brave and honest about most things."

"Except cats."

"Except mysterious cat-induced allergies that defy explanation." Dillon wiped his own eyes, but only out of solidarity with his brother-in-law.

"All right."

"All right?"

"Yes. All right. I believe you. Well, I don't believe you could love someone who doesn't love Kirk, but maybe you're maturing a little."

Dillon just gave him the finger as he bit into his apple. He and Justin hugged before his brother-in-law headed off to work, and Dillon took a couple of minutes to clean up the place before Serena arrived. He needed to get his head in the game. He had a gate to pry open.

First thing Dillon noticed was the blue denim skirt. That boded well. She couldn't have forgotten getting the mint stains out of it, and had to have worn it deliberately. Sure, they were going to the Blue Capri B&B, but it wasn't all about the client.

Second thing he noticed, though, was the upright spine, the hands at ten and two on the steering wheel. She hadn't gotten out of the car to greet him, just popped the trunk so he could add his overnight bag to hers.

Relentless steamroller, he reminded himself. "Morning," he said, casual, with a smile. No leaning in for a kiss.

"Hi." Terse. But not biting. Maybe closer to tentative than friendly, but as long as the hostility was all gone, he could work with it.

"Thanks for picking me up. I meant to tell you, I have to go over some revisions with Philip and told him I'd take him to lunch, so we could head out around one, one-thirty?"

Serena nodded, maybe nodded too many times, but said, "Sure, perfect. Do you need to take my car for lunch?"

"No, Phillip can drive. I'm going to spend the whole day being chauffeured, like the superstar I was born to be."

That earned him upturned lips, and, even better, relaxed shoulders. He couldn't come up with any other jokes that didn't fall flat, but by the time they were walking into the office, Serena had spent a record twelve minutes by his side without blocking him out. Sure, she'd been behind the wheel of her car, but it still counted.

"Okay, see you after lunch." He looked down at her, careful about her personal space but also careful to ensure that she was meeting his eyes.

And how about that? Another smile. It wasn't an 'I love you and can't wait to get you alone' smile, but it wasn't the worst, fake one, either.

He'd take it.

One bite at a time, Serena forced herself to consume most of her lunch salad. Not the cheese, not with the ball of lead she was already digesting, but the greens, and the nuts, and most of the pear. Spending the next hour on I-45 beside Dillon with a growling stomach wasn't on her agenda.

It wasn't that he'd been cold that morning. He'd been perfectly civil. But Dillon was an extremely nice human being, and he wouldn't have wanted to throw her presentation to Mrs. Kirby for a loop by introducing a lot of interpersonal drama beforehand. As far as she knew, it was a façade designed to keep her from seeing his ongoing anger and resentment. It was certainly no guarantee that he would be willing to listen to her later. It didn't mean he would understand and accept what she was going to tell him.

It didn't mean he would understand and accept her.

"Just about ready?" Dillon asked from the break room door, and Serena tried not to jump.

"Three minutes. Meet me in the lobby," she said, standing to scrape the rest of her meal into the trash. When she turned to add a nonsense comment about her fruitless but ongoing quest to establish workplace composting, he was gone.

Okay then.

Serena did her best to shrug it off, going instead to her list of last-minute tasks. Restroom, set email away message, text Anica that they were on the way out, refill water bottle, turn off office lights, leave. If she could just keep checking things off of lists until dinner time, she might just get through without wondering too often what Dillon was thinking. Six hours, tops, and they'd be done with Mrs. Kirby and free to talk without worrying that it would interfere with the main work portion of this trip.

She could be calm and unflustered for six hours.

Squaring her shoulders and exhaling a long, slow, centering breath, she set off to do just that.

CHAPTER FORTY-SIX

SERENA DROVE. She was good at driving, even in Houston's traffic. When she'd turned sixteen, her parents had given her a car, and she only had to pay gas and insurance. It seemed like a sweet deal, until she realized it just meant they could leave all the logistics of whose house she was sleeping at up to her. A couple of boyfriends had tried to point out that, with no one particularly checking up on her movements, she could just stay out all night with them. It had never been persuasive enough to get her to clean out her back seat for them, though. She had a couple of carefully packed milk crates of art supplies she didn't want to accidentally leave at some step's house, so she made a nest for them in her back seat. The trunk was a portable study desk—everything she needed for classes, research projects, college entrance tests. She could quickly find any textbook or composition notebook, no matter where she was. Her study groups always loved her.

So all in all, she was more than capable of navigating the freeways of her hometown. Abruptly short entrance ramps, left exits merging into stop-start commuters, traffic that flowed from seventy to thirty-five and back up to seventy within a mile with no warning; nothing fazed her.

Which begged the question: why, as they drove past the proliferation of billboards and strip malls that characterized I-45 South past downtown, did Serena feel the need to concentrate on such basics as the three-second following rule, and checking each mirror at routine intervals? She drummed her fingers against the steering wheel, not taking her eyes off the road to see if Dillon bought that she was just tapping in time to the music.

Just north of NASA, chain stores to either side and an expanse of cumulus clouds against the cornflower blue sky ahead, traffic stopped. Judging by how hard she had to stomp on the brakes, Serena wasn't paying as much attention to the road as she'd told herself.

She most certainly did not bite her lip. And her neck wasn't prickling with nascent itches. Just because they'd sat in the car for half an hour exchanging barely a dozen words, and all of them work-related, was no reason to panic. Serena had a Plan, after all. And this time, The Plan was open-ended, and depended on Dillon's input. She checked the clock. Five and a quarter hours, maybe less, until she could begin. He'd be willing to listen to her, right? Serena stole a glance at Dillon, leaning back against the headrest, long legs sprawled everywhere. His eyes were half-closed against the glare of the midday sky, but she thought, for such a narrow look, it was a kind of relaxed. If such a thing was possible, Dillon could pull it off. It must be the cheekbones. They were remarkably calming, for cheekbones.

Serena tried to let out a long slow breath without making it sound like a sigh. A smart woman, when coming up with a detailed Plan for after the meeting and tour of Blue Capri, would have put at least a token amount of thought into the eighty minutes they'd spend in the car getting to that meeting. She had nothing.

At least the traffic picked up again.

Dillon watched the telephone poles give way to palm trees as they approached the coast. The occasional field of wildflowers broke up the succession of car dealerships and outlet malls, and a flash of peripheral movement had him tracking a seagull across the brightening sky.

When he leaned forward to retrieve the pair of sunglasses he'd stashed in Serena's glove box, the seat belt bit into his neck. "Hey," Dillon said before he'd thought it through, "who's been messing with my seat?"

Dumb, dumb, dumb. She was going to tense up at the implication that he had a right to personal settings in her car. Even leaving the sunglasses there had probably been a mistake. Dillon turned to fiddle with the belt's height adjustment, avoiding any looks she might shoot his way.

But, "That was Jonas," was all Serena said.

"Oh, I didn't know you'd seen him." Damn her casual response, he'd let his guard slip again. He wasn't her keeper, he wasn't entitled to know her every move; Dillon could hear her mental arguments lining up, waiting to spill forth.

And Serena laughed. Just a quick bark of laughter, and Dillon was able to consign half his tension to outer space. "I almost wish I hadn't. I offered to take him to the movies on Sunday afternoon, thinking we'd see the Pixar movie or something like that."

"No comment."

"Hey, he's thirteen. I was limited."

"And what did you end up at then?"

"Guess."

Dillon mentally scrolled through a list of recent releases, and remembered the anime-inspired action flick. So not Serena's thing. He looked at her over the shades. "No."

"I'm afraid so."

"Oh, Serena."

"Yeah, it was excruciating. Let's just say that I was not the target audience."

Dillon grinned. She was so pretty when she was poking fun at herself. Or, really, all the time. "Did Jonas at least like it?"

"He claims he did. I remember a couple of times, taking him to Disney or Pixar movies when I was back from college for the summer. That was usually fun. I don't know why I thought it would be kinda the same now that he's older." She was getting downright chatty. More tension evaporated.

"You just were off on your timing. Another couple of weeks, you could take him to the summer blockbusters."

"Dear lord."

"Come on, live-action fight scenes, space travel, alien villains? All epic fun."

"Okay, okay, I believe you. But I'm not taking Jonas to see any of it unless you're with me. Let's all go to Platform Nine and Three Quarters and beam up to the USS *Enterprise*."

Dillon would stop grinning, someday. But the summer didn't start for weeks, and Serena wanted him to meet her brother. She might think he was expressing appreciation for her joke attempt, and he obligingly threw out a "Funny girl," to keep her thinking so, but he didn't try to fool himself. Even casually made plans for the future were music to his ears.

"Funny woman."

"Okay, funny woman," he conceded. "Only because no self-respecting child would confuse *Harry Potter* and *Star Trek*. They know the difference between fantasy and sci-fi."

"I could have said the *Millennium Falcon*."

"I'd have been more impressed if you'd said TIE Fighter."

"Or podracer!"

"I knew I should never have let you see that movie."

"Come on, little Anakin was so cute."

"You're trying to torture me."

"He just wanted people to recognize that he was special. I feel sorry for him."

"Pull the car over. I'll walk the rest of the way."

"Across the water?" Serena nodded her chin at the salt marshes that now flanked the freeway.

"Look at that bird!" Dillon sat forward again, fortunately without being attacked by the seat belt this time. "That looks biblical or something."

Serena laughed. "It's a White Ibis. They're everywhere. But they won't ferry you across to the island, so you'd better stay where you are."

Pushing his sunglasses firmly back up the bridge of his nose, Dillon slouched back in the seat again, where he had the best unobserved view of the skirt riding up her smooth thighs. "Okay, you win, I'll stay. But if you mention Jar-Jar Binks, so help me, I won't be held responsible for the consequences."

"He's Dobby's friend, right?"

"Funny, funny, funny girl."

And now Serena's fingers really were tapping along to her driving playlist. She vowed to never admit that she saw why the *Star Wars* prequels were an abomination to Dillon, not if she could get such a dependable rise out of him. It was a delicious power. Mainly because he knew that she agreed, so pretending otherwise was just to torture him.

What if she told him some of the stuff before they got to Blue Capri?

But what if she didn't get it all right? They'd spend a couple of hours with Mrs. Kirby, and instead of wowing her with the pitch, Serena would have half her brain on analyzing what Dillon was thinking about their private lives. As her car rose up the bridge that would put them on Galveston Island, Serena let a calming energy surround her and lift the worry away. A couple of pelicans circled past, and she imagined them scooping up her troubles into their weird throat pouches, dumping them in the bay and leaving her free to get through the work part of the day and, finally, to the personal time.

Maybe, just maybe, it would all go right.

CHAPTER FORTY-SEVEN

BLUE CAPRI B&B WAS BETWEEN the Seawall and the Strand, set among other historic homes with lovely landscaping that lined the letter-named cross streets of Galveston. It had been originally ordered out of the Sears and Roebuck catalog in 1909, when the city was rebuilding after the 1900 Hurricane that flattened the island. The house had been modernized, of course, and bathrooms added to the four upstairs bedrooms to give each guest an en suite. Mrs. Kirby also had a two-bedroom cottage at the back of the garden, and this is where she'd put Dillon and Serena.

"I hope this is all right," she fussed, leading them along the bricked path, past a shaded seating area and small wall fountain. "You do have to share a bathroom, but this way we can sit in the parlor to discuss everything without disturbing the main house guests."

Mrs. Kirby herself was surprisingly modern, given the profusion of antiques and leaded glass and cross-stitching in her home. Her lipstick red cork-heeled wedges didn't match any of the muted blues and creams of the décor. They assured her that the cottage was perfect—Serena tried not to show how perfect it was, if her Plan went well—and embarked on the rest of the tour.

"I'm expecting a couple for the Solaro Room in about an hour, so we'll start there," Mrs. Kirby said, leading them upstairs. "All of the rooms are named after mountains on Capri, and as you can see, I've hung several prints of the Hyde and Sargent paintings from the island. I also have some books written on or about Capri in the bookcase there," she pointed to a set of shelves that also held a wide selection of beach-friendly paperbacks and current release DVDs.

As she showed them the Solaro, the Cappello, the Tiberio, and the San Michele, Mrs. Kirby kept up an intelligent commentary about the furnishings and the history of the house. Dillon was taking notes non-stop, leaving Serena to direct the conversation and take a few shots on her digital camera to supplement what they already had.

"This is all wonderful," she told Mrs. Kirby as they returned to the ground floor. "Why don't you give Dillon and I half an hour or so to organize ourselves, and we'll show you what we've brought down for you?"

They agreed that Mrs. Kirby would head to the Grotta Azzurra—their cottage—once her other guests were checked in, and retreated.

Serena opened her work bag on the parlor's side table and reminded herself to stay professional. Dillon took both of their overnight bags into the large bedroom with the heirloom quilt-covered queen sized bed, and Serena suppressed the frisson of awareness that shot between them when he returned to the parlor's doorway. He'd finger-brushed his hair, but it was still falling insouciantly across his forehead. His jaw held just a hint of dark stubble, and Serena willed herself not to imagine the rough scrape across her belly. She caught the white glint of his teeth as he hitched his mouth into a quick smile, and began to count her breaths to keep herself steady.

Work. Yes, right. Work. She unpacked her color boards and powered up her laptop, cued up the slideshow of their web templates, brochure, and new logo. Checked the time. If Mrs. Kirby's guests were slow settling in, she was going to start blurting things at Dillon and probably a mess would ensue.

Impressed, Dillon added 'watching Serena work with clients' to the list of things he liked about her. The harder edge of certainty she brought to internal meetings was softened by an openness that had Mrs. Kirby nodding eagerly along with her presentation. Dillon had jotted down a few quick descriptions of the Cappello Room, and Serena had added them and a couple of her photos to her website template then showed that page side by side with the existing site, letting the differences speak for themselves. Mrs. Kirby couldn't keep her eyes off of the new version.

And when Dillon was talking her through his plans for the tone of the copy, Serena's left foot—surely not accidentally—slid sideways a little under the table and rested up against his right. Neither of them moved so much as a toe for the further hour that they all sat around the little bistro table, discussing the account.

Not long after six, Mrs. Kirby headed back to the main house's parlor to await her late arrivals, and Serena and Dillon sat back, smiling.

"You were great," he told her, genuine admiration and pleasure she was bound to hear behind his words.

"It went well," she agreed. "I mean, really well. I think she's persuaded to sign off on just about everything." Serena pulled out her phone. "I'm going to text Anica, then I need twenty or thirty minutes to organize my notes. Are you super hungry?" She looked up from the screen and the silver sparks in her eyes just about blinded him. Those were happy sparks, and Dillon had gone too long since he'd seen them.

"No rush," he said. "I'll work on deciphering the rest of my notepad." But before he stood to retrieve it and his laptop, Dillon let the rest of his right leg press up against her left. She didn't press back, but she didn't shift away.

Dillon wondered what the equivalent of silver sparks were in his own eyes, and if Serena ever looked for them. If she was seeing them now.

Relentless steamroller for the win, he thought, and hummed a little "gate, gate, gate" under his breath as he moved to the love seat to start typing.

He lost track of time until Serena stood and stretched. "I'm going to take a quick shower, if you can wait another bit before we get dinner." He looked up to answer, but the things that stretching did to the front of her shirt rather left him at a loss for words. Never mind the silver flecks, it had been way too long since he'd held her breasts. Hopefully his nod was enough of an answer. Serena ducked her head a little self-consciously and went through to the bedroom. Dillon rubbed his jaw and considered shaving. But Serena had once called him 'delightfully scruffy,' so he settled for splashing water over his face at the wet bar, toothbrushing, and a clean white button-down.

He looked around the room, which boasted cute seating areas and a nicely maintained antique sideboard, but not much in the way of fur rugs and large pillows in front of the little fireplace. Not that it was really cool enough for a fire, but he had some hopes that there might be romance later. They'd screwed in any number of settings, of course, but the whole point of the steamroller was to get her to hear and accept his love. The Grotta Azzurra parlor was romantic only in a costume drama kind of way, with the delicate wood legs on the tufted love seat, the candelabra on the sideboard, the fresh flowers on the side table. Frankly, he didn't want to break anything.

Now, the bedroom, it had possibilities. Nice sturdy carved headboard, a mirror on the armoire opposite the footboard, side lamps that cast a diffuse but distinct light across the mound of pillows. The only problem was whether Serena would get prickly and resistant if he headed there as if she was bound to be of the same mind. Sure, she'd seemed fine with his putting both their bags in the same room, but he wasn't going to forget that she could easily move to the other bedroom. Or banish him. So he would be content with the love seat and candelabra, if he had to, but damned if the steamroller agenda didn't also include condoms.

There was a box of matches in the sideboard, along with a small CD player and selection of music. Dillon was flipping through the options when he heard Serena come up behind him. Still crouching in front of the music, he half-turned and, slowly, looked up the length of her body, to her face.

Serena was wearing low sandals with straps that coiled around her ankles and disappeared up her calves, under the fringed hem of a long batik-print skirt that wrapped around her waist and was secured on one hip with a knot that Dillon instantly imagined untying in numerous ways. His fingers, spreading it slowly open. Her hands, letting the whole thing drop as he stood back from her and watched. His teeth, inhaling her scent as he rested his cheek upon her belly. Her torso was hugged by a kind of tie-dye looking long-sleeved t-shirt that played call-and-respond games with the greens in the skirt, and revealed the exact heft of her cleavage. A couple of chains of colored beads dangled over her exposed clavicles, putting Dillon in mind of a string of bright candies, and he could practically taste the sugar on her skin. Silver hoops peeked through the loose waves of her hair, which she'd held tight to her crown with a couple of narrow braids in that fairie queen look he loved.

She was just so fucking gorgeous. He was a lucky man. Well, he sure as hell hoped that he was a lucky man, anyway.

Slowly, Dillon hauled breath into his lungs and rose to his feet. She'd stopped close enough to him that, when he stood, she had to lift her chin to meet his gaze. Close enough that she'd have no trouble reading his avaricious look. Close enough that, if it had been a week earlier, he'd have taken that half-step forward to ensure she knew the instant reaction of his groin to her appearance.

But it wasn't a week earlier. So he stood his ground, silent but speaking volumes with his silence. With his hitched breath, and devouring eyes, too, of course, but the silence was the stronger element, the intruder between them.

Serena watched him a long, long time. Dillon fantasized about mind reading along with all the other fantasies, but his only clue was the way she pressed her glossed lips together, biting just a little, before glancing quickly aside.

"I, um, thought we could go down to Pier 21. There are a couple of good seafood places there? Or there's a Greek place on Seawall that's fun, but...maybe not that quiet. I want to be able to talk?"

Dillon ran his hands through his hair, which was infinitely less appealing than running them through hers. Serena's 'talk?' sent a million calculations and permutations flashing through his mind, but the suitcases sharing a room and the possibility of meeting her brother and, most of all, the low knot in her skirt kept tipping each equation to a hopeful conclusion.

Relentlessly steamrollering ahead, he said the pier would be great.

And so it was. The restaurant they picked had a twenty minute wait for an outdoor table, so they walked past a maritime-god-looking statue and a succession of light poles hung with semaphore flags to the prow of an old sailing ship.

"It's the *Elissa*," Serena told him. "The Official Tall Ship of Texas."

"Texas has an Official Tall Ship?"

"Why, of course. Doesn't California have an Official Tall Ship?"

"I wouldn't begin to guess. What did the *Elissa* do to earn the position?"

"No idea," Serena said flippantly. "I know she was built in 1877, and she docks here, and I think there's something about the—mizzenmast?—that means something. It was all in the research I did for Blue Capri."

"Okay, then. And probably it's the square sails."

"What's probably the square sails?"

"There's no square sails on the mizzenmast, see?" He pointed. "The fore mast and main mast have square sails, but the mizzenmast doesn't."

Serena stopped walking by his side and pivoted so she faced him. "You sail?"

He laughed. "Sure, some. I mean, we never owned a boat, but I am a California boy. I went sailing with friends plenty of times when I was young."

"I thought it was just surfing."

"Oh, I'm a far better surfer than a sailor. Or, I used to be. It's been years since I did either. I've heard there are some decent waves on the Gulf, but I haven't yet persuaded myself to try. The Pacific spoiled me."

"Superstar that you are."

"Superstar that I am."

"You are a man with many facets yet to explore. Surfing, sailing, superstar. So you really know what you're talking about? The mizzenmast is a real thing?"

He couldn't resist tucking a strand of her flying hair back behind her ear. He was determined, in his steamroller way, to keep it light, in the present. He'd spent enough time of late being beaten up by the past. But he'd locked that 'yet to explore' into his calculations, and thought the sums were getting better and better. "Yes, it's a real thing. It's that one in the back. I've only sailed on single mast sailboats, but I still know my fore from my aft, thank you very much."

"I'll just bet you do." And Serena raised her eyebrows suggestively at him.

Dillon thought that, odds were, he was a very lucky man.

Chapter Forty-eight

Their table was ready.

So, this was it. No backing out now. She'd brought up quiet talking time, she'd dressed to please, she'd gathered materials. Altogether, she'd transparently orchestrated the night so there could be no question about Something of Import Happening, and Dillon had clearly not had any trouble reading the signals.

Right, then. She waited through the specials—Dillon nixing a strawberry swirl sangria before the waiter even finished describing its many fine, if toxic to her, qualities. Like the girliest girl ever, or perhaps just a nervous woman, she left the selection of a bottle of wine entirely up to him.

And then they had their wine, the kitchen had their order, and as anticipated, the patio felt private and intimate. The sun was still wandering down towards the bay in front of them, and the conversations of other diners was inaudible beneath the breeze and the occasional clinking of chains for the small boats pulled up into the docks. Serena indulged in a long gaze at the dying light playing in the *Elissa's* rigging, collected her thoughts, and reached for the small sheaf of papers in her bag.

"Is there going to be a test before dinner?" Dillon asked, quirking his head around to try to see.

"Yes, you fail, you get no snapper. It's a harsh rule, but I recommend you accept it graciously."

"Wow, if I'd known, I'd have opted for the crab shack instead."

"No, their test is essay-style. This one is multiple choice." Serena edged her chair a little closer to his and put the papers down on the corner of the table between them. "You're being silly, and I'm a little nervous, and I don't think it's a good combination."

Dillon immediately took her hand. His thumb smoothed over her knuckles, and Serena almost dispassionately noted how quickly just that small affection calmed her jitters. It was really quite ridiculous for her old hang-ups to have so much power over her, when clearly a strong new impulse was lurking in her heart.

"Hey," he said, his voice sweeter than it had been all week. "I can stop being silly. Even though it looks like you're about to make a pitch here." Serena blushed a little, but maybe the dusky light didn't catch it. Dillon went on. "I get that you're nervous. I'm sorry you're nervous. I'm a little nervous myself. And now I've said nervous a million times and it can't be helping."

Unexpectedly, he leaned in and kissed her, soft and quick and lips clinging just a moment before he retreated with a smile. "Aching to do that for hours now."

"Days," Serena said. But mentioning how very long it had been put some of the wariness back between them. She tightened her fingers on his briefly, then smoothed the papers under her palm, and left her eyes on her hands as she began. "Dillon. I'm sorry if I'm being too formal. I really just have one basic thing to say to you. But I realized if I just said it without trying to explain more, it wouldn't be very honest. I think I need to be really honest, I think that's the best thing."

His mouth was dry. Shame to burn a thirty dollar bottle of wine on thirst quenching, but Dillon needed some bolstering along with the liquid. Stupid, foolish idiot move to have kissed her. Now she couldn't even look him in the eye. Him, with his jokes about tests and presentations, so childish. She was right to be nervous, since he clearly was misreading everything. His body language must be making her want to run screaming. Too bad she was his ride home.

Serena glanced up to see Dillon staring off at the ship lights in the distance. He'd settled into the back of his chair, feet planted as if on the verge of scraping it backwards, further away. Well, she knew going in that he might not want to hear her. Their appetizer sat barely touched, the only good thing about the calamari at the moment being the fact that its presence was keeping the waiter away from their table.

She drew in a lungful of briny sea air and made a desperate stab at organizing her thoughts. She was a graphic artist; this was why she'd brought visual aids. "Okay," she said, and this time Dillon looked at her. She so wanted to be able to read the expression in his cobalt eyes, but he was entirely guarded.

"Okay, you don't know this about me, but when Natalie and I first met—I mean, met again, in college—I practically refused to believe she'd been my stepsister. I wasn't remembering a thing about her. She had to write her mom to send up some snapshots of us with our parents before I would agree she was right. It wasn't as if I really thought she was lying. I mean, Serena Colby isn't the most usual name, and she knew things only a stepsister would know. Or someone who'd known a lot about me at twelve, anyway.

"My point is, well, it's the same thing with my brother. I mean, of course he's just a kid, so it's not like he wants to do all that much with me, but I was already in college when Dad divorced Fran, and Jonas was a preschooler. I hadn't met Natalie yet, that was a year or so later, and by the time she had badgered me into connecting with the kid, I already hadn't seen him in so long I figured he would never remember me."

Serena checked Dillon's eyes. He was still giving nothing away. Okay, fair enough, she hadn't managed to get to any of the point yet. "Well, Natalie made me visit him off and on, take him to those Disney movies, but I do the same thing with Jonas as I do with her. Only living in the present. Maybe some of the future, but not much. Not by a long shot. I'm trying to fix it, Dillon, I really am. I even invited my mom and Zane to come over for dinner next week. Just, I guess, not so much building bridges but kind of surveying the site to see if a bridge might stand there someday. I'm being slow about it, probably. I know I need to like, embrace my past or some such mystical realization." Serena laughed some, but Dillon was still stuck in neutral, so she pressed on. "So that's what I do. I keep the past locked in a safe little room, and stay away from things that remind me. Like my parents, for example. I checked my calendar yesterday, and it's been five months since I've talked to my dad, and that was only because neither of us really knew anyone else at Jonas's Bar Mitzvah. My mom—well, we talked for a while, but it wasn't the smoothest. I look at you, and you have no idea how I admire, and envy, your relationship with Shannon. And maybe you have that because you two lost your parents, and I should figure out how to have a good relationship with my parents."

Serena stopped abruptly, shook her head some. "Wait, I'm sorry."

Dillon asked, "For what?"

"Just, I'm getting off track. I'm talking about me here. I shouldn't have even mentioned Shannon or your parents. I mean, not now. Of course later, all you want. Here," she finally flipped over the pages on the table, giving the waiter a little shake of the head when he tried to remove the calamari plate.

"I listed them all. By the time I graduated college and got my first place of my own, I'd lived in twelve houses, between my parents and stepparents. Until second grade with Mom and Dad. Well, he moved out when I was in second grade, but I stayed mostly in the same house with Mom until that summer, then we lived in a duplex close to my new school, until she married Erik. By then, Dad had divorced Alice—she was the one with the evil twins who gave me hives, I told you about her—and lived on his own in some nothing apartment until he married Natalie's mom." She pointed to the number six on the city map where she'd pinpointed the various addresses, best she could remember. "But then Mom and Erik split, so Mom and I moved to a different duplex, were on our own until she met dumb Samuel. Well, you get the point. I practically never stayed at Dad and Tennessee's house, which was later just Dad's, then Dad and Fran's until they had Jonas and sold it. Their new place was way up in Conroe, but that was the last one I used my floor plans for."

Serena moved aside the map, and wished she hadn't made it. She'd hoped it would get a smile out of him, but he hadn't seemed to even look much at it. Hopefully the next part wouldn't fall as flat.

"So when I was little, after I had the hives and Alice and Dad had to put me in a separate room from the twins, he took me shopping for my very own bedroom furniture. I thought it was the greatest thing ever. I'd actually been doing this for a while with my stuff at home. It started with my dollhouse, I think. I just loved rearranging the floor plan. And one day I figured that I could rearrange the furniture in my own room, just like with the dollhouse. Well, the bed was heavy, but I put my back into it and shoved it until I had it where I wanted it."

Serena stole another look at Dillon, to see if he was interested, if he maybe had cracked a half-smile at the cute kid story, anything. But, no. He was listening, but entirely self-contained.

"Eventually I ended up using graph paper and making scale size cutouts of my bedroom and furniture. I even made little 3-D models of it all at some point, but that fell apart ages ago. When I was little, though, I just drew a lot of pictures of my room with the furniture in different places. And when Dad took me to get a whole second set of bedroom furniture, it felt like a huge treat. I'm sure the salesperson was confused about why I was testing how heavy everything was before I would pick anything out." She smiled. "There was a dresser I absolutely loved, with a built-in jewelry drawer, but it was as heavy as sin, there was no way I'd have been able to shove it around on my own, so I passed it up. It was all great, you see? Because I got to rearrange two sets of furniture." She opened the well-worn graph paper pad, with the cover she'd decoupaged as a teenager, and flipped through the succession of room plans within.

Serena was extremely conscious of the fact that Dillon hadn't moved or spoken much since she'd started. She wanted to get it right, tell him everything, but she hadn't thought that would put her into such monologue territory. Maybe she had been wrong to do all this. Maybe he wanted her to shut up and let him eat his fish, which, she gathered from the increased hovering of the waiter, was just about ready to serve.

But she hadn't made a Plan B for a reason. She needed to say it all, as honestly and thoroughly as possible. Okay, then. Onward.

Rather than extract the envelopes with her tiny childhood furniture cutouts to show him, Serena gathered her courage and opened the file marked 'House Plans.' "Okay, so once I'd been working a while at Lanigan, was settled into adult life in Houston, Natalie talked me into serious house hunting. I mean, of course she was looking for commissions with her brand new realtor's license, but she'd remembered all of this bonding we'd apparently done over home decorating magazines and my floor plans and all. I was pretty reluctant at first, but once we started looking at properties I got all excited. I could just envision my own space, setting up things the way I wanted them, all of that. I mean, maybe you remember, I spent the weeks before closing drawing up color schemes, cutting out photos of magazine-spread rooms, all kinds of dreams and fancies." She fanned out a few of her idea pages, to give him the full impact of her not-so-minor obsession.

Big breath now. This was the part she'd been building to, and while Dillon had remained obligingly silent and attentive, she didn't want him to underestimate the import of what she was going to say next. He'd waved off the waiter another time, which maybe boded well? As long as his hunger wasn't driving him to distraction.

Before she spiraled off to a land of crazy speculation—crazier speculation—she ran a finger along the final page in her stack, ready to turn it over. "And that's the way it's been since I bought it. My house, my stuff. I mean, I knew before Saturday that I was freaky about it. I knew that everyone who followed my rules was just indulging me. Well, except Hannah, but you know what I mean. I just thought it wasn't a big deal. That I could have my floor plans and my rules about my space and it was no one's business but my own."

Dillon stiffened a little, but something in her face must have been apologetic enough to keep him sitting, listening.

"You surprised me. Dillon, I thought I could let you in, just a bit, on my terms. I thought we could have a fine time, but I wouldn't need to change, you know? Well," she glanced away, shamed by the admission, but compelled to make it, "I thought there wasn't anything I'd need to change. That I was—well, not perfect, I'm not that arrogant. That I was perfectly fine as is, that there was no reason you'd be upset by my thing about my house."

When he leaned, maybe only a millimeter or two, towards her, Serena felt a rush of relief. The darkness was closing in past the patio, but suddenly his eyes were bright beacons.

Serena wasn't a word person like Dillon. She didn't know how clearly, how even close to clearly, she was explaining herself. But a picture told a thousand words, and images were her strength. Just a little slowly, she flipped over the final photo and placed it squarely on the table in front of him.

CHAPTER FORTY-NINE

HER WHOLE LIVING ROOM had been rearranged. The seating area was closer to the fireplace, and one of the side chairs had been removed. All to leave room for an old steel teacher's desk, repainted in ultramarine and cadmium orange, with a smooth solid black laminate top. There was a wood desk chair with a padded leather seat, a tin miner's cup of pencils and pens, and a blue porcelain bowl with a couple of navel oranges. Smack dab in the center of the black blotter, one pristine legal pad slanted at the perfect angle for a left-handed guy's writing. The light from the window spilled over it all, but there was also a chrome gooseneck lamp arcing on one side.

"If you don't like it, we can change anything. Or if you want to share my study, we can fit it in there. Whatever you want, Dillon. I just want you to have whatever you need. If," Serena pressed her lips together and glanced down at her hands interlaced in her lap, "I mean, if you want to need something from me."

She forced herself to shut up. It was pretty much when she needed him to take over the talking, because her Desk Plan only got her as far as showing him the photo. Serena couldn't remember why making Plan B had seemed inadvisable, because sitting there vulnerable to whatever he was going to say or do next was not her favorite feeling.

She chewed her lip a little more, then opted for some cold calamari instead. Dillon had started running his own fingers along the edges of the picture, and that was good, right? What she wouldn't give for a little psychic power just then. It would have meant the world to her if he would have just grinned and told her it was perfect.

Dillon closed his eyes in a fairly futile attempt to get his emotions under control. He'd known—the universe had known—that she was a maniac about her house. Pushing her on it was at least half the reason he'd moved the table, then refused to return it, in the first place. All those little graph paper room diagrams, though. The firmly dug trench lines of child-Serena's number two pencil marking off each quadrant of the space she had to make her own or feel unanchored in the world. Each diagram labeled 'Pine Street' or 'Glassbury Avenue' instead of the name of a parent or stepparent.

Then talking about owning her own home, the planning and love that went into making it a kind of sacred space for her, an anchor that no one could disrupt through divorce or remarriage. All he'd cared about for his place was that it was easy to get from Shannon, in a good area for him and he'd liked that it had enough room for a big entertainment center and tons of bookshelves. He'd used the in-store layouts at Ikea to be sure he had the right numbers of chairs and tables and rugs in each room. Of course his books and posters were essential to him, but it wasn't like it mattered if they were in the bedroom or the hallway or wherever.

He liked his place. But as soon as he'd walked into Serena's living room, he'd felt invigorated and grounded. The other reason he'd set the table up there was so that he could have the pleasure of working in that space, the window and the room and the essence of Serena everywhere.

And just by refusing to do what she'd asked and work at the island, he'd basically fired a photon torpedo at that essence. He'd beguiled her into lowering her shields, and then casually blasted away.

So it looked like he had been a jerk. He'd yelled at her, actually raised his voice and thrown a temper tantrum to rival the one when eight and his mom had refused to adopt one of their neighbor's puppies. He'd walked out on her. Given her a cold shoulder for a week. Invented this dumbass steamroller philosophy, instead of just freaking talking to her to figure out what had been truly going on with her.

And instead of kicking him to the curb, she'd gotten him a desk. A stunning desk, just the kind of thing he'd love to work at, but better because she'd fancied it up to make it a real part of the room. A part of her house, which, he was seeing, was the same thing as making him a part of her soul.

On top of that, she'd gotten all of these supporting documents, and planned this dinner. That outfit. The knot on her skirt, which had been a fully formed obsession since he'd seen it, no matter the sailing ships and the pelicans on the pier and the table between them obscuring it from his vision.

He should just turn the steamroller on himself.

"Serena."

She looked up, her chin lifting a little resolutely, and Dillon's heart was free-falling. He shook his head a little, remembering the things he'd thought about her since Saturday morning.

"You hate it." She slumped back against the cold metal frame of the chair. "Honestly, Dillon, we can get whatever you like. It was at the flea market, but Natalie and Gillian helped me scrub it down real well before we sanded it so I could put the new color on. The one drawer, that middle one, squeaks, I couldn't bang it out, but it's one of those mousy squeaks, not a fingernails on chalkboard kind of thing."

Dillon dropped the photo on the pile and grabbed her shoulders so he could pull her forward to meet his kiss. Rapacious. The entire reason the word 'rapacious' existed was to define that kiss. He needed to take the soul she was offering, take it and fuse it to himself. Leave no uncertainty, stop her from thinking he would reject her desk. From thinking it was even possible that he could reject the desk. His desk. His woman.

It took her by surprise, her soft lips falling open, but that suited Dillon just fine. They were easier to nip, to suck between his teeth, when she was open to him. One of his hands stayed on her shoulder, anchoring her to him, and the other raked back her hair to mold itself against the base of her skull, her neck and ear freed for further ravishment. Back to her lips, her tongue, her gorgeous smile emerging beneath his kiss. He was almost entirely lost in her. Not totally entirely, fortunately, what with the waiter appearing over his shoulder with two dinner plates. Dillon managed to still his mouth and bring his forehead to rest on hers. His lungs were working fast, his heart beating hard.

"I love you."

Her eyes locked with his, wide from the darkness, silver from the passion. She didn't answer him, but she'd said so much already, both her words and everything that had gone into the desk.

"Serena. You don't know how much I look forward to sitting at that desk. It's amazing. I can't wait. Thank you."

Radiant. Her smile was radiant. It caressed him even as he disengaged from her to sit back and allow the snapper to land at last on the table.

The faint brine added a tang to the air, the breeze cooled her flushed cheeks, and Serena had never felt more at peace. Well, maybe she had, but that kind of casting back wasn't important.

Looking into Dillon's slightly crinkled eyes was important. Nudging her chair closer so their knees lolled against each other was important. Grazing her hand over her neck, still damp from the kisses that were drying against her skin, was important.

"So, you like it, then?"

"Funny girl."

"Funny woman. But I'm serious. Well, okay, you said 'amazing' and I'm taking that as a good thing. Plus, that was a pretty decent kiss."

"Funny Serena. You know damn good and well that the desk is perfect. Much like this yucca relish. Want a bite? I can't believe it's not all overcooked at this point."

She waved him off, busy with her crab cakes and basking in the freely-given 'perfect.' It was perfect, she knew that, and she owed Gillian and Natalie big time for the hours they'd put in helping her refinish it. And for Gill volunteering her brother's pickup to get it from the flea market to her driveway in the first place.

"I'm picturing many fine summer mornings spent scribbling at that desk. I'll keep my stash of paperbacks in the squeaky drawer, that way whenever you hear it open you can chide me for not buckling down to work."

Serena flushed hot again, and reached up to rub at her collarbone.

"What is it? Is the food okay?"

She nodded, shook her head, tried to smile. "I'm fine. This is good, actually, help yourself."

His eyes trapped hers again, this time more assessing than devouring. She like the devouring better, it was a lot more fun. "So what's up?"

"Nothing. I just had a tiny flash of panic, but it was like a habit, not a real feeling."

"Panic." His voice had gone cautious and flat. "Panic doesn't sound like a good habit to have."

"Oh, Dillon," Serena kicked herself for including all of that 'be honest about feelings' crap in the Desk Plan. "It's nothing. I'm just not good at the future talk. I told you, with Natalie and Jonas and all, living in the present. It's just not something I'm good at, and when you said about summer mornings I only freaked for a second. It was nothing serious."

"You do want summer mornings with me? Or you don't?"

"I do," she protested, moving her hand from her almost-itchy neck to take his. "That's why I made the desk. For summer mornings. Just, I'm not good at the future."

He took back his hand, sat silent and thoughtful a moment, but at least his knee still knocked hers. "Don't use that as an excuse, Serena. I'm not just a friend or a half-brother you barely know. Making that desk does say a lot to me, don't get me wrong. But it could just be talking about the present, leaving the future out of the equation. I don't want you to leave the future out, to just brush it off, say you're uncomfortable. I want you to get good at talking about it. To want to get good at it."

Serena's hands were fluttering, restless, and she fought to urge to sit on them. "Me, too. I do want to get better at it. I'm not going to let things end between us because I have trouble talking about next season."

He nodded. "Okay. That's good. I'm glad. But, Serena, do you want to get better at the future for me, because you're maybe worried about losing me if you don't? Or do you want to do it for you?"

She plunked her fork down on her plate and sat back, staring out at the distant lights across the water. Every step she tried to take down that damn path of his, of theirs, he was leaping ahead to some new signpost. Was it too much for him to just accept that she was trying to walk alongside him? She'd already bared so much of herself with her presentation, and the last thing she'd wanted was for him to take that as an open invitation to strip her down further.

What would the Desk Plan call for here, if she'd anticipated such a spot? Well, that honesty thing, of course. Being emotionally open was far from easy, she noted wryly, as if Gillian hadn't pretty much pointed out the same thing to her while they were cautiously maneuvering the almost-dry desk into place.

She turned back to Dillon. "I want it for both of us. I mean, the last thing I'd want is to lose you because I can't talk about the future. But it's another of those walls I've been working on smashing. Or rebuilding, whatever is psychologically healthy to do with walls." She smiled, and got a glint from him in return. "Is that okay? Mentally, I can see that wanting to change like that for myself is the right way to go about it, but emotionally, I'm not all there yet. I guess it takes wanting to change for you, too, to put the sledgehammer in my hands."

"I've got a steamroller if you need it," he said, then laughed at her befuddled look. "Never mind, too dumb to explain." Dillon picked up the photo of her new living room arrangement and studied it for a moment. "Yes, I think it's okay. I think it's more than okay. Maybe because I'm just really selfish about wanting those summer mornings, but maybe because changing for each other is fine, when we're moving towards things that are also good for ourselves."

It was Serena's turn to laugh. "You wouldn't believe how close that is to something Gillian said to me. She's always been the perceptive one, which is one of the reasons I called her about the desk. I needed her ear as much as I did her brother's truck."

"I always did like Gill best."

"Funny boy."

"Funny man."

She leaned in to kiss him, squeezing his hand. "Funny man."

CHAPTER FIFTY

TASTY AS THE FOOD WAS, they barely managed to eat a respectable amount of it, being too busy smiling at each other, reaching out for little touches, stealing quick kisses. Dillon was beyond eager to just get her to himself, so after they paid the bill they took a long walk along the short pier, pausing between street-lamps to kiss. They'd walk, and Serena would pull them onto a park bench, where they'd get lost in each other's roaming hands for a while. Then they'd walk, and Dillon would twirl Serena into a sudden dip, exposing her neck for a series of light nuzzles. Then they'd walk on, meandering, laughing.

"Did you know today is Shakespeare's birthday?"

"Happy birthday, Shakespeare."

"Well, his death date, too."

"You *are* cheerful tonight."

"Hush, funny girl."

"Romeo, Romeo, Romeo, I keep telling you: funny woman."

"Two Romeos, then the wherefore art thous."

"Wow, you're a scholar, too. Sexy. Give us a kiss."

Dillon complied.

"Come on, then, Professor Dillon, lay some poetry on me."

"You are poetry."

"What your hands are doing is poetry."

"Mmm," Dillon kept them dancing across her spine. "Okay, here's a truth about you, from Sonnet Eighty-Three: 'There lives more life in one of your fair eyes/Than both your poets can in praise devise.'"

Serena stopped swaying against him and gazed, arrested, at his tender face. "Wow. That's sweet. Shakespeare was a bit of a romantic, huh?"

"It would seem so."

"And you, what, scrolled through your mental rolodex of sonnets and came up with that? Because if so, I'm super impressed. I don't think I've ever read any except the most famous—mistress' eyes and all that."

He pulled them back along the pier towards the parking lot. "I think the validation from the restaurant is up soon. Let's get out of here before they charge for parking."

"Hmmm. Classic avoidance technique, the redirection. Spill it, Professor Dillon."

Stopping between streetlights so she couldn't see any embarrassment on his face, Dillon admitted, "It's the only one I really know. I mean, I've read probably all of them, between college and everything, but I had to have a poem memorized for debate team freshman year, and my mom couldn't find any poetry besides Shakespeare in the house. I picked that one because, well, I understood what it meant, and I didn't want to do a super popular one so I'd have something no one else had."

Serena almost doubled over laughing. "Oh, you were a smug little teen, weren't you? I bet you wore black turtlenecks to debate tournaments. Admit it."

"Please. It was southern California. Way too hot for turtlenecks."

"Oh, yeah? What then? Black blazer over a black t-shirt?"

"Maybe."

"I knew it. Did you write poetry?"

"Stop it."

"No, seriously, I want to know. Soulful black-clad Dillon, the deepest boy in Los Angeles, was there a black composition book always in your backpack where you jotted down your deepest thoughts?"

"Oh, look, the car. Let's go."

"Wait, wait, did any of your teammates ever ask you what you were so busy writing all the time? Did they sneak open your locker and pass the poetry around while you were in the showers?"

He growled, "Serena."

"Dillon," she grinned back.

"You are actually not as funny as I've always claimed."

She was smug. "Am too."

"Are not."

"Am too."

He narrowed his eyes at her, and she just laughed again. "Here," she handed over her keys. "You drive. I have to text Gillian, tell her I've been swept off my feet by a poet."

Dillon tried to look stern. Failed. Gave up and started the car. "You're not really telling her that, are you?"

Serena's head was tilted over her phone screen, her lips just playing at smiling. She slanted a look at him and it was an electric current. The air in the car crackled between them, and the few short streets between the parking lot and Blue Capri were such a long damn journey.

At last, at last, at last, a closed door between them and the world. Serena locked them in and adjusted the lights while Dillon knelt again in front of the cabinet he'd been investigating when she'd come out wearing her date outfit. He put something slow and jazzy on the CD player and swiveled to light the fireplace.

"It's seventy degrees out there."

"It'll get cooler now that it's dark. Besides, I've spent the past several hours imagining how I'd take that skirt off you. You're going to be very, very naked soon, and I'd hate for you to get a chill."

"Several hours?"

"From the second I saw it."

She did a couple of twirls on the way to meet him mid-room. "I owe Gillian another text. She talked me into this."

"I knew I liked her best."

"I'm getting jealous." She ran her fingers along the placket of his shirt, gently testing the buttons. That movie thing of ripping open the guy's shirt, sending buttons flying, was intriguing but didn't seem plausible. Besides, she really liked him in this ice-white shirt, the brightness against the shadow of his stubble, the cotton smooth and cool under her fingers. "So you like the outfit, then?"

"Oh, yeah." Dillon sank to his knees again, bit lightly at her ribs as he pressed her pelvis up flush with his chest. "Except this shirt. I don't like this shirt. You should take it off immediately."

He already had it pulled out of her waistband, his squared nails lightly scoring her flesh as he wriggled his fingers higher centimeter by centimeter. She was ticklish and turned on in equal measure, but grinding her hips against his solid shoulder did a lot to increase the turned on quotient and give her the focus she needed to lift her top the rest of the way off.

"God, Serena," Dillon whispered, burying his head between her breasts. She was wearing a seafoam lace demi bra, and as soon as he'd seen it, Dillon had shifted his hips to put his groin in insistent contact with her leg. Serena moaned as he sucked her through the bra, and slid her foot up between his legs to caress his full length.

He moaned in response, leaving her damp tight nipples behind. He explored the skin of her thigh, which had emerged through the slit on her skirt when she'd braced her knee against his hip. Dillon nipped her flesh between his teeth, and licked his way to the edge of the wrap skirt. So fast she almost lost her balance, he caught the tail of the bow in his teeth and jerked his head to the side, so all that was left holding her skirt on her waist was one loose knot.

Serena laughed and backed up. She was standing in bra and almost-gone skirt, her candy necklaces and strappy sandals, Dillon kneeling before her with his hands caressing her hipbones. She assessed him. "You are far too dressed. That fire has to warm your naked flesh, too, you know."

"I just want to see you. I need to see you, Serena."

"Well, the feeling is mutual," she said, and stopped talking milliseconds before she added the word 'love' to that sentence. It had almost just slipped out without her knowing about it. No way. No way was she going to sweet nothing her way into that kind of declaration, not without being very sure she meant it, first. She flashed a wicked grin to cover, and poked him in the chest. "Clothes, off, now."

Dillon slowly stood, still holding her, managing to slide closer and wrap his hands around her ass as he did so. She gave a futile little tug at his shirt, but, nope, the buttons didn't go flying. She knew just how to get him moving, though, and went straight for his fly. One zip, and he'd let go of her to unfasten the shirt himself, almost tossing it into the fire before he corrected his aim. His trousers were sinking towards his ankles, and he sat on the little love seat to get rid of them and bare his feet.

Serena retreated to lean on the mantle, watching the firelight play across his chest and arms as he moved. When Dillon was in only his boxers and started to stand, she held up a staying hand.

Silently, never breaking eye contact, she reached back her other hand to unhook her bra. Then both her hands were cupping her breasts as she rotated first one shoulder, then the other, sending the straps sliding down her arms. Dillon sat transfixed. Her thumbs rose over her nipples, rubbed them gently, then hooked the tops of the bra cups and dragged them downwards, dropping the bra entirely but keeping the intent weight of her breasts cradled in her hands, fingernails playing lightly over her tense areolas.

Dillon just stared.

Serena hummed out a low moan and drank in the sight of his long, strong, splayed legs, the twitching erection he stroked slowly through his boxers, his abs tense with the urge to stand and thrust against her, his broad chest rising and falling with ragged breaths. The shadow on his cheeks, the clarity of his eyes. His parted lips and fixed brows and the dark hair that wouldn't stay tidily swept back from his forehead.

He was so damned amazing.

His eyes followed her hands as she lowered them down her torso and reached for the tie of her skirt. She'd never have splurged on the garment if Gill hadn't planted a raunchy image of Dillon unwrapping her from it, 'like a sex present,' that proved irresistible. And it seemed she was right. Instead of simply loosing the tie, she tightened the knot, and Dillon's flared nostrils gave away his impatience as much as his slight growl.

Arching her eyebrow at him, she stepped close enough to hand him one end of the sash. Her look told him not to move, and although he was clearly chafing at the inaction, he obeyed. Serena just loved playing with him. He was always intense, but ready to explore. He let her lead or went galloping ahead as she ran to keep up, but no matter how slow or adventurous or playful they were, he was always Dillon. He was always tender, always joyful, always as aware of her as of himself. Passionate. Hard and sexy and raw, and so into her.

Serena lifted her arms to pile her hair atop her head, just to let him watch her bare breasts shift. It was one of his favorite things. Then, arms still raised, she slowly twirled away from him. The sash anchored in his hand countered her motion, and for a moment the skirt just rotated around her waist. It finally caught up to her intent, though, and unwound from her hips, leaving her in sandals, jewelry, and thong, facing Dillon but closer to the bedroom door than to him.

She turned on one heel and glanced over her shoulder at him. "Coming?" she asked, then added a deliberate sway to her hips as she sauntered away.

Before her fine ass had disappeared through the doorframe, Dillon had dropped the bewitching skirt and gotten his hands on Serena's flesh. The woman was torture. She was every fucking fantasy he had come true. And not just the fantasies about fucking, though he had not one single complaint in that regard. Well, maybe that she had never worn a skirt like that before, but he felt sure he could persuade her to repeat the experience.

The Grotta Azzurra bedroom was all hardwoods and hues of blue. She must have left the blue-shaded bedside lamps on earlier, casting their subdued light across the soft expanse of the pillow-laden bed. Dillon shoved most of the pillows to the floor and spread-eagled the two of them flat to the mattress. Bare limbs pressed together, he reveled in the feel of so much of their skin connecting. He devoured her mouth for a while, hard fierce kisses to make up for the silent torture in the other room. Not that her cunning spin move with the skirt hadn't been enough to make up for it. A removal method he'd not thought of, but of which he approved most heartily.

But they'd been kissing since dinner. He liked the kissing. He liked the kissing a lot. He had missed the kissing during their week of steamroller silence. He had missed the nudity. But he'd had kissing at dinner, and nudity in the parlor. Everything he thought he needed most, when he got it, he just needed something else more. And now he needed more touching. More access to her breasts, her navel, her inner thigh.

Dillon crouched up on all fours above Serena, and considered where to go first. Well, his hand seemed to have decided on its own, as it was already thumbing her nipple, but the rest of him was still considering. So many interesting, delectable options.

Nodding, he sat back on his heels straddling her thighs. Dillon moved Serena so her head was on the only remaining pillow, removing her long necklaces as he positioned her. She was circling his nipples with her nails when he pinioned her wrists together and wrapped the necklaces in a vise around them, draping her arms above her head.

"Hey, I like those beads."

"Don't struggle against your restraints, then, or you might break them."

"Wow. Smug. That's how you're going to play this?"

"And you put this thong on to, what, elicit no response from me?" he plucked at the waistband of the garment, such as it was.

"It matched the bra."

"Now who's smug?"

"Are you saying you don't like it?"

"That's what you heard from me?" Dillon couldn't stop the grin. She was such fun to spar with, always so certain she knew best but ready enough to be surprised by his point of view. He flicked both her nipples at the same time and she twisted her torso, driving her hips up at him. "I like the thong. I liked the bra. I love the skirt. It's my new Number One in the List of Serena's Skirts. You enchant me, head to toe. Satisfied?"

She shook her head at him. "Not entirely. My new necklaces are going to break and this thong is getting really wet."

"Oh, dear, how dreadful." He scooted back and lowered his head so he could lick the trail from her clavicle down to her navel. As if to prove her point, he could smell her arousal, and each breath he took made him harder. The sweet thing about a thong was that the thin stretches of fabric were very easy to grasp with his teeth to pull from her pelvis. As soon as humanly possible, he anchored each of her thighs with a tender hand and paused above her clitoris, gazing with the possessive fervor of a dragon guarding his treasure. Gently, gently he blew on Serena's clit, and she twisted against his hold, moaning his name. Dillon felt magnificent. He would laugh if his mouth wasn't otherwise occupied with licking and probing and sucking.

Through some magic or witchery, Serena had slipped off the sandals and kicked them to the floor, leaving her entirely, thoroughly nude below him. She took advantage of her clever feet to snag his boxers and wrest them half-off, despite his refusing to budge from the kneeling position that gave him such a magnificent view.

"Come on," she urged him, "I want your cock already."

"You come first, then we'll talk."

"Driving a hard bargain?" she tried to tease, but she was panting.

"Mmm," he said, because the hardness and the driving would happen, and soon, they both knew. She could play coy, but her breasts were clearly happy in his palms, and her clit was pulsing with each drag of his tongue.

"Dillon!"

"Mmm?" Lick.

"Dillon!" She refused stillness.

"Mmm?" Skim nipples. Lick.

"I...Dillon, Dillon, I want, I. Oh. Oh. Dillon."

"Mm-mmm?" Pinch. Lick, taste. Thumbs, press, circle. Flick. Suck.

"I. Oh!" And the rest was lost as they rode her orgasm together, exhilarated.

And then, at last, because now he needed it more than he'd ever needed anything, the hard bargain really began. Serena was still moaning softly and pulsing her hips, but Dillon was on the move. He stood to get rid of his boxers and find a condom, and when he came back to the bed he was struck by the intriguing height of the antique. Dillon sheathed himself quickly and reached out to drag Serena towards the edge of the mattress. He ached to be inside her, and standing there, throbbing with desire, her sultry smile just added oil to his fire.

She tilted her pelvis at him and dropped her legs open to either side of his hips, but he wanted more, even, than she offered. Dillon took her ankles and drew them up to his shoulders, then grasped her ass to hold her steady as he thrust quick and deep into her. Serena's gasp went straight to his groin, and he drew back to play the head of his cock at her entrance a moment before driving up again, deeper than before, and again, deeper still. Her ankles tightened to his neck and he looked down at the feast of Serena spread before him. Her graceful legs and the curve of her hips. Her torso arching towards him as her breasts moved sensually with each of his thrusts. Her nipples tightening to peaks he would taste, soon, but not yet, because from this height he could see everything, a high-def sensual feast. His hard cock disappearing into her damp curls, her swollen clit angled to meet his pubic bone each time he sank into her.

Her body. The sheen on her collarbone and her delicious neck, arms still obligingly crossed above her head. Her mouth parted as she licked her bottom lip and he had to thrust deeper again, no more playing; it was time for unrelenting action. Her eyes, clear on his, the look in them as she called his name again and again, as he swiveled his hips slightly to vary the motion and she lost the connected syllables, and then he played his thumbs along the edge of her curls while he withdrew just to her entrance again, the shallow rocking that had her arching further to cling as long as possible to the desperate tip of his shaft. She lost her consonants and was all long vowels and tremors when he bent his knees slightly for one more fast, fierce lunge that kept them united even as she dropped her legs and he fell forward onto her chest and they came with shouts neither was able to muffle in the least.

Without a word, without pausing for more pillows or a glass of water for her parched throat, as instantly as possible, Serena shifted them around so that Dillon was spooning her, enfolding her entirety. Her head was cradled on his arm and his heartbeat thudded into her spine and she pulled a sheet up over them and curled into a ball in his arms.

She'd never felt such an urge to cry after sex. Her limbs shook, part emotion and part aftershock and she wasn't going to analyze the percentages. She held his arms tight to her chest, burrowing down. He was speaking softly, but her head was too far away, the blood pounding in her ears too much of a barrier, and he didn't seem to mind, really. He squeezed her to him, a furnace and an anchor and, somehow, terrifying but completely essential.

And she didn't cry. There may have been a couple of random tears, but he couldn't see them. He finished untangling the necklaces that had fallen loose earlier, and reached over to set them on the bedside table and turn off that lamp. Serena began to relax her limbs as he stroked her hair, except for where she held his other arm tight, a security blanket, a teddy bear, a best friend through a scary night. Dillon was still murmuring, but coherence was beyond her—did he say 'steamroller' again?—and she sighed deeply, and was asleep.

CHAPTER FIFTY-ONE

HIGH LACE-COVERED WINDOWS didn't stop the spill of sunlight across the oak floors, but it did leave their bed in cool shadows. Serena nuzzled her nose into the warm space between Dillon's neck and collarbone, inhaling the morning scent of his skin. They were, of course, naked. He must have gotten up at some point to shut off the other lights and fireplace, but she'd been in a happy oblivion until dawn's early light changed the visual temperature beyond her eyelids.

Before long, he'd changed the temperature of the room, too, and of her increasingly heated body. Then her skin cooled, then heated, then cooled and heated again. Eventually, Serena scooted out from under Dillon, and moved to straddle his back. "The other day, when you were playing basketball—I like the shirtless thing, by the way—I realized how remiss I had been."

"Oh?" He folded his arms under his head and closed his eyes as her hands swept over his shoulders.

"Very remiss. I spend so much time feeling your back muscles, but I never take the time to look at them."

"And you like looking at them?"

"Mmm," she agreed. "Very much. Your back is one of the many sexy parts of your body."

"Do you think I don't feel how you're grinding your clit against me back there?"

"Hush. I'm giving you a back rub and a compliment. If I want to get off a little at the same time, you shouldn't complain."

"Five times. I haven't even brushed my teeth this morning, and I've made you come five times."

"Not yet you haven't."

He reached back and ran one thumb along her inner thigh, and her grip on his shoulders intensified. "That's what I thought," he said, grinning.

"Shut up," she said, pressing her clit into his spine. She leaned down so that her nipples were brushing his upper back with each of her gentle rocking moves, and her tongue swept up his neck to his ear.

"So easy," he muttered, as if his optimistic groin wasn't twitching in response. He arched his lower back and she nestled back against his ass, riding him faster and faster until the entire bed shook beneath the force of her climax. Fifth climax. For the record. While she collapsed on him, panting, he said, "This has got to be the best back rub ever."

"You," she drew in a lungful of air, "are so smug."

"What do you intend to do about it?"

Her head shook on his shoulder. "I'll figure something out."

"Take your time."

And she planted a soft kiss on his shoulder blade, then another, and rested her forehead back on his spine. "I think I will."

Dillon, still a little cautious, quit while he was ahead, but he sensed something tender, fragile and new, in the air. It warmed him. He let it ride.

Eventually, recovered, they took a tender, slow shower and made themselves presentable before heading to the main house for breakfast. It was a group affair, all guests seated around a large gleaming table set with pretty Victorian china and cut-glass serving dishes. There were two older couples, both coincidentally in town for the graduation parties of their granddaughters, who were classmates, and a young military-bearing couple who didn't have much to say about themselves but had the body language of long, close quarters. Accepting Mrs. Kirby's coffee, Tracy requested hot tea for Will; Will passed Tracy the jalapeño jelly as soon as the biscuits started making the rounds.

Serena started a little when Dillon told Mrs. Kirby that she would want tea, too, but kept it together. It was only that it had belatedly occurred to her that they were still there on the job. She glanced over to see that Dillon was taking notes on the dining room and breakfast presentation—fortunately the existing photos of this part of Blue Capri were well done, so Serena didn't have to go back to Grotta Azzurra for the camera she'd forgotten.

She chided herself about being professional, and started talking to the grandparents about the property instead of gazing foolishly at Dillon. She was really an idiot. It was a good thing they had this interlude of work to force her to settle down.

Because she was starting to feel very unsettled.

It was well and good to rearrange her home, give him a desk, admit he made her want to change. Talk about the future some. But that was still not as far down the path as he was, with his 'I love you' hanging in the air. And the fact was, it wasn't his declaration that had her scared. What had shaken her was the intensity of her need for him the night before. The realization that she'd nearly screwed up what was between them, and how very very bad a thing that would be, if it happened.

Mrs. Kirby came back into the room with baked French toast and a bowl of fruit salad. Dillon raised his eyebrows at her before serving himself some strawberries, and she smiled to let him know it wouldn't be a problem for him to eat them, and it hit her, then, that she was really just very idiotic about her own emotions.

Reminding herself every quarter hour about the whole 'be a professional' thing, Serena got through breakfast and a follow-up chat with Mrs. Kirby. After scheduling a phone meeting for the middle of the next week, she and Dillon returned to their approximation of a blue grotto to pack up.

She laughed at the rumpled room. "Well, it won't take much detective work on Mrs. Kirby's part to realize we shared a bed."

"Want me to go jump on the other one a little, try to fool her?"

Serena smiled at her boyfriend. "No. I suspect she knows anyway. Besides, as long as we are the excellent team that we are, our personal life is none of her business."

"Hey, we don't have to go into the office today, do we? I mean, I don't. Do you?"

She shook her head. "I'll send a couple of emails now, but otherwise I'm all yours." The truth of that made her glance up a little bashfully. "What did you have in mind? Want to hide out in Galveston another night? Because I was thinking we could hit a sports bar instead, watch Game Three on the super big screen." The Rockets were back on their home turf and had playoff scores to settle.

"No, that'd be perfect. I just want to check out the beach. Tracy said the 37th Street Jetty is the place to go. That's close, right?"

"Sure, it's just one of the Seawall cross streets, not even that far from here."

"So we can go?"

Serena laughed. "You're quite the eager puppy. Going to take surfing up again, are you?"

"Well, I've lived in Houston more than long enough to have found all this out by now. I'm going to at least do some recon, see if the waves, you know, pull at my soul and all."

She tossed her toiletry bag at him, and he caught it and stuffed it into her duffle. "You are so connected to, like, the earth, man. I had no idea. Let's go walk the Seawall beach a little and then we can grab lunch before heading back."

"As if I'll ever eat again after that breakfast."

"I thought you'd worked up a good appetite this morning."

"Funny Serena."

"That's right, Surfer Dude. Funny Serena. Ready to go?"

He scooped up their overnight bags, she grabbed her work tote, and off they went.

They found parking a few blocks from 37th and descended the concrete steps to the beach. The tide was about half-out, and the beach was lined mostly with small family groups up and down the entire Seawall. Older kids were in school, but there were moms with swim-diaper-clad toddlers and preschoolers wielding plastic shovels everywhere. Plenty of older couples, too, some sedentary, some taking what looked like routine constitutionals along the packed wet sand. And, as promised, the surfers in the distance.

"Decent peaks," was Dillon's appraisal. "Not the best."

"Enough to tempt you?"

"Maybe. Sometime. I'll take a look at my short board when I'm home, see what condition it's in."

They skirted a chubby three-year-old charging the waves and a clump of the seaweed that populated all of Galveston's beaches. Dillon held his shoes, but Serena had been able to slip her low-heeled sandals into her shoulder bag, and when she saw some intact purple and grey clam shells, she scooped up five or six, all barely thumbnail sized. Dillon plucked them away, then stepped into the surf to rinse them for her.

"Thanks," she said, kissing his cheek and slipping them into her pocket. The wind grabbed her hair as she turned, so she pulled it all into a ponytail and looked up at him. Dillon was staring out at the water, his feet still submerged with each wavelet that came in, a faraway look in his eyes. "Are you dreaming of the good life in California? Do you miss the Pacific?"

He reached a hand for hers and they went on to the jetty, climbing the granite slabs of the sides before stopping to lean against each other and slip their shoes back on. Soon they were several feet out along the path, the water breaking to either side of them, with few people and only the wind to catch their words.

"I don't miss it, actually." He pulled them down to sitting, tucking her shoulder under the arm he wrapped around her. It felt perfect, and Serena tried to figure out if working up a natural conversation or just blurting was the way to go. She had no plan. She hated having no plan, but Dillon tended to throw them all off center, anyway. "I liked growing up where I did, I had a lot of fun as a kid. Mom and Dad...they were good parents. I think you'd have liked them."

"I'm sure I would have."

"Well, it's academic. It's been a decade, you know that? Any rate, I didn't surf much after their accident. Justin tried to take me a few times, that was one of his schemes to get me out of the house and back into the world, but he can't surf for shit." Dillon nuzzled her neck. "Even though I know you think he looks like a surfer dude."

Serena giggled. She hadn't meant to gush or anything, but clearly Dillon had noticed her awareness of his brother-in-law's hotness quotient. "I only like the tall, dark, and handsome sort myself," she said.

"Funny girl. The point is, while I can tell you that the tubes are infinitely better on Malibu and there's no way I'd get any air on those breaks, I'm extremely happy to be here instead of there. My only real family is here, and you're here."

Right, plunging in it would be, then. The sun was warm, the wind was playful, the water wasn't entirely brown. Best to take a deep breath and dive. "Dillon, about what you said before."

He grimaced a little. "I know, I'm rushing you. I'm sorry, Serena, I really am. And I don't expect—that is, it has been made clear to me that I, poor orphan Dillon, am very eager to be settling down with my life and creating a nuclear family of my own. Also, I apparently bottle up bad things and hold grudges. Sorry to shatter you illusions about my perfection." He paused so she could kiss him lightly. "I am sure I love you, you know. It's not that I'm inventing the emotion because it suits my long-term goals. But you have to get there your own way. If you get there." He glanced away, then bent his head to hers again. "I hope you get there. But your way. I'm not going anywhere, I can wait."

Serena's eyes were watering, and not from the salty wind. Dillon wiped her cheek with his thumb.

"It's really okay, you know. You gave me the desk, and that was so amazing. Brave of you, and so important to me. It means the world to me, and," he waggled his eyebrows and gave her that grin, "I'm hoping to spend the next few nights at your place, so I can get some use out of it. In fact, I'm hoping that you can help me break it in, if you know what I mean, and I think you do."

Serena blew out a laugh and nestled her head so she could hear the steady beat of his heart beneath her ear. "You're tireless."

"That's what you get when you date a younger man. Tons of sexual stamina."

"I knew I picked you for a reason."

"That's how this happened?"

"Well, sure. I looked around the office and thought, 'who here can make me come four times in one morning?' and my gaze fell on you."

"Five."

"Smug."

"Proud. And correct." They kissed, a slow slow kiss that Serena felt to her toes. "But I'm glad you noticed what a stud I am. At last. I'd only been panting after you since the interview."

"Well, I might have noticed earlier. But I figured something out about myself recently."

"Oh, yeah? What's that?" Dillon wrapped the bulk of her ponytail in his hand, cradling her skull and running just one light finger along the nape of her neck. He knew it would make her shiver.

"It's about emotional honesty, and being an idiot."

His eyes crinkled as he looked at her. "An idiot, eh?"

"I am frequently an idiot. When I'm jiggy with excitement because I'll see you soon, and can't stop smiling like an idiot. When I'm hit so hard with conflicting signals that I run and hide like an idiot instead of figuring it out. When I knee-jerk react to something unexpected, like being told you love me."

Dillon. His face was sober now, his grip on the back of her head slack. He'd gone still, except for his eyes, bluer than any water on the Gulf Coast could ever hope to be, tracking back and forth across her face.

Serena offered a tentative smile. "So my New Plan—I ran out of other plans, and you know how I like to have a plan—my New Plan is to stop being an idiot."

"Okay?"

"And to be emotionally honest. Well, that was part of the Desk Plan, but it seemed to be a good idea, so I'm keeping it as part of the New Plan."

He nodded. He didn't point out that she was babbling. "The Not Being an Idiot plan?"

"Right." She nodded, and noted in doing so that his hand had tightened in her hair again. She wondered if he realized how very intertwined they'd become. Well, whatever happened, he couldn't just up and run off from her, not without taking half her ponytail along with him. Absurd, but comforting. So she continued with the dive.

"And since I'm an emotionally honest non-idiot, it seems like I shouldn't be scared by how much I need you. How much I want those summer mornings, and then some fall mornings, and winter evenings, come to that."

"Serena." His voice had gone rough.

She put a caressing hand on his cheek, and interrupted him, "I am still learning how to not be an emotionally dishonest idiot, Dillon. It won't be overnight, and we have things to learn, both of us. But I want to learn. I want to follow this New Plan with you, for you, Dillon. Because I love you, too. I love you, and I want you to live with me."

"Serena." He wiped at his eyes, the other hand tight on her nape, holding her to him.

"See, now I'm grinning like an idiot again, and it's so damn hard to kiss you when I'm grinning like an idiot."

Dillon had a plan for that, though, and together, they managed just fine.

Epilogue

"Put the heat on?" Serena called from the bathroom.

"I will not put the heat on, you Texan wimp. It's October."

There was only a slight chill in the air, but Serena was wearing her #34 jersey for the Rocket's season opener, and little else. She came through the hallway, asking, "Do you want me to have to change?"

Dillon stopped half-way to the dining table with the serving bowls in hand, and just looked at her.

In truth, his expression did plenty to heat her from the inside out, but she pretended to shiver, rubbing her arms. If doing so happened to jiggle her unbound breasts, that was hardly her fault.

"Serena," Dillon growled, depositing the bowls in an untidy heap on the table. "We have guests coming in an hour."

She stepped back towards their bedroom, and he followed. "You're suggesting I dress more warmly, then?"

"I'm suggesting we don't have time for this. You haven't even started your salad yet."

Serena shrugged, closing her eyes a minute as the fabric slid cooly over her eternally wanton nipples. "So?"

"And," Dillon said, hands on her waist now and backing her up against his low bookcase full of sci-fi classics. She'd put her foot down when he moved in, insisting that he cull his collection down to a reasonable size. She'd turned a blind eye to the number of book boxes he'd stashed in the bungalow's attic, though, so it counted as a compromise. And a good compromise, at that, since it also brought the sturdy bookcase with the hip-height perch into their bedroom. "I haven't brought the folding chairs in off the porch yet."

Since it had been delightful the first time, Serena shrugged again. "So? Gives people a place to sit if they show up before we're ready."

Dillon's cobalt eyes were fiery enough to assure Serena that his protests were nothing but token ones. She hitched her jersey up so he could see the Rockets-red panties she wore. His palms pressed her thighs further apart. "If you'd worn something proper, we'd be ready on time. You know Jorge is always early."

"I texted Bubba just now, asked them to pick up some tamales from that place on Studewood. They'll be late."

"Doesn't mean Janice and Miguel will be."

Serena ran her hand up Dillon's chest, stopping to admire her engagement ring as she stroked his pecs. Dillon looked, too, then pressed forward until Serena's legs wrapped around his hips, her arms around his neck as he pulled her tight to him.

She smiled, smug. "I knew I could distract you."

"The dinner party was your idea, smarty pants."

"In case you didn't notice, I'm not wearing pants."

"Funny girl."

"Funny woman," she corrected, for at least the hundredth time, tilting her pelvis into his hardness to make her point.

Dillon's mouth paused long enough for him to say, "Funny fiancee."

And, for at least the hundredth time, Serena gasped, overwhelmed by the surge of emotion. She took Dillon's beautiful strong face in her hands, staring into his steady eyes, and said, "Your funny fiancee, Rocket Man."

Never breaking eye contact, Dillon stroked her core, watching her expression do whatever stupefied things it did when she was loved by the man who loved her. "And don't you forget it," he said, low and intense and confident.

Smug man. She'd show him.

Just as soon as he was done showing her.

If Serena didn't have time to arrange the chairs so everyone could see the TV and reach the snacks without the space feeling crowded, well. It was a small price to pay for making sure Dillon knew exactly how warm their house needed to be, for all the days of their lives.

ABOUT THE AUTHOR

Melanie Greene is a native Houstonian. She shares her life with her hometown hunk of a husband and children so amazing they defy superlatives.

You can find her at www.MelanieGreene.com or www.facebook.com/MelGreeneBooks.

Follow her @dakimel